Dragon Code

Garnett,
Best of wishes,

Mae

Dragon Code

The Evil of Torlen

MARK MATTHEWS

authorHOUSE®

AuthorHouse™
1663 Liberty Drive
Bloomington, IN 47403
www.authorhouse.com
Phone: 1-800-839-8640

First published by AuthorHouse   07/01/2011

ISBN: 978-1-4634-1151-0 (sc)
ISBN: 978-1-4634-1150-3 (dj)
ISBN: 978-1-4634-1149-7 (ebk)

Library of Congress Control Number: 2011908755

Printed in the United States of America

Any people depicted in stock imagery provided by Thinkstock are models, and such images are being used for illustrative purposes only.
Certain stock imagery © Thinkstock.

This book is printed on acid-free paper.

Because of the dynamic nature of the Internet, any web addresses or links contained in this book may have changed since publication and may no longer be valid. The views expressed in this work are solely those of the author and do not necessarily reflect the views of the publisher, and the publisher hereby disclaims any responsibility for them.

ACKNOWLEDGEMENT

Special love and gratitude go to my wife and sons for their patience and understanding of my quest to vanquish evil from the lands. Armed with sword in hand, or in my case a computer, I press onward with the noble cause. Their tolerance of my goal is phenomenal.

This book is dedicated to not only my parents, but my mother and father-in-law as well. Their guidance and support is invaluable in everyday life.

A great deal of gratitude goes out to Cindy Savage who has taught me perseverance and will power goes a long way in the writing industry. Her 'never give up' attitude helps drive me continually onward and inspires me to reach higher goals.

I would be amiss if no mention was made of Bret, my friend of twenty five years. He is my sounding board and makes life easier by having someone to confide in and help work through life's obstacles. May you be blessed with long life and prosperity, my friend.

SELONOTH

A lone dark figure stood upon the parapet high above the landscape far below. His boots clacked against the cold stone as he paced, peering to the west with each pass. Wind stirred his hair and robe while his evil thoughts focused on revenge.

The tyrannical quest for domination of all lands about him had been thwarted some years earlier, nearly costing him his life. Then, with renewed malevolence he undertook the construction of a new army and fortress as well. Now he stood ready to overtake all that were before him. Confidence and a new evil plan were now held close to his heart, for he learned many things during his exile and recovery.

"Long indeed have I labored to form a new, superior force that will do my bidding. These outlanders believe I have perished in a far away land, never to be heard from again. They have no idea how wrong they were. They are all *fools*!" Holnok fumed aloud as he circled the great tower. "My strength is greater than ever. For years I toiled in secret building the vast mountain fortress of Selonoth, breeding my minions for the sole purpose of wiping away the vermin lying before me. Time has come once again to release my armies and seek the Sacred Six for my own. This time however, the items I seek and their hiding places are known to me," he said as a wry smile came to his lips.

"They will be unable to withstand my power. Puny outlanders, I hate them all. I shall see them bow before me while standing over them as their High Lord," Holnok ranted as furor rose within him. "I will destroy their homes, lands and any that dare stand in my way!"

he said, breaking into hideous laughter that echoed through the open door and down the long darkened hallway.

Visions of burning cities, bodies littering the ground, and having the Six under his control filled his mind. *Fairy magic will not be enough to stop me this time,* he thought. Hatred lingered for the race whose ancestors banished and shamed his father. Magic or not, he would bring them to their knees, making them swear allegiance to him and beg for mercy before the end. *I will conquer them in due time. First, I will possess the Six, then I shall turn my new powers on those pesky, pointy eared intruders,* he thought. *They will pay dearly for meddling in my plans.*

"The young outlanders that accompanied the fairies to Mindaloth will pay as well. Using powers that should rightfully be mine, they destroyed my fortress and sent my armies into hiding or set them free. Bah! Curse them. Curse them all," he said, speaking aloud once more. "Young, worthless fools! I shall have dues paid to me. They cannot hide now, for I know their faces. I have seen them as they haunt my dreams!

Once more, glory filled his mind. Riches, women, land and dreams of power danced before his eyes. A slow, dark smile formed on his lips. Abruptly, his face turned horrible as anxiety rose up and swept him away in a frenzy of anger. No longer could he contain his thirst for vengeance. *It is time to set my glorious plan in motion,* he thought.

Stopping suddenly, he whirled and entered the main chamber that stood behind him. His harsh voice boomed as he strode the hallway summoning forth his servant.

"Natrae, where are you, cur. Where do you hide, imp! Your master requires your presence. We have much work to do and my bidding will wait no longer," Holnok spouted as he stood waiting, annoyed. His eyes narrowed into slits as his patience wore thin. Again, he began to pace. "Come, you miserable dog. I command your attendance."

Pattering footfalls approached quickly from a narrow hallway to Holnok's left. Natrae entered, looking much older than before. Evil ways did not agree with his stature, he appeared bent and tired. The once strong, youthful exterior had vanished. His hair was dirty, clothes loose fitting and soiled. Groveling, he came before his master as a sad figure of a man, a shadow of his former self.

"How may I serve you, my liege?" asked Natrae, wringing his hands and licking his lips as he knelt peering through glassy, distant eyes, fidgeting all the while.

Holnok stared at his servant indignantly. Revulsion swept over him as he gazed at the pitiful, cowering form. If Natrae had not previously saved his life, Holnok would have slain him as he knelt before him. Instead, he aimed a swift kick at his servant which narrowly missed his head.

Natrae whimpered loudly but said nothing to further agitate his master. Silence was the best recourse.

"Send forth more Zenex riders. Have them spread through the lands to the homes of the outlanders that were once your companions, your one time friends. Or so they said. Now that you have rid yourself of those usurpers, you know where your allegiance lies do you not, fool?" Holnok said, with belligerence ripe in his voice.

"Of course Master, I serve no other than thee. I have always been loyal to you my lord," said Natrae with a whine, still fearful of reprisal. Sweat beaded his brow as he awaited another form of retribution for his master's anger. His eyes squinted at the stroke that would surely fall upon him. "I live to serve you my lord, I only . . ."

"You live," Holnok interrupted, "simply because you crave the wealth and power that shall be mine when I conquer these lands. You do not fool me Natrae. I know the desire for a kingdom of your own to rule as you see fit burns within your heart," said Holnok. Then suddenly, he softened his tone. "However, a promise was made to you, one that shall be kept. For you have been a worthy servant to this point. Glorious rewards shall be bestowed upon you. Patience is all that is required now," he said grinning.

"Thank you my lord, I am not worthy of your generosity," replied Natrae, as he stomach churned with excitement.

*   *   *

Magnificent, opulent, and beautiful thoughts of his own kingdom filled Natrae's mind. Drinking from a golden chalice, he strolled through his fortress, his royal silken robe flowing from his shoulders, the finest clothing clung neatly to his body. A jewel encrusted silver crown rode atop his head, reflecting the brilliant sunshine which bore upon him as he entered the courtyard. Turning to stare at his dwelling which rose high into the sky, its gleaming white walls impenetrable and glorious, he smiled. Maidens swooned to him as he came forth to greet them, while soldiers bowed or lowered to one knee as he passed. Cheers and shouts of joy and love came from the people of his kingdom as they caught sight of their lord and king. Tears welled in his eyes until his masters voice rang in his ears once more as his thoughts quickly faded, focusing back to the black, cold stone before him.

*　　*　　*

"Go now. Carry out the orders you were given. Do not fail me, for my wrath will be terrible if you do. Your future kingdom depends on my victory," said Holnok as he whirled, quickly disappearing down the darkened hallway behind him, never giving another thought to Natrae.

A large wooden door creaked with protest as Holnok slowly pushed his way into a small room to his right. The only furnishing was a comfortable high backed chair and a tall knurled solitary wooden staff floating inches off the floor in the room's center, suspended by unseen magical force. Dim light gleamed upon the polished stone floor from high above, coming through several small windows near the tip of an enormous cathedral ceiling. Hundreds of candles lined either side of the walls, burning dimly as they cast flickering shadows upon the reflective black stone.

Holnok withdrew a fist sized red gem from his cloak and began to mumble softly, unintelligibly. Gazing at the crystal admiringly, he began to stroke it back and forth, up and down, his fingers admiring its cold hardness. All the while he muttered to himself, seemingly conversing to the object itself to confess his admiration or love for it before placing it atop the staff.

A brilliant beam of white light emanated instantly from the crystal, spiraling upward, spreading wide above Holnok, who gazed intently at its images. Slowly, he walked to his chair and slumped in it, peering keenly at the floating scenes before him while smiling mischievously.

"I see you. I see you *all* clearly now," he said, speaking to the images. Pleased at hearing his own voice, he continued. "You cannot escape the Stone of Sight. It sees all I desire. Each of your lands and homes are known to me and I am coming for my possessions. MY Six! You will give them to me freely or die when my forces destroy all you love and take the items while you lay dead at my feet." Again, his hideous laughter reverberated from the lifeless walls.

"You have slain the riders sent to your lands. But no matter, I shall send more, for my army is vast now, even beyond your pitiful reckoning. Eldon of Hatar and Verion of Eldarn, I know you all too well. Undeniably you have grown more skillful indeed. Watching you from afar for a long while as I healed the wound put upon me by your friend Baytor has taught me much. But, the fool paid with his life for his error of daring to stand against me. Now outlanders, with my new forces you have no hope. It is futile to hide that which I shall possess."

Above him danced images of the company members who had partaken in the destruction of Mindaloth, his fortress that once lay in the Bottomless Lands. He saw them smiling, laughing, working, living the happy lives he despised them for. Wrath began to seethe from him. Gripping the chair arms tightly as he spoke to himself, as was his want, he slowly grew incensed.

"You never know when I am watching. You have no idea I can see you. Soon enough you will fear the name of Holnok once more, then you will realize there is no escape from me. I now have powers your minds cannot even comprehend. Many interesting things lay in the depths of Morog when I returned there. The Stone of Sight is but one of them. Enormous hidden evil power and magic lay there, waiting, calling to me. Prepare yourself fools! My hordes will be upon you soon and I will pluck your precious artifacts from your hands." Holnok let loose a dreadful laugh which brought great joy to him.

Quickly, he rose from his chair and collected the crystal from the staff, neatly tucking it away, but not before openly admiring it once more. He proceeded to his sleep chamber with an uncharacteristic grin upon his face, knowing his visions had been set into motion. Still, he remained unsatisfied. The burning within him was nearly uncontrollable. Resentment swelled within his heart and he was unsure if it was anger from his original plans being foiled or that the powers he desired brought about Mindaloth's downfall and his failure.

"One ill turn deserves yet another, my outlander friends. Soon it shall become clear who your master is. Certainly it cannot be the pitiful humans you call kings or lords. Nay! It is I, Holnok, High Lord of the Jarcoth. The future ruler of your world. Prepare to bow under my reign and if you do I may allow your families to live. But, I shall spare no mercy for you, my friends. You shall hand me the Six willingly or meet your death."

Holnok rose up and spread his arms high above him and laughed.

Return of the Dragons

The sun glistened from Trimlin's scales as his rider peered at the winged shapes following closely behind. Verion sat atop his dragon's dark blue scaled back as they slowly circled with four of his offspring in tow. Gynexa, the black dragon, glided to his left. Verion's life partner and future queen of Eldarn, Aleeza, sat astride her back.

"Come, catch me if you are able," said Verion loudly over his shoulder as the wind whistled through his hair.

"If you insist on hurting your own pride, then I shall aid your cause, husband," shouted Aleeza in reply. "The first one to the giant oak, wins!"

She banked Gynexa hard right, cutting in front of Verion, then dove straight downward to the earth, with Trimlin now rocketing close behind.

"Let them have their victory my friend," thought Verion to his dragon. "After all, she is my beloved partner and Gynexa, your offspring. They will both take great joy in it, and I will swallow my dignity for their sake," he chuckled.

"So be it, rider," replied Trimlin. "Though, we could indeed make it a close race, could we not?"

"Indeed. She could win by a heads length perhaps," laughed Verion. "Catch them."

He smiled broadly as his mind wandered back a few short years, when together, he and his wife fought for their lives in a far away land. They undertook a quest to destroy the spreading evil that endangered all races and lands about them, including each of their homes. They crossed many miles, fighting several fierce battles along way. Eventually, they reached the Bottomless Lands, where they fulfilled their destiny of driving the High Lord Holnok from Mindaloth, his malevolent fortress.

Verion promised himself these thoughts would be driven from his mind forever when the quest was over. After all, happiness was boundless in his present life. His beautiful wife was now by his side and the dream of binding together all peoples alienated for many ages was successful. Plus, Trimlin and his mate Keltora brought eight new dragons into the world, begetting power and magic once again. The future king could ask for nothing more.

However, even during this, the happiest time of his life, dread secretly grew within him. Fear of the High Lord's return swelled in his mind. Though mortally wounded, Holnok could indeed have escaped the final battle with his servant Natrae's aid.

This fact haunted Verion more often then he cared to admit. Did the evil lord indeed live? Will he return? Can he be stopped once more? These questions gave Verion agonizing headaches. But, since his life partner did not possess the gift of Seeing, she could not sense his worry, pain or growing despair. So he did well to suppress his discomfort and emotions.

Years passed quickly since Holnok was driven from the lands to the east. The After Years brought unification of all races as it was centuries ago. Peace now covered the earth like a warm blanket. Trade between kingdoms and races was taken up once more. Messages flowed freely in what became a large extended family of peoples. Even the Malmaks, the Cyclops race from the Caves of Doom, visited the humans often. They were particularly fond of the city of Eldarn, taking up trade with them as it was many years ago. Verion grew close to the one eyed giant named Murn during their adventure to destroy Mindaloth. They remained very close, visiting one another often and teaching one another many crafts.

Then there was Ono, Verion's small leather-skinned flying friend with the bulging eyes, who proved himself invaluable to the quest. Though, once a servant to the evil lord, he betrayed his master. Ono despised Holnok for enslaving his race and destroying their home. Ono supplied Verion and the companions information along the way, leading to Holnok being driven out.

Zot, Ono's mate, would visit as well. She was introduced to Verion during the festival which was held in Ono's honor, in fact all Grendar were now looked upon with reverence. Each of the pair's subsequent visits were surprisingly entertaining. Their mannerisms took some getting used to if you first laid eye upon them, but they were loved by all nonetheless.

All races held high honor for Ono and his kind. Without their aid, the quest would have most likely failed. Once the Fairies gifted Ono and his entire race with speech, the creatures began to travel far and wide. Some even took up residence in towns filled with humans, beginning families and living in peaceful coexistence with the tall ones.

Verion's joining with Aleeza united the Quantar people with his own. His sister Nira joined with Eldon of Hatar. Jinarl, of the Arton people, wed Zarah, Eldon's sister. Even Murn wed a fairy named Katima. They made a particularly interesting couple when viewed together. The company that once traveled as one to defeat evil was joined forever in friendship and some were betrothed. However, the thought presently on Verion's mind was the continuing training of the young dragons. Pride swelled within him as the group glided in a precise formation over the sleepy little village that was Verion's home. He had seen many lands on his prior quest, finding special attractiveness in them all, but he dearly loved Eldarn the best. Though, Avior, the home of the fairies, was always on his mind as was the race of immortals themselves.

A gentle spring time mist lay nestled in the valley as Verion steered the dragons to a field behind his home. Gliding through the clouds, the moisture covered his face as he went, invigorating his senses. The five large shapes landed with resounding thuds. They were indeed a magnificent bunch, just as Verion's father predicted. Of the eight young dragons, four remained in Eldarn, one of which was Aleeza's. One bonded with Jinarl and now lived in Tarsis, the sea port near the Sea of Songs, home of the Arton people. The final three were with Keltora, who remained by Nira's side in Hatar. Eldon had bonded with one of the three.

"Your offspring is a blessing my beloved friend. They are far beyond my hopes and visions," thought Verion silently. His thoughts went forth into his dragons mind, for they were bonded, as with all riders and dragons, being chosen for one another in this fashion. If the pair shared a connection of telepathy they become a team.

"Your power and magic shall bring prosperity to the world once more. Majestic dragons will fill the skies again. Pride swells in my heart for you and the young ones as well."

"Many thanks, rider," retorted Trimlin, turning an eye to stare at Verion as he drew closer. "I, too, am pleased with them all. Though, I do miss my mate, Keltora. But the little ones do keep us busy do they not." Trimlin stood on his rear legs letting loose a skyward fireball. He thudded back to earth and began to purr as the young ones replicated his actions, making Verion laugh aloud. The adolescent dragons recently learned to breathe fire, a feat which he kept a close eye on for fear of setting the town ablaze by well meaning, but playful offspring.

"Yes, a fine bunch indeed," he said aloud. "I shall return tomorrow for more training. Go now my friend, rest and stand vigilant as always." Verion quickly looked about him to see Aleeza approaching. Hurriedly, his thoughts pushed forth to his dragon once more.

"I have an uneasy feeling Trimlin, though I cannot say why. Be heedful during your watch, for I am uncomfortable as of late. Something is afoot, perhaps only my imagination. Nonetheless, stay aware."

"No harm shall come to you Verion, I promise this. Five pair of eyes roams the skies from above. Evil shall not come upon you unseen. Rest well and worry not, my rider," retorted Trimlin, as he slowly turned his massive head from side to side ostensibly searching for a hidden foe.

Verion patted his dragon's neck as Aleeza came to his side, kissing her husband softly. She clasp his strong, large hands within her own and gazed into his eyes.

"Shall we have supper, I'm sure you are famished," said Aleeza with a quick grin and wink. "Our day has been long and joyful, especially since I was victorious during the race, but you look worried my love. What is it?"

"Worry not, I am simply tired, for the day has been demanding," lied Verion. "Indeed you did win the race and I believe my love has become a better rider than I," he chuckled.

He detested openly deceiving his mate, but as with the secret he held during the journey years ago, he felt it was in her best interest. Believing he could spare her any grief from his ill feelings, he maintained his silence.

Time passed and no harm came to Verion. Nonetheless, unpleasant feelings and dreams remained with him. Several times he yearned to talk to his sister, Nira. After all, she wore the Dragons Eye amulet, which gave her unlimited Seeing ability. If danger was spreading westward she would know. In many ways he regretted she was in Hatar with Eldon. Communication was much slower than he desired and he was not powerful enough to read her thoughts from a distance. Often, he wished to speak to her in person, alone. Since that was rarely possible, he settled for visits as often as he could. Dragon rides to the plains proved quite pleasant in fact.

Finally, no longer able to bear the feelings of danger, he spoke openly of his concerns to Aleeza, for he was swept away with guilt of not candidly revealing his thoughts to her.

"My love, I wish a journey to Hatar. I yearn to lay eyes upon my sister, plus Trimlin misses his mate and I would enjoy Eldon's company once more. Also, I must speak to you of growing uneasy feelings in my heart which haunt me," he said, running his fingers through his hair, which had grown long. "Evil is on the move once again, I sense it. Though, I have no proof of this, only a feeling. Nira would know for her powers are great. I seek her counsel."

"I knew you were disturbed by thoughts you held within yourself. Though, I did not press you, knowing you would come to me when ready," she said smiling. "A journey would indeed be welcome. It has been overly long since we last rode from the boundaries of Eldarn. A visit is in order, my love."

Verion smiled, then embraced her. He kissed her softly, remembering many of the reasons he felt deep love for his wife. Even without any Seeing ability, she seemed quite able to read his mind whenever she desired. A small smile formed on his lips and quickly widened.

Evening came, bringing its grey light upon Eldarn. A gentle breeze rose against Verion's face as he watched the mountains veil themselves in the deepening darkness. Knowing he would soon be venturing forth once more brought relief to him. The smile he wore quickly faded as thoughts of encountering evil pressed to the forefront of his mind. Rest came in fragments throughout the remainder of the night, as attempts to relieve anxiety failed.

Morning light came softly upon the small cottage as he readied himself for departure. Truly, he felt reluctance at departing Eldarn. For, if malevolence was indeed spreading as he feared, the safety of his mother and father were a great concern. His heart was torn. Yet, it seemed bearable leaving since his inclinations could indeed be wrong. Nonetheless, it was firmly in his mind.

Verion decided to visit his parents one final time before the journey. Though he previously discussed the plan with them, he thirsted for their counsel before the actual departure. The journey to Mindaloth and lessons learned were discussed at great length. Confidence swelled within him, much more than the first adventure which he unknowingly became embroiled in. Now, there was a good possibility he headed into danger willingly, or on the other hand, not at all, for his uneasy feelings could be nothing more than misgivings of Holnok's survival, he thought.

The night crept slowly by as the foursome spoke openly of concerns and memories from the past. Some of which from Verion's childhood he wished his parents had indeed forgotten. Nonetheless, they made him smile and lightened his heart. Finally, he returned home filled with past recollections and happiness as he strode hand in hand with his wife to their cottage.

The moon was overhead, smiling brightly upon them as they crested the small ridge leading to their home. Verion whisked Aleeza from her feet and carried her across the threshold, closing the door with his foot. Though it was late, the pair found time for one another.

Once more fog filled the low lying valley, caressing trees, mountains and the earth itself with its wet, cool touch as the couple awoke. Verion breathed deeply and dressed quietly, slipping from the room to prepare his wife's meal.

After a hearty breakfast the pair walked hand in hand to the stable where they saddled horses, smiling all the while. Provisions were well stocked and joy filled Verion's heart. Wanderlust gripped him yet again. Still, the nagging worry for his parents held him closely. The last time he departed Eldarn for adventure, Nira, his sister, was by his side. His life had changed dramatically since then, confirmed by peering over his saddle at Aleeza.

She is incredibly beautiful, he thought. *It is no wonder I am so happy. My dreams and wishes have all been fulfilled. There is peace in all our lands, I love my wife dearly, and we have new dragons. Now we journey to Hatar with much joy and anticipation.*

Then, thoughts of Holnok returned, forcing their way into his mind. His horrible howl when Baytor stabbed him, echoed in his ears. Verion could still see the evil lord's face twisted in pain as he thudded to the stone floor near death.

He pushed the visions and thoughts away momentarily. Were the recent images a figment of his imagination from the beginning, nothing more than horrible dreams. Perhaps he fabricated the entire thing so as to have an excuse to visit Hatar. His brow furrowed as a frown formed on his face. Making quite sure Aleeza saw neither, they swung into their saddles simultaneously.

"Well, we're finally off," he said as they moved past the well made house he built with his own hands. Constructed of wood and stone it was perhaps the best home in Eldarn, though certainly not the largest. He preferred cozy over large, though it was more than enough for two and some occasional guests. A sturdy wooden fence surrounded the plot of land the home sat on. Another small bit of handy work from Verion, who was a skilled craftsman in many arenas. Pride in everything he touched was quite evident, even down to the smallest detail and intricate designs on things he laid his hands upon.

Aleeza on the other hand, enjoyed not only helping build things, but she was an excellent gardener as well. Manicured hedges lined the walkway to the sturdy wooden front door. Flower boxes decorated several window sills in which beautiful arrays of exotic plant life sprouted forth. Flora of all types grew in abundance on nearly every side of the house, except the rear. That space was reserved for a garden in which the most bountiful, lustrous fruit and vegetables in the entire valley grew.

Each year at the farmers market, she struggled to keep up with the demand of buyers that made quite a to-do over her wares. Yet, somehow she managed, with Verion's help, to turn no one away unsatisfied.

Often, Verion teased his wife, saying their home no longer looked as a warrior's dwelling should, but that of a farmers. She feigned great insult as this, but secretly a grin formed on her lips.

The pair wore sizeable smiles as they rode eastward. Verion's parents agreed to tend the garden and house in their absence, which was a welcome help to both. As he grew older, Verion began to realize the sacrifices his parents made for him during his youth and even to this day. Some were small and others quite sizeable in his estimation. He made a mental note to thank them in some way upon his return. A special handmade gift or party perhaps, he thought.

"Trimlin, my large friend, today begins a new journey. We head for Hatar to visit your beloved mate as well as seeing Eldon and Nira. You know the way, but stay within mind's reach as always," said Verion moving forward and pushing his thoughts forward.

"I long to see Keltora and grow thrilled to be underway once again," came Trimlin's thoughts into Verion's mind as the dragon sped quickly overhead in a low pass. "It shall be excellent experience for the young ones as well." A massive roar broke the early morning silence as Trimlin expressed his pleasure.

Verion smiled and patted Brandor's neck as they rode forward. His trusted mount whinnied and snorted loudly, showing his delight as well. Verion's bond with Brandor was as special to him as was that of his dragon. He loved his horse dearly, even equal to the dragons.

The pass through the Whispering Mountains leading to the Plains of Hatar laid easterly, two day's journey from Eldarn. Verion wished to see the Watching Hill once again before crossing into the low lands. He camped there with Nira during the first journey. Since then, at Verion's insistence, it had been restored to its former glory. An eagerness to have Aleeza lay eyes upon it was buried within him. Now, it slowly rose to the surface.

"I have a light heart once more," said Verion, smiling at his wife. "It has been overly long since we have journeyed forth. Traveling makes my heart glad and all I love is close by. I have you, the dragons overhead, Brandor under me and I press onward to seek my sister and friend, it is a perfect day."

Verion glanced momentarily to Haldira. The ancient sword, one of the magical Six Holnok so desperately sought, hung silently from his waist. For a moment prior to the journey he considered leaving it behind before starting out on the path, but once more, evil stirred his mind into an uneasy state. Though, in hindsight it was a senseless thought, for he never parted from his sword, even in these times of peace.

"I am pleased at your happiness. I, too, will delight to see old friends. Stepping foot on a trail once again gives me great pleasure as well," replied Aleeza. "We must make yet another journey before summer is upon us, for my father and our lands are due for a visit soon."

"So we shall, love," said Verion. "I am quite fond of your father and a visit to Raza will be time well spent. I miss the old man."

Verion rubbed the ancient jewel that hung round his neck, a gift from the kindly old woodworker from the land of Quantar. It proved to be quite valuable and powerful in several ways. Since he received the Jewel of the Tareen, he freely communicated with Brandor and other animals as well. A power he greatly enjoyed. He was born with limited mind reading ability toward men, but his sister possessed a much greater natural ability and she held the Dragons Eye Amulet, another of the Six, which made her communicative powers toward humans and creatures alike nearly unlimited. Now however, Verion shared a small taste of her talent and found great pleasure in it.

Shadows of the trees grew tall and thin over the path as the pair traveled the great road to the east. The day passed quickly, as did the clear, cool night. Daylight came in a rush of yellow over the tree tops, skittering down the path to strike the travelers as they stirred from their bedrolls.

Pressing onward in this undisturbed fashion for two days, they slowly reaching the Watching Hill on the eve of the third night. Its ascending path was no longer overgrown and rocky. A smooth, winding trail leading directly to the ancient outpost now lay before them. Quietly moving Brandor forward, they slowly climbed toward the enormous structure.

As the pair crested the hill, Baarta, the highest point of the Dimlor Mountains, came in to full view. It was known as the Halo of the Sun, a sight which always made Verion smile, for he loved the mountains. The eastern sun rise earned the great mountain its name, for it formed a golden halo of light round its peak. As a boy, Verion spent much time here playing among the ruins, keeping imaginary foes from entering Eldarn, thereby protecting his kingdom. Not including his thinking spot, this place was where he spent the most memorable days of his childhood. It stood it shambles then, but now it had been restored to its former glory.

Verion smiled at Aleeza's response to the battlement. He stood admiring her grin and wide eyes. Her mouth hung agape as she strolled along the walls, gently running her fingertips over them as she went. She had not viewed the outpost since Verion and the townsfolk completed their work upon it for her focus lay with dragon training and her own riding lessons.

The dragons played a large part in the rebuilding as well. They carried huge amounts of wood and supplies to the site, much to the pleasure and relief of several pack mules and large draft horses. At least, according to Verion, who spoke plainly to them. Also, there were many great stones that required hoisting or hauling a great distance and dragons were the logical choice for such work. It required very little effort for a animal of such size to carry things that took thirty or more large men to move a few feet.

The nagging thoughts of Holnok's survival drove Verion into action shortly after his return from the destruction of Mindaloth. His father the king asked for volunteers, which nearly every man in the town lent a hand, for the love of the Parta was great indeed. They started early the following spring, taking nearly fifteen months to complete the work. Now though, it was a sight to behold.

"You remember well when my father and I convinced the people of Eldarn to rebuild this forgotten outpost. If ever evil is upon us again, it shall be manned with many stout hearted warriors of our village, men and women alike. I pray we have no call for it, but we shall be prepared nonetheless."

"Nira spoke of this spot during our talks, but I never imagined . . ." she let her voice trail away into silence. "It is so beautiful, so . . ."

Suddenly, Verion sensed eyes upon them as they stood near the cold, stone walls. Calling for silence, he listened intently, clutching the jewel under his tunic.

"Shhhh, quiet!" he said softly, holding a finger to his lips. "We are watched, I feel we are not alone. Thoughts come to my mind . . . dark and foreboding they are. Ready yourself. I care not for the feeling that sweeps over me," he whispered as he drew Haldira from its sheath.

Aleeza lay an arrow on its rest and slid the nock onto the string in one fluid motion.

Before he could speak again the night's stillness was broken. From the darkness, a Zenex and rider sprang forward with a terrible growl coming from the beast. Its slathering jaws snapped and popped as it rushed forward. Aleeza's arrow flew straight and true, thudding home in the creature's heart. It fell as the rider tumbled to the ground, instantly springing to its feet, a Tulak grasped in both hands. The creature warrior rushed instantly to Verion's position.

The Tulak bore a club head on one end, a spear point on the other. It stood nearly seven feet in length. The rider, a Sorn, jabbed several quick thrusts at Verion, who nimbly dodged or blocked the attacks. Then, with amazing speed and skill, the Sorn reversed his swing. The club head caught Verion squarely in the chest.

Verion barely saw the blow coming. Though he prepared for the impact it struck with greater force then he anticipated. He rolled away from his enemy as his chest grew tight with pain, the air forced from his lungs. Gasping, he lunged forward, eyes watering from lack of air. Every movement caused searing pain, which he fought to ignore.

"Quento Misra Darest," he gasped. Haldira sprang to life instantly as a familiar blue glow engulfed the edges as red flame overtook the length to the hilt. Charging forward, still breathless, he swung the enchanted sword high, releasing its power on the Sorn. It severed the Tulak in half, catching his enemy off guard. The Sorn, momentarily dumbfounded at the turn of events, stood frozen. That was all the time Verion needed. With a quick graceful move he severed the head from his foe. Its lifeless body thumped softly onto the ground at his feet, the head came to rest nearby. The entire battle had taken mere moments.

Verion grabbed his chest and crumpled to the ground wheezing as Aleeza reached his side, concern etched on her face. He flashed a quick grin between grimaces of pain from the slightest of movements. His body became chilled, yet the impact burnt hotter than flame itself.

"My chest is filled with fire, I cannot breathe and it causes great pain to move. Use your powers, my wife. Heal me, please," said Verion, grunting and groaning as he slowly lay flat on the ground.

Aleeza knelt over his prone body as she had done years before while saving his life from an arrow wound received during an attack on their previous quest. Then, they were simply companions on the same journey. Now her concern was much different. Placing her shaking hands over his chest, she began to chant quietly, attempting to heal her beloved husband.

"Naron Tono Maye," she whispered softly, moving both hands in a circular motion inches above Verion's chest. The Dragons Life ring responded immediately, engulfing her hands in an orange glow that quickly grew to intense, vibrant yellow. The magical healing ring worked its miraculous power on the prone, still shape of her mate.

Verion's eyes fluttered open as the pain slowly began to subside, until it was completely gone. Breathing deeply as a smile formed on his face, he slowly sat upright, with Aleeza's help. Again, another deep inhale was taken. Satisfaction washed over him as his chest expanded fully while taking a deep, long lungful of air.

"My survival without you would be short lived I believe," said Verion, only half jokingly but smiling broadly nonetheless.

"You must rest. We shall use the battlement tonight for shelter. Sunrise will bring a new meaning to our journey, for your premonition was indeed correct, husband. Evil has been taken up once more, it comes yet again from the east," she said, pointing eastward.

"I wish to rest as you suggest, but first we must gaze upon our new enemies. Neither of which creature I have laid eyes upon before today," he said, while making his way to the forms lying before him.

Verion strode to the bodies, the Sorn first. It reminded him much of the Zarns he battled previously. It bore tiny scales upon its dark, leathery skin. Sharp claws protruded from long fingers and sharp teeth filled its mouth. This creature was much larger and more muscular, not hunched forward like a Zarn. It stood upright, even wider and taller than Verion, and moved with surprising speed, skill and agility during the attack. After staring intently at the body for a long while, sadness taking his thoughts.

Did Holnok magically curse the Zarns once more, turning them into even more horrid beasts. During previous battles, Verion felt remorse for the Zarns, now those feelings welled within him yet again. For, he was sure evil magic created this being. Next, he turned to the Zenex.

He knelt beside a dark, thickly furred horse sized body mounted on squat, powerful legs with padded feet. Its large head held boar like jaws with exceedingly long, sharpened tusks for ripping and slashing.

Verion shuddered briefly. Realization of emergent evil swept over him like a tidal wave, filling every corner of his mind. His worst fears were brought to fruition. He knew in his heart Holnok survived the destruction of Mindolath. Once more malevolence was upon the earth, spreading cruelty and destruction as it went.

"Let us rest, then we make for Hatar with haste. We shall send warnings to all races that evil has awakened. So begin the Days of Despair," said Verion softly. "In my heart I believe we shall not see home again for some time to come."

Aleeza simply nodded and frowned. It was the first time he had seen his wife frown in many months. Rarely did she ever show displeasure at all. Verion knew she desired his rest and recovery, but she would not argue with his decision for haste. Then, his mood softened. He felt need to reassure her in some small way.

"I am fine. Trust me, you have fully healed my wounds," he said, taking her hands into his. "We must move at first light," he said, staring into her eyes and tenderly touching her hands.

The moon rose full in the star dimpled night sky as the pair unfurled bedrolls, kindled a fire and curled close for warmth to fend off the cool spring night air.

REUNION AT HATAR

The easterly sun rose brilliant, glowing behind the Dimlor Mountains. The warming rays struck the battlement early, though they did not immediately chase away the chilly morning air.

Verion donned his cloak as he saddled Brandor and Deema, Aleeza's mount. Speaking softly to Brandor, he expressed joy at having taken to the trail with his mount under him again. His steed answered in kind, quite pleased at the attention and exercise. Once horses were ready, the pair swung simultaneously into their saddles, grinning at one another.

The winding path began a gradual descent before striking a southerly trail toward the Whispering Mountains. Tall hardwood trees glimmered as sunlight touched upon the early morning dew that clung comfortably to their leaves and branches.

Verion peered skyward toward five shapes, the largest of which would perform a maneuver, then each of the others would duplicate. *Trimlin makes an excellent father. The young ones have learned so much already*, he thought, before refocusing on the trail which now turned evermore southward.

His dream of bringing the race of dragons back to the earth was becoming a reality. Pride welled within him as the five dragons flew low overhead, momentarily blocking out the sun. A broad smile grew on his face as Trimlin gave a roar when he caught sight of his rider emerging from the thick tree line.

"We shall arrive by late afternoon," said Verion happily. "It has been overly long since we have visited our friends. Though now, with last night's evil events, we cannot tarry as we would have liked. Counsel and the strength of the Six are called for now."

"I am worried, Verion. Do you believe Holnok lives hidden in the east as Ono said? Did those creatures come from his lair? This means he seeks the Sacred Six once more and our homes and friends shall be in danger yet again."

"Yes Aleeza, I am sure he lives and all you have said is true. The bearers of the Six must unite once more to finish our quest from years ago. This time, we must ensure it comes to end, for I shall not allow evil to touch Eldarn, no matter the cost."

Then, Verion went silent momentarily as he reached his mind outward to the dragon.

"Trimlin my friend, we shall reach Hatar by nightfall. Take your beloved family and fly to the city. Find Keltora and let my sister know we draw near, though most likely she is already aware we approach," said Verion, staring skyward.

"As you wish, my rider. However, I will leave Gynexa overhead in case. She will be your eyes, if I have your blessing," replied Trimlin as he dipped low overhead.

"An excellent idea. So be it. Be off now and keep watch, we will join you again soon," said Verion, as Gynexa gave several quick rolls, then began to slowly circle overhead. Trimlin bellowed a roar and quickly disappeared from sight with the young dragons in tow as they winged southward toward Hatar.

Husband and wife pressed on several more hours, eating light foods from their packs as they went, stopping for no other reason except to enjoy watching Gynexa fly above them.

Golden rays of the late afternoon sun began to slowly give way to night time's dusky shadows as they plodded their way across the open plains.

Soon, several riders appeared on the southern horizon with two riding forward. Many well armed soldiers rode behind them, their armor glistening in the fading light. Verion instantly recognized his sister and his life friend, Eldon. As the band of horses approached in a lope to meet them, Verion's smile grew wide.

Verion embraced Nira and kissed her cheek, then turned to Eldon with another embrace and firm handshake, grasping his forearm. Aleeza kissed Eldon's cheek and hugged her sister in law.

"I have missed you both. Too long has it been since we have laid eyes upon one another. There is much to speak of, some of which is troubling indeed," said Verion, while tilting his head to peer behind his friend. "Why do the King's Riders accompany you, my friend," he asked with a serious look.

"Our times have been dark of late. We have slain creatures never seen before. My intention is to be not taken unaware. The royal guards follow at my father's orders," replied Eldon, sounding concerned. Even as he spoke, his deep blue eyes scanned the surroundings for unnatural movement.

"Then you have seen them too? They have entered your lands," said Verion, surprised. "A tall scaled rider on a large darkened boar like creature. We slew one of each the night prior to this."

"Indeed, they are the same. The beast is a Zenex, and the rider, a Sorn. We have heard rumors from our spies to the east they are called these names," said Nira.

Verion took notice his sister looked as if she hadn't aged a day since their last meeting. Maturity was in her eyes and she glowed from a combination of love and happiness. Inwardly, he grew pleased at her obvious happiness. Love suited her well, he thought, smiling.

"Come, let us move to the city. We shall be safe under cover and there is much to speak of," said Eldon, still watching his surroundings.

The small company mounted, turning southerly once more as a warm soft breeze caressed their faces. Within several hours they reached the concealed city of Hatar, which for the most part remained the same as Verion's last visit. The city was still indeed concealed, now however, it stood encased by high walls with large sweeping gates pointing northerly and a smaller entrance to the south. Sentries patrolled the top most portions of the spiked battlement walls.

"Lo! Lord Eldon and Lady Nira approach. The gates, open the gates!" the sentry yelled from above. Moments later the huge doors swung silently inward. The riders passed slowly through as an enormous thud resounded at the latching of the entry behind them.

Verion and Nira, during their first encounter with the people of Hatar, shared metallurgy secrets in exchange for the ancient art of concealment. It appeared, Verion thought, the plains people retained much of their forging knowledge they were taught. Their walls and small towers were impressive and expertly made, standing tall and strong against the skyline. They were mixtures of steel and stone, holding many portals to fire arrows or spears through.

"Yes Brother, the people have learned much. The structures before you were by order of Eldon's father. The king deemed it necessary in these evil times, for he feels wickedness will not be quelled so easily this time," she said, reading her brother's thoughts. "We prepare ourselves for battle with new wicked forces, the likes of which we have never seen. It is a sad time indeed."

"So it is, Sister. I have named them the Days of Despair. I believe it is fitting. If the gods watch over us we shall put evil to flight once more. Aleeza and I have spoken of this on our trek. Nonetheless, I greatly desire your counsel as well. For, you know and see much beyond our borders, far more than I."

Verion was proud of his sister. She had grown not only powerful but emotionally and was looked upon with great favor in Hatar, being wise and kind to all who knew her. Verion knew this for he sensed it not only from Eldon but the people of Hatar as well. Her Dragons Eye amulet made her as magically potent as a fairy in many respects. She learned its full potential from the mystic fairies of Avior and put its strengths to good use in her new home.

As the group slowly ascended to the western edge of the city the King's home came into view. Verion spied the large statured man he had grown to love as a second father, standing, awaiting their arrival. King Rolnor hadn't changed. He looked as physically commanding and wise as Verion remembered. Even with more grey streaks gracing his long black hair, he stood fit, broad shouldered and an impressive sight of a man. This fact was quite evident to Verion as he was nearly crushed under the King's embrace when he dismounted.

"Welcome once more my honored guests. I am pleased to see you both well," said Rolnor smiling, gently clasping Aleeza's hand in his own. His large arms engulfed their shoulders as he started up the stairs to the great hall where food and drink were brought forth for all.

Rolnor's hall was warm and welcoming as usual. Even during the daylight, a small fire burnt brightly in the large stone fire pit that now lay in the center of the massive room. A silken banner of the rattlesnake crest of Hatar hung motionless over head, making the king appear even more royal. The hall, both inside and out, always impressed Verion who marveled at the woodworking skills of the Willons. Though not as impressive as the Quantar, the Willons were skilled carpenters and craftsman. During the recent days of peace the two united and shared many secrets, hence various new skills for both the races, including metal and wood crafting skills.

They sat talking of their first meeting years ago. Then, of all happenings since their last visit. Time flew quickly as darkness encompassed the sweeping plains when the talk turned to the approaching evil from the East.

"I feel we must unite the Six and ride to meet this challenge as before," said Verion, rubbing his finger tips over Haldira's handle. The cold steel gave him odd comfort as he probed its length as was his want when he grew uneasy.

"Holnok's forces have grown beyond reckoning. They are tenfold the size of our last battle. He has grown wise and cautious since his near death. Secretly, he bred this army for one purpose and one purpose only, to capture the Six and to kill all who stood in his way. His hordes will not be convinced to flee to their homes, for he is their creator and master," said Nira softly sighing before continuing.

"He paces within his stone towers, gazing west. I see him clearly. Having discovered our homes and knowing the items he seeks, forces shall be sent forth against us. For, long ago Natrae the Betrayer supplied him with this knowledge. Now he sends out scouting parties to catch us with our defenses down, perhaps, to capture the Six easily. If he is unable, he will send forth mass armies to take them. But, his mistakes lie in underestimating our increased powers, and secondly, he feels we are inferior to him. This is a great weakness, though he is unaware of it. He shall learn of it before the end comes."

"We have sent warning to the Fairy's to hide their city once again. Though, we are sure they have already done so. Nira has also connected with Katima's mind. She is well, as is Murn. They await our arrival at the Caves of Doom. Nira sensed we would move together in that direction. Our arrival shall be within the week if we move steadily," said Eldon.

"So we come to it once more. We must band together and discuss a plan. Like old times, eh?" said Verion smiling, attempting to lighten the dark mood which silently crept into the room.

"No matter how great your powers, you are severely out numbered. There is no chance of turning the forces away, as in your last encounter. You no longer deal with thralls, now you face killing machines bent on obeying their master's commands. Stealth and secrecy will not be enough. Though, I would have not thought your past plan to work either," said Rolnor, smiling broadly. "Perhaps I have lost my sharpness for battle in my old age."

"I am sure you have lost nothing, my liege," said Verion truthfully. "I hold great value in your counsel and it will stay with me as I travel. If what I have heard is true, even if all races band together we are not strong enough to defeat the forces that shall march against us. Once again I shall seek the fairies aid. Perhaps they will fight in force. This will greatly increase our chances, for we have all seen their magic first hand."

"There is more," said Nira quickly. "Rumors swirl several Ancients have returned from the Mystic Isles. It says they now reside in Madaria, east of the fairies Protected Realm of Avior. No one knows if this is true, for the Ancients have spoken to no other race as of yet."

"Hope rises yet again. The Ancients are undeniably more powerful than the fairies, next to the gods themselves, and would certainly able to defeat Holnok and his hordes. We must also seek their aid. Let us make for the Forest of Dreams after we visit the Caves and Avior. A dragon must wing to the Sea of Songs, to summon Jinarl, Telesta and Zarah from Tarsis," said Verion.

"During the Ancient Days, over five thousand years ago, Ancients inhabited our lands. Then came the First Years, three thousand years ago, they created the Tareen wizards and witches, of which, the fairies are their descendents. The Fading Years followed as the Ancients returned to the Mystic Isles, nearly twenty five hundred years after arriving. The Tareen have since faded from the earth in all but tales and lore. No one knows why or where they have gone. The Ancients however, remain, for they are immortal like the Fairies. They are also passive, though very powerful. I do not believe they will aid in Holnok's destruction. But, that remains to be seen," said Rolnor, with raised eyebrows.

"I wish to meet them for myself. At one time the fairies captured my imagination. Upon our first encounter, they proved very powerful indeed, as in the tales. Perhaps, when the world is threatened to slip into darkness forever the Ancients will change their ways and lend aid or knowledge," said Verion, sounding resolute. "We cannot tarry. With your permission my King, we will take our leave in one day's time."

"I trust your judgment, Lord Verion. I know your powers have grown since your last adventure, but nonetheless, take heed of all travels outside these lands. For danger and evil will follow your company relentlessly. There is no place you may hide, with the exception of the Protected Realm of Avior or the Forest of Dreams in Madaria, if the Ancients do indeed inhabit it as in the days of old," said Rolnor.

"Let us make preparations. We must be off on the second sunrise from this day," said Nira softly. "Now let us take rest, for the moon is waxing and I am weary of evil talk this night."

The moon rose full and bright overhead as Verion slipped next to Aleeza for his night's sleep. His mind filled with thoughts of evil coming forth to burn and pillage once again. Desire grew within him to send word to his parents, warning them to be cautious, even in their beloved Eldarn. He fell fast asleep in Aleeza's arms as his mind slowly drained itself of thoughts.

As morning came, Verion stood gazing from the balcony outside his room as Aleeza drew nearer to him, sliding her arm around his waist. She stood silent and withdrawn for a long while before speaking.

"I envy your sister. She can do something for you I cannot and jealousy is in my heart," she blurted out suddenly. Her voice carried sadness and disappointment laden thick in its tone.

Verion's head snapped to his left, looking squarely in her eyes. Disbelief registered on his face. Never had he sensed jealousy of any type from Aleeza, let alone toward his own sister.

"I am unable to read your mind, where she can read any thoughts she desires," Aleeza continued with a frown, her head hung low. "I wish that power as well."

"Rest assured my love, there are many times I would rather she not have that ability," Verion chuckled and smiled. "Envy is not needed, my beautiful wife. You have but to ask for my thoughts and they shall be known."

He turned, raising her face to his, looking into her green eyes once more. "I hold nothing from you. You know all thoughts within my mind, though admittedly, sometimes you need to ask before I speak openly of it. Do not carry a heavy heart, my love. Jealousy is a wasted emotion. Come, let us eat a meal. I'm famished."

They entered the main hall hand in hand, smiling as they came. The king sat talking softly to Nira and Eldon.

"A fine day greets us Lord Verion and Lady Aleeza. You have slept well I hope," asked Rolnor. "Both of you appear rested and happy as usual."

"Quite comfortably as always, my king," replied Verion as he pushed in Aleeza's chair beneath her. "Your fine city of Hatar always brings forth our joy."

Greetings were exchanged as large meals were brought quickly before them. No talk of evil activities were discussed this morning, for they knew what the quest would entail and th ifficulties and dangers soon to be awaiting the group. Once the friends took to the eastward path there would be no turning back.

The first part of the day was spent readying provisions, sharpening weapons, and ensuring all were in agreement of their travel route. Then, abundant, jovial conversation flowed as the friends gathered to recount first meetings, adventures, and their new lives since they separated. Hours passed quickly as the sun slowly hid itself behind the western horizon.

Verion sat quietly alone, staring at the reunited dragons soaring overhead in the waning light. Secretly, he wished he could speak to Aris, the fairy queen. A great respect and love for her race was with him since their first meeting. Though, her ability to enter his mind no matter the distance was disconcerting, he grew used to it and desired her counsel. Now, a visit would be delightful, for many questions inundated him. Ones he knew only the queen could answer.

Darkness was upon them as Rolnor summoned them for a meal. Again, talk began quickly and stretched far into the night. Moon light flickered between high clouds as each bade good night, knowing the sunrise would bring another adventure for the foursome. Weariness held them tightly as they made for their rooms. Anxiety slowly rose within Verion.

"Tomorrow it begins once again," he said while undressing. "Dread fills my heart, though I carry hope in our friends. We have stood against much as a company, now we journey forth to end our lands misery and fear."

"Perhaps things you wish for shall come to pass," said Aleeza. "Mayhap the Ancients shall stand by our side with fairies and the Six. None know the future Verion, only time shall play out our fate. No matter how powerful the magic, none may see what is to be."

"Nonetheless, with you by my side, all is well," smiled Verion. "Strength flows between us. If I have you, we are destined to succeed."

Aleeza remained silent and slid into bed, patting the spot next to her. A smile graced her beautiful face.

"Come, you need rest," she said, patting the bed again. "The bed is warm and soft and your queen desires her king."

Verion awoke smiling, as soft whistling of bird songs wafted through the open window. Slipping from bed, he dressed quietly, taking care not to disturb Aleeza. Striding to the balcony, he slid his magical sword from its sheath, turning it over again and again in his palm. He began to run his fingertips over Haldira contemplating the day's journey and the new quest before him. Subconsciously he traced the rune letters that ran the blade length, while thinking of his father who presented the sword to him.

The previous quest taught him a great deal by forcing him to grow from a naïve boy to a battled hardened man in a very short time. Since then, confidence in his decisions was at its peak. He felt mature and proud of his life. Love for Aleeza filled every fiber of his being and he fulfilled promises of visiting life friends from distant lands. He was a man of his word, that fact made him swell with pride. What type of king would he be if his word held no value or could not be trusted, he thought. Yet, he wondered how his father would handle this journey, what counsel would he give.

Inhaling a deep breath of the cool morning air, he turned to face his wife, who now stood behind him smiling. She was dressed and ready for travel. Hand in hand they slowly walked to the stables.

Rolnor stood waiting for them, dressed simply in tunic and pants with a large tan cloak flowing from his shoulders, as it stirred gently in the soft breeze. A broad smile graced his face as he embraced the pair with his large arms. Grasping Verion's shoulders, he stared into his eyes. Rolnor's stern gaze held Verion's as he spoke.

"Once again young lord, farewell brings us together. Now you set forth without knowing what end lies in wait. You are a future king, I have every faith in your decisions. Lead well, as I know you will. Bring those I love home safely, including yourself and your lovely life partner," he said, smiling now. "Stay alert, for your movements will be difficult to conceal. No more shall I say."

"You have always provided wisdom to me my lord. I will heed your advice to the letter if I may. For, only the gods know where our path will take us. Though, hope lives in my heart knowing the Ancients have returned. Messages shall be sent as often as we are able. Farewell for now, my King. Do not despair or let darkness enter your heart," said Verion softly.

The four mounted together and rode from Hatar as the sun broke the easterly horizon in its full splendor. It showered the riders with its spreading warmth as they went.

Verion glanced overhead, smiling broadly as nine dragons glided above them. Trimlin and Keltora saved the company's lives on several occasions during the previous quest and now their numbers had multiplied. Faith swelled within him as thoughts of numerous dragons and fairy aid came to his mind. Even more exhilarating was the prospect of the Ancients joining their cause.

Joy gradually built in his heart, for his thoughts turned to Aleeza. The sole notion in his mind was bliss whenever his wife entered his sight. Love occupied every thought as he pushed designs of worry and despair from himself with force. Turning to his wife, he smiled a heartfelt grin.

Sound of his sister clearing her throat caught his attention. Her smiling face stared back at him as he frowned, shaking his head. Light laughter filled his ears as he began to mumble under his breath.

"I admit this part of our togetherness was not missed," he said aloud. Now incapable of hiding his thoughts from Nira no matter his determination, he grew frustrated. Embarrassment swept over him as he realized she read every thought, yet he was furtively pleased to be near her again. Delight welled within him, yet it was short lived as he rode further eastward into oncoming malice.

The group turned northerly, bypassing the Battle of Ages which lay to the east. They rode for the stone bridge joining the land of the Willons, Eldon's people and the Quantar, Aleeza's home.

It laid many leagues yet to the north. Verion recalled the way from his first quest, as he rode to the front of his companions and took the lead.

Conversation abounded during the the journey while the group steadily pressed forward for two days with no hint of danger around them. This troubled him, for he fully expected to be pursued or attacked during the trek. Even his sister remained silent during the ride, she had not alerted once. It seemed unnatural and unnerving as he rode steadily forward.

I know we are watched, yet sense no eyes upon me. Why have we not been attacked? I am sure Holnok seeks us. Rolnor advised me to be wary at all times. Still, we travel freely and unhindered. There is something amiss here, though I cannot understand it, he thought.

"Agreed Brother," said Nira, smiling. "There is something odd about our journey to this point. Perhaps, it could be we have nine winged guardians above us. None would dare come against us, even with large numbers. It would be foolish at best. Nonetheless, there is something foul at work. I sense it, but it is quite distant yet."

This was one time Verion was pleased his sister read his thoughts. Confirmation of his growing discomfort helped soothe the uneasiness. His mind quickly read Eldon's and Aleeza's thoughts. They, too, felt the same, though neither uttered a word.

As the sun sunk behind the western horizon, Verion called for a halt to make camp. They reached the bridge unopposed. The next morning would bring them into the land of the Quantar, his wife's homeland. Verion was sure they would receive a warm welcome. One he would enjoy, for he was very fond of King Cytan, his father-in-law. His kind face and gentle eyes topped a muscular frame that lay hidden beneath his simple clothing. He was a stately man that Verion carried great respect for. In expressiveness and mood he was the opposite of Rolnor.

After the meal, despite no sign of the enemy, Verion posted a watch throughout the night. Aleeza volunteered for the first duty. Meanwhile, Verion slept well, despite sleeping alone. Eldon awoke him for the last watch where he enjoyed the rising sun as it crept slowly over the tree line to the east.

The sunlight gently sifted through the tree tops and onto his face as he sat solemnly, deep in thought, motionless for some time until his companions began to stir. Troubling thoughts were pushed away as pans began to clank and clatter for a meal. Joining the group to aid in building of the fire or preparation of food, he was put to work immediately. Nira asked for some kindling wood, sending him off into the forest, which still lay thin about them.

Wildlife moved freely about him showing no signs of concern which put him at ease as well. Then, Holnok entered his mind. He wondered why the High Lord turned to hateful ways. Was it always his demeanor to covet treasure and riches or had something from his past drove him to resent—no, hate—outlanders and fairies. Baytor once told a story of Holnok's father being stripped of power and banished from the wizard world of the Tareen. Why seek revenge for something so long ago. The fairies were merely descendents, why punish them.

Never could he be allowed to possess the Six, for if he gained their power the world would fall under his control. That thought lingered with Verion for a long while as they traveled that day.

After a delicious meal from his sister, the companions took to the trail once more, riding until the bridge came into view. There, Verion made camp, though it meant a delay, he needed time to think clearly and be alone, feeling a plan would come to him. The sunset turned the night sky orange as it sank from sight. Aleeza came to her husband and sat silently by his side as he wrapped his strong arm around her.

STONE OF SIGHT

"Ah, my outlander friends, I see your dragon clan is growing. Now, you attempt to gather the original company that brought about my downfall in Mindaloth. Good! For, I wish to ensure you are all together when I bring about your destruction," said Holnok, speaking aloud to himself, as was his way.

Sitting comfortably in his lone chair, staring at the images dancing above him, his eyes fixated on Haldira hanging by Verion's side. As he watched the future king ride slowly to the City of Life, a slow wicked smile grew on his face. Revenge entered his mind in a great rush.

"Come closer within my grasp young fools. You save me great effort as you come toward my lands," whispered Holnok. Then, suddenly, he rose in a flash of anger. "Why should I tarry any longer? These cretins have deprived me of my wants for too long. I shall *take* what I desire. My forces will sweep you all away."

With that, Holnok rose, gently lifting the Stone of Sight from its staff, tucking it securely away. But, not before openly admiring it once more, then he strode from the room into the hall where Natrae paced nervously.

"What did you see my lord? Do they approach as you have foretold?" asked Natrae nervously, licking his lips, shaking with anticipation. Dreams of his future kingdom danced in his mind.

"Indeed. They are making for the land of the Quantar people. I shall send forces to intercept them. Perhaps I will only burn the city. Providing of course the imps surrender to me first. If they do not, they all shall die, including the bearers of the Six," said Holnok before letting loose his horrible, hideous laughter which echoed down the cold stone hallway.

Then, Holnok stopped suddenly. An alarm went up from the guards near the gates of the fortress. He rushed to the western most window with Natrae in tow and peered out. A lone cloaked figure approached, walking slowly as he came. Several guards rushed forward to meet him, their long pikes raised, preparing to use force to halt his progress. Their warnings went unheeded. Then abruptly, they froze in place like grotesque stone statues as the hooded figure continued without losing his stride. He glided past as if they didn't exist.

The heavy fortress doors groaned open slowly, moved by some unseen force. Once the intruder gained entrance, they quickly clanked and locked shut as he passed.

Impossible, thought Holnok. *It takes many strong men to open the fortress gates, yet there are none in sight. What trickery is this.*

Holnok drew his sword and rushed to the great hall, preparing to meet the figure on the outer stairs. As he arrived, a flash of light caused him to shield his eyes momentarily. There, in his hall stood the cloaked and hooded figure, motionless.

"Who is this fool that dares to enter the High Lord's halls uninvited," asked Holnok in a demanding tone. "You provoke my wrath coming before me without kneeling! You shall beg for my pardon ere I slay you here in Selonoth. I am . . ."

"Silence," the hooded figure said in a near whisper, abruptly cutting off Holnok's ranting. The stranger's voice, though low, was crystal clear, projecting itself throughout out hall while drowning out Holnok's tirade.

Holnok's voice left him. Unable to utter a sound, his hand clutched desperately at his throat in fear, gasping for air that would not come. The sword he held fell to the floor with a resonant clank of steel meeting stone.

The figure strode past Holnok, his face still obscured by his hood as he lowered himself gently into the high backed throne chair.

Natrae cowered in a nearby corner as his master fell to his knees before him, trying desperately to speak, wheezing for breath. His face was horribly twisted as he fought for air that refused to enter his lungs. His eyes locked with Natrae's, silently begging for aid, yet both were unable to move. Holnok was frozen from magic, Natrae from fear.

"I have come to form an alliance, to offer my aid to you Holnok. Do you accept?" the figure asked simply, unemotionally. "You would benefit greatly from it. This is my oath to you."

Holnok could do nothing but nod his head, still clutching his throat. Without warning, he fell forward to all fours, drawing in precious gulps of air, though his voice remained silent. Pale color began to show in his skin once again as he inhaled deeply.

"I am Torlen, an Ancient from the land of the Mystic Isles. After nearly three thousand years my people have come back to these lands. Rejoice, for I am here to aid you in your quest for the Sacred Six," said Torlen quietly, almost imperceptibly.

For the first time in his life, Holnok was speechless. Slowly he rose, staring openly at the hooded figure. His breathing slowly returned to normal as he apprehensively inched toward Torlen. The intruder sat motionless, his head turned downward. Shadowed by the cloak hood, his face remained unclear and hidden.

The High Lord's eyes went wide in disbelief that this man, this being, would dare take his throne, treating it as another spot to rest his frame. Slowly, fear welled within him, becoming clearly fixed upon his face. Sweat beaded his high forehead as the stranger raised his eyes to stare at him intently.

"How is it you enter my lair at your whim? What aid do you carry that gives you such power? Show me your face if we are indeed to have this alliance of which you speak. I have no time . . ." again, Holnok's voice was muted as Torlen's hand moved slightly.

"My, you are an impatient one are you not. It is no wonder you are a failure" quipped Torlen quickly, his voice growing louder now. "I am far more powerful than you could ever imagine Holnok. There are many things at stake which you do not even begin to understand. Your pitiful attempt to possess the Six is a disgraceful effort, one which nearly cost you your life at the hands of your former commander and a mere group of outlanders."

Holnok felt flushed with wrath. He simply suffered setbacks during his efforts to hold the Sacred Six, they were not disgraceful by any means, he thought, as fury clutched him. No one ever defied him by using merely his name without the proper respect of lord, master or High Lord. Then, to dare to call his quest 'pitiful' was nearly all he could stand. Clenching his fists, he seethed with anger. His eyes narrowed into slits. Yet, he managed to remain silent as Torlen continued. His voice was lost more from fear than rage.

"Long has my race maintained peaceful ways. Since we are immortal, I have had much time to ponder our existence. While my people have always remained passive and possess no desire to attain higher aspirations, I feel the pull of power and ownership of greater things then what is held on the Mystic Isles. So, seizing the opportunity to return to this land and strike out on my own accord, I fixated on Selonoth for your thoughts are so easily read. Aid has come in your quest for domination of this world."

"Then, you mean to help me and serve by my side?" asked Holnok forwardly, as a dry smile formed on his face. Dreams of destruction and domination formed in his mind on a grandiose scale, one larger than he ever imagined possible.

Torlen gave an icy laugh that chilled Holnok's blood. He shrank in fear. A look of shock covered his pale face as he fumbled back from the throne chair. His goals of power and glory instantly disappeared from his thoughts. Standing staring blankly, he felt alone, isolated and confused.

"With a single thought you would vanish, never to return. You fool! Do you think I would share power with one so inferior? I shall allow you to remain alive and by my side as my commander. But, my dear Holnok, pay that price and you shall receive what your heart desires the most, the Sacred Six, for your very own. What say you," asked Torlen coldly.

The Ancient being neglected to tell Holnok once he used the Six for his own plans, they would be rendered powerless. Then of course, by the time Holnok received them they would contain no value or power. He also omitted facts the Six could render all races as mindless thralls under his control, leaving him in total mastery of the earth. Holnok's status as commander was no more than a thin attempt at a ruse.

Holnok was unaware of this as he stood dumbfounded. *Commander! What manner of trickery is this. I am High Lord, not some mere servant*, he thought. *Never will I agree to this. Perhaps I can slay this fool before he speaks again.* Several moments passed as his mind worked quickly, attempting to grasp all that happened in the short time since Torlen arrived. His guards were immobilized or dead, the fortress breeched, he was nearly choked to death, and the stranger never lifted a finger. His mind jumped forward to the future. *Perhaps I could attain the Six as promised, then find a way to destroy Torlen in secret. Until then I will agree to whatever is necessary to hold my treasures.* As he spoke a wry, deceitful smile formed on his lips.

"I agree to your terms without question," said Holnok, nearly choking on his own words, forcing them from his mouth. "All I ask is to be informed of all that happens. Agreed?"

"Agreed," said Torlen quietly. "You have my oath. Knowledge of all that happens, if it concerns you, shall be shared."

Torlen rose, throwing back his hood. Holnok gawked openly, as a gasp came from the corner where Natrae remained hidden, immobilized by fear.

Torlen was an incredibly handsome man. Dazzling long white hair adorned his head, lying braided down his back. His features were smooth with a face that held eyes shining with the brilliance of the sun, but the color of the sea. Radiant garb, filled with silver, white, and gold adorned his body as he stood tall and strong, appearing as a god in the evil hall he now occupied.

Again, Holnok shrank back, fighting the urge to bow before this god like being. *A perfect being*, Holnok thought as he turned his eyes from him, unable to withstand the vision. He lowered his head and slowly began to kneel.

The rapid patter of soft footfalls was heard as Natrae scampered from the room, openly weeping as he fled.

"What are thy wishes, my lord," asked Holnok, with humility in his voice. "I will do thy bidding without question my liege."

"So you will my Commander, and you shall be rewarded well," said Torlen grinning. "Walk with me, we shall speak together."

Though hesitant, Holnok slowly rose and followed. Never did he dare draw close to Torlen, he strode behind him and to one side or the other, not having courage to look upon him or gaze at his face.

So it was, Holnok became a servant to his own lust and greed. Answerable to a powerful, magical and frightening master.

CITY OF LIFE

"I am ready to move," said Verion with vigor. He slept well, when he did sleep. The sun refreshed him as it struck his face, for the morning came clear and bright bringing sounds of singing birds to his ears. Outwardly, he smiled. Tinkling of pots and pans being packed came to him as he strode from the camp. Pausing briefly, his mind reached out to his dragon.

"Trimlin my friend, it is time. Send Jarnea to Tarsis. Have her to fly north until reaching the sea, then search the shore line for the great city. She will be able to speak with Jinarl or Telesta, they will understand her thoughts. Pass along that I wish he, Telesta and Zarah meet us at the Caves of Doom with all speed. The dragons may carry them hither."

"I will send her now, my rider, with haste," replied Trimlin to Verion. "We have patrolled all night, seeing no signs of danger about you. Your journey this morning should be worry free."

"Many thanks, my friend. I must hasten, the companions await me. We will speak on the trail as time permits. Stay safe and farewell for now."

Verion returned to camp still puzzling over the fact evil had not been sighted. *Were the Zenex and their Sorn riders nothing more than a fluke? Perhaps evil is not marching forth as I previously believed. Yet, all signs make it so. How has evil escaped my sight if we are indeed hunted. Will Holnok wait until the Six have gathered once more then attempt to take them. Yet, that would not bode well for him, since our powers could unite.*

Deep thoughts held him as he saddled Brandor for the day's journey. A disquiet, brought on by rising thoughts and worries, formed freely in his mind. In his heart he knew his first impulse was true. Even Nira confirmed what he knew, and if anyone would know, she would certainly be able to foresee it. The fairies would certainly have answer, he thought. Katima will know.

A warm, gentle touch landed on his shoulder. Turning, he prepared to greet his wife and grew surprised to see Nira by his side with an uneasy look on her face.

"I must speak openly before we depart. It is a matter of some concern," she said solemnly.

Verion knew it was urgent, he sensed it. His sister was never one to be so grave unless it was called for. Except in battle, she was normally smiling and joy filled. Worry welled within him as he gathered his friends round, listening intently as she spoke.

"Something is amiss with Holnok. No longer can I see him," she said with a hint of frustration. "His thoughts have been hidden from me. What magic he possess or if my own powers have faltered, I do not know. Nonetheless he is gone from my vision."

"Has he departed his lair? Does he come forth?" asked Verion quickly, as panic came in a flash. "Are we to be waylaid then."

"I do not know," said Nira, her frustration plainly growing. "He was there, staring westward. I could see him plainly. Suddenly, he seemed . . . frightened. Madness took him. Terrified thoughts came to me as he ran through his fortress, sword in hand, then he was gone from my Eye. Now, I sense nothing. Only a haze remains. Foresight is gone and I am unsure what to make of it."

Sudden fear gripped Verion. He felt without seeing his foe clearly it was indeed a bad omen.

"I am wary of this. Yet, I cannot imagine Holnok finding some secret source of power or magic that enables him to hide from you. Let us ponder it as we move. We must tarry no longer," said Verion quietly. "Perhaps your visions will return as we draw closer."

Clopping of the horses shod feet were lost in the depths of the forest as they crossed the stone bridge leading to the land of the Quantar. The morning dawned unusually cool, causing each rider to don cloaks against the chill as they took a trodden path leading to the tree line. Unlike their first journey to this land, where Verion first laid eyes on Aleeza, this trek was with purpose, not simple adventure as before.

Verion's excitement grew as he rubbed the jewel that lay under his tunic. It was a gift from Raza, a woodworker within the city. Named the Jewel of the Tareen, it seemed to beckon to him upon his first visit. Many fascinating powers were held within it, most of which he learned from Raza on the return journey home, some he found by himself, accidently. Any forces or magic lying within the crystal had not reached their full potential yet, he was sure. Still, he had no way to unlock them, or at even learn more of them.

While riding and eating their fill, the sun warmed their faces as it filtered through the tree tops. Time passed quickly as scents and sounds of the forest continually rose to greet them. Riding in file for the most part, each of the company was alone with their own thoughts for a great distance. They spoke little, for Verion sat in contemplation of Holnok's disappearance.

Again, the day drew on without event and once more Verion grew increasingly uneasy. His sister lost her sight of the enemy and no forces had beset them yet. Mere puzzlement turned to a dull throb inside his head as he searched for answers. Gloom crawled into his heart, holding it closely as he rode deep in thought.

Two days of near silence slowly fell away unnoticed as the Stone Heart Mountains drew closer. Verion loved these mountains nearly as much as the Dimlors that lay near his home. He felt comfortable riding forward in peace, though still quite alert. The ancient trees grew thicker on either side of the path that ran to the north, gently rising as it went.

The company halted on several occasions to give horses long drinks and fill water skins from one of many gurgling, clear streams that ran alongside or beneath the path.

As they crested a small ridge Aleeza brought forth a small flute like instrument and played four quick notes, then quickly tucked it away.

Within seconds, Verion's eyes caught movement ahead. Instantly they were surrounded by many shapes descending from trees or stepping from behind large boulders.

"Welcome home Aleeza," a figure said as they approached her. "It is good to lay eyes upon you all once again. Long has it been since your last visit. Your father and our people shall rejoice at your coming."

"It is good to see you as well, Brodell. I am joyous at my return, though I have much business with my father," she said. "Perhaps we may speak later. Now, I must be off to see the king," she said as she slowly rode past.

"He is expecting you. We sent word as soon as your company was spotted," replied Brodell, as the group rode from sight, still following the trail before them.

King Cytan, Verion's father-in-law, stood awaiting their arrival. He, too, like Rolnor appeared the same. His long blonde hair flowed down his back. Green eyes peered out from a kind, slender face. His familiar cloak draped his shoulders, as he stood silently with folded hands.

Verion was pleased to see him. He carried great respect for the soft spoken man. In many ways Cytan reminded him much of his own father, quiet and wise, yet physically strong and keen of mind. He held the kings counsel in the highest regard.

"Hail, my lord," said Verion, as he dismounted and knelt before the king. "We have been away too long, my apologies Sire. You look well, the gods smile on you."

"Rise my son," said Cytan softly, gently taking Verion's hands within his own. "I have missed you as well and it is obvious my daughter has flourished in Eldarn. She is as beautiful as ever. Love sits very well with her" he said, making his way to embrace her. "Come, one and all. Let us eat while we talk of many things that bear discussion."

They entered the royal hall of Cytan. It was simple, yet elegant and well kept. Numerous wooden effigies of kings long past stood on pedestals near the walls to either side. Most stood with hands folded before them in a peaceful gentle manner, much like Cytan himself. Others held swords with royal cloaks flowing from their backs in action like poses. Verion guessed those were the kings or nobility that had not returned from the Battle of Ages many years ago.

Banners hung on each side of an intricately carved chair placed on a small rise at the furthest end of the hall. A lengthy dining table sat in the center of the wooden floor, with benches placed on either side. The table ends held high backed chairs. One seat was never allowed to be occupied, for it was a memorial to Cytan's wife, Aleeza's mother that died many years earlier.

The king placed himself squarely at the head of the table as the others gathered on either side. Food and drink were brought before he had fully seated himself. Greetings and polite recognition went to all those who served him. Verion admired that quality in him. Cytan never ignored any servant or common person in his kingdom. He would always listen and heed their words while being overwhelmingly polite and well spoken. No one was beneath him, though he ruled them all. His reign was fair and just and the people held a genuine adoration for him. Cytan's kingdom flourished with love, peace and respect.

Verion vowed to take some of these qualities and keep them with him during his reign and his life. Cytan's calmness and temperate ways earned him great respect from the future king.

After they had eaten and drunk their fill conversation turned to their previous journey and times since they last visited Quantar. There was a great deal to speak of, for Verion did not visit nearly as often as he would have liked. Though, messages flowed regularly between the kingdoms, it was not enough, he thought.

They spoke of many things as day waned into night, bringing forth a starless sky which held only a sliver of moon. Much news of the world outside the City of Life came to Cytan.

Tidings were mostly pleasant, yet sadness and evil doings were spoken of as talk of Holnok and his minions eventually came to the forefront. However, the king was aware of a great deal already.

The king sat patiently and heard all that was said, while the companions told their tales of the journey thus far, being attacked by Zenex and Sorn alike. Concern grew on Cytan's face as Nira spoke of no longer being able to see Holnok.

"Yes, evil comes to us once more," said Cytan quietly, a hint of sadness in his voice. "Holnok is returning and with him are rumored to be creatures and beasts of large numbers. Even more savage than the last. Again, my people begin to stand guard in towers and man our walls. It is a cheerless time, peace has left our valley."

"Agreed, my liege. We have named them the Days of Despair," said Verion. "Have you any news of the evil lords comings and goings?"

"Only what my spies bring to me. Holnok has built a mass fortress yet again. This time however, it lies carved in a mountain side. There is no open way to assail it unseen. Only one side remains exposed, the front. He views much from the dark towering pinnacles, for it is believed he holds new dark magic close to him. After his escape from Mindaloth, he was ferried away by his servant, Aleeza's cousin, Natrae. They made for Morog, where they discovered many ancient secrets and long forgotten things. Things that should have remained lost to time. Now, Welkar's evil will spread for a second time, thousands of years after the Battle of Ages."

"Then, he found the beasts and their riders there?" asked Eldon. "The creatures are unlike any we have ever seen."

"No, Lord Eldon," answered Cytan. "These creatures were created from his labor within the foul depths of his lair in Selonoth, the Tortured Lands, in his tongue. Surely he fashions many other evil beings we have not yet seen."

"What does my liege know of the Ancients? It is rumored they have returned. Do you hold any truth in this?" asked Nira with interest. "We wish their aid for the quest, if we may."

"It is said they have indeed returned. East of the Protected Realm of the fairy's land, across the mountains, lies the Forest of Dreams. They have taken up home in Madaria, which has returned to its full splendor I am told, though none have laid eyes upon it to this day. It, like the fairy's Avior, has many spells and enchantments about it. None shall discover it unless led there by the Ancients themselves. Most will not travel within the forest. It brings fear and dread to them."

"Then we make for it with all speed," said Verion, his anxiousness rising once more. "We must depart for the Caves of Doom at the new sun. There, we can join with Murn and Katima. Jinarl, Telesta and Zarah should meet us there, if Jarnea has already made it to Tarsis. Then, we shall press onward to Avior to again seek the aid of the fairies. We must move with speed to Madaria from there."

"Ah, Lord Verion, I see some things are yet unchanged," said the king, with a growing grin. "It has been too long since your vitality and youthful ways have graced my halls. I shall not try dissuading you from yet another quest, for it is futile, but go with warnings. You will not face mindless Orna or Zarn on this quest. Hate filled, wrathful beings simply wishing to kill for their master is what awaits you now. Their glory comes from battle and conquest, nothing more."

"Each of us previously faced these creatures. We shall use due caution in our travels. However, I believe we will encounter them again, as you have foreseen, Father," said Aleeza. "I, for one, will welcome Katima's aid once more. Perhaps she can persuade the fairies to lend assistance to our cause as before. Our success was due in part to their protection and knowledge."

"We may rest easy with the knowledge we have one fairy on our side even as we speak," said Verion with narrowing eyes. His thought process worked rapidly as he silently planned the future of the quest before ever departing the City of Life. Abruptly, the voices of the others seemed distant, hollow, apart from him as he slowly rubbed the jewel under his tunic. Slowly, he began to realize a voice was echoing in his mind. He quickly recognized it was Aris, the beautiful queen of the fairies.

"I am waiting for you Lord Verion," came clearly into his mind. "Your quest will bring us together yet again, seeking aid no doubt. I carry news as well. Come to Avior."

He shook his head slightly, trying to rid himself of the nuisance within. *My imagination is playing tricks,* he thought. *No, I am certain it was the queen's voice. She beckoned to me and knows my wants already. We must hasten to Avior and have her counsel.*

Yet again, her voice entered his mind. "I see within your mind. There is much you do not know yet. Holnok has aid, very powerful aid that could lead to the ruin of you all, even with our support. Be wary; come to me with all speed after the Six form once more. I shall be waiting. Farewell."

"Verion . . . Verion!" shouted Nira, trying to break her brother's trance. "What is wrong? Are you ill?"

"I am fine," he said, holding up his hand to silence and reassure her. "Aris has just spoken to me. She entered my thoughts, saying Holnok has gained a powerful ally by his side. Though, she did not say who or what it was. We are commanded to reform the Six and make to Avior with all speed. So be it. Tomorrow we depart as planned. Let us make for the Caves."

The companions, as well as the king, looked shocked. Verion ignored them all momentarily as he rubbed his temples, contemplating all Aris said to him. He felt overwhelmed and frustrated he could not arrive at Avior sooner. Taking the dragons would speed the trip, but then he would be without horses if he required them. Certainly they go on foot after that, but in turn, would be moving slowly once more. Either way was not quick enough, he thought.

The question was put forth to his companions for open discussion. It was agreed they would ride their steeds to the Caves of Doom, then into Avior where they would stable them until able to return. Dragons could be used from that point on if there was a need to move instantly and rapidly. At least, that was the plan to this point.

With the dilemma solved, each bade good night to the king and made for their comfortable rooms. Verion paced restlessly for some time, until his wife's calming voice spoke to him, summoning him to their bed. Mumbling under his breath, he wondered if Aleeza's voice calmed him from an unseen magic or was it simply his great love for her that soothed him.

During the darkness of night he rose silently and began to pace again as was his way of thinking through his troubling thoughts. His mind worked slowly, methodically etching out every detail he could imagine. Things rarely went as planned, he knew that, yet he felt at peace attempting to prepare for whatever may come. The previous quest left him with a comprehension of battle and perhaps even an insight to Holnok's mind. Both his planning and the understanding of his enemy filled him with confidence. Only one concern stood in his way. It was a major one at that. What aid did Holnok receive? This was a puzzle with missing pieces. One only Aris could solve for him.

Returning to bed mentally exhausted, he fell fast asleep, getting what rest he could before dawn's light spilled through the open arched window to his left. He was unsure if he slept, though he felt pleased with himself for solving most of his mind's questions concerning his plan.

The four companions were joined by the king as they prepared for the journey. Cytan looked solemn as he strode toward the stables. His gentle face carried a wrinkled brow upon it as he stopped, facing Verion.

"I stand before you at the moment of your departure once again. At our first meeting you were asked to care for my daughter and I do this for a second time. She lives a joyous life and though gone from my lands, the knowledge in my heart she is safe, is enough.

Before the company heads into the lair of death once more, we stand together yet again. Care for my daughter, your wife. Protect her at all costs, for you know she is precious to me," said the king sadly. "You both are all I hold precious to me."

"Sire," said Verion softly with a bow. "I shall do as you ask for I dearly love your daughter and would sacrifice myself if it would mean her safe return. You carry my oath no harm shall befall her as long as my body draws breath. We shall return as soon as we may."

"Remember that Holnok is always watching. He sees and hear much. Since he entered Morog with a great wound upon him, he has only sought one thing, revenge. I imagine for a long while he forgot about your treasures, only thoughts of the company occupied his mind. Now again, he seeks the Six and your death would please him greatly. Travel with care."

"Even as we speak here his forces are growing. Yet, I feel we shall triumph. I hold hope within my heart. Keep faith, my king. Our eyes shall be open with step. You have my oath."

"I trust your words, young lord. Go with speed and watch to the east . . . always."

Verion rode slowly from the gates, the giant doors quietly closing behind him. Turning to take one final glance at the city that was his second home, he smiled before riding onward without looking back a second time. Glimpsing quickly overhead to the cloudless blue sky he saw Keltora and Trimlin circling above, keeping a keen eye on the travelers as they went. They rocked from side to side acknowledging his gaze as the sun flashed now and again from their scaled bodies. The young dragons rolled and sped through the sky chasing one another blowing small fire balls at each other's tails.

Pleasant memories flooded to him, recalling a time when Trimlin was immature and full of mischief. The young dragons were well trained, thanks in part to his many hours with them, but mostly it came from their parents. Pride for each of them filled his heart. Nonetheless, he chuckled softly at their antics as he rode for it helped him push evil thoughts from his mind, even for a short time.

The group pressed northward at a steady pace, aiming for the mighty Helix River. As before, the hidden ferry would carry them across the water toward the Caves of Doom.

This was a replay of his previous quest, Verion thought. One difference was this time Natrae did not ride alongside the group. Natrae the Betrayer, as Jinarl named him, sent messages to his master Holnok of their progress as they drew closer to Mindaloth. The company was waylaid several times due to his treachery. One attack nearly ended Verion's life. If Aleeza had not healed him with the Dragon's Life he would have surely perished. Each time during battle Natrae hid himself until the fray ended.

Finally, he was caught in the act of sending messages to Holnok. Verion put a sword point to him, then they marched to a prison at the Caves of Doom. However, within weeks of capture, Natrae slew his guard and escaped. Now, Verion sat wondering what became of him. He felt remorse and pity for the man that once rode by his side, sharing food, drinks, and camaraderie with him. Holnok promised his servant wealth, a kingdom and more, a dream that constantly danced before Natrae. So, he betrayed the bearers of the Six to his High Lord for his twisted dreams.

Now, he lived by Holnok's side. Verion was sure of it. It was guessed the two went far to the east, perhaps to Morog as Ono had foreseen. Regardless of where they hid, Verion felt Natrae's dreams were wasted. Never would he live to see them to fruition. Verion could not and would not allow them to pass. So, with these thoughts running through his mind, he rode steadily forward to assail evil once more. This time however, he would see Holnok dead. Intentions of never having evil return again, was now his singular purpose. Holnok would not escape this time.

Natrae's fate was less clear to him. Thoughts on this subject were indeed cloudy. He felt the Betrayer deserved death, to be quickly taken from the misery and false dreams possessing him now. Yet, perhaps there was hope to return him to his former gentle ways, as he once carried proudly during his time among the Quantar, before evil took him.

"Perhaps he should be given another chance," said Nira as she rode quietly beside her brother. "Who knows what life he lives now? I have seen him in my visions, constantly terrified, looking worn and hard to recognize. Though, I am sure it was him the Eye focused on."

Verion made no comment about his sister reading his mind this time. He was pleased to have her counsel and view on many matters. Chuckling softly to himself, he was struck by the fact his younger sister came to him often during their youth for advice and counsel. Now, the roles reversed themselves. Nira's aid and advice was powerful and trusted, being next only to Aris.

Life has a funny way of weaving itself, much like a giant spider's web, he thought as he rode in time with Brandor's gait. *My sister is far wiser than I in many matters. We trust her with all of our lives if it indeed comes to that. My protection is no longer needed. After all, I merely carry a magical sword, where the others have powers far greater and more valuable than mine. Though unspoken leader of the company, how I was chosen. All here are future kings or queens, even Murn is a leader of his clan. Yet, the responsibility falls to me. It should have never come to me. Though, I cannot shirk leadership. What type of king would recoil from his duty.*

Verion's head began to pulse rhythmically from his doubting thoughts. After the last quest they fled his mind, he hoped never to return. Yet, they seemed to have returned with vengeance.

Slowly picking their way along the tree line, they came to a wide grass filled hollow. Verion took pleasure in the smell and feel of grass. He dismounted and walked a short way simply to feel the softness beneath his feet, though he used the horses rest as an excuse to amble for a distance. Brandor snorted in response to his comment, seemingly insulted.

Gradually, the trees engulfed them once again as Verion remounted and pressed forward, the smell of grass still in his nostrils. The ground slowly began an ascent that took them higher and higher, over and around until they reached a peak overlooking the entire valley floor below. The ground fell away steeply before them as they sat atop the highest summit. The sun shone brilliantly on their faces for it was mid day now. Verion breathed deeply and smiled. The peaceful valley stretched far beyond sight in any direction. One clear path turned downward.

This is why evil cannot overcome good. All would be lost. The lands would be brought to ruin and all before me now would be gone. Never to be seen again, he thought.

They sat for a long while simply admiring the majestic sight before them, then reluctantly he called to move as a hawk screeched and launched from a nearby branch, soaring high on the wind currents.

After many leagues camp was called to be made as waning daylight fled the sky with speed. The group rode all day with no danger upon them, which still sat uneasily in Verion's thoughts.

Shadows disappeared as all light faded, while darkness engulfed the travelers. A deep silence lay heavy about the camp as stars grew thick, twinkling brightly overhead.

Fires were to be lit for food and warmth. *It would also lift my spirits,* he thought. As the group huddled round talking quietly of the final day's journey that would lead them to the Caves of Doom, Nira became alert.

"Something approaches from the north. It is still far off, but closing on us as we speak. There is no malice in this creature. We are in no danger," she said softly. "I believe our friend is near."

Then, Verion's ears picked up the sounds of flapping wings approaching. His eyes narrowed in the darkness, searching for the smallest of movements. Within seconds, he spotted a tiny shape fluttering between the trees, its large eyes nearly glowing in the night. Immediately, he recognized Ono.

"Ono . . . Ono," he called softly. "We are here my friend, come to me," he said in a near whisper.

Ono's dark, leathery wings beat a steady rhythm as he approached. His squat body landed nearby on an overhead tree branch, surveying the ground intently with his large eyes, before hopping to the ground near the fire.

"It has been too long my little friend," said Verion, bowing low before the Grendar. "I have missed your company. You must visit Eldarn more often. It has been months since we have laid eyes upon you. What brings you this way, in darkness no less?"

"My Lord Verion," said Ono, returning the bow. "I bring news as in our days of the quest," he said, with his usual crooked smile, as he slowly swayed side to side. "Since the Grendar are free to travel the lands at will, we have learned much that may interest you. I travel at night simply because it is easier for my old eyes to see. They are far too sensitive for long journeys during daylight in my declining years," again the crooked smile formed on his face.

"Greetings from Hatar, friend of the tall ones," said Nira, smiling broadly. "I am pleased to see you well. Tell what helpful news you carry."

Ono's eye went wide. Nira had gone unnoticed standing in the shadows. He fidgeted and bowed awkwardly.

"Greetings, my Lady Nira. Forgive me for not catching sight of you. The Grendar send love and respect," said Ono, bowing several more times before turning to Verion once more.

"We enjoy lives in many new places since our freedom was granted to us," he said, bowing yet again to Nira, whom the Grendar worshipped as their savior. "We know Holnok has returned. There is a new fortress called Selonoth high in the Tortured Lands, lying far north of the ancient evil battlement of Morog and east of the Forest of Dreams. Many new evil things, horrible creatures and beasts now grow there, and his numbers are very large indeed. Ten fold his strength at Mindaloth."

Ono paused, staring at the four that sat by the fire listening with great interest. His head moved from side to side as the firelight reflected from his saucer-like eyes. It appeared to Verion that Ono was searching for unnatural noises nearby. Then, the little creature continued.

"There is even more news my friends," he said, now shifting from foot to foot. "A stranger entered Selonoth. We believe him a powerful wizard or magician."

"Alas, that is ill news indeed, Ono?" said Nira. "How do you come by this."

"Another Grendar, Poso, was performing scouting duties when he came upon Selonoth unlooked for. Then, he sat and watched the fortress for some time, learning all he could. A shadowy figure approached the battlement and the guards tried to assail him, but the figure froze them where they stood. The great doors opened and he entered unhindered. Very powerful magic must be with him. I fear for the tall ones once more."

"Then, you discovered Selonoth by accident? And this stranger of which you speak, is he still in Selonoth?" asked Eldon.

"We heard rumor of strange beasts roaming about, so my race set forth to gain more knowledge. My kind does not venture to the east often, for it is believed to still hold evil. We discovered Selonoth, and by chance we saw the stranger. He still resides there," replied Ono.

"Once more we are in your debt my little friend. I am uncertain how our race survived so long without your aid," said Verion with a large grin. "You have done well. Though, there is one final thing, Ono. What you can tell us about the stranger? What did he, or she, look like?"

"This, I do not know, for the figure was hooded and cloaked," the creature replied.

"Perhaps we shall find out what we face as we move to the fairy lands. They may have used their powers of sight to see the stranger, where as we cannot," said Aleeza.

"I shall return as information comes to me. Be watchful tall ones, danger is spreading," said Ono, jumping into the air, hovering before the group. "I take my leave and shall return when able. Never turn your eyes from the east."

With that, he disappeared quickly into the darkness that now lay as a blanket of blackness around the campfire, closing in around them as they pondered Ono's words and prepared for sleep.

"Then rumors reaching the west are indeed genuine. Holnok survived and we must face him once more. This time I pray to the gods for a different ending," said Verion.

"Each us knew in our hearts evil survived Mindaloth. Though we pushed it from our thoughts, it returns to haunt us. I for one vow to end his wicked ways," said Eldon.

"We should rest now," said Nira. "Our destination will be waiting for us soon enough."

HOLNOK'S MISERY

"My lord, why not simply go forth and kill the outlanders, then take the Six for our own?" asked Holnok, his voice shaking slightly. "They are unaware we watch them as they move. The element of surprise would be ours. Quickly, we could hold the treasures in our hands and begin to make this world bow to our power."

"There is no need," said Torlen in his soft voice. "They are bringing the Six to us even as we speak, for the young fools believe gathering enough might around them will cause our defeat. Little do they know our plan is much larger and their insignificant attempt will fail. I am certain they will try to enlist fairy aid and seek my kin for the same, unaware the Ancients will not support their cause. For they are too peaceful to wage open war upon us. Be patient my commander, the treasures are coming to me."

"The fairies have hidden Avior from my Stone of Sight. I cannot locate their Realm, even though I have tried with all my will. Can you see them master? I greatly desire revenge for my father. Hate seethes from me, I shall see them conquered before all others. With your blessing of course, my liege."

"It is puzzling to me as well, my friend," said Torlen with a furrowed brow. "I have been unable to see into their world. It should be a matter of ease, for Ancients are more powerful than their kind. It is a mystery I was pondering before you broke my thoughts when you barged in unannounced."

Holnok stood frozen in fear, feeling certain he would be struck down or made to disappear for his mistake. His palms grew slick as his stomach knotted tightly, waiting for a slight movement from Torlen or a spoken language he had never heard before. He was convinced it would send him spiraling into some barred hole deep in his own dungeons or find himself on a torture rack, begging for mercy or perhaps something far worse. An involuntarily flinch caused him to close his eyes for a moment to regain composure. Then Torlen spoke, breaking his thoughts of a horrible end.

"Perhaps my kind has already aided the fairies with protection? Nevertheless, I will discover their precious city and destroy them with the others. Their time grows short enough. You will indeed have the revenge you so desperately seek."

"They have had much time to perfect their arts my liege. Often I have attempted to seek their hidden city, but to no avail. Mayhap they are more powerful than we imagined? They have always been my bane of existence," said Holnok flatly. Then he realized the err of his comment.

Torlen stood quickly, his eyes flashed with pure anger at the suggestion other beings could match powers against him.

Holnok retreated several steps as Torlen appeared to grow in size before him. The High Lord cowered to his knees, burying his face against the stone floor, awaiting his fate from his new master. He was certain he drew ire from Torlen with his words, bringing forth his own doom.

All light was sucked from the chamber; no noise carried on the air. Silence reigned as a void of darkness surrounded Torlen. Then the floor shook beneath his feet. His voice rumbled like thunder as he spoke, making his commander shudder uncontrollably.

"My domination shall be complete. No race dare stand in my way. *I* am the master of this world," said Torlen. "They will bow to me or shall be wiped from this earth."

Then, light and sound returned as quickly as it departed. Torlen sat quietly in the throne chair once more, showing no hint of the anger that possessed him mere moments before. He rose and began to pace slowly.

"The outlanders have not yet reached the Caves. The bearers are to meet there. I have foreseen it. Send many Gorlan forth with orders to capture the outlanders. If they resist, kill them all and return with my treasures, for I tire of waiting" Torlen said as a smile grew on his face.

A muffled scream was heard from the corner, followed by footfalls. Natrae fled from the room in near madness. His shrieks were lost in the depths of the fortress as he disappeared from sight.

Holnok stood on wobbly legs, afraid to lay eyes upon Torlen. His eyes fixated on the floor before him, quaking all the while.

"As you command master," he said with a crackling voice. "I will carry out the orders myself," said Holnok, bowing several times nervously.

"It appears you must, for your servant has fled your side," said Torlen with a sly smile.

Holnok shuffled from the room. As the doors closed loudly behind him, terror gripped him. He ran mindlessly down the hall as if chased by invisible demons, his mind gripped with uncontrollable terror. Wedging his body into a dark corner he cowered for a long while, unable to move, frozen in fear. He fought a great urge to sob openly.

Finally, he composed himself and headed for the lower level of Selonoth, to the home of the Gorlans. He issued their orders and drew back as they howled and shrieked their approval. The baying deafened him. Holnok watched as they bound from the fortress with all speed, running on all fours as they went.

"I must regain control of Selonoth. But how! Torlen seems invincible, having more power than in the tales of his kind. Patience, yes, patience, I must hold a sliver of hope I shall find a weakness to use against him," said Holnok in a near whisper as he strode the halls.

Meeting of the Six

Verion rose early to speak briefly with Trimlin. He sent the dragons to scout ahead in all directions, even rearward. Only Trimlin remained with the group as they moved for the Caves before sunlight lit the eastern horizon. Verion was inwardly excited at the upcoming reunion with his companions, Murn, Katima, Jinarl, Telesta and Zarah as well. He could not have been more pleased with his life friends. After all, he indeed trusted his companions with his life several years ago during the quest to Mindaloth. Though in hindsight, he did not actually choose them, they came together by happenstance. Nonetheless, they grew close to one another and he was going to rejoice at their reunion.

The days passed quickly as the riders followed the trail to the east. It ran through many ridged hills and stony slopes that dropped away sharply here and there. From an over looking cliff they could see water flowing far below, passing through a narrow, rocky gorge. Their path however, turned sharply southward for a way, until turning back to the east across gullies and washes, some laden with green grass. The company stopped for rest and allowed the horses to graze peacefully as the travelers took food and drink.

The sun was at full strength as Verion remounted and began to move. Further on, the land turned colorful once more. Grasses and bushes were thick and abundant with flowers growing sporadically along many folds of the land. Some ridges were steep and would not dared be traveled upon, forcing the riders to navigate around them, slowing their journey even more, thought Verion.

Though, at this point he was relaxed and few worries were upon him. Several days travel wore away while his mind filled with memories of his allies as he rode. Then, sounds of the mighty Helix River flowing in the distance came on the breeze. Verion felt he owed his friends from Tarsis for his new found fondness of the water. Though mountains still captured his heart and love, the water had grown on him. He became quite enamored with it.

During his visits to Tarsis, he developed an affinity for the sea and all running water. He thrilled at the experience of being on open waters aboard a ship. Never before had he felt the waves beneath his feet, it was exhilarating to him, a feeling he would carry throughout his life. With each subsequent visit to the sea port he enjoyed a voyage, no matter how short.

The company neared the calmest part of the river, the eastern most boundary of the Willons. There he began searching the shoreline for the hidden ferry. Verion began to grow increasingly uncomfortable, sensing the company was being closed in upon by an unseen force. Desperately he scanned the surroundings for signs of unnatural movement. Though he saw none, he continued to hurriedly load the ferry and pushed off.

"Nira, do you . . . ." he never finished his sentence.

"Yes, there are many beings nearly upon us, they come from the east," she said, pointing toward the opposite shore. "They move with speed and with numbers much larger than ours."

Verion was gripped with panic. His worst nightmare was unfolding before his eyes. Suddenly, he felt helpless, trapped on a ferry with little defense. It was unnerving at being barely half way across the waterway and vulnerable. Then, he paused as terror gripped him. Suddenly his mind whirled as he groped for a plan to save his companions.

The shoreline consisted of low lying plains which extended for several leagues north, until reaching the mountainous terrain of the Caves. There was little shelter to be taken if they needed to defend themselves. Even if they could reach shore before being besieged they would trapped in the open. A rocky, sparse tree line lay close by, perhaps with luck they could reach it in time to secure small cover.

"Oars! To the oars, quickly. Row with speed, NOW!" he yelled frantically.

Eldon grabbed the oars, throwing one to Verion. They cut into the water with ferocity. Both men pulled with all their strength, straining against the handles as the ferry slowly approached the shore. Even pulling with every ounce of power, the horses and companions aboard made for slow going. The ferry seemed to inch along if indeed move at all.

His head swiveled to and fro in search of danger, certain he would be too late. Arm and back muscles burnt under the strain of rowing, yet he knew there was no time to stop. If he faltered it would mean certain capture or death. Time moved agonizingly slow as the oars splashed feverishly into the water. Finally, the shore was reached as he flushed with anger at being taken unawares.

The company quickly secured the ferry as Verion spoke silently to Brandor, sending the horses for cover as their riders ran toward protection. Verion knelt behind one of the few trees spotting the shoreline. Nira and Eldon found large boulders to conceal them while Aleeza nimbly climbed one of the few trees over Verion's head, acting as the company's eyes.

"What do you see Aleeza?" asked Verion quietly, realizing they could never make thick tree cover before they were beset.

"Many dark shapes come toward us. I have never seen them before. They run on all fours, dark and fur covered, like wolves. Only, they are enormous and carry weapons upon their backs," she said.

"They growl and snarl as they come. They are nearly upon us, less than league away now," said Eldon, his keen senses picking up each sound. "Voices? Yes, voices come on the wind as well."

"Prepare for battle my friends," ordered Verion. "We are to be besieged once again. Let courage grip your heart. Stand fast and aim true."

The company drew swords and readied arrows as the beasts reached their position.

The Gorlans skidded to a stop seventy yards from the shoreline where the company lay barely hidden. Slowly they advanced. The leaders head turned from side to side searching for the slightest movement. Then the beast rose to full height on his hind legs and sniffed the air.

"The man-things are here. I smell them. Find them, they go to Torlen. If they resist, kill them," he snarled, as the three dozen creatures began to fan out, inching slowly toward the river's edge. "We must have their trinkets. Hunt them, now."

Verion felt vulnerable. The river lay rearward, there was no hope of escape there. They were being enclosed in a semi-circle. A feeling to protect the others grew rapidly, quickly becoming overwhelming. Even if he sacrificed himself for their chance at an escape, he would risk it. His sister and wife were about to be slain if action wasn't taken quickly. Trimlin could not be used for defense, for the creatures were nearly upon them, advancing far quicker than he anticipated. It was up to him to divert their attention, hoping the others could flee or slay as many as possible before making an escape.

"Quento Misra Darest" whispered Verion softly, as Haldira sprang to life.

The nearest Gorlan instantly sprang for his position. Not even Verion's whisper was hidden from the creature's sensitive hearing. The beast leaped forward, drawing its sword in midair and attacked within a mere moment. But it was not quick enough.

Verion was ready. He stepped nimbly to the side, swinging Haldira in a rapid, high arch. The creature fell before him headless. Haldira's blade length glowed red as he charged recklessly forward. A war cry came from his lips, momentarily bewildering the Gorlans. No longer did he care for his own safety, the thought of his companions being taken or slaughtered was too much to bear.

The leader gave an enraged howl and charged Verion with three others by his side. Aleeza and Nira fired simultaneous arrows, slaying one to the the leaders left. He fell pierced through the heart and eye.

The remaining Gorlans charged Nira's position in a wave, aware of her as she stood to fire. They charged forward, standing on their hind legs as they came, while drawing swords in an amazingly graceful motion. They hurtled onward to attack.

Eldon sprang before Nira, sword in hand, preparing to defend her to the death. His blade shone bright in the sunlight. His face wore a stern, determined look.

"Come! Come closer so I may send you back to the darkness from whence you came!" he yelled, as the creatures were nearly upon him. Drawing his sword up high, he waited to strike.

Suddenly, several of the attacking creatures in the lead were gone. Piles of ash lay scattered before Eldon's feet where the Gorlans stood moments before.

Verion's head swiveled quickly as a great horn blast came from the tree line, followed by many roars and tremendous shouts. He knew this sound. The Malmak had arrived.

The Gorlans, realizing the larger threat, stopped their advance on the company and turned to charge a large rise behind them. Now they fought in self defense. They rose to full height, standing over nine feet tall, higher than the largest Malmak and raced to meet the new intruders.

Verion watched Murn lead his warriors into battle. The giant wore his magical armor and helm he bore during the previous quest. He was protected well and carried his familiar war hammer and axe as before, swinging freely as he came.

Two Malmak were slashed and knocked to the ground, overtaken by the Gorlan's speed. As the beasts prepared to deal the Malmaks death blows, an arrow entered the side of its head, flying swiftly from Aleeza's bow. He fell backward with a thud, as the other turned to ash.

A beautiful red haired figure immerged from behind a thin tree, radiant light coming from her hands as she came. She sent blasts of magic into the remaining creatures, turning them to smoldering piles of cinder and dust. The remaining Gorlan howled, turned and fled to the east.

Verion raced to the wounded Cyclops warriors. He summoned his wife with a quick glance. Lightly she ran to his side kneeling before the bleeding giants. Their chests were slashed deeply from the Gorlans claws.

"Naron Tono Maye," she chanted softly, using the spell previously used to save Verion's life on their first quest and mend his body at the Watching Hill. Slowly her hand circled atop the Cyclops' large chest. The wounds began to heal before Verion's eyes. He urged her onto the next warrior, where she repeated her Dragons Life magic.

Verion lifted his gaze to Murn standing before him. He rose and grasped Murn's forearm tightly with his two hands.

"I am indeed pleased at your arrival my large friend. You arrived none too soon," said Verion, smiling and moving to embrace Katima.

"It is good to see you both. Despair was upon me before your arrival. I acted foolishly from fear for my companions."

"Katima had foreseen the Gorlans approach. We came with all speed," said Murn with a smile, removing his helm as he spoke. "Pardon our timing. You bravery saved them all for they would have been discovered and overrun if you had not distracted the enemy."

"I owe you a debt my Lady," said Eldon, bowing low before Katima. "You have saved us from capture or death. Thank you for my life, but more precious to me than that, for Nira's."

"My friend Eldon, you owe me nothing. I am pleased you are all safe," said Katima softly. "Come, let us proceed to our home. There is much to discuss."

Even after battle and still shaken, Verion took great pleasure in Katima's voice. For, fairy voices sounded much like music to the ears, delightful and pleasing to the listener.

Once remounted, the group cut toward the tree line bearing to the northwest. In time, they came to a long, deep valley that lay lush with thick tall grass and ancient knurled trees. Verion knew the Caves lay on the northern slope near the river that wound through the valley floor far below. Though hidden from sight from their vantage point, the flowing dark waters of the mighty Helix River could be faintly heard to sensitive ears. They began their descent after a brief respite from their saddles and a small bite to eat and refreshing drink.

The journey went quickly as the Caves of Doom came into sight before he realized the company had traveled a great distance. The sun was nearly gone from the sky as the travelers arrived. Smiling broadly at the familiar view of the cave entrance, he saw before him, Jinarl, Telesta and Zarah. A stranger stood silently by Telesta's side. He was introduced as her life partner, Milar. They had wed during the fall after Verion's last visit.

Jinarl and Telesta, brother and sister, came from Tarsis near the Sea of Songs. Verion met them as they aided the company during his initial quest to Mindaloth. Zarah was Eldon's sister who was a life partner with Jinarl. She departed Hatar for her new home near the sea after the return journey from the Bottomless Lands.

Verion was greeted warmly upon his dismount as he hurried forward with much delight.

"Greetings my sea faring friends," he began, grasping Jinarl's forearm. "I have missed Tarsis and the sea a great deal but I have missed you most of all. It has been too long, but nonetheless, you look well."

He strode to embrace both Zarah and Telesta. Introductions were made to Milar as well.

"My pardon for not aiding in your defense," said Jinarl with a frown. "We were away on a scouting trip, patrolling the borders. Katima warned us of danger and asked us to stay behind with the rest of the clan, in case of attack here."

"We fared well with the aid of Murn and Katima and returned safely thanks to her visions and magic," said Verion. "I do not believe that the four of us could have conquered the beasts."

"Come my friends, Murn's clan has prepared food for us. We may speak over a meal," said Jinarl.

The company, now nearly at its old strength, was seated once again at the table that always brought a smile to Verion, for it was oversized to the point of making him feel as a small child. Karth, Murn's brother, along with several other Malmak, brought forth several large trays laden with food and drink.

"Eat, my friends. I am sure you desire food and rest. This will aid you, at least in part. Rest shall come later. Eat, drink and tonight you may even bathe," said Karth chuckling with his deep resounding tone.

Verion stood and grasped Karth's forearm, at least as much as his hand could encompass. Likewise, Verion's arm nearly disappeared within the giant's grip. He grabbed up Verion by the shoulders and stared at him, smiling as the outlanders feet dangled high off the floor.

"Welcome back, young lord of Eldarn. Too long has it been. You look well and strong . . . for an outlander," he smiled again.

"It is good to see you, my large friend. You speak true, it has been too long since we have set eyes upon one another," then he paused and leaned close to the giant's ear. "Karth, your crushing me," he whispered as the giant set him down gently to the floor, still smiling.

The future king then began conversation immediately, for it pressed into his mind with a nagging ferocity to work through many things he wished wise counsel for.

"I am unsure where to begin," he said truthfully. "We shall speak of pleasantries later. Let us make council for the reason we are gathered here once more. Our previous mission failed, for Holnok still lives. I have known this for some time, but yet held hope my feelings and visions were wrong. Alas, as we sit here within safety, we all know he has returned."

"During our journey, we, too, have seen visions of Holnok," said Telesta. "He is alive and well, it is certain. Malice and fear shall be upon us once again."

"Images of him came clearly until recently. I knew of Holnok's survival as well. The visions came plainly prior to Verion's arrival in Hatar," said Nira, as her brow furrowed. "Once Katima spoke to me and I begged for counsel, she foresaw our journey to the Caves, so we deferred any talk for now so all could hear her wisdom."

"True," said Katima. "I have foreseen our meeting, as well as our path from here, though many things remain unclear. Now, Holnok has aid from an Ancient named Torlen. This adds a great deal of difficulty for our new quest."

"Who is this Torlen of which you speak?" asked Aleeza quizzically. "You say he is an Ancient. So it is true. They have returned to our lands. I have always believed them to be peaceful. Why would he take up arms and turn to evil ways? What could he gain?"

"His wish is to gain this world for his own," said a soft, melodic voice from the rear of the chamber. "Hoping to enslave all and become their only master."

All heads turned in the direction of the voice to see two tall figures standing in the shadows. Both slowly came forward seeming to glide as they came, their movements, slow and graceful. It immediately reminded Verion of his first encounter with the fairies.

The male was dressed in colors of the lightest blue with fine golden lace upon the sleeves and neckline of his flowing, layered robe. The woman bore similar fashion except blue was replaced by a mixture of faint yellows and white. Radiant hair, much like that of Torlen, lay braided down the male figures back while the woman wore hers loosely over her shoulders. Their faces were smooth and pleasing to look at. Both wore smiles as they approached the company, their hands were neatly tucked inside their garment sleeves. They paused near Verion, looking directly into his eyes before proceeding to sit at the opposite end of the large table.

"I am Setorin, Torlen's brother. This is our sister, Renara. Perhaps we may answer your question more thoroughly, Lady Aleeza," said Setorin in his melodic way, as he slowly uncovered his hands, placing them on the table before him. "Torlen has always been one to desire more than he possessed. He yearns for treasures and valuables of his own, never satisfied with what he held. Now, with your world in turmoil once more, he seized an opportunity to gain that which he desires the most, a world of his own, being master to all and equal to none."

"So, you can stop him, or least lend aid to us in our cause?" asked Verion quickly, attempting to hide his rapidly rising hopes.

"Our magic is centuries old, our race immortal. We have watched you from afar, never interfering with your causes or petty differences. Now, because of Torlen, we have become embroiled in your troubles. Our descendents the fairies have done well to stem the tide in your favor, but I fear their power is not enough. Though, they have gained more power and knowledge than we could have ever foreseen."

"You will help then?" Verion repeated, somewhat impatiently still seeking a sign of aid.

"Lord Verion, your cause is noble indeed. Since the beginning of our time we have kept peaceful ways. Even as your races banded together for the Battle of Ages to defeat Welkar, we took no part in it, with the exception of one. Though, we watched from the Mystic Isles with great interest. But now, your peril is far greater than Welkar. We will aid in your defense of Torlen, he should not be your burden. He is of our race and we shall aid in his downfall, unless he chooses to revert to his pure ways."

Verion smiled inwardly while remaining stoic on the outside. He hid his exhilaration well, pushing his emotions deep within, trying desperately to hide them from Setorin and Renara.

"Torlen fears the Six. Yet, his desire for them is even greater than that of Holnok. It burns within him, eating at his mind and soul. He knows if he possesses them he can rule this world for his own while he himself would remain its sole master. The Sacred Six could perpetuate his downfall as well, thus he must gain their control. It is a dual edge sword he perches on precariously. However, his lust and greed drive him."

For the first time Renara began to speak. Fairy voices were described as enchanting, beautiful and melodic in nature, perhaps even hypnotizing. Upon hearing them for the first time, Verion agreed. However, once Renara spoke, it seemed a goddess from Valla itself stood before him. His mind went blank. The heart within his chest beat with a force unlike he'd ever felt. Her voice captivated his mind and gripped his heart. Sitting entranced by her words, he would willing do anything she ask of him, even hand her Haldira if she would but extend her hand for it.

The mystical trance was broken as Aleeza whispered in his ear, though the words were hazy and vague. His head shook to clear his mind.

"The good for which the Six were designed may be turned to evil in the wrong hands. Torlen knows their secrets and powers, though he will not share this with Holnok. Long ago, when the Six were created, our visions could not have foreseen their possible evil use. Torlen will spread malice like a plague upon the earth. He will control every being of all races, making them mindless thralls to his smallest whim. Great black cities will be raised. Darkness will cover the sky, shadows will hide creatures and beasts that shall roam at will, enforcing their master's wishes. Ruler of all, he would become unstoppable, consuming all happiness and joy, growing ever more powerful as he devoured it."

"I had been watching Holnok from afar, before the arrival of Torlen. He has been watching us with some type of crystal I have never seen or even heard tales of. Its powers are used to espy us," said Katima, sounding puzzled. "Can you say more."

"The Stone of Sight has been retrieved. It is ancient magic from Morog. One never recovered after the defeat of Welkar for none would dare enter the evil place. So many things remain as they have been for ages. He came upon it during his concealment after your company drove him from Mindaloth," said Renara. "It was once used to view the future. Though, Welkar bent it purposes for his own, using it to spy on his enemies and much more. It aided him greatly during the Battle of Ages. Though in the end it betrayed him and he perished for his ignorance."

"Lady Nira, you can no longer read Holnok's thoughts or see him simply because Torlen will not allow it. He has blocked any Seeing abilities into Selonoth. None will be able to penetrate either's thoughts. However, he is not as wise as he believes. For, there are many among us more powerful than even he was aware of. Our parents, Delthas and Laveena, are among two he cannot remain hidden from. They will have counsel on our course of action. We must make for Avior, for they visit the fairies as we speak," said Setorin.

Verion's hope rose up to grip him tightly. His stomach was knotted with excitement and optimism. Confidence he could bring about the defeat of Holnok came to him. But, Torlen was a problem he did not anticipate. How could he, a mere human, compete with a magical being far more powerful than the combined Six. Would Setorin and Renara be able to protect the company while bringing about his downfall? If they would only lend aid, then Verion had a plan.

"Come, let us forget evil for now. We will speak of it when we reach Avior. Now, let us rest and feast, for you all are weary after the journey. We shall leave on the second sunrise," said Katima.

After the large meal, Murn met with Verion, who sat rubbing his stomach mumbling aloud of the quantity of food he consumed. The pair moved outside the cave entrance and stood among the dragons that landed nearby. Verion looked on with pride as they slowly weaved their way between the winged guardians, patting each one's neck as he went.

"I have missed you my friend," began Verion. "It has been many months since our last visit.

Your cave now carries a woman's touch and your loin cloth has been traded for breeches and tunic as well," he said with a growing grin. "But have no fear, I mean no disrespect. My house also carries many of the same touches upon it," he said, now smiling broadly.

Then suddenly, before he could respond, Murn stopped in his tracks as his face went expressionless. He turned his head from side to side, looking for the source of the unfamiliar voice. His giant hand glided back and forth rapidly on his bald head.

Verion sensed he was puzzled, for Murn's way was to scratch his head when he was truly at a loss for an answer. Apparently, this was a huge question.

"What is it Murn," asked Verion, easing his hand to Haldira, he senses instantly turning to alert.

"A voice speaks to me. It is a sweet sound, unlike any ever heard. Yet, I am unsure of its origin. It is female, young and glorious to hear," he said, still running his large hand over his bald head. "She speaks in common tongue and musically."

*　　*　　*

"It is Jarnea," a voice came into his mind. "I can sense your thoughts, my rider. You have been clearly chosen for me. I am your guardian."

Murn was speechless. He stood with his eye wide, staring at the young purple dragon that moved closer to him. The giant went motionless as she lowered her head, staring directly into his eye, pushing her thoughts into his mind.

"I will be honored to have you among us here at the Caves," replied Murn, now wearing a shocked look upon his grey face. "I have heard how riders were chosen. Never did I imagine being blessed enough to have a guardian of my own. Welcome to your new home, Lady Jarnea. My love and respect shall be yours for as long as I draw breath. Of course, provided you are willing?" said Murn, bowing.

"It is destiny Murn, for I can read your thoughts. We have become a team. So it shall be. I am delighted, for it is a dragons dream to have a rider," she responded. "My life shall be spent her among the hills and caves of the Malmak."

Then, to show her pleasure, Jarnea stood upon her hind legs and let loose a roar and a small fireball that lit the night sky.

*　　*　　*

At that moment Verion understood, for he heard Jarnea as she spoke freely to Murn. The magic Tareen jewel gave him the ability he was once jealous of his sister for, the capability to hear and speak to animals, including the dragons. Though he used it seldom, he was fond of pushing his private thoughts or orders to the dragons when needed. Rarely would he speak aloud to them if others stood near.

In that instant he knew he lost another dragon to a friend. His joy was overwhelming as Murn turned to him, still wearing a befuddled look upon his face.

"I spoke to a dragon," he said, sounding surprised and exhilarated. Even more so than when Verion divulged Katima was attracted to him. "Her name is Jarnea, I have been chosen as her rider. She belongs here at the Caves."

"I am pleased for you. She could not have chosen a more worthy rider," said Verion honestly. "Let us spread the good news, it will delight everyone. Happy tidings would be welcome in these troubled times. Come, my friend."

The pair returned to the cave entrance where most sat gathered before an open fire that roared and cracked in the silence of the night. Though it went unnoticed, drowned out by the company enjoying ale and conversation. A cheer went up as the news was announced, pushing dread and malice from the company's mind for a short while.

Verion was joyous for his friend, yet he felt a twinge of remorse at losing another dragon. He knew it would pass in time, just as losing Luntar and Plyno had left him sensing loss. But, in the end, it was his dream to bring dragon magic back to the world. Possession of the dragons could not be held solely for himself, so grief was pushed from his mind and it became filled with happiness once more for his giant friend.

Finally, the evening drew to an end as the moon rode high in the star filled sky.

The Return of Natrae

Verion paced in his room, slowly contemplating all that was spoken during that day. *If Torlen is indeed as powerful as is told, then our quest will be nearly impossible. Perhaps Setorin and Renara will defeat him alone, leaving Holnok to us for his fate. One which I will ensure is carried out this time. He will not escape again*, he thought as his mind grew weary. He undressed and slipped quietly into bed with Aleeza and slept soundly, exhausted.

Rising early, he dressed quickly and slipped from the room, deciding to visit the dragons before the company awoke to meet the morning. Slipping from the cave entrance silently, he walked among the sleeping forms before him. Keltora circled high above, patrolling for danger. Trimlin's purring reached his ears as he approached. He wrapped his arms around his dragons neck and squeezed. This time he spoke aloud.

"My beloved friend, tomorrow we depart for Avior. Another quest is upon us. One I am sure you will play a part in before all is done. Keep your eyes wide, for we face great magic this time, the likes of which we have never seen. I am unsure what hidden powers or forces await us. Stay alert and keep your young ones close. I worry for them. Though they have learned a great deal, I dwell on their well being nonetheless," said Verion.

"We will keep you safe as we may, you have my oath. It is my duty and honor to protect you, rider. All shall return safely. Humans and dragons alike," said Trimlin.

Then suddenly, Keltora's voice entered Verion's mind.

"Verion, there is a lone figure approaching from the east, barely walking, stumbling with each step. He is worn and haggard but moves nonetheless," she said. "He wanders aimlessly as he approaches the river."

"Bring him forth Keltora, perhaps we may lend aid," said Verion quickly. He sprinted to the cave entrance, raising alarm, calling the company forth.

Shouts and ringing steel met his ears, then echoes of footfalls were heard as he turned to see Keltora gently carrying a limp, lifeless form in her talons. She dropped low, landing before Verion. He scooped the stranger in his arms and carried him quickly inside, laying him on the table which Nira had covered with furs and blankets for his body.

Before them, lay a thin underweight man dressed in tattered clothing. His eyes were sunken and dim. Long, dark hair lay matted to his face, with skin pale and drawn tightly to his frame. Holes were worn in the bottoms of his boots, he bled from a multitude of scratches and cuts.

Verion wondered if his efforts were too late. He bent closely to the man's nose, listening and feeling for breath, while his hand covered his chest, feeling for signs of life.

"He lives yet! Let us lend aid, for he shall not survive much longer without it. Bring food and water quickly," said Verion. Then abruptly he ran from the table, down the hallway to his room. After rustling through his pack he pulled forth a crystal phial with translucent green liquid within it then bolted from the room. Returning to the main chamber he gently lifted the stranger's head allowing several sips of green Silnoy to pass his lips.

Silnoy was a fairy gift from his previous quest. Named the Liquid of Life, it would sustain a body through bleakest of times. It was blessed by fairy magic and could heal even when near death.

The figure began to stir. His dark eyes opened into slits as he began to moan softly. His limbs moved slowly, wiping the matted dark hair from his face. Suddenly his eyes grew wide as he shrieked in terror, leaping from the table, wedging himself into a nearby corner. The form shivered wildly and whimpered for mercy as the company starred at him in bewilderment. From across the room a deafening roar came from Murn as he charged the helpless figure with rage on his face, his eye wide with fury. He extended his arms to grab the cowering form, intent on killing him. Then he stood frozen, bound by magic, struggling mightily to no avail.

"I shall release you but you may not harm this defenseless man," said Renara as she walked to his side. "No death shall befall him while he is frail and helpless. Do you agree?"

The Cyclops could do nothing but simply nod his massive head. His eye was fixed on the stranger which remained cowering in the corner.

"Murn, what has come over you?" asked Verion quickly as he moved to his friend's side. "What madness possesses you?"

The giant stood breathing in heaves, his skin wet with sweat as he strained against the magic that held him. Finally, after several minutes to control himself, he relaxed. He simply glared at the cornered form, his face twisted in anger. Then he spoke, his voice resonating through the room.

"Natrae," he said, still pointing a massive finger at the huddled mass of the cowering man.

Gasps were heard from around him. Verion was stunned. His eyes darted to the figure as he searched every inch of the stranger's face, searching desperately for some way of bearing out Murn's accusation.

"That is not possible," said Verion as he slowly advanced, kneeling by the whimpering stranger. He extended his hand to slowly clear away the hair covering the man's eyes and forehead. Drawing a quick breath, he stared with disbelief at the gaunt face before him. Murn was right. It was the conspirator of the company, Natrae the Betrayer. Verion rose quickly with his eyes wide, though he remained silent. For a long moment he stood silent in shock.

"Long have I waited to lay my hands upon him. He brought about not only my brother's demise, but gave us away to Holnok as we traveled, nearly bringing about all our deaths. Coward! Cur! I shall kill you with my bare hands," said Murn as he lunged for Natrae once more. Again, he was frozen, held in place by Renara's magic. His eye was wide with ire, his hands outstretched to seize the betrayer, who whimpered loudly between sobs.

Renara walked quietly to his side and gently touched Murn's hand.

Instantly, he was expressionless, standing as a statue.

"He shall be fine," said Renara softly. "I have simply driven away his anger, returning him to his good natured self. Anger can fill his heart quickly, can it not?" she asked rhetorically.

"His brother's death weighs heavily upon him. He swore revenge," said Verion, unable to take his eyes from Natrae's shuddering form. "Baytor's demise brought great grief as well."

Sudden pity swept over Verion, though hate and distrust still swelled in his heart. *I know what Murn feels and why, yet, look at the pitiful man before me. He is a shell of a human being. No matter how great my hate, I cannot willing harm him now.*

"Natrae, you will not be harmed. Come, eat and drink. Silnoy alone shall not sustain you," said Verion with softness in his voice.

Verion's emotions were greatly divided. He caught Natrae betraying the company's secrets to Holnok, then marched him to the caves at sword point for judgment. Murn desired his death but Verion allowed him to live. Then, during captivity, Natrae slew his guard and escaped back to Holnok. It was obvious he had not been well cared for as was his dream. Natrae once fantasized of his own kingdom with riches, servants and women, but his dreams fell into ruin with the fleeing of his master from Mindaloth. Now, he cowered before Verion, huddled in a mass of shivering flesh.

The years had softened Verion's hatred, unlike Murn's who still held tightly to his promise to slay him upon sight. Three deaths were attributed to the Betrayer. Baytor, Bolo, and the guard all fell to him. These acts would likely never be forgotten, thought Verion.

Verion extended his hand to Natrae and patiently awaited a response. Slowly, the Betrayer turned his eyes to Verion, peering through cold, grey eyes. Then, their hands met. Verion gently pulled him to his feet, helping him to the table as the company looked on in disbelief and utter silence.

Food and drink were brought before the sullied man, who stared openly at the plate, wringing his hands in his lap while alternating glances between it and Verion.

"It is safe, I assure you," said Verion with a slow smile. "We did not save you only to place poison in your food. Please," he said, moving the plate closer to Natrae, "eat, it will aid your strength."

Verion remained silent as Natrae ate and drank his fill with a ravenous hunger. His eyes shifted from one company member to the other. Verion read Natrae's thoughts, knowing he was expecting to be struck down any moment by a wrathful companion. He jumped sporadically at sudden movements or sounds within the chamber. Then, he spoke between bites.

"Holnok has become a servant to Torlen," he said simply while chewing voraciously. His drink spilt down his tunic as he gulped its contents. "He is a prisoner of sorts."

A collective gasp arose from the group. They stood in shocked silence, yet listened intently for more intriguing news.

"Lies! We can trust nothing that comes from his faithless forked tongue," boomed Murn. "I hold neither trust nor belief in anything the Deceiver speaks. Do not let him spread his deception any further."

Natrae seemed undaunted by Murn's lack of faith as he continued, for, hunger and weariness overruled his fear.

"An Ancient named Torlen entered the fortress, promising Holnok the Six after he used them for his own purpose. Holnok is now his commander, but he is nothing more than a miserable servant. Also, the High Lord has an ancient stone from Morog, the Stone of Sight, it makes him aware of all you do. Torlen has not sent forth the forces for he knows you are coming to him. Now, he bides his time, before unleashing wrath and fury upon you. He cares not whether you live or die, only thoughts of the Six, all of which he knows the spells for, occupies his mind. There is a great desire burning in him to destroy each of you and make thralls of all on this earth."

"Why have you come here, fool! Does your master guide you, seeing all you say and do here among those with courage, unlike yourself," asked Jinarl with vehemence. "Let us end your misery to ensure Holnok hears no words of our plans."

"He has spoken no lies," said Verion quickly in Natrae's defense. "We have been aware of all he speaks to this point, though he possessed no way of knowing this. All that was said has been open and truthful."

"Folly I say, my Captain. You do not trust this trickster with your life do you, Verion?" asked the giant.

"No," said Verion quickly. "Yet, that does not undo the fact he speaks openly. Our wisdom and knowledge is held safe within us and he has no want for it. He has not sought answers, he is merely speaking that which he knows as truth."

Renara stepped forward, gingerly placing her hand on Natrae's head as he fidgeted beneath her touch. She stood silent for several moments, then stepped away.

"He speaks the truth from fear. Nothing spoken was false," said Renara quietly. "He came here simply because it is a place he knew you would all be found together. To give you warning and aid in some way is his only desire. In his mind, Holnok cannot reach him here among the company. Fearing for his life in Selonoth, even more so than here, he came forth. I see honor and courage that is yet to be brought forth within him."

"Honor! What does this creature know of honor. Baytor was slain by his deceitful means and the vermin structured my brother's death. Coward, I say! One that should have been slain when his treachery was discovered, for he caused much pain and grief to this company. Many among us swore to kill him upon sight. Now you say he holds honor and courage! Bah!" said Murn with with anger rising. "I will certainly not protect him from Holnok or anyone else."

Setorin walked slowly to the front of the company, staring at them momentarily. His face wore a sullen and grim look as his eyes locked on the company one by one.

"Then who will slay him?" he asked calmly. "Take up your weapons and strike him down. Have your revenge you so desperately seek. Ease your mind by killing this pitiful form of a man. End his miserable existence," said Setorin emotionless, pointing at Natrae. "Do as you will with him."

The Ancient seized an axe from the corner and lay it on the table for all to see. He now stood expressionless as his eyes continued to rove over the companions.

"Take it up, strike him down," he said calmly. "Your hearts call for it. Now the time has presented itself to part with your bane. Slay the Betrayer. Vengeance is yours for the taking."

Natrae fell to the floor cowering, pressing his face against the cold stone, whimpering and weeping openly.

Verion stepped before him and held steadfast. Natrae's thoughts of fleeing or dying swirled furiously within Verion's mind, for the Betrayer was nearly mad with fear. It took all his energy to push the powerful visions from him with force.

Setorin stared at each of the company. Verion saw his eyes change to grey, his garb became dark. He seemed to grow in size as he spoke, though Verion remained silent and unafraid. Perhaps it was simply a trick of the mind, he thought.

"Here is your chance. Reap the vengeance you have carried in your hearts for years, gnawing at your souls and minds. Hate consumes your every thought. You have waited for this moment. Is there none among you who will do this deed you have sworn to do? Kill him if it is your desire. Destroy him now," said Setorin, again pointing a finger at a helpless Natrae. "Pick up the axe or draw your sword and do this deed."

"Stop it! You see what he is doing? It is a test. There will be no death here. We do not have that much hate within us to kill such a pitiful defenseless being. Look at him," said Nira, nodding Natrae's direction "We speak only of vengeance when our hearts are hot with pain and grief. Mine has passed. I will not allow any of you to slay him. Not even you, Murn. Though I love you dearly as a friend, you shall not do this deed, I will stop you if need be. For, you know it would not bring back Baytor or your brother Bolo from Valla. Let this matter be healed in your heart. End it here. You, all of you, are better than this."

Then, she spoke quickly to Setorin with anger in her heart.

"How can you stand and ask us to murder for revenge. We are not Holnok's thralls that kill on command or whims. We do not stand before you as puppets. None of us shall do this thing you ask. It is heinous and malicious."

The companions were dumbfounded. A mere mortal spoke with vehemence against the most powerful beings ever to grace their world. A thick hush fell over them all as they stared blankly at Setorin. They waited with baited breath for a reaction from the Ancient.

"Well spoken Nira," said Setorin as he returned to his former self. Then, after a another long uncomfortable silence, he spoke again. "I beg for pardon from all of you. Indeed it was a test. For, if blood lust was truly in your hearts, then our aid would not be given.

None would have been allowed to harm Natrae, for he is powerless. Yet, I sense this man will play a part in your journey and he must accompany you on the trek to Madaria and beyond."

Verion's eyes went wide, his jaw dropped open. He glanced at his companions to see a similar reaction from them all, even Murn. *Had Setorin gone mad? What possible purpose could Natrae serve? This will certainly make for a troubled journey*, he thought. *The man that led us into several traps and much more, will now ride alongside as one of the company again. Perhaps Murn was right, death would have been kinder. To what end or good could this come to now. Is Setorin's vision correct? Natrae, serving a purpose to our journey, I feel it is to no avail, it is certainly folly.*

Natrae was led away by Renara to a bath and fresh clothing as Setorin spoke once more.

"Even now as we stand, my sister is removing the fear and evil from Natrae's mind, essentially wiping his memory clean. Unfortunately, he will not remember any of you. His memory shall begin today. Though, he may indeed retain feelings of joy and images of his youth. Once, he was a man of honor before evil took him in the City of Life. That man shall again return. Trust him with your life if you must, for he will now defend each of you to the death with his own."

Again, all stood silent, stunned by Setorin's power and magic and shocked Natrae would return with no memory of the evil he partook in. The death, treachery, and service to Holnok he performed would be gone forevermore.

"Come my friends, let us walk outside to breathe the fresh air and clear our minds," said Verion. He needed time to ponder Natrae's sudden appearance and the events since his arrival. "Let us make the most of the day, for we depart at sunrise."

The company stepped silently from the cave, reeling from happenings of the last several hours. They sat in stillness for a long while as the brilliant midday sun warmed them. Finally, Verion broke the hush.

"My friends, once more we are moving toward evil," he began. "My heart is heavy for we did not slay Holnok at our first meeting, though we tried. I take blame for this. But, I carry great hope since we shall have Ancients by our side. Yet, Natrae will bring out our distrust and anxiety once more, even though he shall be a different man when we lay eyes upon him again. Let it not interfere with our quest. We must not obsess over his past deeds. Concentrate only on the quest at hand and embrace the new Natrae."

"You are to blame for none of this," said Jinarl solemnly.

Murn, his eye narrowed, immediately opened his mouth to object but words never came.

No sooner did Jinarl finish than Renara, Setorin and Natrae came forth from the cave entrance. The company stared open mouthed once more. He was now clean shaven with flowing hair laying loosely down his back. He wore clean fitted clothing giving him a strong youthful appearance once again. A broad smile graced his face and each step was light. A gleam of happiness shone in his eyes. Though still thin, his frailty seemingly vanished. Now, he stood upright and proud.

"Greetings to you all my friends, my name is Natrae. I am pleased to make your acquaintance," he said still smiling. "Renara has said we are to journey to Avior. I have never seen fairies and shall relish the opportunity to do so. There is much I would learn from them. May I sit among you?" he asked, motioning to a spot beside Verion.

"I would be honored," said Verion truthfully. "Rest here beside me."

Verion often wondered what Natrae would have been like ere evil took him. Now, he knew. A smile formed on his lips. Though it was impossible to completely remove thoughts of hate and distrust toward the man sitting before him, he tried nonetheless. Natrae appeared to be a remarkably handsome man since worry had been lifted from his face, his mind effectively emptied.

Again Verion marveled at the magical power of the Ancients, which turned his mind to Selonoth. Could Torlen defend Selonoth? He was an Ancient and would possess as much power as his brother or sister. Could the company defeat one with so great a power? His brow furrowed, as thoughts of adversity and death entered his mind.

Pain and hardship are only days away now. How can I devise a plan to defeat such a being that can grow in size at will, or hold a Malmak in place with a single thought. Is it folly to hope for victory. Yet, it must be done or our lands will be consumed, he thought.

Natrae sat talking comfortably among the companions, none of whom he carried any memory of, not even his cousin Aleeza.

Verion toyed with the jewel dangling from his neck as he reached out to his friends minds, reading as many thoughts as he could. They seemed pleased at the changes within Natrae, for he was pleasant, even humorous at times, sparking laughter within the group as they talked freely. He was intelligent and well spoken. Murn however, held the most reservations for the change.

Verion wondered what event or thought pushed Natrae to evil. He made friends easily and was enjoyable to be near, but something, somehow, pushed him into darkness and greed.

I may never know, thought Verion. *Now he is among us a changed man. I will give him every chance to prove himself and pray he doesn't fail us, for he surely not survive a second attempt at deceit. One among us will certainly bring about his end quickly if he falls into the grasp of evil once more.*

The company was summoned for their evening meal. Time began to slip away unnoticed as evening shadows lengthened against the cave entrance. The companions entered, each bearing a healthy appetite. Their dinner proved very pleasant indeed as earlier joyful talk resumed, even Murn wore a smile. Verion was glad Selonoth and Torlen were not the topic of conversation.

As the sky twinkled with star light, Verion sought sleep in preparation for the next day. Before turning in for the night he ensured provisions for the company were readied for early departure. He bade good night to all before heading to his chamber only to find Murn standing patiently at his doorway.

"May I have a moment of your time my lord," asked Murn. "I have need to speak before our journey. There is much I wish to know."

"My friend, I shall always have time for you," said Verion honestly. "Speak openly. What fills your thoughts? I would imagine most of your troubles shall be easily read."

Verion needn't have asked since he had already read Murn's thoughts as he approached.

"I have spent the day with the Betrayer and though I still do not fully trust him yet, he seems to have indeed changed. Do you sense any difference since his return."

Verion was genuinely shocked. Certainly, the first words from Murn should have been his continuing hatred for Natrae.

"Firstly, my large companion, I would not call him the Betrayer any longer. It could be . . . awkward," said Verion smiling. "I, too, shared your thoughts of mistrust. I have probed Natrae's mind to the best of my ability and found no malice or evil within his heart or mind. But, I am not as powerful as Nira. Let us consult her in the morning, we shall speak then."

"So be it," said Murn quietly, though not completely satisfied. "It is strange indeed to have him among us and will freely admit I carried a great desire to slay him. Though, it seems to have passed. Perhaps the Ancients have driven it from me."

"Your wife is a magical fairy my friend. I believe she had a great deal to do with it as well," said Verion smiling broadly. "Though your thought of the Ancients could be correct as well."

They stood for some time, discussing Natrae, dragons, and a new quest. The moon shone high above the cave entrance as the pair bid good night and parted. Verion felt drained mentally and looked forward to a soft bed and a good night's rest. Slipping quietly into bed, he curled tightly against his wife and slept.

A large red winged woodpecker beat a sporadic rhythm on a tree outside Verion's open window, rousing him from a deep sleep. He knew as before, that each step was taking his company closer to evil and malevolence. Dread rose within him, though he pushed it from his mind. Knowing his sister, and others would read his thoughts no matter how well he hid them disconcerted him, yet there was no way to prevent it, for they were far more powerful than he. Rising with uneasiness in his heart, he focused on his wife.

Aleeza came to his side as he dressed slowly. Hand in hand they walked to the main chamber, as the company slowly trickled in. Setorin and Renara sat at either end of the table, seats of honor according to Murn, who forfeited his spot to allow Setorin the head seat. Katima did the same for Renara as well.

"Let us move toward Avior quickly," said Renara softly. "We must tarry no longer. If we delay, Torlen shall see or guess our intentions."

Verion never tasted his food. He ate automatically, almost by reflex. His mind was occupied with seeing Avior and the fairies once more, pressing on to Selonoth, and mostly of Torlen and Holnok. Baytor fell to the last quest at Mindaloth. Though he tried to keep this from entering his mind, it rose to the forefront. Constant danger would be upon them once they stepped from the Protected Realm. He glanced at each face around him, seeing their smiling faces suddenly brought horrible images to him. He saw his companions falling one by one to the quest. Suddenly, he felt ill and weak. His stomach twisted and churned inside him, making him nauseous.

Rising quickly from the table, he excused himself. But not before he caught Renara's eye and stopped suddenly, staring openly at her. Instantaneously, the images were gone; his mind was now clear and worry free. The nausea was gone.

Renara simply smiled and nodded to him. Then she came to take his hand within her own. Leaning close, she whispered that all was well now, then returned to her seat. Verion sat shocked and amazed. Still staring at Renara he grew flushed, then turned away. Embarrassment gripped him. Feeling the entire company was staring at him, he rose quickly once more and regained his composure.

"Before we depart, I believe we should welcome Setorin and Renara as our leaders," said Verion. "They will steer our company to victory, I am sure."

"Lord Verion, the company remains in your hands. My sister and I simply come along to provide advice and to aid with defense from Torlen. You must make your own decisions as you did on your past quest," said Setorin, looking into Verion's eyes. "Final fate lies with you. It rests solely in your hands."

Though Verion was the undisputed leader of the last quest, shock registered on his face at Setorin's words. Why would he retain his leadership role when the Ancients could lead? This made him uncomfortable. He compared it to being in charge of his own father. How could he possibly tell an immortal race of powerful beings where to go, how to act, what to think. The thought was inconceivable. The only recourse was to start the quest, contemplating it as he went onward, for he believed open discussion would be to no avail. With any luck, the Ancients could be convinced to lead the company. Though, he had grown used to having his way and the company was led to victory several times in the past under his commands.

Secret fear of failure grew stronger. What if this attempt to quell evil came to a horrible end and all trust in him was lost or many perished. His future decisions would be questioned and perhaps ignored. To this point only one had met a fateful end, Baytor. What if other members of the company fell. The sorrow and pain would be too much to bear in his heart forever.

"Come my friends, we are wasting precious time," he said quickly. "Let us move forward to visit our allies in Avior."

With that, Verion walked from the cave to speak to the dragons. Telling them of the route and plans, commanding each to follow as they could, though the company would be out of sight once they entered the forest. Its magical protection from sight would prevent it even from the air.

The dragons took flight, rocking from side to side, as the company formed to make the trek toward the ferry that would carry them into the Shimmering Lands. They rode steadily forward, reaching their transportation within several hours. They loaded quickly and crossed the river without incident, only the growing ill feelings Verion carried with him were not be seen, but they accompanied him nonetheless, like heavy invisible baggage.

He still bore concerns over Natrae as well. Though he did indeed seem changed, Verion promised himself to maintain his guard and watch his friend closely.

The Ancients

V erion rode forward into the Shimmering Lands, the home of the fairies. He had never entered on horseback before, it was always by dragon or foot. The trees still glittered and the rocks sparkled as they had done on their first quest and the forest itself seemed sentient, it opened and closed to your wants and needs. Still yet was the bewildering rearward path that disappeared as you moved forward, making it impossible retrace your steps. You were at the forests mercy once you stepped into the magical place.

On his first trip, a powerful spell protected this land. It brought forth dread, thoughts of despair and hopelessness, pulling your mind into deep, dark places filled with doubt. Since the initial quest it had been removed for many years. Now, he was sure it was in place once more. However, since Katima was with them on this trek, she most certainly protected them from the magic when they entered if indeed it was still present.

Hearts were strangely lightened as the company moved forward. Verion rode in peace as the path passed quickly beneath him. Brandor was relaxed, keeping him at ease as they pressed onward. His mount showed signs of concern or danger as his tail flicked at flies that drew to close. The two spoke silently as they rode onward. Verion greatly enjoyed his new found telepathy with animals, it came as a great aid when needed and keeping ones conversations private. He could confess his deepest fears and doubts and never have them known by any other, unless of course his sister was able to sense them first.

Nothing appeared familiar to Verion as he stared at his surroundings. Once, Murn said this land changed with each visit, no matter how often you stepped foot upon it. Since Verion usually arrived by dragon during his visits in the years after the quest, he had never noticed it before. However, it was quite apparent now, for nothing seemed recognizable. No land marks, trees or rocks seemed the same. In short order he had lost all sense of direction, yet he plodded onward knowing the fairies would appear in time. Often he wondered if it was a test of some sort, to see if he was worthy of entering the land and finding the hidden city.

They wound steadily upward and round several tall peaks, each higher than the last. Rays of the sun sparkled and bounced from the path before them. Verion was unsure if it was real or yet another illusion of this land. Nonetheless, it was beautiful and mesmerizing to him. Eventually, their descent began, leading the company to a wide open green hollow. Once on level ground their path led round the feet of a low hill which carried them to an even wider, broader valley. A ridge of tall hills stood before them as they turned what Verion believed to be northerly. Though he was truly unsure what his position was.

Little time had been given to genial greetings during the journey to this point. Then a thought came to Verion. He had not spoken more than a few passing words to Milar, Telesta's life partner, since their introduction. Making it a point to ride by his side, the two became acquainted as they pressed forward. Verion thought he was a pleasant enough man, quiet spoken to be sure. At times he strained to hear Milar's voice even in the silence of the forest. Nonetheless, he found him intelligent and gracious and took an instant liking to him.

The sloping hills brought a gentle breeze as the horses carried their riders higher yet again. Verion called for rest on several occasions as the day slowly wore away. A point was made to stop near the abundant running water they neared often. Horses drank deeply and riders filled their skins. In this manner they rode at length up and down again and again, through hollows and valley floors with glimmering trees and rocks sparkling all the while.

They spoke for several hours as they pressed onward. Though Milar heard the story several times, Verion was asked to repeat the tale of the Fall of Mindaloth, as it had come to be known. Parts were difficult to be repeated, for they brought painful memories from the past. Ones that Verion tried to forget. Nonetheless, he left out no details.

The path took them to level ground once more. Now the company made its way through a small flat round grassy spot with trees taller than most. Here, Verion finally recognized the forest. It seemed similar, yet he was unsure if it was indeed the same spot.

They had come upon the circular opening where the fairies met them on the previous journey. There before them stood the two fairies they were familiar with, Aris, Queen of the Protected Realm and Qnara, her daughter. A stranger stood by Qnara's side. A tall handsome man, as was typical with their race, stood proudly smiling as the company came.

"Greetings to all," came Aris's voice, sounding as light and enchanting as ever. "The others await us," she said, slowly walking to the edge of the tree line, which parted before her.

Verion was unsure who the other's were. He grew anxious and hopeful. Perhaps it was aid for the quest, he thought. With any luck it would be vast numbers of fairies and Ancients to accompany them, though he held little hope of that. Fairies, like the Ancients, kept to themselves, rarely meddling in affairs of other races, hence the reason they were misunderstood, for some took it as being unfriendly or even hostile. Yet, nothing was further from the truth.

Aris's voice entered Verion's mind, an occurrence that still disconcerted him, but one he had grown accustomed too in his own way.

"I see Natrae is among you once more," she said, pushing her thoughts forward. "It was wise of you to spare him not only now, but during your previous quest as well. I feel he will play a large part in your future. Guard him well future king, for your quest rests on his shoulders."

"He was near death when Keltora found him. Renara aided him in becoming pure again after the malice of Holnok took him. For the second time I have been told of his importance, though I do not understand. He remembers nothing of his evil ways. Of what use he will be to the company is yet to be foreseen," replied Verion. "Many here hold doubts."

"You will not regret your decision," she thought once more. "Honor, courage and trust will prove his worthiness before all is done. His safety should become vital to you. Without him, you will fail. I have foreseen it."

Verion was mystified why a great deal of importance was placed on a man who carried with him no memory of his past life before a mere few days ago. Nonetheless, he knew Aris was the wisest of the fairies, so her words never left his mind, though puzzlement remained. Many burning questions were left unanswered, ones which he greatly desired to know, especially concerning the Betrayer.

The company dismounted as the trees separated showing a clear path to Avior. The travelers made their way to the small cottage that housed them previously. It was magical, appearing large enough to house perhaps three or four of the company, though upon entering it was very large indeed, holding as many as needed.

Verion smiled, as joy grew within him. He loved Avior and spent many days here after the quest and in subsequent visits, growing very fond of the fairies. They freely shared history, magic and friendship with him. He was quite proud of the open admiration the fairies bestowed on the dragons during his visits. If he survived this quest, he would ensure they would have another opportunity to spend time with the winged creatures yet again.

"This is Zydor," said Qnara, facing the group with a brightened face. "He is my life partner and will accompany me on any adventure we undertake. We were joined shortly after Verion's last visit."

Zydor nodded smoothly as all greeted him with a rousing cheer.

Verion was delighted yet another fairy would be among them as the company pressed forward and he felt joy for his life friend Qnara for her joining. Zydor stood nearly as tall as Verion, who stood over six feet. When he turned his gaze to you it held tightly, for his blue eyes were piercing and bright.

"Now my friends, we have much to discuss," said Aris. "There are new faces among you and more yet to meet. We shall begin with introductions, then discuss the evil loosed upon us once more."

Two figures entered the large room as the queen spoke. Renara and Setorin rose quickly and bowed low. A dim glow of light clung neatly about the pair as they approached.

"Greetings, Mother and Father," said Renara. "It is good to see you well."

"May blessings be upon you, my daughter," the delicate figure of a woman said with a soft voice.

"This is Laveena and Delthas," announced Aris. "Setorin, Renara and Torlen are their offspring. They grace us with their presence, traveling far from the Mystic Isles to walk among us once more."

The two nodded in unison, then smiled as they walked a wide circle around the table as the company sat silent and unmoving.

Verion's mind went blank, stricken with Laveena's beauty, which was even greater than that of Renara if possible. Though, Laveena was thousands of years old, she was extraordinary to behold. No sign of age was upon her. She possessed a loveliness that he never beheld. Smooth flowing white hair lay perfectly over her shoulders. Her head was circled by a woven ring of silver which held a small dangling jewel to her forehead. Eyes that held the brightness of many stars peered at him. Smooth, flawless skin could be seen on her face, neck and hands. Her delicate, soft robes clung neatly to her thin, graceful frame in layers.

Verion felt small and insignificant as she approached. He tried desperately not to stare, though his eyes were drawn to her involuntarily. Frantically, he attempted to hide his thoughts from his companions, especially his sister. Shame took him as Aleeza slipped her hand into his.

The pair dressed in nearly identical attire as their children, except each bore a small necklace with an emblem, the design of which Verion could not see clearly. At first glance it appeared to be three overlapping triangles. Though, the significance of it was unclear. Wonder took his breath at the sight of the immortal beings that stood mere inches away.

Verion quickly noticed all men in the company sat slack jawed as well, staring at the calming beauty of Laveena as she passed. Again, shame took him as he tried to pry his eyes from her. Then, Delthas spoke and broke their stare.

"May O'Tan bless you all," said Delthas, pausing momentarily before continuing. His voice, though masculine, was gentle and harmonious to hear. "Long have we awaited your arrival. There is much to discuss. We should begin with that which is on all our minds, Torlen. He is young, coming into the world barely fifteen hundred years ago. There is still much for him to learn. Though he is powerful, he is not so great as to not be defeated. He will learn this in time, before his end."

"Does this mean you will destroy him," asked Zarah bluntly. "Our victory shall not be stayed."

Verion was shocked at her question. In essence she was asking parents to destroy one of their own children. The words hung in the air thickly, like attempting to stir hardening cement.

Delthas seemingly did not hear her, or chose to ignore the question. Then, Laveena spoke.

"As with your expulsion of Holnok years ago, you made the choice his own," she said softly. "Lady Zarah, Torlen will choose his own fate. He may revert to his glorious ways and become even more powerful, or choose to face that which will bring about his shame and banishment. Perhaps even death."

"Then you will go forth among us to drive evil from our lands," asked Natrae, his hope rising. "Though the Sacred Six are indeed powerful, what chance would they stand against forces and magic such as your own, my lord," he said with a courteous nod of his head.

Verion, wearing a startled expression, stared openly at Murn expecting to see a similar reaction. Natrae's comment astonished him. Since Ancient magic was used upon him, it was no wonder Natrae fit in the company with ease. Even while openly discussing assailing his former master to an Ancient he showed no signs of his former self. Verion noticed he took great interest in all that was said since Renara performed his cleansing, as he called it.

"As you know, we have been impassive in your affairs until now. Our peaceful ways were ended with the sin of Torlen. Though the Fairies have become most powerful indeed, I do not believe they can stay Torlen. So, my people will aid you to drive him from D'Enode," said Delthas.

"D'Enode?" asked Telesta quizzically. "I am unfamiliar with this term."

"The story is simple Lady Telesta," said Renara smiling. "D'Enode in our language means Realm of Bliss. It is what you call earth. Long ago O'Tan, He Who Creates, and E'Lenoria, She Who Loves All, created your world. The mountains separating the Protected Realm and Madaria are named in her honor, for she greatly loved this world and took enormous pleasure in its creation, forming rivers, valleys, and mountains then shaping them with her own hands. She nurtured the world as it grew, giving it many colors and hues that delighted her. O'Tan himself fashioned the dragon race and bestowed great magic upon them. In turn, the race of men became blessed by them thereafter, hence the alliance between men and dragons. Their son, T'Ord the Mighty, was the lone Ancient to ever aid the children of D'Enode in battle. He fought in the Battle of Ages," she paused, seeing the astounded look on the company's face. She smiled momentarily.

"Our parents are descendents of the Creators. They have lived over six thousand of your years and have seen much. Now, they return from the Mystic Isles. The mightiest of the Ancients stand before you here in D'Enode. They come to aid your quest," she said, staring with open admiration at her parents.

"Please daughter, thank you for the praise, but be seated. Let us deal with what is at hand," said Laveena softly with a smile. "Your brother has brought much grief and shame to us."

"We are truly humbled and honored by your presence," said Verion with a low bow. "Only in tales have we heard of your race. Now you stand before us, willing to aid our cause to drive malice from D'Enode. We all," said Verion with a sweeping motion of his arm, "carry respect for your power and immeasurable knowledge. We shall not judge your kind from Torlen."

"We must march to Selonoth and destroy all within its walls. It is the only way," said Milar, his face showing no expression. "If Torlen must fall as well, so be it."

"We must not form a plan as of yet, Milar," said Delthas, holding up his hand. "First we shall journey to Madaria. There are certain steps that must be taken ere you attempt to overthrow Selonoth. Perchance a plan will become more apparent once we reach the peace of our sanctuary. Once there we shall have a long council."

"Then perhaps we should rest and depart with the rising sun," said Verion, turning to the company. "Rest as you see fit. In the morning we shall meet here once again, ready for travel."

The company broke asunder but Verion was restless and anxious yet again. Attempting to make a viable plan for attack was his only thought. Patience usually abounded within him, except now he felt more urgency than calmness. Taking Aleeza's hand, he strode from the cottage and walked among the fairies. There he saw many familiar faces and spoke at great length to them, most of which was in their own tongue. He learned a great deal during the After Years of peace. He prided himself in his knowledge of this race, for his admiration was boundless. A promise was given to summon the dragons for their enjoyment when he returned from his journey.

Weariness took him as the night wore on, yet he departed with gloom, wishing to stay upon his hosts even longer. Knowing the morning would bring his advance to the east, he sought his room for needed rest.

Verion sat on the edge of his bed with Aleeza, his brow furrowed. Even though he trusted his wife with all his thoughts, some he tried to solve or work through on his own accord. Finally, he spoke to her.

"Do you believe Natrae has some purpose among us or is it yet another odd test from the Ancients?" he asked of Aleeza. "It was told to me I am to keep Natrae safe or our quest will fail. Long have I thought of this, seeking an answer to this riddle, yet it eludes me. What aid could he possess that is held invaluable. Can it be in battle, or some way I cannot foresee."

"I believe Setorin knows that of which he speaks. His race is far more powerful than what we have seen. I trust Natrae now. He is as he was years ago before coming to the City of Life," she said. "The man you see before you is how I remember my cousin."

"Aris has said as much," said Verion. "I am sure Setorin is true, and the queen as well, though Natrae's true use is hidden from me yet. It haunts my every thought. Perhaps I should take counsel with Aris yet again."

Verion slid into bed and pulled the covers close, quickly drifting to sleep in Aleeza's arms.

Morning sifted through the trees begrudgingly. Sparse sunlight filtered through low lying clouds that lay thick in spots over the valleys and mountaintops. Thunder rumbled overhead as a gentle mist fell from the sky.

Puzzlement greeted him. Each time he had been in the Realm, it was protected by spells of the fairies. It not only hid the city from evil eyes but even weather was kept at bay. An unseen magical spell covered Avior and the fairies maintained the weather within it to their preferences, which was always comfortable. Now though, it was raining. He was unsure if the magic had somehow been broken or stripped away. Pondering this, he strode toward the door enjoying the sweet smell and feel of the tender rain on his skin.

He stood at the entrance, his mind reaching out to Trimlin. They spoke of the departure to Madaria. Verion bade the dragons watch the surrounding lands, though he knew the company would be unseen heading for the Forest of Dreams. Stepping back inside as the company formed for a meal before their departure, he was greeted by all as large plates and bowls were brought forth, much to Verion's pleasure and delight.

"I have not seen Setorin and Renara or their parents? Are they ready to depart?" asked Verion. "I long to ask many questions on the way. There is much that needs answering."

"They are gone. I have been told we never see them arrive or depart," said Katima. "Before their departure they spoke an oath to meet us at Madaria."

A shadow passed over Verion's heart. Even though he carried an oath to be met at Madaria, his spirit sank. He wondered if the Ancients could actually bring about the downfall of one of their own kind regardless of the evil that possessed him now.

"How is it that rain falls and thunder claps overhead, Aris?" asked Eldon quizzically, seemingly reading Verion's mind from earlier.

"Since the Ancients have returned they taught us much about protecting the city, yet allowing nature to be around us if we desire it. Our city is still hidden from evil and on occasion we allow the weather to be more than the illusion you are used to," she said softly.

Verion simply smiled and chuckled. He was amazed each time he met the fairies for they seemed to surprise him in one way or another. Even after spending many days among them learning their ways, customs and language he found them full of wonder.

"Come my friends, we must be off," said Verion still smiling. "The road to the east gets warmer yet with the unknown and approaching wickedness. It beckons us."

The company moved forward fifteen strong, two of which were new to Verion and one was re-born. He rode beside Milar and Zydor, growing closer to them with each stride forward. Natrae was surprising as well. Even though he had done much evil prior to this quest, he was now an pleasant, amiable man with Verion actually enjoying his company. He noticed Natrae was putting on weight, filling out to his former self and his spirit reflected the change. The light hearted and quick witted demeanor was refreshing during worrisome times.

Verion knew most still struggled with their feelings concerning the Betrayer. Now, Natrae was among the company as a friend. Still, a level of distrust and hatred was bound to him. It may never dissipate, he thought. After all, things had gone ill during the first quest due to his treachery. He was unsure if Natrae would ever have true friends. Though it would be very difficult, Verion was going to try and give him a chance to earn his trust and respect. After all, the entire company was nothing more than strangers to him now that his memories were taken from him.

None complained about the light rain that fell, for it invigorated them. It brought the smells of spring upon each droplet, though the season had indeed passed. The glittering trees put forth unusual fragrances Verion couldn't identify. A sweet floral scent he had never experienced rose from the trail with each step. It brought contentment as he traveled, making the day disappear without notice.

The trees that lay thick about them began to move away as a clearing came before the company. Katima had summoned a resting spot for the night. The rain stopped and the ground was magically dried for bedrolls. A fire was made and a rather large meal prepared as Verion strode from the camp, admiring the forest as he went. It was then, as he passed Zydor, Verion noticed for the first time the fairies carried swords and daggers with them. On the previous quest they relied on magic alone, now they were well armed. This brought a smile to his face, for the fairies could be doubly potent.

Then, as he sat in thought of Holnok and Natrae, Trimlin's voice came into his mind with an urgency.

"Verion, many dark shapes come this way. They are spread out among the lands. The wolf creatures come with the beasts and riders and many humans. The host marches this way. They are beyond count, rider. What are thy commands," he asked.

"I shall take counsel. Do not attack until I speak with the company. We must decide what is best. Excellent job my trusted friend," replied Verion as he sprinted to the camp.

Verion burst into camp breathless and gave news of the advancing forces. Shock and despair gripped them as he spoke. The company's whereabouts were not known to the enemy yet. Unless Torlen had somehow used his powers to find them. Perhaps he was indeed powerful enough to break the fairies spell over their lands. Only one explanation remained, thought Verion. The hordes did not hunt them, they headed for the cities of all lands about them.

"Torlen and Holnok have sent many forces upon the lands. They come this way as we speak, the dragons have spotted them. There are many, enough to blacken the lands. Gorlans, Zenex with Sorn riders and many other shapes. Most likely Jarcoth, Holnok's kind, march with them."

"I cannot see them," said Nira quickly. "They are hidden from me as with Holnok."

"You shall not be able to," said Zydor. "Torlen has blocked himself and his servant from our seeing. I am sure his creatures are magically protected as well. It must be how they came upon us unawares."

Suddenly, there was a small flash of light from the tree line. As the company turned to stare, Renara and Setorin stood silently, smiling at the group. They immediately joined the conversation.

"My parents have removed his spell, even from Madaria. No doubt this shall infuriate Torlen. To have his magic overcome will not bode well. Retaliation against all the lands is certain," said Renara. "I am afraid the war has begun. We must send word to all lands to prepare for battle. Evil forces move at will now."

"How shall word reach our lands? They lie many miles from here, we are cut off from them," said Zarah with concern evident in her voice.

"Our people have many talents Lady Zarah," said Setorin. "Even as we speak, an Ancient is appearing in front of each of your leaders giving counsel for the impending tide of approaching war. Your people shall not be taken unaware. They shall have help from our race."

Verion stepped forward and lowered to one knee, followed in turn by the company.

"We can never repay you for your aid. Your power is great and we know evil shall be put to flight or perish in its attempt to overthrow our lands. Our people are all worthy warriors and will fight until none remain, if it comes to that. Evil will meet more resistance then ever they believed possible."

"Rise, all of you," said Renara softly. "We are not your gods, simply their descendents. We have had thousands of your years to perfect magic and crafts which you cannot fully understand yet. Though someday you will. Then D'Enode will once again stand as the Realm of Bliss as it was many years ago in a time long forgotten by all, except my race. Our power is simple and pitiful compared to O'Tan or E'Lenoria. Those are the true gods of this world, we are simply of their blood. Now come, you should not rest this night, you are safe here. Move forward to Madaria after your recover strength. For, now even greater haste is upon us."

Another sudden flash came and the Ancients were gone.

Verion told Trimlin all that passed. No attack was to be set into motion unless the company itself was attacked. The dragons were to remain vigilant throughout the night. However, he decided dragon aid would benefit each city.

"Luntar, fly north to protect your home in Tarsis. Junia, go forth to our lands in Eldarn. Plyno, you as well must safeguard Rolnor and the people of Hatar. Finally, Eptus wing to the City of Life, give your strength to the Quantar. Evil shall not reach our lands. Be safe and wary my friends. Go now and be strong my beloved young ones, return when your work is done."

Returning to camp, he told of his decision. Sadness and worry for the young dragons filled many minds, which was easily read as Verion searched their thoughts.

"Worry not," he said. "They are strong and keen of wit. All will be safe and return soon. Six guardians remain overhead, our force shall be protected as will our cities. For each has many brave warriors within their walls. Now, Ancients and dragons will aid in their defense."

The company moved quickly but wearily through the Protected Realm, moving all day into the next night. Finally, they reached the E'Lenoria Mountains, its passes led to Madaria. Once more camp was set. This time rest was to be taken, for the company could go no further without needed respite. Weariness gripped them as they unfurled their bedrolls.

Verion stared at the towering mountain range before him. The lofty peaks and crags jutted to pierce the blue sky. Thick, blanket like clouds ringed the summits allowing the younger dragons to take rest unseen. Verion could make out Trimlin's shape appearing occasionally as he drifted through the bank of billowing softness. Meanwhile Keltora patrolled in slow circles just within sight. Nira's voice brought his attention back to camp.

"You need to eat to keep up your strength," she said. "One cannot head for battle on an empty stomach."

"I'm famished," he said, as Nira handed him an overly full plate. "With blessings on our side, battle still lay yet far away. In my heart I hold this hope and pray to our gods to make it so."

Again Verion's eyes went to the mountains. He had never passed the E'Lenoria Mountains before. He had been to their south, across the great river where Mindaloth once lay far below in the Bottomless Lands. But, he had never been any further east than where he sat now.

Anticipation welled within him knowing he was heading for the fabled city of Madaria. That thought alone was exciting enough, but now he felt wanderlust grip him again even though danger would be drawing closer with each step.

He felt reasonably safe since he would be entering the Forest of Dreams, the land of the Ancients. There, he yearned to gain new allies and life friends as well. That is, if the Ancients made friends of men. Perhaps they only arrived here to retrieve Torlen, then return to the Mystic Isles from whence they came, leaving the world as they found it. Could they leave when great need is upon D'Enode? After all, Trimlin warned them of advancing forces. Was attack even possible near such powerful lands? He was sure the mountains, though sacred to the Ancients and other races, held no special place in the heart of their enemy. They would attack without mercy. Battle now drew near.

His focus returned to the empty plate before him. It was time to rest for the night. He stood, cleaned and stowed his plate, then looked for Renara and Setorin. They had gone. Answers to his questions would come, but not quite yet.

The company started off early, making for the pass with speed. It led through the heart of majestic mountains towering on either side of them. Snow covered peaks rose high above, filtering down into tree covered slopes, dark in spots with thick, old trees.

Then, in the distance, baying came on the winds, breaking the silence. Howls and snarls grew louder as the company peaked the pass. Trimlin's warning roar came from above as dark shapes began to fill the tree line ahead. Instantly, the horses were sent to safety to the rear, far from sight.

I was right, he thought quickly. *Once we departed the Protected Realm we are hunted. Safety only lies in the Forest of Dreams now. It is too late to reach the border before we are besieged. We must make a stand here, for we cannot go backward to the Shimmering Lands.*

Verion looked ahead, seeing Zenex bearing their Sorn riders with speed. Gorlans ran beside them on all fours. They wore light armor with swords on their backs and helms on their heads.

Columns of Jarcoth warriors were holding positions on each side of the trail ahead. The company now lay vulnerable even as Verion watched. Helplessness clutched his throat like a vice, making each breath a struggle. He mustered his strength and courage, instantly working on a plan to protect the company from grievous harm or capture.

"Find cover," he yelled quickly. "Stay close if you can. Archers fire at will. Swords to me, we stand ready," he said, rallying much of the company to him.

Natrae was the first to reach his side, sword drawn. Eldon, Milar, Murn, and Jinarl followed as the dark wave of shapes broke upon them.

Arrows flew quickly from behind trees as the archers picked their marks carefully. The shafts thudded into their targets with deadly accuracy. Sorns fell from the backs of the Zenex as they came. Gorlans were pierced many times before remaining still.

Jinarl summoned Dragons Might giving him the strength of many Malmak. Bodies flew from beside him as he struck deadly blows. Swords, shields and helms alike were halved as his blade sung a mighty song.

Katima, Qnara and Zydor sent magical light blasts in all directions. Piles of ash were all that remained of those that stood before them. They created a path of destruction and protection around the company. No matter their effort, the enemy gained ground, slowly forming a tightening circle around the company.

Amidst the fray, one Gorlan rose to his hind legs and came forward. All horde movement around him ceased. He approached within mere yards of the company and spoke to them.

"We have come for the trinkets you carry man-thing. Give them to us and you may return to your homes unhindered," the beast said in a near snarl. "Deny us of our wants and you shall all be slain and we will take them from your dead bodies and we will feast upon your carcass."

"Tell your master he shall have that which he desires. We shall give them to him willing when we destroy Selonoth, he shall know their full power and see it firsthand. He will come to understand why he fears us," came Verion's voice clearly breaking the hush that lay around him.

The Gorlan snarled, threw back his head and howled, then lunged for Verion. As he did, the sky above him blackened momentarily. He was gone in an instant as Trimlin's great talons closed around him carrying him high into the air, never to be seen again.

Howls and shouts of terror arose from the enemy. The dragons had remained hidden in the clouds. Now, the predators were the prey. Above them in a large circle were six very angry guardians, waiting for an order to destroy the ground forces. Bellowing roars filled the air overhead, shaking the ground beneath the enemies feet.

The dragons brought fear to the enemy unlike any they had ever known. They cowered and covered their ears as the guardians drew nearer the earth. Some threw harmless spears or shot many arrows to no avail.

"Hear me! Return to your master and give him our warning. He may depart while he is able, or be destroyed," said Verion, though doubt gripped his mind even as he spoke the words.

So much evil strength came against him now, he wondered what lay in store for the company as they drew closer to the Tortured Lands. Would they meet thousands, perhaps tens of thousands of the enemy? Even bearing the Six, they would hold no chance against so many, even with fairies on their side. Could the Ancients be their saviors. They had said they would only lend aid with Torlen. How could they simply stand by and witness battle without aiding the cause. Anger began to rise in his heart as the dragons broke his thoughts.

Again, roars came from overhead. Verion knew the dragon's patience was waning. It did not sit well with them to watch their riders become encircled, trapped within an enemy ring. Verion decided he would give the attack order soon, but tried one last attempt to avoid further death.

"Go now! I will hold the death from above no longer. Leave with your lives, or die here," he said. "Time to choose is upon you. I wait no longer."

Verion's thoughts reached to Trimlin, who swooped low, laying a single fire blast where the lone Gorlan stood moments before. The boulders and stones turned red hot before the enemy's wide eyes. The Jarcoth warriors recoiled instantly. They were seen retreating over the eastward rise of the pass but the Zenex, Sorns and Gorlans were not so easily convinced.

Over five hundred banded together for a charge, deciding to tempt fate. They made a dash for the front line of the company, moving with surprising speed. The mass covered a mere twenty yards before being burnt to ash. Trimlin came from the north, Keltora from the south. They passed one another in mid air, raining fire upon the small horde.

The remaining enemy made a quick decision. They turned, shrieking and baying as they went, returning east to their new master, who would undoubtedly seek revenge.

The company reformed quickly, desiring to make for the safety of Madaria. Verion instinctively took a head count of his companions, finding them all present and miraculously unharmed.

Verion grasped his Jewel and spoke to Brandor and Deema. The horses whinnying drew closer each moment as the small herd thundered to their owners sides. All mounts returned safely and were a welcomed sight to the exhausted company.

"Let us press forward quickly," said Verion. "Madaria awaits. We are not safe in the open. Seek the safety of the forest, we must move now. Come, let us be off."

The dragons circled above watching the surrounding lands. This time no movement was detected within their sight.

The day passed uneasily as hours dragged slowly by. None let their guard slip. Verion's head turned to and fro at every sound. He was sure the enemy had gone, though he knew it was only the beginning. Finally, the Forest of Dreams came upon them.

FOREST OF DREAMS

Verion noticed nothing mystical about the forest. He expected to gaze upon a giant walled city or large fortress looming above him. Only trees and rocks met his eyes. Small gurgling, crystal clear streams flowed throughout the land. He thought of the spell protecting the Shimmering Lands of the fairies. It was powerful and gave doubting, misguided thoughts that led even the most stout hearted astray and left them wandering aimlessly. He felt no such spell here.

Secretly, Verion read the thoughts of his companions and sensed no such disorientation. With that, he was satisfied, at least for the time being. He rode easterly unsure what he searched for. Knowing he would recognize it when it came to him he traveled forward as the company rode single file along the path laid before them.

His head turned from side to side often, listening to the sounds of the forest. It reminded him of any other wood, except bird songs were merrier and wild creatures and beasts did not flee at the sight of intruders. They strolled happily alongside the trail without a care.

Weariness of battle was still upon him as he rode forward even with a blissful feeling inside. Realizing the company could take no more, he called for camp to be made. *Rest and food shall recoup my strength and diminish the aches and pains in my body*, he thought, as he dismounted.

Surprisingly, the forest seemed eerily similar to his homeland of Eldarn. He saw very little difference. It made him comfortable and happy even though this was no time for joy since his journey was for a perilous purpose, though he could not help himself. He began to smile and delight grew within his heart, though he body was drained of all energy.

"I feel it too," said Nira as she stood by his side, reading her brother's thoughts. "It is said that only happiness dwells here."

"Another spell?" he asked quizzically. "There is magic at work here, I feel it."

"I am sure of it. Perhaps we shall learn more upon our arrival. Though there may be little time for such talk of magic held within the trees."

"Then let us be off at first light, for urgency still grips me, regardless of the joy I feel."

Verion slept soundly that night, despite his lingering fear of attack. If there was only one safe place left to rest, save Avior, this was it. He slept as if on a feather bed instead of a bedroll on the hard ground itself. The company woke refreshed and ready for travel after a small but hearty breakfast.

The future king led the company forward, though he knew not his direction or distance yet to travel. The road wound this way and that. First turning northerly and climbing for a great distance, then descending to the south to touch once again upon the forest floor. Gentle breezes were with them as they rode, never was the wind or sun harsh upon the company. As in the Shimmering Lands, as they neared the banks of a flowing stream they stopped to fill skins or to allow the horses their share of the crystal blue water as well. They rode comfortably onward for many leagues.

The ground slowly rose once again, bringing them to a narrow tree laden slope that fell quickly away to the south. They rode in file for a great distance until coming to a wide hollow that descended gently to the floor below. Tree shade offered protection from the sun which shone brightly overhead, but it was not overly warm. Comfortable indeed, thought Verion.

As with Avior, no path appeared before them, so Verion rode forward until a sign would come to him. None of the company had ever entered this forest. It was new, uncharted ground to all, so seeking aid from his companions would be to no avail, for no clear direction was seen and counsel would be no help. In fact it had been ages since Men or any other race strode willingly through the forest.

Verion prided himself on his tracking ability and his knowledge of the wood and mountains, yet as he rode forward he was uncertain if he was not traveling in circles. Like Avior, he felt certain it was protection for the city.

Rumors of many queer happenings surrounded this place. Tales would tell of men and horses traveling through the wood never to be seen again. Large, strange beasts were glimpsed, noises and sounds were eerie and odd at best. It was avoided at all costs, even if it meant many days travel going out of your way to avoid the deep wood. The reason it bore the name the Forest of Dreams was because the Ancients once occupied it. It was told that your every wish awaited within its borders. However, after their race departed, men shunned the land and grew afraid. Terror rose in them after stories grew to tales and then to legend.

As he guided Brandor through the hanging tree boughs, statues of men and women were found throughout the forest. Some stood alone, some formed a silent stone circle, as if in deep meditation or a form of muted council. The faces were unfamiliar as they stared forever forward. They wore unfamiliar garb, similar to that of the Ancients, yet different in many ways. A mixture between the race of men and Ancients come to his mind. Though, until recently he had never seen or laid eyes upon an Ancient before and these figures looked similar yet different. Their expressions were peaceful and serene.

"Who are these beings?" asked Natrae, startling Verion, who rode in deep concentration and unaware he drew near. "They stand like majestic lords and ladies of realms that no longer exist. A memorial perchance, or a place of worship."

"I cannot say," said Verion truthfully. "Their faces are not known to me. Perhaps they are kings of old I have no knowledge of. Yet, they are vaguely familiar."

"These are the great wizards and witches of the Tareen," said Zydor, overhearing the question. "They once lived in this forest, during the Fading Years. They abandoned it after that. No one knows where they have gone, they simply disappeared. As you know, we are their descendents. They were the first race the Ancients created. There are many great . . . ."

His sentence fell short as a flash of light ahead drew their immediate attention, causing quite the commotion as hands gripped swords and axes alike.

Directly in their path, standing on a large boulder like a podium, stood Delthas and Laveena. They gazed upon the company, smiling, motionless. Then they spoke softly.

"We have anxiously awaited your arrival after witnessing your conflict with the enemy," said Delthas softly. "You used cunning to defeat a vastly larger force. Well met my friends."

"Please, this way," said Laveena as she turned and walked over a small grass covered rise behind her. "Madaria lays in wait and welcomes you all."

As Verion crested the small knoll to the sloping path the city came before him. Four enormous arches rose high above the earthen floor. Each met and joined at their peak, directly above the city center. Beneath them lay pointed spires atop smooth, white towers, six stories in height. A large outer circular ring led to eight progressively smaller rings held within. Covered arched walkways led from one circle to the next. Each ring bore small windows and vaulted doorways on the outer side. The city was filled with gentle light; its walls were white and silver intermingled with forest and earthen hues.

Fragrant grass abound in and around the city covering the forest floor in every direction. Flowers bloomed at will as you passed, some giving forth aromas that held you tightly in place longing for more of the sweet scent. The bouquet made all things around you crystal clear, bright and beautiful. Thick white trees bore broad golden leaves laced with the most delicate of silver veins within them. Thinner, but not less tall, were trees woven throughout the structure itself. They rose to the sky from the open courtyards and walkways, spreading their long branches here and there. Their leaves were of pale yellow that rustled softly in the gentle breeze that came against the company's face.

"The city could not have been there moments ago," said Verion bewildered, rubbing his eyes. "My eyes have never left the surrounding forest, yet here it stands towering before me."

"Ancient magic," quipped Zarah. "The city, like the fairies Avior, will only be seen when it is revealed to those who seek it. Providing they are good at heart. Evil should pray they never lay eyes upon it, for it would drive them mad or be their last sight on this earth. I know this from legends and tales of my youth."

As Verion watched, Laveena stepped toward the outer most ring. The air itself seemed to bend and shift shape. It appeared she walked through still water that hung unseen before her. It rippled gently, then hung unmoving once more. No trace of her entry could be seen.

Verion dismounted and moved forward with wide eyes. Slowly, he extended his hand to feel the hidden barrier, watching it swell and contract to its original form within seconds. He smiled, then ran his fingertips over the invisible wall again, admiring the way it danced and moved before him.

"What magic is this," he said aloud. "Never would I imagine such craft possible. This is nothing more than some trickery is it not. An illusion perhaps."

"You have much to learn yet, Lord Verion," answered Laveena. "Your race will gain this knowledge in time. It is a protection of great magic. Vileness shall never pass. The protection comes from D'Enode itself. This was once part of E'Lenoria's sanctuary that she offered to all who sought it if need would arrive arise. Now, the time has come for its use once more. Once our home lay in the City of Life when our creator occupied Madaria. Now, it is our sanctuary."

As Verion entered, soft, gentle music reached his ears. Voices sung a melodic tune that stopped him in his tracks. He was mesmerized by its enchanting notes though the words were strange to him, a language he never heard before. The source remained hidden from his eyes though he sought its origin. Murn's giant hand on his back moved him forward once more.

They entered a softly lit, cool, comfortable circular room with white curtains riding a temperate breeze. A large oval table laden with food and drink sat before them. Laveena motioned them to sit, which went unnoticed by some as they stood in awe of their surroundings. Verion's voice brought the company to the table.

He was struck by the warmth and cleanliness of his surroundings. Woven cloths with intricate designs draped the table tops. Great chairs at either end of the table were now occupied by Laveena and Delthas who each wore a circlet of gold on their head. Lesser chairs sat round either side. Colors were soft and well blended, giving a peaceful, harmonious feeling to the travelers.

Verion felt more tranquil than ever before. No aches or pains begot his body, his mind was clear of evil thoughts. He held no worries or wants within his heart.

"Once again we come together with a great deal to discuss. This is the final respite in your journey before undertaking the quest to Selonoth. There will be no place to seek aid nor relief once you leave these walls. Ask what you will, for all shall be answered," said Delthas in a quiet voice, his expression unchanging.

"How may we defeat Torlen?" asked Verion simply. "Holnok is mortal and possesses no great magic, except perhaps that which he bore from Morog. He can be slain in combat, But, I know of no way to slay or drive out Torlen. He shall be too powerful."

"Torlen is indeed powerful, though he has forgotten one simple rule of our race. When the gods created us they made it so we can do no harm to others, unless they take action against us first, hence our peaceful nature. For, if we turn to evil ways the magic within us will rise against the user. Each attempt to use his powers for evil will consume the good that once dwelled within, making him horrible to behold. None has ever done so before, so the end result cannot be foreseen. Though, heed my words, it will be terrible and malevolent. His magic will slowly fade as he transforms into a thing none can predict, even with our magic," Laveena said with a slight frown.

The company sat open mouthed at the revelation. Fear rose among them all, even Verion, who sat imagining what form of wickedness he would face. Dismay held his thoughts tightly.

What form of creature or beast would Torlen become? He must know of this curse. Did he find a way to defeat its hold on him? Would he retain his magic even against the malice that gripped his shape? thought Verion.

"If we force Torlen to use his powers, we will speed his transformation, stripping him of the magic he will use against us. I would rather face an unknown being or creature than magical spells," said Natrae. "Flesh and blood can be slain, magic cannot. We should march against Selonoth soon. After all, we do move with powerful allies by our side."

"I agree. Considering all that has been spoken, we have no choice. We must face whatever shall come our way, no matter how perilous," said Telesta.

"We have faced mere beasts and creatures before, but never magic to this extent," said Murn. "Natrae is right, powerful aid shall be with us, fairies and Ancients walk by our side. We can deal with the minions that come against us, let magic deal with Torlen."

"Selonoth will unleash all its fury as you draw nearer. Once you leave this forest, you will be hounded to lengthy ends, perhaps to the demise of you all," said Laveena.

"Fairies can see the future. Is there no way we can see what is to be," asked Aleeza, staring at Laveena. "Certainly your race bears power to foresee our doom or victory."

"Yes, Lady Aleeza," responded Delthas. "We possess the power which you speak of. However, now we deal with an Ancient that turned to evil ways. It clouds all we see. For, his magic changes our visions with each passing moment. There is no way to predict what comes."

"Then let us speak of a plan. If our destiny cannot be seen, we shall face it as it comes before us," said Verion, his frustration rising. "Will you accompany us for the destruction of Torlen and Holnok? Or will you place a spell upon us to aid our victory."

Verion thought how similar this moment was. During the company's previous quest he convinced the fairies to lend aid in the quest to overthrow Holnok. Now, he stood before the Ancients, attempting the same feat. Knowingly heading into a magically protected land worried him. Though, he felt confident they could succeed with magical defense or aid. His stomach churned with anticipation while awaiting a response, for he felt success or failure would hinge upon it. No matter the power of the Six, Ancient aid would ensure their victory.

"Setorin and Renara shall aid your cause," said Delthas. "They are as powerful and knowledgeable as any among us. They can halt their brother's madness, if the gods are willing. But know this, they will not slay their own kind, only aid in your cause to revert him to former ways or abet his downfall. For now, there are no other options."

"Then it is decided. We shall move toward the east with speed. Let us depart on the second sunrise," said Verion. "Tomorrow brings discussion and planning after a needed nights rest, for now I am weary. Sleep well my friend."

THE MAGIC OF TORLEN

H olnok stared intently at Torlen from a darkened corner. His face pressed against the cold stone wall as he peered out from his hiding place, his eyes squinted in the dim light.

There is something different and strange about him, he thought. *He seems darker than before. His clothes, hair, and eyes, all seem dull. What magic could he be performing on himself? Why would he dare such a thing? Perhaps my eyes play tricks on me. Before, he would know when I approached, though now he holds no idea I stand near. It is curious, for I could strike him down without warning and be rid of him. He holds no weapons, it would be an easy matter. No, no, I must not. First, he must give me the Six freely, then I can deal death upon him. Yes, I shall bide my time. It is my only hope while he lives.*

Holnok smiled outwardly to himself. His mind began to devise a plan to rid himself of Torlen but fear stayed his hand from acting yet. However, if Torlen could help him gain the Six, then perhaps he could suppress his loathing long enough to gain his desire. An upsurge of hatred caused him to clench his teeth as he watched from the shadows. His hand slowly went to his dagger, then he released it as dread returned in a rush.

Just then, Torlen called for his commander, startling the lurking Holnok from the dimness of the room. He scurried forward, trying desperately to hide his thoughts as his boots clacked loudly in the silent hall as he came,

"I am here my liege," said Holnok, scuttling forward, dropping to one knee before his new master. "You summoned me, my Lord. What are thy new commands. I live to serve thee."

Then, a sudden revulsion swept over him. For those were the exact words his previous servant had spoken to him causing disgust and hatred, wishing his death as he knelt before him on many occasions. A glimpse into Natrae's world had now entered his twisted mind, nearly causing him to heave. His head swam in a sea of misery at the thought of becoming a filthy, downtrodden wretch.

"It has begun," said Torlen quickly. "They are moving against us. Dragons, Ancients, fairies and men. We are to be besieged, my Commander. They believe we will fall in defeat, that they have a chance of victory against my might. Fools!" he cried. "I shall show them the err of their ways. Soon this world shall be mine."

Again, Holnok's teeth clenched. For he knew Torlen would betray him. Always, he referred to the world as his own, much like any time he spoke of the hordes, or the Six. Holnok began to realize that he would never hold his treasures. They would be kept from him, secreted away in a magically sealed vault or room to which he could never enter. Hope drained from his mind as he knelt before his master. A desire to burst from the room seized him, yet he knelt motionless.

Torlen stood quickly, startling Holnok. Then he walked to a westward facing parapet, opened the doors and stepped onto the lifeless stone, ire rising within him.

"I will raise up the lands against them. Their journey shall be one of great peril and hardship. The likes of which even my brother and sister could not foresee. They will all die before reaching Selonoth."

Torlen grew in size before Holnok as he lifted his arms to the sky and began to mutter. The sky itself blackened in an instant. The ground began to shake and rumble before the fortress, in many places the earth rose, forming jagged, twisted mountains before Holnok's eyes. Black swamps formed and deep fissures spotted the landscape. The terrain lay broken and twisted from malice. Darkness covered the land, light was held from touching the earth by thick black rolling clouds that rumbled and roared as lightning flashed overhead giving a life to the horrible scene below.

Holnok shrank back in fear as he caught sight of Torlen, who, even as he worked his magic, grew dark and deformed. Terror rose within him as he cried out and ran from his master's sight.

Uncontrollable fear carried him quickly to his chamber where he slammed and bolted the door behind him. Though, in his heart he knew it offered no protection. He paced rapidly as thoughts of dread and mind numbing terror overtook him. Forgotten were his plans of domination and power, now he merely wished to stay alive long enough to see his plan to fruition. Since the Ancient's arrival he lived in constant fright and dismay. Only is his finest moments would he dare to think of the Six any longer.

A flash of light turned his attention to his doorway. There stood Torlen, dark, terrifying and foreboding, barely able to fit inside Holnok's bower.

The High Lord knelt to one knee quaking before his master who darkened the room, blocking out light with his massive size. He quaked with pure terror and dread.

"You left my side during our finest hour, my Commander," he sneered. "Why do you cower so? Do you fear me? We are allies are we not?" asked Torlen mockingly.

"Y . . . Y . . . Yes, my master, I am certainly your ally" stammered Holnok, now dropping to two knees. "I serve thy whims and obey thy commands, my lord. What would you have me do?"

"Nothing as of yet," said Torlen, his voice rumbling within the tiny room, shaking the walls with its power. "The time will come when you will lead our forces into battle, but it is not yet. The powers draw closer even as we speak. Soon, they will be well within our borders. Then, we shall snare them, for they must not escape. The treasures will be mine and the outlanders destroyed. Let their legends speak of their fall before this, my battlement."

Holnok still craved the Sacred Six for his own. He would do anything to possess them, even lead the charge into battle to pluck the items from the company's dead bodies and claim them for himself, then depart unseen away from Torlen. Yet, fear drove hope from him as soon as the images of grandeur and victory entered his head. His head rung like a giant bell from Torlen''s voice. Yet, he was frozen and quelled his thoughts.

However, if he could overcome his dread he would head to Morog along with the most faithful of his Jarcoth guards and any that would follow. There, he would rebuild and start anew, away from Torlen and Selonoth. Then, when the time was right once more, he would strike at the outlanders. For, he still harbored visions of holding D'Enode for his own, sharing it with no one, especially Torlen. He felt certain the once the company was slain, he could possess their trinkets and turn the powers on the monster before him.

"As you wish, Master," he said with a devious smile, as thoughts of domination drove away his fear. His hate was pushed deep where even Torlen could not sense it. "I shall proudly take our forces forth to complete the destruction of the outlanders which I have dreamed about for many a night."

"So be it," said Torlen, "I am sure you will prove yourself in battle, my Commander."

Torlen read Holnok's mind easily this time for he held no desire to hide these thoughts from his master, attempting to deceive him in any way he could.

Holnok dared to gaze upon Torlen. His god-like appearance was gone. Now, his hair was blackened, eyes filled red with hate. Huge arms hung from wide shoulders leading to hands which held fingers half as long as Holnok's forearms. His massive chest heaved in and out with each breath. A creature had come forth from within, towering several feet over Holnok who groveled before the thing that once seemed to him as a god. To Holnok's misery, it seemed to be growing as well. What the beasts final appearance would be, he could only guess.

"I shall return victorious my lord," said Holnok proudly, mustering his courage. Images of possessing the Six gave him hidden daring as he rose to face Torlen. "I shall bear the Six to you after the company's destruction is complete."

"Yes, you shall," said Torlen grinning, revealing sharp, fang like teeth. "And shall be well rewarded for your effort. The Six you prize shall be yours alone. I promise this to you. I know your heart, I feel your lust for the treasures that draw near. Soon, my Commander. Hold faith and patience close to you. Ummmm, I feel your hate, it gives me hope for you yet."

Suddenly, Holnok turned his eyes away, fearing his deepest hate and deceptive plan had been discovered. Instantly, panic rose from his stomach, spreading through every inch of his body until his vision became blurred. His heart pounded rapidly and with a fury he thought would burst within his chest. Finally, he blurted forth speech.

"I live to serve you, master," smiled Holnok inwardly as he spoke the dishonest words, for the only thought he held was to destroy Torlen and possess the trinkets for himself.

"Go now. You head for glory. The lands shall be stained with blood once again. As it was thousands of years ago, so it shall be again. Only this time, we will not be driven from my kingdom. We will occupy the earth, making the lands my own," said Torlen, his voice rising as he spoke. "Kill them all! Let none alive."

Holnok scampered from the room to find the lower levels of the fortress where unnamed things dwelt. Now he despised the darkness he once loved. For, he bred many things here for evil purposes, but at this point they frightened him. He was unsure if their allegiance lie with Torlen or if he still held control over them all.

Then, his mind turned to his hatred for the company. *This is their doing. If not for their meddling at Mindaloth, I would be High Lord of earth, never having to lay eyes upon Torlen. Now I fight two battles, one within my own fortress and the other comes from the vermin that dares to go against my might. Which one is the greater threat. I must find a way to kill Torlen, yet I must have the Six to end his existence. Bah! Troubles abound by my side and I see no clear path to the end. What shall I do,* he thought as he moved mindlessly downward.

Finally, he came upon the entrance to the lower levels. He moved with caution, his eyes shifting from side to side as he went. His once self confident air fled him as he jerked and twisted to see the source of every sound while slowly descending into the depths of Selonoth. Then, he reached the den of the Gorlans.

"Time for battle is upon us. Prepare yourselves, we go forth at dawn," said Holnok. "It shall be a glorious day. The races of this earth shall bow before us."

"What do you know of battle," the Gorlan snarled as he rose on hind legs and moved closer. The beast now stood only inches away, towering over Holnok. "You are a puppet that will lead us to death."

Holnok grew incensed, fury instantly welled within him. His heart went black and cold. No longer could he contain himself. His blood boiled within his veins from anger.

"I alone have created you. You will obey *my* commands!" shouted Holnok, mustering every ounce of courage within him. "Perhaps I should inform Torlen you are unwilling to fight for your creator and master. I believe he would cure your cowardice for you," he said with vehemence in his voice.

Holnok's anger grew even larger, providing a new strength and resolve. He was furious his plans had gone awry. Now he was a servant to a beast and his own minions questioned him. It was more then he could stand. He drew his sword with speed, pointing it at the Gorlans heart as his face reddened with fury.

"You can die where you stand, or fight without question," he spat. "Choose now! For, if I slay you, I will simply create another to take your place. Speak your allegiance or perish here in the darkness."

The Gorlan stepped back, lowered to all fours and spoke with a humbled voice.

"We serve our creator, Holnok," said the beast. "We shall die for him without doubt."

"So be it," said Holnok, satisfied with the oath. "Speak to the mass. We shall stretch across the land as a black wave, crushing the outlanders and their friends as they draw near. Death will find them soon. Glorious war is upon us my friends, let us feast on their fear and their carcasses. We move at sunrise, TO WAR!" Holnok shouted amidst the frenzied howls and snarls of approval from the Gorlans.

He spun quickly, his cloak flowing behind him as he went, the sword still in his hand. He slammed the door behind him as he exited the tunnels. Confidence overwhelmed him once more. His step was filled with pride and poise now. Hate and loathing gave way to supremacy and hope. His stride was long and his head held high.

I will lead MY minions into battle and we shall see the fall of these fools that rise against us, he thought. *Then I will find a way to defeat Torlen as well. I shall regain control of my kingdom, as it was before.*

His mind was firmly made up as he strode with conviction to his chamber. Torlen was gone, the room lay empty. Again, he closed and bolted the door and paced rapidly.

THE DRAGON HEAD SHIELD

As Verion stirred from bed, his heart was heavy. He did not dread battle, but fear of losing one or more of his companions in a war that would soon be upon them, haunted him. He felt confident they would be victorious, yet at what cost. Facing potent magic, especially after seeing the extent of the powerful Ancients, added worry as well.

He jumped slightly at a soft knock at his door. Nira stood in the entrance, smiling.

"Come, let us speak privately," she whispered. "I know your fears, they are stirring within you. Release your burdens to me. Let us quell them now. Come."

"There was a time when we needed to be side by side for you to read my thoughts," said Verion, frowning. "Now, they are unsafe no matter the distance," he said as his face changed to a slight smile.

"Brother, you know I mean well. Your thoughts are easily read with or without the Eye," she said, smiling. "Besides, if I can sense them, many others can as well. Tell me what troubles you, we have always spoken openly, perhaps I can help."

"It is as it was during our first journey. I fear losing a companion to the quest. I am unsure how it would affect me," he said honestly with sadness in his tone. Then he turned and took his sister's hands within his own. "I fear for your safety and Aleeza's as well. Though all the company is held dear to me, both of you are the most precious of all. I do not doubt your skill in battle, but I dread magic. Who knows what we shall face or the power it will bring forth."

"Fear not, Brother," said Nira, smiling once more. "I have foreseen our end and it is indeed an end, but none meet their death.

Yet understand it is only a vision. I have no way of knowing the truth in it all. I only know what the Eye shows me."

Renara came upon them unseen, moving silently down the hallway. She walked gracefully to Verion's side, placing her hand on his shoulder.

"My parents summon you forth. There is magic your dragon must take part in it" she said softly. "Bring Trimlin before us my lord," she said, before turning and slowly walking away.

She disappeared from sight before Verion could utter a word. He wore a puzzled expression as he turned quickly to face his sister. Nira looked equally quizzical as she shrugged.

Nonetheless, he did as he was commanded. He strode outdoors as his thoughts reached Trimlin, who glided before him within seconds, his low rumbling purr evident.

As the dragon landed Renara returned followed by the entire company at her heels. Next came Delthas, Laveena, and Setorin.

"We have brought you hither for a Blessing," said Laveena, turning to the companions gathered before her. "It has been nearly five thousand of your years since this has been done. Not since the days of the Dragon Code have mortals lay witness to this ceremony. Now, you will behold true dragon magic.

Delthas stood before Trimlin motionless and silent. The dragon stared at him intently, then to Verion's surprise, he nodded in response to Delthas. The Ancient stepped away from the guardian and retrieved a shield Setorin carried.

He held up the gleaming black and silver artifact. It was shaped as a replica of a dragons head. Its forged face stared back at Verion, seemingly alive, watching his every move. He shook his head quickly in disbelief. The image faded as the shield returned to a simple piece of steel.

"Not since the Battle of Ages has this shield been seen. The mighty T'Ord carried it forth into battle. He alone fought alongside all races of D'Enode to drive evil from this world. It was merely a shield then, no enchantments were upon it. However, this day it will become blessed by powerful dragon magic, as with Murn's armor. Behold, Trimlin shall utter his power. I bequeath a onetime gift to enable him to bestow his powerful magic," he said, walking to Trimlin's side once more.

"The time has come, my dragon friend," he said, holding the shining shield aloft before the dragon and nodding slightly, his head barely moving.

"Reto Bara Sola Nor," said Trimlin plainly in the common tongue of men for all to understand.

The shield lifted from the hands of Delthas to hover beside him in midair. It glowed momentarily, then sparkling light engulfed its shape, spinning and swirling, encompassing the shield. Mesmerizing radiant beams flickered and shimmered, shooting outward, then faded.

Verion thought it reminiscent to the power of the Six when used against Mindaloth.

Delthas seemed satisfied as he retrieved the shield that hung before him. He smiled and strode before Verion, handing the blessed shield to him. Verion's head bowed instantly.

"As T'Ord led the races of your world into battle, so you shall lead your company into Selonoth and beyond. This shield cannot be pierced by any magic or weapon known. Along with Haldira by your side, you are formidable to all who would rise up before you. With the new sun you shall set forth to the east to bring about the fall of evil that once more comes to threaten your world," said Delthas with a smile.

The company gawked openly, standing momentarily motionless. Glances were exchanged though they all remained silent.

Verion turned the shield over many times. It was light as a feather. Again, the image of the dragon seemed to stare at him as he gazed upon it. It felt alive as his hands ran over its surface, tingling his fingertips. His eyes turned to Delthas who smiled back at him.

"I have no words to thank thee for this gift and shall carry it with honor. Though not T'Ord the Mighty, I pray to our gods for his strength and courage in battle. For his legend is still told to this day," said Verion.

"May it serve you well, Lord Verion," said Laveena quietly. "Though it is not one of the original Six, it will aid you greatly in the end. After all, one of your gods bore it forth. Only one of great bravery and courage may lay hands upon it."

Verion smiled half heartedly, feeling overwhelmed, yet pleased. Something Delthas said struck him as queer. *What did he mean by* it protecting me from Selonoth and beyond? There is nothing that lay further east except Morog itself. Laveena said it will aid me before the end. The end of what?, he thought. Momentarily he pushed it from him to speak to Trimlin.

He smiled again, genuinely this time as he walked to his dragon and began to pat his neck. Then he spoke in a near whisper.

"I knew in my heart dragon magic would return one day," thought Verion, as his smile widened. "This is only the beginning. Now you have given a gift that is next only in greatness to yourself. Thank you, my friend."

"Though Delthas seemed to speak to me for only a moment of your time, he said a great deal," replied Trimlin. "It was told to me that magic from my heart and soul are held within the shield from the blessing. I shall always be with you now, protecting my rider even though I may be far away. He commanded me to say that when all is over you shall learn the secret of the Dragon Code for yourself. The power of the Blessing shall be yours."

Verion stared at the shield again, then to his dragon who gazed intently at him through his bright yellow eyes.

"Tomorrow brings battle once again," thought Verion finally. "Take care of yourself, your mate and the young ones. Stay close as always for I am sure you will be needed."

Trimlin launched into the air with a roar. He turned his head back over his wing to look a final time at his rider before disappearing over the tree tops, rocking from side to side as he went.

"Come, we must discuss our plans. But first, a meal to aid our minds with thought," said Renanra. "This way my friends."

They were seated in the comfortable room of their first meeting and much food was brought forth while conversation began immediately.

"We must ready provisions and weapons for our journey," began Verion. Then he turned to Setorin and Renara. "Your presence will be of great aid to the company. The company shall stand ready for whatever Selonoth will bring."

"Spoken as a true warrior with a brave heart," said Delthas quickly. "You will indeed need all of your bravery. I have foreseen terrible visions of things that await you. You will be challenged with each step. Torlen will look to the west for your arrival. The company will not come unseen. There will be no element of surprise for your companions as you move forward. Be prepared for battle which shall come quickly after you depart."

Verion stared ahead silently in quiet contemplation. His eyes narrowed several times as his brow furrowed sporadically. Then, his eyes moved to Haldira and his newly blessed dragon shield. Without thinking, his fingers ran slowly over the shield, feeling the tingling once more.

Does it hold a life of its own? I feel as though it tries to speak to me, though nothing is heard. Mayhap Delthas could aid me, he thought, turning back to the conversation before him.

"We are ready," he said simply. "Together, we will face whatever evil is unleashed upon us.

Strength beyond reckoning is held within our group. The companions carry the power of the Six, magic and dragons are by our side. Victory against Selonoth and its forces shall be difficult, yet I hold great hope. Now, if it pleases my lord and lady, we wish to rest and forego evil talk for a short time."

Verion and the company rose and bowed to Laveena and Delthas, who nodded in response. Then he turned and strode from the chamber when the voice of Aris entered Verion's mind.

"You shall find aid on your trek, though it will not be looked for," she said, her thoughts pushing forward. "Your company will grow to large numbers, which shall serve you well when needed. Trust them all, for they have allegiance to you and your company."

"Of whom do you speak, my Queen," thought Verion in answer. "Who would aid us? We have members of each race. There are none left to travel by our side. Trust in who?"

Aris remained silent, her voice had left his mind leaving him with yet again more unanswered questions. Verion chose not to inquire any further for he trusted the queen's visions. He turned to address the company once more.

"My friends, let us take rest and make what preparations we must. Meet here at the new sun. We make for the Tortured Lands tomorrow," he said softly. "Haste is needed now."

The company broke asunder. Some made preparations, others wandered outside to stare east, some remained at the table to talk among themselves. The conversation was of things other than evil.

Murn, Jinarl and Eldon came to Verion's side as he slumped against the wall and slid to the ground breathing deeply of the night air. He smiled as the coolness went deep into his lungs.

"It seems we are destined for danger once more," said Verion, expressionless. His stare was focused on the magical force field surrounding the city. "Aris has spoken to me once again."

During the previous quest, Verion held his tongue, not openly speaking of the queen's prophecy, which was of doom. Now however, he kept nothing secret. He had learned to put complete trust in companions, sharing all of his relevant thoughts with them.

"Was a prophecy of doom placed upon us once more," asked Murn, his eye widening in fear.

"No, my giant friend," replied Verion. "It was told we shall receive unlooked for aid in large numbers. Though, she would say no more and I asked no further. We must wait and see what our paths brings us now."

Suddenly, Nira's shape was seen running from the meeting room. She hastened to the small group with distress on her face.

"Come! Our lands are besieged. Come quickly, hear the news yourself," she said with desperation and panic in her voice as she bolted rearward to the hall.

Verion sprang to his feet and sprinted to join the company as his mind raced with horrible thoughts. Renara and Laveena sat side by side as he burst forth into the room.

"What news! What of our lands?" he asked with dismay in his voice as he burst into the hall. "Please, I must know, does my family yet live."

"Your family is well for now. Though, even as we speak preparations for battle have commenced. Zenex, Sorns, Gorlans and Jarcoth move to all lands. None of the outlanders will willingly submit to evil. They use steel and valor as weapons to defend your homes," said Laveena.

"Why! What does Torlen or Holnok hope to gain through attacking our lands," asked Verion, more speaking aloud than asking directly. "He must know we are coming to him. Why attack the innocent now. Our peoples have not wronged either of them, why are they assailed."

"That is the exact reason he attacks, Lord Verion," Delthas chimed in. "It is his way of making you choose. You may stay your present course to face him or depart on dragons to defend your homelands, perhaps saving your loved ones. He is hoping your heart will outweigh your quest. Though he greatly desires the Six, he can later hunt you one by one and take them. He fears their united power, so he attempts to separate them. His magic is fading, he is becoming a beast. One which is no longer any semblance to the beauty and peace he once possessed."

Delthas moved toward the company, gliding once more, his long robes flowing round his feet. His eyes roved over each companion, causing many to cast their stare downward. Then he spoke.

"With his magic gone he no longer possesses the ability to sense you. This terrifies him, making him lust for the treasures even more. The power of the Six can still revert him to his former self. Yet even now, he slips deeper into the abyss of darkness. Though, even as a beast his mind is keen. He knows all will fear him and he may yet still rule D'Enode if he possesses them, for no power could rise against him in his horrible form. None would overcome him."

"We must depart now," said Verion quickly. "Let us take the battle to him, since he desires it. This must end before our lands are destroyed and loved ones are lost forever."

"Patience my young Lord," said Laveena. Her soft, calming voice came through the stillness. "Your time for battle draws nigh. Let not hasty actions rule your mind . . . or heart. Death will surround you soon enough. Though the future is unclear, I see your parents will yet live. They are valiant warriors. Worry not for their safety, for it will cloud your mind. Concentrate on what lies before you" she said with a smile.

Verion's shoulders relaxed. His red face returned to normal color as ire and worry left him. He noticed Katima now stood by his side. She used fairy magic to remove his troubles, he was sure. He smiled and nodded at her, silently thanking her.

"So be it," said Verion softly. "Sunrise cannot be upon us soon enough." He turned and left the hall once more with Aleeza following closely.

"My husband, wait," she called as Verion halted. "All will be well, you will see. Our lands have many great warriors among them. They will turn away any evil that comes against them. Dragons protect them as well. You have already sent them for protection."

The company formed around Verion as the two spoke. Some wore frowns, others stood expressionless, lost in their own thoughts.

"It comes to us yet again," said Zarah, her eyes roving over her companions. "Danger is but a breath away. This time the evil ones will not escape us. It must end here, there will be no eluding our strength."

"Agreed, no matter where our fates lie, we must ensure the end of the malevolence," said Eldon. "Regardless of our destinies, we must venture forth as a company to see the end of the wickedness. It shall be a great task indeed. We are many days travel from Selonoth, meanwhile, evil spreads upon our lands like a darkened shadow."

"What shall our course of travel be? We do have dragons after all," stated Natrae. "We could go on horses or foot as well. Though, by foot we would lose several days, many miles still lay before us."

"We shall go on foot," said Verion. "Mindaloth was a wicked, broken land. One in which horses would have been no use. I believe Holnok will surround himself once more with wastelands and even if the fairies hid our dragons as they had previously, there is a great risk in that strategy. For, I believe Torlen will expect us to come from the sky, not by foot."

"It will take us five, perhaps six days to reach Selonoth from here," added Nira. "My brother speaks wisely. I, too, believe Torlen will search the skies. For, I sense it. The mind of Torlen and Holnok are returning to me. I sense their protection is fading."

"True," said Katima. "If Delthas is correct, as Torlen turns to more beast than man, his magic and protection will fade. I have seen their minds as well. Holnok is fearful, yet hopeful. He secretly prays for the destruction of Torlen so he may rule again."

"He has lost his servant Natrae and he is forced to take matters into his own hands," said Jinarl. "Certainly it sits ill with him, forced to do another's bidding without aid to carry his orders to and fro."

Then, suddenly, all movement stopped. All heads turned to Natrae, who stood with wide eyes. His head tilted to one side as he tried to contemplate Jinarl's comment.

"I do not understand. Of what do you speak, Lord Jinarl," asked Natrae. "I have never served any man, let alone Holnok. You speak blasphemy against me. Am I to be named as an evil thrall. Your words are cursed and harmful to my honor," said Natrae, resting his hand on his sword.

Verion stood frozen. No words came from his lips. Panic rose within him as he searched desperately for an explanation to give to his former enemy. Then, he hung his head and sighed.

"Natrae, my friend, let us speak privately if we may," said Verion sullenly. "There is much to discuss. There are things you must know before we go further into the Tortured Lands. Tis news of a good man who once walked in the shadow of darkness, yet, he made his way to the light and became righteous once more. Though, I cannot see the end, I believe it shall become a a tale of the ages."

Verion's form faded into the distance with Natrae by his side disappearing in the shadow of a nearby tree. The company, still silent, moved to the great hall once more.

Hours passed slowly as they sat silent. None dared leave. Aleeza paced to and fro as she anxiously awaited Verion's return. Murn sat sharpening his axe, creating the only sound within the room.

Finally, Milar's hand raised up, calling for silence. His voice came clear and soft.

"They come this way," he said in a near whisper.

Verion entered beside Natrae, whose face was pale and drawn. He wore no expression, only a distant blank stare. Gazing at each of the company individually through hazy eyes, he halted momentarily, then wandered mindlessly down the long hall to his left. The sound of a door closing and locking echoed within the chamber.

All eyes swung to Verion who looked tired and worn. His eyes seemed glassy and remote as he gazed at the companions briefly before he spoke.

"His misdeeds, at least all that were within my knowledge, are now known to him," said Verion softly. "He knows the full account since the Second Coming. Many questions were asked of me and he became shocked and confused when I answered, yet he listened intently nonetheless. I sensed two things; one is he believes we will never place faith in him. Secondly, he is not worthy to be among the company."

"Will he go forward with us?" asked Murn. "I have grown used to the new Natrae. Desire for his death has left me. Since his cleansing he has become tolerable." Which was Murn's way of saying he enjoyed his company and friendship.

"Yes," said Verion simply. "I also felt his hatred for Holnok. I believe vengeance fills his thoughts toward his former master."

"I sense the same as well," said Nira, joining in. "His heart is quite loyal to our cause. He has no evil or malice within him any longer, at least, not toward us. Now it is directed at Selonoth."

"Still, we must wonder if it is wise to have him beside us," said Zarah. "Our path lies many leagues to the east, yet the Betrayer shall remain at our side. Perhaps the old villain is indeed gone, or perhaps not. Does he have our full trust? I ask all of you here."

"You have witnessed the change for yourself, yet you still hold doubt," said Eldon. "I for one stand firm to my faith in his change."

"I hold blame alone. For I misspoke and now we are forced to chose if Natrae shall join us," said Jinarl.

"Lord Jinarl, better it be known now than on the road to destroy Holnok. A mere slip of the tongue may have indeed set things as they should be. For, if Holnok lays eyes upon him, who could foresee what hold he may yet have," said Verion. "Now, Natrae must choose to follow us or remain behind. Do not forget it has been foretold he will aid the cause in a way none here can."

"Aris, Delthas and Laveena have said we must have him by our side or the quest will fail," said Eldon. "So be it. I believe he should stay by our side."

"Come, let us rest. The hour grows late," said Verion quietly before any others spoke. "We will need all our strength for what lies ahead of us. We will take council with a new sun. Good night my friends, rest well," said Verion as he rose. He proceeded down the hallway with Aleeza's hand in his.

Verion's night was restless. Dreams of Natrae reverting back to evil danced in his mind. He saw a wicked Natrae battling with his pure counterpart, each filled with wrath and fury. Verion watched helplessly as the two locked themselves in mortal combat for the right to vanquish the other and live on. As the combat faded, it became a scene of Natrae bowing at Holnok's feet, swearing his allegiance. The scene turned quickly to Natrae standing by Verion's side fighting to the death as the minions of Selonoth assailed them. The pure Natrae stood bloodied and showed no mercy to the evil that came against him. Then, the visions were gone.

Verion lay sweating, tossing in bed when Aleeza's hand on his shoulder woke him. He rose and began to pace to and fro within the room. His brow was furrowed as he mumbled softly to himself, then he turned to Aleeza.

"I have no worries," he said. "I know in my heart Natrae is a good man. I will stand by him in all that comes our way. His heart is true to our cause, not to Holnok. I feel it and sense it."

Aleeza simply smiled and patted the empty side of the bed. Verion went to her side. He lay, attempting yet again to sleep. This time he slept exhausted for the few remaining hours until the dawn came.

He was weary as he dressed. Sleep evaded him for many hours during the darkness of night.

His eyes were reddened, aches and pains begot his body. Yet, he smiled at Aleeza, saying nothing of his discomfort and fatigue.

The company slowly gathered round the table for a morning meal. Conversation was at a minimum. The room fell silent as Natrae entered. Uneasiness lay a veil of silence over each of the companions. Tension grew thick around them, enveloping them all like a smothering, wet blanket.

Verion pushed an empty chair toward Natrae with his foot and nodded to it. Natrae moved silently toward the vacant seat. Verion smiled at him and rested his hand upon his shoulder, gently squeezing it, then continued his meal silently.

A hush came over the companions. None spoke openly, though many pair of eyes shot quizzical, even concerned glances to one another. Heads turned slowly from side to side as if to not disturb the fragile stillness laying heavily over the table.

Natrae's soft, low voice shattered the silence like a giant bell ringing within the room, startling many around him.

"I am now aware of the offenses I have done," he began. "I beg you not to hold them against me. Madness possessed me, though, I cannot explain how or why. I remember being happy long ago, yet it seems like a dream. I vow here and now to follow this company, giving my life for the quest if need be. Evil has fled my mind and heart. As it was many years ago, so shall it be again, for I am a new man once more. If there is any here who doubts my loyalty or my allegiance, speak now. I do not wish to travel with hate or distrust among us. I shall say no more."

Again, the room fell silent. None dared move, though all were uncomfortable as Natrae's eyes touched each companion one by one. Some averted his gaze, others simply squirmed.

Murn slowly lifted his giant frame from his chair, his eye narrowing at Natrae. He bent forward to rest his large hands on the table, staring at him. Then, he stood upright and began to pace as his booming voice filled the air.

"You," said Murn, pointing a large grey finger at Natrae, "caused the death of my brother. You slew Baytor with your own hands. Both died with honor, but needlessly. One of my guards is dead as well. I swore an oath to slay you with my bare hands if ever I laid eyes upon you again. Now you sit before us and ask us to trust you. My answer is . . . yea. You shall have my trust."

Murn's words shocked and bewildered the entire company. Verion was perched near the edge of his seat, preparing to come between the two as he had done previously. Certainly Murn would attack, he thought. He did not look forward to attempting to stop a nine foot tall enraged Cyclops. Secretly, he hoped Katima would use her magic to bind him. Now however, he sat gaping at the giant. All thoughts of aiding Natrae were lost to amazement.

"I trust and welcome you. Why you may ask? Two reasons, Natrae. One is that Ancient magic is strong and I truly believe you carry no memory of your deeds, ere Verion spoke of them. But most importantly is I have watched you closely as of late, waiting for you to deceive us or revert to your old ways and send message to your former master. You have done neither."

Murn paused and walked next to Natrae, towering over him, looking down into his face.

"At one time I also distrusted Baytor. Yet, he proved himself to be one of the most honorable and courageous men I ever knew. In my heart, I give you a second chance, for I feel you have the same honor and courage within you as well my friend. Forgiveness for your evil ways is yours and I welcome you to the company."

Verion nearly tipped from his seat. He gazed at the flabbergasted company, most of whom he sensed carried the same worry of seeing Natrae pulled apart by Murn's own hands before any could contain him. He found his voice quickly. His mind worked rapidly as he rose.

"So it shall be," he said swiftly. "Does any here have any doubt or mistrust in our re-born companion?"

The room remained still and silent as Verion scanned the faces before him. He glanced at Murn, then smiled and nodded to him. He knew it was difficult for Murn to forget his hate. To give the Betrayer a second chance took great courage, which is one of many reasons Verion greatly admired the Cyclops and they had become fast friends.

"Now, it is over. Never again shall we have talk of the old Natrae," said Verion to all. "From this moment forward he shall be named Fenorl. In my tongue it means 'the forgiven one.' Do any object?"

Again silence reigned within the room. The company appeared frozen by some magical spell. Verion caught Laveena's stare upon him. She smiled broadly and nodded as her thoughts pushed into his mind.

"Well done young lord," she said. "Yet again you have made a wise choice. Your trust and vision will become clear for all to see. Though it may come unlooked for in the darkest hour."

Verion smiled and turned away, attempting to hide his thoughts of pride from her. Images of his mother rewarding him for a job well done flashed in his mind. He flushed and grew warm.

"Let us move," he said. "The sun is nearly upon us. There is much ground to cover and our fate awaits us. We shall meet it in combat. My heart calls for an end to Holnok and his evil ways."

With that, he grabbed up his pack and lifted it on to his back and strode to the doorway.

"Farewell my lord Delthas and my lady Laveena," he said with a low bow. "We shall meet again soon."

"Of that, I am sure," said Laveena, waving a hand slowly. "Fare well Verion of Eldarn, son of Parta. With great interest we shall be watching all you do young lord. Always watch the east."

Rustling of packs could be heard as the company readied itself for the journey. Once outside the companions turned east. Verion however, made a quick detour to the stables with sadness in his heart.

"Brandor, my trusted friend. Yet again, I must leave you behind. For, I know not what dangers lie before us," he said aloud, with sorrow. "I shall return to you in time. Be patient my companion. Enjoy the rest while you can. Look after Deema too," he said with a slight smile.

Verion patted his neck and stroked his muzzle. He stuffed his hand in his pack and produced a large ripe apple which Brandor accepted immediately. Then he strode to join the rest of the company as Brandor's thoughts of farewell came into his mind.

The force field flexed and returned to normal with the passing of each member, with Verion exiting last. He turned and looked back, still fascinated with the invisible shield of protection. He smiled at the thought of someday possessing the great magic for Eldarn.

The company headed east with speed and purpose, moving through the Forest of Dreams with low conversation flowing freely. The travelers made attempts at keeping talk happy, yet it seemed to revert to evil as often as not. After some time, the talk ended from despair.

Verion felt remorse at leaving his horse behind. For the second time in his life he was forced to move forward without his mount. The first was during the march to Mindaloth. Though before, he had little time to contemplate his feelings since his mind was occupied with matters of the company, it now began to gnaw at him as he strode forward.

As they pressed onward Verion marveled at the beauty of the forest. Though his home was thick with ancient tress and mountainous, this land seemed enchanted, even more mystical and beautiful to him. Crystal blue water falls came from tree laden slopes that rose high toward the sky. The clear, cool water flowed steadily down gurgling streams that cut through the forest floor. Only faint foot trails were perceptible to his trained eye. Birds fluttered and wild beasts roamed about the company as they moved. Verion was blissful, if only for a short while.

The day moved quickly. Before Verion realized, the sun had reached its zenith. He called for a meal to be prepared as he wandered away from camp and slipped from his boots to dangle his feet in the cold water. A sudden joyous feeling swept through him. Elation overwhelmed him. Flashes of his parents, dragons, life friends and special moments in his life danced before his eyes. The water itself seemed to speak to him, to understand him and occupy his mind.

Then, sounds of flapping wings came to Verion's ears, breaking his euphoria. He quickly slipped on his boots and ran to the campsite. His hand rested upon Haldira as he arrived.

A dark shape fluttered between the trees coming toward the company. Its form was small and flew alone. Verion knew the black figure that appeared. He turned his head quickly to his sister, who was smiling, then he caught her eye as she nodded to him. He rose and stepped forward.

"Hail Ono," said Verion loudly. "Come sit with us my winged friend."

Ono turned and flew to the company, landing directly in front of Verion, who gave a low bow to the little bugged eyed creature. Ono bore a crooked smile on his face as he awkwardly returned the bow and spoke.

"Greetings my friends," he began. "I have been directed to bring news for your quest . . ."

"Ono, what know you of our quest," interrupted Verion, with obvious surprise in his voice.

"Aris has spoken to me," he said simply. "She summoned me here. Her words came into my head, so I sought you out as she commanded. I have searched very far. Never has a Grendar traveled in the Forest of Dreams. The fairy queen told me where to search."

"What news can you share," asked Verion. "Tell us the full tale. For it is of great importance."

"It is said Selonoth has raised up the land around it walls. Holnok himself marches forth with many beasts, men and creatures by his side. He comes this way with a great army. There is no place to conceal yourself once in the Tortured Lands. They will trap you and slay you all. There are too many," Ono said as he flapped his wings quickly.

"We have faced large numbers before and survived. We shall do so again, my small friend," said Verion. "Holnok himself is leading the hordes you say. Hummm, that is curious indeed."

Ono's head tilted from side to side as he recalled several of the battles for Mindolath in which the company fought his former master, Holnok.

"There is more," retorted Ono. "Good news for your cause and the company. Hexart has heard word of your march to Selonoth. He and a very large group of a mixed band of warriors await you at the borders of this forest. Orna, Zarns, and Crutad anticipate your coming. They have sworn allegiance to you. Since you have given them their freedom, they wish to fight by your side now."

Verion's mind instantly turned to the fight for Mindaloth. Hexart was a large, muscular human warrior of the Crutad, who once fought for Holnok. Verion set his people free from evil. Hexart swore allegiance to Verion that day. The Orna were creatures Holnok created to do his wickedness. They, too, were set free. Now, it appeared they would fight by his side as well. The Zarns were common men that once followed Holnok's father. However, once they turned to evil ways a great magic was placed upon them, turning them into creatures. Verion was sure they yearned for revenge. Now he felt they would have their chance.

"How many would you say stand by Hexart's side, Ono?" asked Verion. "What strength in numbers do we speak of."

"Perhaps four thousand," replied Ono flatly. Again, his wings fluttered wildly. "Does this please my lord?"

Verion's eyes grew large. He envisioned perhaps several hundred or even one thousand warriors. Quickly, his hopes grew as new plans formed in his mind within seconds. Though no force of such size was expected to aid the quest, it certainly would not be turned away. It was foreseen strength would indeed come, but Verion never dreamed of such a large scale.

"Indeed it does, my little companion. Let us move forward to meet them," said Verion, turning to the company. "It bodes well we have unlooked for aid in such numbers," he said. "Our strength is growing."

"Can we trust them?" asked Zydor suddenly. "We have no way of knowing if they have fallen under Holnok's grasp once again."

"Hexart and the others live and die by a warriors code. They shall never allow their lands to be overrun again, especially by Holnok and his new forces. They will fight to the last man or creature if they must," said Verion.

"They are trustworthy," interjected Qnara. "I will gladly fight by their side. They hold no love for their former master and seek revenge, perhaps justice as well."

"They fight for their freedom once more," said Ono. "Free will is theirs now. They do not wish to be Holnok's thralls ever again. So they will stand against the spread of malice, for it also threatens them as well. Hexart has told this to me."

"Then let us delay no longer," said Verion, shouldering his pack. "Let us be off. Forward my friends, new hope awaits us."

The company moved with even greater expectations in their hearts. The welcomed news lengthened their strides toward the forests edge as talk resumed once more. This time it was of hope and gladness. Dread and gloom had been chased away. Verion wondered if the fairies had placed a spell upon the travelers to help ease their minds for a time.

Eagerness filled Verion's mind. *Four thousand,* he thought. *Perhaps O'Tan smiles on us and the quest. Traveling undetected will be bothersome now. There will be no hope of hiding such a force, unless the fairies can use magic. Nonetheless, that shall be dealt with when it arises. For now I am filled with faith once more. This is the aid the queen foretold to me.*

Then, Renara's soft, musical voice came into his mind like a soft gentle breeze of a spring day against his face.

"Four thousand against tens of thousands young lord," she said. "Stay your hope. Many will die, and the company may fail. Do not be overly confident, it could lead to our downfall. You must keep reason by your side. For the direst of times is yet to come."

"True, my lady," thought Verion in return. "Yet, do not deny it is welcome aid. Now we have a force which will take the wicked ones unawares. This bodes well for us. Does it not?"

"Indeed," replied Renara. "But, you now face a force larger than you have encountered before. Caution is my only warning."

With that, Renara's thoughts fell away and he heard no more. The music left him.

Nighttime came upon them quickly. The sun hid its face behind the E'Lenoria Mountains to the west and her sister the moon slowly rose to its full splendor high above. Camp was made at Verion's request. He started a small, warm fire and sat before it rubbing his hands together as Fenorl came to his side.

"My lord," said Fenorl hesitantly. "May I sit? I have much on my mind I wish an answer to."

Verion smiled and nodded to his left as Fenorl lowered himself into the spot.

"Do you bear faith in me," asked Fenorl bluntly, expressionless. "I yearn to free myself of this heavy heart that burdens me. A life of trust and honor is what I covet, yet it eludes me in all I do."

Verion was momentarily speechless. He stared intently at Fenorl, unsure what brought about his question here and now, though the answer was readily apparent.

"Of course I hold faith in you, my friend," said Verion, smiling. Why do you ask? Speak your mind. I sense turmoil within you and feel you possess a great desire to prove yourself."

"Yes," said Fenorl quickly, staring at the fire. "I know all here have accepted me. But, words often veil the truth. I wonder who among us trust their lives to me. I do not recall giving trust, or being trusted, in my lifetime. At least not after my cleansing."

Verion's brow furrowed. He wrung his hands before the flames, then turned to stare into his friend's eyes. Images of fear when Natrae betrayed the company and was caught sending messages to Holnok sprung into Verion's thoughts. The hate and loathing within his eyes on that day remained with Verion since. Now, the re-born Fenorl sat before asking for trust and honor.

"Fenorl, none here speak ill of you. All trust you. If they did not, they would speak words of doubt. I have traveled many leagues with most of this company and they are good at heart and true in word. If there was one here holding secret loathing or fear, I, or my sister, would know. Worry not, you will prove your valor I am sure," said Verion, studying Fenorl as the dancing yellow flames cast soft light on his face.

"You are a worthy man and will make a great king," said Fenorl. "When all is done, will you have me in Eldarn. For, I no longer have a home. I shall not return to Quantar just yet. It would bring me great pride to call your lands my own."

Verion's throat tightened as he was choked with thoughts flowing into his mind from Fenorl. He felt lost, abandoned and confused.

His heart was filled with sorrow and remorse, doubt and worry rose within him. Verion closed his eyes, shaking his head slightly to break the thoughts.

"We would honor your presence. After all, I am wed to your cousin," said Verion smiling. "I will help build your home with my own hands," he said laying his strong grip on Fenorl's shoulder. "It may not be the kingdom you once desired, though I think you will find it pleasurable nonetheless. You are welcome in Eldarn among the warrior folk."

Now, happiness welled within him. Overwhelming relief and joy flooded Verion's thoughts, replacing the dark, dreary notions that assailed him.

"We should rest," said Verion. "Come, find sleep. We have a long, arduous day ahead."

Verion strode to his bedroll and curled close to his wife who slept soundly. His sleep did not come easily. Dreadful visions and thoughts pushed into his dreams, which were many. He stirred fitfully throughout the night, trying unsuccessfully to rid himself of the fright they brought to him. Terror gripped him many times as he lay in a cold sweat, rolling about fitfully.

His mind was filled with scenes of Fenorl falling in battle and the quest failing from Verion's lack of protection for his companion. He had been warned several times of Fenorl's importance, yet he failed in his duty even after the foretelling of doom. Images of evil sweeping over D'Enode due to his inability to follow the warnings swarmed his mind.

He sat upright, staring into the blackness around him, wondering if anyone had probed his terrible, dread filled dreams. Attempting to sleep, he curled next to Aleeza and prayed to the gods she would provide her usual comfort for his rest.

The sky glowed orange in the east as the sun broke the horizon. Birds chirped happily as Verion rekindled the fire for a quick breakfast. Urgency grew within him as he sat stirring food in a pan. He felt an immediate need to meet with Hexart, though he was unsure why. This day would bring the borders of the forest within sight.

The company moved steadily through the wooded refuge of Madaria. None grew weary as they pressed ever forward. Verion stopped only for light meals and drink as time slipped past quickly.

The sun was minutes away from sinking below the western horizon when the travelers reached the edge of the Forest of Dreams. Verion did not slow his pace. He pressed forward from the tree line, leaving the security and protection of the forest behind.

THE TORTURED LANDS

Eerie silence met Verion as he strode forward. He expected many warriors awaiting their arrival of his company. His eyes scanned the surroundings, covering each inch thoroughly. He wondered if Ono had been mistaken or perhaps the forces had a change of heart, deciding to flee rather than fight.

Instantly his heart sank. If they had indeed abandoned the cause, then plans he made and high held hopes would be dashed. New strategies would need to be put into place before the company could go forth. He was unsure if disappointment or fury took him. Yet, he felt guilt at feeling ire. After all, their aid had not been promised, merely foretold.

No, he thought. *Hexart and his clan were vicious warriors. They would not run from death. Certainly they would meet it sword on sword, not cower and retreat. It was not in his races nature to recoil from danger.*

Yet, as his eyes moved over the landscape again, he began to lose faith. Ono had raised his hopes with news of the freed minions of Mindaloth standing shoulder to shoulder with him. He tried desperately to believe in Ono, for he had never given false information before. However, the land stood before him empty and broken with no aid in sight. Despair took him as he began to pace to and fro.

Then, from the north came a sound to Verion's ears. The marching of many feet came from behind a bleak, tall hillside. Scores of shapes drew into focus as they crested a smooth knoll a short distance away. Men marched forth toward the company as a chill wind blew from the east. Smooth skinned, bald warriors wearing light garments of red with leather covering their chest and back came onward in a wave. Each bore leather gauntlets on their wrists. Their curved swords and axes gleamed as they drew near. Some carried a bow with many quivered arrows and short swords on their belts.

From the thick tree line to the south came the lizard like Zarns, the reptile like creatures whom Verion pitied for their doomed destiny. He and Trimlin destroyed several hundred, perhaps thousands of the creatures during the last quest. Yet, he felt sorrow at doing so. Images of the attacks secretly haunted his dreams to this day. The short, squat, grayish black Orna brought up the rear of the unlikely column, their strong muscular bodies lurching from side to side as they moved forward.

Spear tips shone in the dusky light as the creatures came forward with their wide, misshapen noses and long arms and overly large hands swaying as they came. Orna were not the most intelligent of the races he met along the way, but nonetheless, they cared not for slavery of Holnok. Verion knew they would fight as hard as any other race. His only concern was his inability to communicate with them. They spoke in grunts, cackles and gurgling noises and the Zarns simply hissed like an angry snake.

"Worry not my lord," said Katima softly as she moved to his side. "We have given Ono and his race voices, so shall it be with the Orna and Zarn," she said waving her hand several times atop the approaching horde.

Shock registered on the creatures ugly, twisted faces as they slowly realized human speech came from their wide, thick lips. The Zarns reacted in kind. Their indistinguishable clicks and clacks gave way to a mostly human voice that rose quickly among their ranks. Though they retained a great deal of hissing in their speech their lizard like voices could now be easily understood.

"Hail, warrior allies" said Verion, stepping forward to grasp Hexart's forearm. "The company welcomes you all."

Hexart's battle scared face stared back at Verion as a smile formed on his lips. His muscular frame made even Verion appear young, small and weak. His broad shoulders carried thick, well shaped arms, and a narrow waist sat atop powerful, solid legs.

"Once again we meet, my lord" said Hexart, with a bow. "Yet again, malevolence has brought us together. Though we stand shoulder to shoulder for this quest."

"I grieve our meeting must be so. Yet, your forces are most welcome," said Verion honestly. "This time however, we face a far greater challenge than before. New dangers await us, some of which shall test our strength and will."

Then Hexart pointed to the east and gave news Verion dreaded to hear.

"We spied enormous forces approaching in the distance. They will be upon us soon. Many new minions march by Holnok's side, the likes of which we have never seen. My scouts report they are perhaps a few hours march from us, perhaps less, for they move quickly," said Hexart.

"What shall be our plan, Verion?" asked Murn. "If we still possess the advantage of time, we could perhaps ensnare them somehow."

Verion gazed to all sides. The land was similar in nature to the Bottomless Lands of Mindaloth. Though there were no steaming geysers, poisonous fumes or bottomless holes to navigate as before, it still held malice in the land itself. It was a hard cruel land. Peaks rose high into the sky, jagged and deformed. Nothing lived upon the earth. Trees, shrubs and bushes were gone from sight. The land was black, not darkened from a passing cloud or nighttime, but it lay before him as a cloak on the land, sucking life and light into the ground itself. The landscape was hard and unforgiving, like the steel of a sword. Black swamps and marshes dotted the landscape for many leagues.

"I will take Trimlin and ride ahead," said Verion finally. "Prepare for battle in my absence. Pass word to the others. We shall not be long, but I must know what we face."

"They will see your winged beasties," Snarat, the Orna leader spoke to Verion for the first time since receiving his voice. "If you rides'em Holnok will knows you're ere."

"Yessss, he seesss all that happensss," Turlk, the leader of the Zarns hissed.

"My friends," said Verion smiling. "I am sure our presence is already known. Perhaps I may attain aid for the dragons for the problem of which you speak. They were unseen by evil eyes on our first quest, perhaps it can be so again."

Verion asked Katima to join him at his side. He felt magic was a viable recourse for the remaining dragons. *Unseen death from the sky bodes ill for the enemy*, he thought.

"My Lady, once, you made the dragons invisible to evil eyes," he said. "Can you perform this magic again?"

"Indeed," said Katima as she approached. "Not only shall they remain unseen, but they are protected as well. Great magic is upon them. However, I make no promise that Torlen or Holnok shall not detect them, for I know not what magic they hold."

"I am in your debt, my lady," said Verion, before gathering the company to reveal his plan.

"Murn, Aleeza and I will take dragons to scout ahead. Nira, you seek a vantage point for shelter and attack. You shall see all that happens with the Eye and will know what needs to be done when the time is right if I do not return" said Verion, smiling at his sister. "Remain safe, all of you. We shall return as quickly as we may."

Verion's mind reached out to summon his mighty blue dragon who circled low overhead.

"Trimlin," he began. "Bring Gynexa and Jarnea with you. We head to danger, my friend."

The dragons landed with thuds, shaking the ground beneath Verion's feet. All three were purring their low rumbling contented sound as the trio swung onto their lowered necks. Silently, he spoke to his guardian.

"There are large numbers upon us again," he said. "We must survey the land and see what routes we can take for defense or escape. Fly slow and easy, we are unseen above them."

"Our strength is fivefold since Mindaloth," replied Trimlin. "The enemy, no matter how large their numbers, will not reach the company unhindered."

With that, Trimlin bellowed a roar and was airborne, followed closely by Gynexa and Jarnea.

Immediately, Verion saw black shapes dotting the landscape. They were far closer than he anticipated. All other information had been correct. There were great numbers advancing toward the companions. Ten thousand or more marched to the west in search of the Six. Despair and hopelessness welled in his heart. A premonition of death came to him as he rode high in the sky. Frowning, he thrust it from his thoughts.

The enemy spread across the only path Verion could see. Jutting, serrated peaks and twisted mountains stood on either side of the mass as they filled the valley floor. There was no escape.

There are so many. What chance does our small company stand against this," thought Verion as his eyes scanned the shifting and undulating dark horde. *Even with Ancient magic and dragons, we will be overwhelmed.*

Again, he shoved these thoughts deep within himself, knowing his mind was not sacred. For, many of the company could sense his thoughts quite easily. He would not willingly dash their hopes with thoughts of dread or death. Unbeknownst to him as he rode high in the sky, Nira was frowning even before he finished his thought.

Steering Trimlin over the center of the column with Murn and Aleeza on each side of his dragon, they formed a wedge. Silently he thanked Katima for her protection upon the guardians as they dipped low over the enemy unseen.

Below him were armored Gorlans with shields and swords on their backs. They ran forward on all fours, moving with speed. Zenex beasts carried their Sorn riders with ease over the rough terrain, snarling as they advanced. The human followers of Holnok, the Jarcoth, brought up the rear in a great mass, marching tirelessly onward to the west. All wore some type of black, crudely made armor. It is not much, but more than enough to offer protection in battle, he thought.

Then, Verion spotted Holnok himself amidst the shapes. His black cloak flowing rearward as he marched determinedly forward. He appeared angry and dreadful, a deep scowl on his face. A mighty sword hung on his side, shining brightly in the dimness of the day.

Suddenly, Holnok's thoughts came to Verion as he drew closer. Verion knew he was indeed harboring hate and anger. Though, this time it was directed at Torlen, not at the company. Also he sensed his foe still desired the Six, but his disgust toward Torlen was overwhelming his mind. Holnok hated his master's power; it drew fear from deep within him. Verion felt an odd sense of regret for the evil High Lord, though he couldn't understand the reason. Perhaps, because it was the same feeling Holnok gave to Baytor for most of his adult life. The young future king genuinely missed Baytor. He perished during the first quest, at the hands of Fenorl no less. Now, that seemed as a different life time ago.

Verion's concentration focused back to the earth as the forces moved below him. The desire to attack gripped him tightly. He knew even with only three dragons he could inflict great damage to the enemy, perhaps even scatter them and send them fleeing to the east. He held his desire to begin their destruction. One lesson learned from the previous quest was rash actions could make matters worse. A plan was needed, so he steered the dragons rearward toward the company.

The earth shook as the dragons landed. The trio dismounted quickly and approached their companions.

"I am sure you know all we have seen," he said. We have no recourse but to fight, unless we turn and flee to our homes. We are trapped here within the pass. Peaks lie on either side and the path is smothered with forces from the east," he said.

"The dragons shall attack the sides of the formation, forcing them to cluster in the center. They will stand close together, unable to fight and shall be wedged shoulder to shoulder. Hexart, your forces will attack there while they are at their weakest. Anyone possessing magical power will take a high vantage point to either side and protect those on the ground. Bearers of the Six to me, we remain together through the fray. Never lose sight of one another if possible."

Verion paused, staring intently at Fenorl. He sensed his hope of being chosen to stand by his side during combat.

"Fenorl, you are with me. You must bear the shield," said Verion, sliding the magical dragons head shield from his back. He remembered well the command to ensure Fenorl's safety. "May it guard you well," he said, smiling.

Fenorl attempted to speak, but his voice was lost as Verion quickly turned to Murn.

He placed Murn's helm on his large friends head as the giant knelt before him. He stared into Murn's narrowing eye and spoke.

"Stay close, for I need your protection," said Verion with a grin. Years ago, Murn swore an oath to protect Verion with his life. The giant would certainly honor it as long as he lived. The Malmak's strength and cunning in combat where renowned to all present. Verion now relied on it. "I need your protection not for myself, but for Fenorl. It has been foretold he must survive or our quest is doomed, he cannot fall. Presently, he is our most valued friend."

Murn's eye went wide, his mouth opened to speak but Verion hurriedly turned away.

"Trimlin, it is time to go skyward. You lead one side, Keltora the other. Wait for my signal for our timing is crucial. Stay alert always."

"We are ready, rider," said Trimlin into Verion's mind as he launched into the air. "The guardians await your signal."

"Archers to the rear. Draw swords when needed," ordered Verion, striding to a nearby hilltop, gazing easterly. He stared intently at the dark shapes now drawing closer to the company's position. Faint mumbling came from his lips as his brow furrowed while stirring the ground before him with the toe of his boot. Several plans, none of which he was sure would work, sprang into his mind. Finally satisfied with the plan he made, he rejoined the company, yet, doubt lingered in his thoughts. He found his resolve, deciding the strategy would keep the company safe. Dragons to the sides, magic protecting all, and the Six defending the center along with Hexart's warriors. *It shall work, it has too*, he thought.

"Prepare for battle," he yelled. "Draw swords and ready yourselves. Take positions, they are nearly upon us." Sounds of ringing steel filled the air. "May the gods be with each of you."

He turned to take a final look back. The fairies had scrambled up the hillsides and stood in waiting, their hands glowing, each a different color. Aleeza, Zarah and many warriors stood shoulder to shoulder with arrows on their rests, ready to fire. The company formed a line seventy paces to the front of the archers, with the remaining warriors in a semi-circle between the two. The remaining companions were spread to either side. Each wore solemn looks upon their faces.

Murn's eye peered at Verion intently from under his helm. He simply smiled and nodded in response.

Verion's heart raced with fear. Never had he faced such a large number of enemy before. Pure adrenaline kept his moving, his mind racing all the while.

"Do not be afraid. We are strong and carry courage within our hearts," shouted Verion.

A sudden flash of light drew his attention. There stood Renara and Setorin. Verion's thoughts of defeat instantly fled him. Victory would belong to the company this day, he thought. Now the most powerful beings known stood by his side and the company was most certainly saved no matter the number that came against them.

"May the gods smile on you all, young king," said Renara. "Sadly, we must depart."

No sooner had she uttered her words when another flash of light came and they were gone. Verion's heart sank instantly. He counted on the Ancients for great magical feats though he still kept three fairies by his side giving him great hope. Katima, Zydor and Qnara remained. He knew all too well their powers and he was satisfied they would protect the companions. They must, he thought.

There was no more time to contemplate the Ancients sudden disappearance. Holnok, along with a small band of Jarcoth warriors, approached. The remaining mass laid nearly two hundred yards away. *That distance could be covered in a blink of an eye*, he thought. *The Gorlan and Zenex could move with incredible speed, I have seen it firsthand. I shall watch them closely.*

Verion swallowed hard and strode forward with Murn and Eldon by his side. He knew at this distance he could be overrun in a moment. They stopped fifty paces apart from the evil entourage before Holnok spoke.

"I have come for what is mine," he said simply. "If you give the Six to me freely you may depart unharmed. Though I greatly desire revenge for the destruction of Mindaloth, I grant you safe passage to your home lands unfettered. Deny me, and I will take them from your dead bodies. However, there is no need for bloodshed this day if you part with your treasures."

Verion stood expressionless, staring openly at Holnok. This was the first close look Verion had gotten of his nemesis. Though dressed in black he seemed regal and proud, not the haggard coward he saw in Mindaloth that needed to attack from the shadows.

Still, he sensed dishonesty in Holnok's words and his heart gave him warning. He attempted to quarrel with the dark figure before him but his words were lost. In some strange way he was mesmerized by the High Lord's voice. It came on the air as a melodic tune from a glorious harp.

Instantly, he thought of the fairies. Holnok's voice had the same effect on his mind, the words rose and fell like beautiful music from Valla itself. If another spoke it was grating to his ears. His only desire was to hear Holnok. He felt a father figure in whom he held great faith and respect for spoke to him with soft, kind words. Obedience to his every command without question would have been the High Lord's for the asking.

Suddenly, Aris's voice came into his thoughts, pushing Holnok's outward. It filled every corner of his mind, sweeping the High Lord's voice out like a great wave of water smashing against a rocky shore. Quickly, his thoughts became his own once more.

"Beware young lord," the sweet voice said. "Do not let him speak overly long lest you fall under his spell. Holnok has learned ancient magic in Morog. He wishes to bind you with wickedness. You must stay his words, for they shall hold your will and take your strength."

Verion shook his head, feeling confused, bewildered and suddenly drained of strength. The Tareen jewel that lay round his neck grew warm as Verion reached upward to stroke it gently. Slowly, he turned to gaze at each of his companions, then drew a deep breath and spoke.

"Nay, my High Lord Holnok," he said loudly. "I believe you would indeed grant us safe passage to our lands, then you and your master Torlen would sweep through them to destroy us all. You say your minions will take them from our bodies, then let it be so, for it will be far more grueling then you imagine. You will never possess the Six for your own as long as one of the company draws breath. Never will you hold the things not meant for evil hands."

Holnok's ire flashed in his eyes at the mere mention of Torlen. Insulting as it was coming from the young imp of a future king, he knew it was true, Torlen was indeed his master.

"You choose death then," replied Holnok with a harsh voice, his dark eyes narrowing. Then, quickly, Holnok's tone changed, its sweet sound rising once again. "Verion, son of Parta, future king of Eldran, leader of the magnificent company, imagine the power and glory we could hold together. None would dare stand against us young lord. We could rule this earth side by side. You could possess all of your desires with a mere word. Rid yourself of these fools that stand faithlessly by you now."

Verion fought desperately to retain control of his thoughts, slowly slipping deeper under Holnok's control. His head pulsed with pain as he struggled to reclaim his own will, yet the melodic voice ensnared him tightly. His palms grew slick with sweat. A helpless feeling swept over him, taking him further into the darkness. Again, he shook his head to free himself from the harp like music in his head as he now gripped the Tareen Jewel under his tunic.

"I possess all a man may desire," replied Verion calmly, struggling with his composure. "I carry love and happiness in my heart and life friends stand by my side. It is more than you could ever dream of. Riches and power have no grasp on me. Abandon this folly, and live among us as a good, honorable man. Turn your minions on your true enemy, Torlen."

As Verion spoke, Fenorl silently came to his side, standing straight and tall. He wore a resolute look upon his face as he stared at his former tormentor. The dragon shield glimmered in the light as it hung from Fenorl's arm.

Holnok's eyes went wide. His face twisted in disbelief, his cheeks reddened with anger. Then, he quickly regained composure.

"So, the cursed Natrae has found solace with those he betrayed," said Holnok calmly as a smirk formed on his lips. "Why would you allow this vermin to stand by your side? The murderer of Baytor and betrayer of your company! You should wish his death. Slay him like a rabid beast or torture him on the rack if you would. Much have I desired to lay eyes upon him since his cowardly departure. He fled his master's side like the craven fool he is. Yet now he stands before me wishing to do me grievous harm no doubt."

"My name is Fenorl," he said proudly. "I am aware of the evil you instilled within me. I did your bidding from fear of pain or death, with empty promises from your silver tongue of power and kingdoms to spur me on. Your voice and pledges no longer bind me. Now, I have been reborn. Your malice is dead within me. I stand in defense of my new homeland of Eldarn. You shall go no further, Holnok. Get you gone from here, for no good can come from your presence."

Holnok laughed his shrill, horrible laugh. His voice lost its appeal momentarily as it sliced the air like daggers, making Verion shiver fleetingly.

"Reborn you say!" mocked Holnok with his graveled voice. "Nay Natrae, or Fenorl if you choose. You are not reborn, merely fooled by these outlanders who feign their friendship while they cackle behind your back, distrusting your every word. You are as naïve and foolish as ever, you cur! Never shall you be extended trust, for you are faithless. Though the outlanders will indeed say they accept you, it is merely deceit on their part, for they hide their hate well. They wish your death as much as I. A task that should have been carried out long ago."

Verion extended his arm to hold Fenorl from attacking Holnok. He simply shook his head, halting Fenorl where he stood.

"Your words are slippery indeed for they are coated with poison, Holnok," said Verion. "It is proof you know nothing of our races. For, I trust Fenorl with my life and our bond of life friends with him is true. I will die protecting him if need be, as he will do for me. You will never understand forgiveness or friendship, yet you long for it. I sense it within you. Again I ask you to abandon your ways. Join us to drive Torlen from D'Enode, or die before ever laying eyes upon him again."

Anger flashed in Holnok's eyes. A shadow seemed to grow from his form, extending toward the company. It hung momentarily, then faded as quickly as it was seen. This time his poise was lost.

"Then it begins now," yelled Holnok. "Hear me! Death will find you all and I will hold the Six for my own. Prepare to die," he said, turning away to rejoin his awaiting forces. Then, he turned back quickly with a swift movement, staring at Fenorl. His eyes narrowed as he pointed a long finger at his former savior. "You will be the first to fall, traitor! We will see if your new master's vow is true. For you shall die defending him, then he will fall by your side."

Verion placed his hand on Fenorl's shoulder again and smiled.

"He knows not what he speaks. His words are tainted and corrupt, his mind filled with hate. Anger controls his thoughts," said Verion, smiling. "Knowledge of the future is not within his power, he owns only the fury burning his heart. Holnok has no hold on you any longer."

The foursome returned to the company solemnly. None spoke as they stared toward the mass, awaiting the headlong charge they knew would come. The horde began to stir as Holnok approached. Their frenzy grew with each step.

Verion silently instructed Trimlin to lay fire between the forces as the enemy drew near. He commanded him to wait until the final possible moment.

Quickly, the sky darkened as a hail of shafts flew from the rear of the horde. Then they came. The black shapes, growling, snarling and yelling, rushed forward in a tidal wave of flesh.

Destruction of all before them was their goal. None would remain alive, unless Verion's plan worked to perfection. Even then, Verion had misgivings of all leaving alive.

"Attack" shouted Verion within his head, pushing his thoughts firmly to his guardian.

Instantly, Trimlin unleashed a wave of fire running north to south between Verion and the enemy. The remaining dragons followed his lead to the sides. They flew west to east over Holnok's forces, propelling hellish flame and fire earthward as they went along the edges of the enemy, forcing them into a tightly bunched throng filled with terror and confusion.

Shouts of horror went up among the mass as they searched the skies for the source of their death. Some ran aimlessly into the open waste lands seeking what cover they could find. Others ran eastward toward Selonoth, or sought shelter in the mountains. Hundreds lay in smoldering piles of cinders. Some fired great waves of arrows skyward to no avail. They missed their mark or bounced harmlessly earthward again.

Thick smoke and the stench of burnt flesh reached Verion's nostrils. He waved his hand frantically before his face, trying desperately to assess his situation. Vaguely through the haze, he saw dark shapes approaching the company in a rush.

"Fire!" he yelled to the archers.

A storm of deadly shafts flew through the air, striking home with fatal accuracy. They thudded their targets with sickening sounds. The bodies tumbled and piled before the rushing mass. Still they came onward. Gorlans were nearly upon them, with Zenex and riders close behind. The archers fired at will as the mass came relentlessly forward.

The Gorlans effortlessly switched to two legs, drawing swords and shields as they came. The Zenex rushed among the company with reckless abandon. Furious fighting began as the din of clashing steel filled the air. The Crutad blew a war horn that rose far above the battle noise, spurring the vicious bald warriors onward. Hexart's voice cried out and called his clan forward.

Arrows, pikes, axes and spears met the enemy as they bolted into the throng of warriors. The Sorn riders tumbled from their slain mounts ready for battle, only to be quickly swarmed by Hexart's awaiting force. Battle cries went up from the Crutad, Orna and Zarns as they engaged in life and death struggles.

"Quento Misra Darest," cried Verion as he called upon Haldira. His sword sprang to life. Its blade glowed brightly before bursting forth with flame over the length. It shone like a beacon on the battlefield as fire trailed the singing blade of death.

"Forward," he yelled above the clamor. The companions rushed onward into the fray of humans, beasts and creatures alike. They pressed ahead slashing and cleaving all who stood before them.

The dragons continued their assault from overhead, destroying great numbers of the enemy as they flew low in rapid passes. Their bellowing roars drowned out horrific screams that echoed from under them as their fire rained downward. Large swatches of ash and cinder lay beneath them.

Murn's axe and hammer swung with precision, slaying many around him. Death surrounded him as he stood steadfast with a dagger protruding from his thigh. His pace was furious with no regard given to the blood flowing freely from his leg.

Verion's sword sung a deadly song as it sliced through blades and shields alike. Nothing withstood the magical steel that fell time and again.

The fairies sent blasts of colored lights zipping past the companions, incinerating all it touched. The enemy was reduced to smoldering ash, much like a dragon's blast.

Verion stood shoulder to shoulder with Fenorl, who fought with years of pent up fury and frustration. Blades shattered as they struck the dragons head shield he carried. He pressed forward with determination etched on his face, slaying many before him as the battle progressed.

Eldon's Dragon Scale armor turned aside all weapons that met it. Blades were broken or shattered as they struck his chest. However, his left arm carried a deep gash from a slicing swing of a Gorlan sword. He bled profusely, yet fought on with force and strength.

Jinarl and Hexart were struck by arrows. Yet, they did not slow their furious pace. They fought onward cutting a swatch through their foes that came one after another.

Verion searched frantically for Holnok during the fray, but he was gone. Unsure if he magically disappeared or retreated, his eyes scanned the battlefield as best he could. Yet, there was no sign of the High Lord. Like Renara and Setorin, he simply vanished.

The enemy was dumbstruck. Disbelief registered on the human faces, while howls came from the beasts. The small band held the great horde from advancing or gaining ground as flame and death surrounded them.

The battle pressed on with ferocity. Suddenly, at its peak, the enemy stopped. They quickly turned to face east, hearing a recall audible only to the horde. The battle ceased immediately as the enemy retreated at a frenzied pace to the broken lands of Selonoth. Weapons, bodies and smoldering ashes were all that remained of the fallen horde.

The dragons pursued them, cutting down more of the terrified horde as they fled. Thousands lay dead or smoldering spread across many leagues until Verion's thoughts reached Trimlin, calling the guardians to his side. Only two remained in the sky. Trimlin and Keltora maintained their skyward vigilance as the young ones rested on the ground, forming a scaled wall of protection around the company should their enemy return.

"Well done, my friends," said Verion as his companions formed around him. "We have held for now. Quickly, tend to the wounded. They may be regrouping as we speak."

The fairies and Aleeza used magic to heal wounds. No traces of the hideous injuries remained after the mending, not even scars were seen. All bestowed thanks upon their healers and indeed many were injured during the fray, warriors and company members alike.

"Why did they abandon the battle?" asked Aleeza quizzically.

A flash of light came from inside the circle of dragons. Renara stood alone, smiling.

"Torlen summoned them," said Renara. "I heard his voice plainly. All plans he held shall now change, I am sure. Knowing a frontal assault will be to no avail he shall devise yet another more devious scheme. You are more powerful than he imagined. Great pleasure is mine to hold, seeing that the company fared well indeed," she said, staring directly at Verion.

"My lady," said Verion bowing low. "They were kept at bay, that is all. They will return in larger numbers, it is almost certain. Our cause would have benefitted from your aid. Though we held our ground well against the size of enemy we faced, we have not seen the last of them."

"Apologies," she replied. "My intention was to indeed aid you in battle, though I was delayed in Selonoth. Seeing an opportunity that held great promise to gain knowledge, I seized it."

Verion gaped at her slack jawed. His brow furrowed as he struggled to comprehend her statement. He was sure he heard correctly. How could Renara have been in or near the fortress? He ran his fingers through his long hair, temporarily lost in thought, until he found his voice.

"Selonoth!" said Verion after a long pause. "Within in the fortress itself. You walked its halls and chambers," he asked with amazement in his voice.

"Indeed, my lord," she said softly. "I have discovered many things. Some of which are of great interest."

"Forgive me, my lady," said Verion. "Pardon the interruption and my confusion," he said, slightly ashamed of his impatience.

"Setorin and I were able to slip into the fortress since our brother Torlen has lost a great deal of his power," she said. "He has turned into an enormous, horrible beast with his magic all but gone. His body has been cursed and corrupted. It was a simple task to gain access to the fortress since he no longer senses us. His minions are terrified of his presence; they dare not defy him in any way. Many have fled from his sight. It was indeed their master that recalled them from battle. His plan is to await your arrival and destroy you himself. Though, I would imagine we have not seen the last of the forces that come against you."

As was his way, Verion's mind reeled with possibilities and plans. *Horrible beast!* he thought. *What type of beast? Do we have the power to defeat him, even without his magic? Can he be more powerful than we expect? Who stands beside him if the minions have fled.*

"Yes, lord Verion, Torlen is indeed very powerful. But, it is no longer a magical power. Or at least very little remains with him," she said calmly, reading his thoughts. "Now it is simply pure wickedness that drives him. In his heart he knows human form shall never return to him. This causes him anguish, which in turn creates great ire. His wrath will be as large as his form."

It was always disconcerting to Verion that others could read his thoughts. Even though he grew up with his sister having the ability, it still set him slightly aback. It became a habit for him to push feelings deep within himself so as to not be easily read. Yet, now, Nira possessed the Eye, the fairies easily read his mind and the Ancients were even more powerful. He would have to concentrate much harder to suppress his worries, he thought. Furtively he wished for a power to bar his mind from others. His mind was an open book to one as powerful as an Ancient, it was useless to resist even if he wished it.

"What are we to do? Can we defeat him?" asked Verion solemnly. "There must be a way we can conquer the creature."

"His form is so large he can no longer reside in Selonoth," she said. "Pacing before the fortress, he waits, aware you will come to him soon. He must simply be patient. Though, at times, it tears at his soul. His only thought is revenge and he blames each of the company for his monstrous form and failure to retrieve the Six."

Verion remained silent for some time as he gazed at each of the company one by one. The companions must face a monstrous Torlen, along with Holnok and his forces, posing a unique problem he had not foreseen. He imagined his company would come against incredible magic and unknown powers, however this news changed his strategy. For, he would face a creature larger than he had ever laid eyes upon. Several options quickly came and went as his mind worked furiously. He paced to and fro as all eyes followed his movements. No words were uttered from the travelers as he mumbled softly to himself.

Finally, Verion halted. He stood staring eastward, his eyes narrowing into mere slits.

ONWARD TO SELONOTH

"Let us make camp here tonight," he said. "I do not believe we shall be attacked again, at least for awhile. We are weary from battle. Let us eat and rest as we may."

With that, he strode away while glancing to the sky to see Jarnea and Gynexa patrolling above him. Trimlin and Keltora had landed to take rest while he stood deep in thought. He walked to a bent, twisted rise a short distance away and began staring to the east.

A gentle breeze carried the smoke and stench from the smoldering ash piles to his nostrils. During his first quest he recalled feeling anger toward Holnok for sending so many to their death needlessly. That fury began to take hold again. Thousands were destroyed today. Again it was uncalled for, he thought. Greed was something he didn't understand. He couldn't fathom the emotion. Nor could he comprehend the pure malice to destroy lands, enslave other races, or create creatures and beasts to do ones malicious bidding.

Earlier, as he attempted to reason with Holnok, asking him to forego his desire to hold the Six and regain honor, he thought Holnok would agree. He sensed the evil lord was tired, disappointed, even sorrowful beneath his facade of hate. Once Holnok saw his former servant Fenorl restored to his pure self it brought forth his hate and anger instantly. The High Lord's jealousy sprang into Verion's mind when he laid eyes upon his old servant. That moment swept away any hope of converting him to good.

He felt a twinge of pity for him. Even though he had slain innocent villagers, tried to kill his companions, and created creatures for evil, Verion bore sadness for Holnok's hate and wickedness. Nonetheless, he yearned to complete his task of driving him from these lands or destroying him once and for all. Along with his new master Torlen, they must both fall. It was a daunting task before him. One he knew must be carried out no matter the cost. Feelings of compassion could not stay his course or hand when the time was upon him.

While sitting deep in thought the company gathered silently around him, giving him unspoken comfort. Hexart, Turlk and Snarat came to stand with the companions.

"What number of our warriors fell," asked Verion slightly afraid to hear the answer.

"Over two hundred, my lord," replied Hexart. "They fought and died with honor. None could ask for more. Valiant warriors to the end."

"Too many," he said sadly. "We grieve for their loss. Yet, you speak wisely, for they died a noble warriors death and free."

The pain of loss hung thickly in Verion's mind, swirling and twisting into a dull ache. He knew battle brought with it death, yet he agonized over each of them. The hurt never faded from his mind, even in his later years.

Many among the group read Verion's thoughts. Knowing his turmoil, they came to provide counsel if needed. However, he remained stoic and quiet, barely even noticing their presence. It was his way to muddle through his own feelings and emotions no matter how difficult or long it took. The fairies could remove his grief within mere moments, but that was not his wish. A desire to solve them alone gave him a sense of accomplishment, no matter how small.

Murn's giant hand came to rest on Verion's back as his large frame lowered beside his friend.

"I thank you all for concern," said Verion with a sincere smile as he faced the company. "I am fine. How could I not be? I am surrounded by life friends and others who share my burdens. You ease my grief by your presence. None could wish for finer companions to stand by their side."

Verion read many thoughts around him. Concern and worry mixed with pain and anguish came to him. Each was troubled for their Captain. The emotions nearly overwhelmed him. So many thoughts entered his head in a single moment he fought the desire to shout aloud. He kept his composure, reassuring his companions he was fine. His hand subconsciously rubbed the jewel under his tunic as the crushing thoughts began to fade. They were being blocked out as he concentrated on the necklace, though he was unsure why. *Could it be the jewel holds power to soothe my mind as well, or did it simply block the plethora of thoughts from me. Either way, I am grateful and can study its value later. Perhaps I have learned yet another use.*

He realized Aleeza's hand was in his as he was gripped by incredible guilt. A feeling of neglect swept over him. It did not come from his wife, but from within his own heart. He felt for most of the journey he ignored her, though it was quite unintentional. Sadness took him as he gently squeezed her hand. Murn sat on his left, his wife on his right, and yet he felt alone.

Finally, a voice broke the silence. Verion's sister began to speak and he welcomed her words for it brought small comfort to him, especially since he felt dejected.

"So, Brother, would you care for a meal? I am sure you are famished," she said with a wink and a clear light laugh.

Verion couldn't help but smile in return. Happiness slowly began to return to his heart and mind, pushing out the dread and gloom that occupied it moments before.

"I would indeed eat my share," he said, grinning as he rose, striding to the open fire.

"Of that I am sure," said Nira as she prepared a overly full plate.

Conversation began immediately from the entire company, including the warriors. They sat close by one another and spoke of their previous quest. It felt odd for Verion since the united group sitting beside him were his enemies during the first adventure. Nonetheless, the warriors themselves told a side of the story Verion had never heard before, the view of Holnok's minions.

Fenorl took great interest in the tale as well, though they spoke of his betrayal, it did not affect him this time. However, he listened intently, his face twisting and contorting in disbelief at times.

Though great danger was near, a relief of anxiety was welcomed as darkness closed about them with great speed. Winds began to rise, slicing through the camp with increasing ferocity. The silver orb of the moon hung high in the sky, quickly disappearing behind thickening clouds before Verion called for shelter. Cracks of tremendous thunder filled the night as the company searched desperately for respite from the approaching storm.

Then, the sky loosed itself upon them. Pounding, stinging rain pelted the travelers as they crammed themselves under overhangs or any refuge they could obtain. Though it was of little use.

Verion was wet and miserable. There was no nook or cranny he could wedge himself in to for any small amount of comfort. Earlier happiness fled him as claps of thunder intensified and the great rumbling noise shook the earth itself beneath his feet. Mumbling to himself, he wondered when the deluge would come to an end. It seemed to last for an eternity, even growing in force as he sat soaked from head to toe. He was alone and downtrodden as despair clutched at him with cold icy fingers. He shivered wildly as gale force winds seemed to push the rain into his skin as it fell. The onslaught lasted several hours before the storm broke and began to move from overhead.

He was sure the storm had been magical, perhaps a warning to turn away from these lands. Yet, he would not allow it to deter him. It hardened his resolve to move forward and push wickedness from the lands forever. His face showed his anger clearly as he pulled the boots from his feet and drained the water from them.

The fairies started magical fires which burnt brightly, yet he never felt warm throughout the night. Even after wrapping himself in his cloak and huddling amongst his companions round the blazing flames the effort was futile. It was a struggle to feel anything at all, only the wetness that engulfed him held his senses.

His thoughts were filled with Holnok's face and the sound of his voice. Quickly, he sat bolt upright. Had he heard his name being called? Was Holnok summoning him? It must have been the storm, he thought. Then, weariness finally came, his body could withstand no more. He fell back and slept, though only in fractured pieces.

When he awoke, Jinarl stood watch. They whispered greetings as Verion prepared a morning meal for all. The coldness had not left him as thoughts of Holnok reentered his mind. He began to grumble to himself, quite unhappy, his mood turned foul. Pushing the High Lord forcefully from his mind for fear of being discovered or read, he turned his attention to home.

Slowly, one by one, the company awoke and formed round a fire he built. Nira and Katima assumed cooking duties for the company. Meanwhile, Verion attempted to dry his cloak which he had cast aside for it gave him no comfort at all being still wet. He felt a tingling chill that ran clear to his bones.

"Today may be the final day for such luxuries as a hot meal," announced Verion as the company ate. "We head deep into the Tortured Lands. There will be no respite, for we cannot tarry overly long in any position. Urgency is upon us, yet, we know Torlen waits for us at the end. It is what lies between us that gives me concern presently. I feel Holnok and his forces will attack once more before we reach Selonoth. Surely his desire to hold the Six for his own, without sharing the knowledge with his master, is his only thought. Be wary; let no movement before us go unseen. The dragons will watch above, yet stay alert nonetheless. Let us move forward."

"Verion speaks wisely," said Nira. "I have foreseen another attempt to take the Six. Holnok does indeed hope to gain them before they reach Torlen. He will lead his forces against us yet again."

"Agreed," said Qnara. "His thoughts betray him. Desire for the Six has changed. Once he held visions of capturing D'Enode with their power, now he craves them to destroy Torlen. For, he fears him greatly and yearns to bring about his masters downfall through their magic. In an odd way our fates are closely intertwined."

"Then let us go east, for I wish to be rid of Torlen also," said Verion. "We will deal with Holnok as the time presents itself."

Verion shouldered his pack and turned eastward, striding toward the rising sun. *We have been set on the destruction of Torlen. Perhaps we could revert him to the glorious being he was. Why are we firm on his death,* he thought. He moved the company forward at a quickened pace as Fenorl came by his side while they moved.

"You fought bravely Fenorl," said Verion honestly. "You have some skill with a blade I see. I would imagine you learned it in Quantar, for there are many worthy swordsmen there. How did the shield fare during combat?"

"I am alive due to the blessed shield. It saved me many times," he said, smiling. "I came to give thanks for use of the magic. Never did I feel a blow, yet it turned all aside with ease. It bore no weight upon my arm during the fray. Truly, it is a wonder."

"There are no thanks needed. Most among us have magical abilities, or ancient items which aid us greatly. You did not. Therefore, you were the wisest choice to carry the shield," said Verion simply, choosing not to reveal the importance of his safety. "Nonetheless, I am pleased it aided your defense and kept you from harm. Though, I believe when we face Torlen, I shall ask to have use of it once more."

Fenorl look horrified, his face twisted and his mouth fell agape.

"I feared as much. You will deny me a chance to defend our homelands and stand by your side, my lord," said Fenorl, anxiety building in his voice as his eyes widened.

Verion looked upon him with a kindly pity that caused Fenorl to lower his gaze.

"I do not believe even with the mighty dragon shield on my arm and Haldira in my hand, I will be a match for Torlen. It will take all the power of the Six to stand against his form. A power which you do not possess, my friend. I would indeed have you stand beside me if you held such a gift. Nonetheless your aid is needed. Your task shall be to defend and lead the company in my stead. You shall lead the warriors. They shall need a Captain. Keep them safe, for you also be the guardian of the company as well."

Verion paused, then placed his hand on Fenorl's shoulder, gripping it firmly. He knew his friend felt rejected and worthless at that moment. The future king's eyes filled with softness as he spoke again.

"You will find your calling during battle," he said. "Of that, I have no doubt. You have already shown valor and strength on this day. None doubt that it will continue to grow and come forth. Many here stand in awe of your battle prowess. You earned great respect this day."

Fenorl simply smiled, somewhat miserably. His eyes could not meet Verion's gaze. He chose to stare intently at his boots as he strode by his Captain's side.

"May it guard you well then, my liege, for it is certainly fit for a king." he said finally.

The land stretched before the company for many leagues. The mountain pass lay far behind. Before them stood broken, low lying marshes and swamps, which brought forth gnats and mosquitoes by the thousands, swarming the company whose march disturbed their resting places. The land lay moist and soggy before them as they slogged onward.

The day was windless and the sun bore on them mercilessly. Verion grew hot and weary, his going was slow and he desired shelter. Sweat beaded his brow as he trudged continually onward. His thoughts drifted to riding the dragons forward, avoiding this leg of the journey entirely. Though he abandoned the idea, for he held secret hopes of encountering Holnok again, not for battle, but for another chance to persuade him from evil. He felt an odd compulsion to try and sway his mind to good once more. If he failed to dissuade him from his malicious quest, then he was sure it would end horribly for one of them, perhaps even both.

Time stood still as the company inched their way across the stench filled bogs. Several times the company was forced to free a comrade's foot that became entrenched in mud and slime. The day was an eternity as the group crept forward. Dark water surrounded them with each step. Often, Verion felt as if the earth itself tried to pull him down into the liquid murkiness to be lost forever beneath its blackness. They moved at a monotonous pace. Finally, after many hours of exhausting physical labor, they reached solid ground once more.

They fell about, filthy and worn. Great hunger and thirst rose within them as they sat grumbling to one another. Happiness of the previous night had long since fled them.

"The next stage is upon us now. Fear not, we are on hard ground once more," said Verion.

Quickly, he pulled off his pack, slumping to the ground as a great thirst took him. He drank deeply from his water skin, then rummaged through his pack, pulling out the crystal phial of translucent green liquid the fairies bestowed upon him during his previous quest. He took one sip and immediately felt refreshed. Silnoy was made from the waters of Fairy Lake and was blessed by their magic. It rapidly invigorates the mind and body of a wary traveler. It was indeed the same phial used on Fenorl when he was rescued by Keltora.

Verion thanked Aleeza for storing it within his pack prior to their departure from Eldarn. Her foresight provided him great comfort at that moment and many more to come.

Murn shared his liquid with Fenorl. Due to his size he had received two phials, one of which still remained untouched. He gifted it freely to his companion to aid his recovery and strength.

Feeling refreshed, Verion quickly called to move forward. With hard ground under his feet he looked to regain some lost time from the trek across the swamps. He pressed onward with renewed vigor, walking many leagues before halting to stare eastward.

Selonoth stood silent in the far distance. Though it still laid three days march away, anxiety intensified within him. He slowly gazed at his surroundings. The land flattened only before the battlement, providing no location for defense or shelter for that portion of the journey should they require it. The company would be exposed and vulnerable, they would also be visible for many leagues before their arrival. Any hope of a stealthy attack was gone, which was also an advantage to the company, for no harm could come upon them unseen.

"We have few choices," said Verion, while still surveying the broken, foul lands they now stood upon. "We cannot remain hidden from evil eyes much longer. Though, I am sure they know we come. As Renara said, they are waiting for us to arrive and bring the Six to Selonoth."

"We must go forth and create a diversion," said Hexart, as his scared face twisted into a smile. "This day is as good as any other to die. It shall give you time to draw closer unseen. Perhaps you can defeat this Torlen with your powers if surprise is on your side. He shall busy himself with us while you strike at him."

"Nay," said Verion sternly, sounding like a scolding father figure. "There are many ways to approach Selonoth. None will sacrifice themselves needlessly. Though regardless of our path we shall end up before the gates of the fortress. There is no way to assail it from the rear and we may not move to the sides or our journey shall end quickly. Nothing but rock and stone await us there."

"We doesss whatever the othersss do," hissed Turlk. "We rid ourselvesss of evil too. Long have we waited to ssslay the bad onesss."

"Use yur' magic," blurted out Snarat. "If them fairies can make your beasties disappear, make warriors do it too."

Verion's eyes went wide as if he was physically struck. *Could it be that simple! I was so preoccupied with an elaborate plan I missed the simplest of all. Of course, we could be hidden,* he thought.

"Snarat, you are brilliant," exclaimed Verion. "It shall work, I am sure. The gods smile on you," he said, placing his hand on the Orna's shoulder.

Verion smiled as Snarat seemed quite pleased with the compliment. He began to rock from one foot to another as a gurgling sound rose from his throat.

He turned to the fairies with wide eyes and a smile. His hope soared once more.

"It is possible, is it not," he asked with an anxious tone. "After all, Snarat is right. If you can hide the dragons, you can certainly bestow the same protection upon the company and all the warriors."

"Yes, my lord," said Qnara. "We can indeed protect the company from evil eyes. It will be a simple matter. However, I am unsure if Torlen can see through the magic. He may yet retain enough power to see us plainly as we approach. Nonetheless, we shall try."

Verion was momentarily ecstatic. Anticipation swelled in his heart as his veins pulsed with adrenaline. Then, Qnara's words sunk in deeper. Perhaps Torlen could see the company's approach. If he did, then all hope may be lost. Even with many warriors at Verion's side, dragons overhead, fairies and the Six around him, the quest could end miserably. Surprise would be lost.

Suddenly, all went quiet. Verion heard the sound of wing beats approaching from the east. He jerked his head around to locate the source, his hand found the hilt of Haldira as he whirled. He saw the familiar shape of Ono approaching. The little creature landed before him, breathing in heaves.

"I have found you! I have found you," he exclaimed. "If I would not have seen the dragons, I would still be searching. I bear news you must hear," he said as his eyes grew large. He began to hop from one foot to the other as was his want when he became nervous, reminding Verion of a small version of Snarat.

"Slowly, little one," said Verion smiling. "You are among friends, breathe deeply. Steady yourself and report your news."

"Holnok has fled to Morog," blurted Ono. "He departed with a great number of his force to journey to the ancient battlement. After his defeat at the pass, he turned eastward and marched steadily until lost from sight. We did not follow, but it is the only place to go for such a force."

Verion's happiness left him in an instant. Confusion replaced his joy. Why would Holnok not attack again? Why flee now when the Six were nearly in the palm of his hand?

Then, as if reading Verion's mind, Ono continued, still hoping to and fro and eyes bulging. His wings began to flap rapidly as his excitement grew.

"My spies tell me his fear of Torlen was too great to bear," continued Ono. "Secretly, he hopes your company can destroy the beast of Selonoth. This will make him master once more. It appears my friends, you have two great battles that must be fought to vanquish evil from these lands. Neither journey will be easy for they are many leagues apart and shall be watched closely."

"Indeed, my friend," said Verion solemnly, suddenly feeling drained and exhausted. "We will press onward to Selonoth first, then to Morog, which lies many days journey to the southeast, across the great Bilana River." said Verion, raising an arm in that direction.

"Thank you little one," said Verion as he knelt to pat Ono's head. "The company would be lost without you. Even with all our magic, your advice is looked for and revered" he said smiling. "Sit with us and take rest and food, for your deeds have earned it."

"Are you all willing to finish what we have begun?" asked Verion, turning to his companions. Many days of travel lay ahead of us, with great danger at each stop. There is no shame in striking out for your homelands."

Murn's booming laughter filled the air. His hands ran over his bald head, while smiling at Verion.

"My lord," said Murn. "None here would be separated now. The need for togetherness is greater than ever. We will face whatever lies in wait for us as one, as we always have. You humans are such a funny race," Murn said with a chuckle, his eye roving over the company.

"I could not speak for you all, my giant friend, so I sought your answer. Though, in my heart I knew what lay in your mind," said Verion smiling. Then he turned to Hexart and Snarat. "Will you travel by our side as well?"

"We would not depart before the heat of battle. Shame would be upon us all," said Hexart quickly. "We will travel to any lands regardless of the leagues that lay between them if it means driving evil from our world once more."

"We be there too," said Snarat. "We not miss killing the foul things. Orna go too."

"Zarnsssss go with outlandersss," hissed Turlk. "Old evil mussst face the new evil."

Verion took a great deal of time to consider what the Zarn had just spoken. He still felt remorse for them, those who were cursed when they followed Holnok's father ages ago, then turned to evil ways enacting the magic that turned them to creatures. They became the reptile like beings before him, cursed forevermore due to their ancestors foolishness, dreams of power and lust for greed, much like Holnok himself held in his heart.

Now that they possessed voices, Verion felt a peculiar sense of kinship to them. He desired to help them become human again. It was not their own misdeeds that brought about their transformation, it was their ancestors that were first cursed, not the Zarns that stood before him now. He was sure it was an impossible feat to restore them to human form, but he kept it close to the forefront of his mind.

He pondered the bizarre turn of events that led Holnok's previous minions to defy his rule and aid in driving him from all lands. Once, those same thralls raided outlander's villages, killing many innocent people in search of the Six. Now, they desired the ancient power to be use against their former master. They trusted Verion, for he set them free from wickedness on his first quest. They viewed him as a savior and bestowed honor upon his name.

He had slain hundreds, perhaps thousands, of all their kind. The dragons and the companions engaged them on several occasions. Each time it fared poorly for the enemy. Now they stood by his side in a combined effort to duplicate what was done in Mindaloth.

All three races cherished the freedom Verion gave to them only a short time ago. Now, they revered his name and held him in high reverence. They would fight to the death for their leader.

The sun hid its face as it sunk behind the western horizon. Dusk turned the sky a burnt orange as Verion dug pits in the camp. Katima used her magical powers to summon forth fires within them as normal.

Verion became restless as he sat staring east at the distant lights of Selonoth, wondering what forces awaited him there. Was Ono's information right? Had Holnok fled to Morog with his minions in tow? Did Torlen await the company's arrival in some horrible form? Were there still numerous forces by his side or did he stand alone ready to face the company he knew was coming to him? Perhaps they held such a great fear they all fled to Morog with Holnok.

Then he had a thought, one of which he did not share. His mind reached to Karnell, the young dragon.

"Go forth. You must summon Garold. Beg for his aid, for our need is dire. We seek his strength, for our very lives may depend on him. Fly with speed my friend. Rest only as needed," he said.

His mind began to ache when Murn came silently to his side, his large form blocking the moon from view. Verion smiled, for he enjoyed the giant's company a great deal. He felt a special bond with the Cyclops. Since their first meeting when Murn's brother Bolo lost his life in battle, they bonded to one another for inexplicable reasons. Murn was a confidant, a fearless warrior and a trusted friend.

"You should sleep, my Captain," whispered Murn as softly as his deep voice allowed. "Choices come easier when one's mind is not throttled by weariness."

Verion swelled with pride at being called Captain by Murn. For he, too, was a leader. Yet he followed Verion without question on every occasion no matter the circumstance.

"The same could be said of you," grinned Verion. "Though I admit, your presence is a comfort to me," he said, staring upward into Murn's eye, which seemed to glow in the flickering firelight.

Verion thought how terrifying the giant's face must look to an enemy when it was filled with wrath, his eye glowing with fury. He shivered suddenly as the stray thought struck him. Though Verion feared no man, creature or beast, he held no desire to ever stand against an angry Malmak in battle. He chuckled slightly at the absurd thought.

"Something fills your mind, does it not," asked Murn quizzically.

"Honestly my friend, I have many things astir in my thoughts," said Verion truthfully, still smiling. "I am concerned about Torlen. Though I am unafraid for myself, I worry for the company's safety. Especially my sister and our life partners."

"I, too, have thought of this," said Murn as a slow smile spread over his face. "I believe we can defeat the beast that was once Torlen. He will be powerful and no doubt terrible to gaze upon, but we have the strength within our company to bring him to his end."

"Even if we bring about his downfall and all survive, we have another long journey to Morog, a place that no man has laid eyes on for hundreds of years. Only in tales does it live for me. Yet, here we sit speaking of besieging it," said Verion. "Tell me Murn, why did we come on this quest. Will we ever be rid of evil even if we slay those that hunt us now?"

Murn turned his eye to the east, sitting silently for a while. Then, he ran his giant hand over his head. His gaze turned to Verion as he grinned slightly.

"In my heart I believe evil never entirely disappears," he said in a low rumbling voice. "As with the tides washing on the shore of the Sea of Songs, evil ebbs and flows much like water. Wickedness remains constant, though some simply turn their head from it. While others, like us, face it and try to push it back from whence it came or destroy it. We should have learned our lesson from Mindaloth."

"What lesson is that?" asked Verion quizzically as his mind searched for the answer.

"We drove Holnok from his fortress and the earth itself swallowed the evil place. Yet, we face his malice once more. Not to mention, even if we had slain him another would take his place. Nay, my outlander friend, I do not believe evil ever truly dies. It simply goes unnoticed until it is so large that none can help but see it. Then they must succumb or fight against it."

Verion ran his fingers through his long hair as he contemplated all Murn spoke. He knew evil was never truly gone. It was just hidden away until moments like these. Even now, many in the world carried no idea what transpired here on the plains of the Tortured Lands. In fact, they were most likely engaged in their own battles even as Verion sat thinking of them. Forces were waging war on his homeland as he sat by a warm fire thinking selfishly of his own demise.

At this very moment friends and family could be dying at the hands of the minions of Selonoth. He thought of his parents, king's Cytan and Rolnor as well. Even images of the kindly woodworker Raza entered his mind. Ire began to rise within him, then a familiar calmness took hold. He never turned to see which fairy calmed his anger, but he knew all too well his feelings were being read. He pushed silent thanks from his mind to the one who removed his dark thoughts, whoever it may be.

He refocused on his Cyclops friend sitting by his side.

"You are incredibly wise, my enormous friend," said Verion with open admiration. "The Malmak have a truly great leader of their clan. I am proud to call you my friend and hope someday to be as wise as you. Your counsel is always held close to me."

"My friend, it is I who is honored," replied Murn. "You carry burdens with each life and death decision you make. I do not envy that. Yet, you are steadfast and true to your purpose. A warrior's heart and an elder's mind is held within you. Though it is an odd combination," said Murn as he chuckled. "Nonetheless, it is one I respect and admire. Most importantly, you are a true friend. One I trust my life with. I shall follow you wherever our roads may lead."

Murn laid his large hand on Verion's back and fell silent. Neither spoke as they sat staring to the east once again.

"Alas for us all if the quest fails," said Murn softly. "For if we indeed survive and fall short of driving out malice, our lives shall be ruled by never ending shadow. There is none left to come to our aid. Even the fairies cannot save all races and the Ancients will not interfere."

"True words no doubt. Then I say we must have victory or perish in the attempt. For I shall never willingly bow to wickedness and despair. No race shall ever be enslaved again."

Before long, stirring arose behind them. The company began to rise from slumber. Eldon, Jinarl and Fenorl came to join their friends. Silence hung heavy in the air as the companions sat motionless next to one another, staring to the east. The day dawned bleak and windy, much like the feelings in Verion's heart.

"Come friends, let us take a meal, we have far to travel this day," he said solemnly. "We must have our strength with us."

Verion rose and stared at each of his company. Sudden dread gripped him. Forceful, clear thoughts of a companion falling to the quest seized him like Murn's hand. He struggled to shake the feeling, but to no avail. Nira caught his eye and though he returned her smile, it was empty and hollow. He was sure Nira read his thoughts and doubts. He grasped his jewel and began to concentrate to block them from her, and others as well.

Is it foresight, he wondered. *This cannot come to pass. By my life or death, I shall not allow it. Did Holnok somehow put the image and fear there. Was it true he held more power and magic than believed to do this feat.* Verion tried to shrug the unexplained event away, however, the seed had been firmly planted and continued to grow.

Immediately after breakfast, the call to move forward went out. Impatience now welled in his heart. He desired to face the evil before him. Each step would be agony, for it became a burning feeling he could not rid himself of. Facing his fear would be the only cure.

Torlen Comes Forth

"Nira, we must know what lies in wait for us," said Verion softly, pulling her gently aside. "Use your magic. The Eye will see if we are to be taken unaware."

Verion watched as Nira closed her eyes momentarily, then quickly opened them to meet his gaze.

"I see no enemy before us, with the exception of what lies in Selonoth," she said. "Their size is small I believe. The Eye tells me the battlement is nearly empty. Only a minor force remains."

Verion was astounded by the news and of Nira's power as well. Previously when using the Eye, she would sit and make incantations to summon forth the hidden power. Now however, her skills had grown beyond even his reckoning. He was proud his sister equaled the magic seeing ability of a fairy. Only a few moments concentration brought the visions to her clearly. Her words became apparent after the shock of her unbridled power and his jealousy had dimmed.

"Ono spoke truthfully then," said Verion. "Yet, explain why we had foreseen Holnok attempting to waylay us again."

"My visions are not only of what is, but what could be," replied Nira. "Perhaps Holnok's fear of Torlen did indeed drive him thither to Morog, changing the earlier image. For now though, he shall not hinder us, unless of course my sight is incorrect."

"Of that I doubt, my Sister," said Verion smiling, as he placed his hand upon her shoulder. "You have never led us astray yet. I shall follow any counsel you give, for your mastery of the Dragon's Eye is complete.

Brother and sister hurried to catch the company as they pressed onward across the twisted wasteland.

Verion began to imagine Torlen drawing nearer. He felt evil close to him, about to befall the company. His stomach churned with anticipation as his hand grasped Haldira. A sudden urge to draw his sword seized him. Any moment Torlen would appear before him to engage in deadly combat, he was sure of it. Quickly, he surveyed his surroundings, searching desperately for something amiss. Nothing came before him, yet his heart told him to be wary.

Then, a flash of light drew his attention. The sound of ringing steel met Renara and Setorin as they appeared before Verion, who held a drawn sword. Embarrassment took him. He froze in his spot, mortified and embarrassed.

"I beg your pardon for my folly," said Verion, slightly ashamed. "My thoughts were occupied with . . ."

"Torlen," said Renara, cutting off Verion's voice. "And rightly so, my young lord. For, he comes this way. He bore no love for Selonoth, it had no hold on him so he abandoned it in search of the company. Now, he approaches," said Renara, pointing a slender arm to the east. "The beast will be upon you soon. You must prepare."

Combat with men or evil thralls put no fear in Verion. However, Torlen was different. A giant beast formed by powerful, ancient magic now approached intent on destroying the company. He would bring all his hatred and frustration to bear on the companions. Verion was sure the beast no longer cared to possess the Six, it marched forward with pure loathing and malice bent solely toward the company and all who stood before him.

Even with all his magical power and ancient knowledge, he had been foiled. Rage was now his only emotion. He would make the bearers of the Sacred Six pay for his failure. No longer could he regain his grace or beauty, now he simply wanted revenge. Verion knew this, yet he was unsure how. It came to him clearly as he gazed to the east and held his jewel in the palm of his hand. Its warmth soothed him as it glowed dimly in his hand.

Verion summoned his inner fortitude to fend off momentary panic. He turned calmly to his companions, slowly replacing Haldira in its sheath and sliding his treasured necklace round his neck, tucking it securely away. He gazed at each of them as a thin grin grew on his face.

"Our time has come, my friends," he said softly. "Battle is upon us once more. However, Torlen holds promise of our most difficult challenge. He is but one, not the hordes we are used to, but nonetheless he will be formidable. More terrible than any we ever faced. I am sure Renara speaks wisely of his power, so beware. We must now shape our destiny here in this forsaken land. May the gods watch over each of you."

"The creature will arrive soon," said Setorin. "He is nearly upon us. My brother comes hither, bent on death and destruction of you all."

Verion sprinted to a small rise that afforded him the best view. As he gazed eastward, his ears caught sounds of movement, yet he saw nothing. His thoughts went quickly to his dragon as a plan came plainly to light in his mind.

"Do you see him, Trimlin," he asked quickly. "Does the beast approach? Is he near?"

"Indeed, rider," replied Trimlin. "It comes this way with some speed. The thing was not visible before, though now I clearly spy the beast now."

"He used the last of his magic keeping himself hidden from our eyes," said Nira, also reading the dragon's thoughts. "Now it has faded, his power is nearly gone, for even I may sense his thoughts."

Verion returned to the warriors who stood in wait. He placed a hand on Hexart's shoulder, gazing solemnly into his eyes.

"Swords, arrows and pikes will be of no use this time my friend," said Verion solemnly. "Flee to your homelands if we fall, for much hope will be lost. You have fought valiantly and with great honor. There is no fear among you. May the gods grant you long life, my companion."

He turned to Turlk and Snarat, staring at the creatures with a smile upon his face. He bowed to them as they stood in amazement of a future outlander king paying them respect. The extent of which they had never known before.

"Your aid was most welcome and each of you is a warrior I was proud to stand alongside and defend our lands with," said Verion with another bow. "I fear only ancient powers and magic are needed here. You are free to depart with your honor."

"We will ssstay," hissed Turlk quickly. "Zarnsss will sssee the quest through to itssss end."

"My warriors stay too," replied Snarat, "We don't run from big human beast. Even Orna want thing dead. We attack with the rest."

"Agreed," said Hexart as he joined the trio. "True, we do not possess magic. But our blades are sharp and can do great damage. Perhaps we can draw it from you, then, you can use your magic on it."

Verion never expected the warriors to depart. Yet, he felt a need to offer the chance, thereby allowing them to retain honor in the event they chose to return to their own lands.

Fenorl came to Verion, handing the shield to him with a frown, his eyes were cast downward.

"Worry not," said Verion. "If I fall you shall carry both shield and sword for me. You must return them safely to my father, the king. He shall reward you well. It is your destiny if my death is to be here this day."

"I care not for rewards, my lord. The grief would be unbearable, speak not of such things. Though I shall proudly do as you ask if I must, while bearing a heavy heart all the while and forever more," said Fenorl.

All thoughts fled Verion as a terrible growl came to his ears. From behind a large peak directly east of the company the noise rose up on the wind. It was close, shaking the ground under his feet as it reverberated through the low lying hills and surrounding peaks.

A shadow came over them suddenly. Many of the warriors cowered, raising their arms overhead as they crouched in terror. They were taken by fear and despair, crying out to their gods as they trembled.

Verion sprang into action. There was no time for hesitation. Many lives depended on his actions within the next seconds and he held no intention of faltering now. Secretly, terror seized him, though it remained hidden deep in his heart.

"Together, the Six to me, peril is upon us!" yelled Verion. Quickly, he turned to Renara. "Can we be seen by the creature?"

"Yes," she said softly. "You are veiled only from Holnok and his minions. Torlen still retains enough magic to see through our spell. His greatest magic has faded, yet he still holds some powers no matter how small."

"Quento Misra Darest," said Verion, pulling Haldira free once more.

Haldira sprang to life. Burning flame engulfed the blade as Verion bound effortlessly to the nearest hill with the other bearers close behind him. The dragon shield glistened brightly in the dim light as he held it closely to his body.

He swept the landscape with his gaze. Then, Aleeza cried out.

"There! He is there," she said pointing to her right.

All heads swiveled to follow her finger. An enormous fifty foot creature approached, roaring as it came. Giant, thick legs propelled the beast to its destination. Long, heavily muscled arms swung by its sides. Its shoulders were exceedingly broad and the beast's chest was thick as a mountainside. Its head bore giant spiraling horns protruding from the skull. The beast slathered and gnashed its massive jaws as it came. Its eyes glowed red with fury.

Verion was unsure if fire or rage lay captured within them, perhaps both. The thing did not lumber forward as he expected for one of such size. It moved with ease and rather nimbly as it weaved through the foothills, shaking the earth as it came. As it drew closer Verion could see spiked protrusions coming from the forearms, with a ridge of similar extensions running down its back. Huge fang like teeth shown pale yellow in the sun as the jaws open and closed to bellow its rage. Each large extremity held four clawed digits the size of a tall human.

Renara quickly stepped forward. She waved her arms rapidly before her. The beast bellowed with rage, stopped in its tracks. It pounded the air with all its might. Waves of blue light rippled above Verion and the company where the creatures enormous arms struck.

"This shield will slow him momentarily. He will break through it in time," said Renara over the beasts pounding and bellowing. "What are your orders my lord," she asked Verion bluntly.

Verion knew he held precious little time to think of defense. Now, thousands of lives were in his hands. The company and all warriors stopped and stared at him, awaiting their instructions. He began to sweat. His eyes narrowed as his stomach tightened like a vice. This was no time for fear to grip him, he thought. He stared at Hexart and smiled as complete calmness washed over him.

"Perhaps it is a good day to die my friend," he said. "Though, it will be an end of legend."

Then he turned quickly to the company and spoke.

"The fairies will use their magic against him when he breaks through. It should provide enough distraction for the Six to attack. When we bring the beast down, Hexart and his warriors will swarm him doing whatever damage they may. If he rises, pull back before we are all destroyed. Regroup and we shall summon the power of the Six against him when he is weakened. I carry a plan for dragon power as well."

Before another word was spoken, Torlen charged forward after a thundering boom filled the air. The shield had given way. Now, if possible the creature's anger had increased.

Magical blasts flew from behind Verion, striking the beast's chest and face. It stopped, rocking to and fro, its arms raised to protect its head. The beast roared with fury as it began to lash its massive arms outward in hopes of striking any who stood before it.

Then, Verion knew his plan was flawed, he switched thoughts in mid stride.

"Now!" yelled Verion aloud. Those standing nearby were taken aback by his outburst, unsure what to expect next for this was not part of the plan.

Instantly, the sky darkened with a massive shape, unlike any had ever seen. All eyes went skyward, searching frantically for the magic that befell them. Then, from behind the tallest mountain came a black dragon whose shape filled the air. It bore yellow stripes upon its wings and red markings on his face, its body nearly three times the size of Trimlin or Keltora. It was Garold, the immortal father of all dragons, protector of D'Enode.

He swooped upon Torlen grabbing the beast by its shoulders, carrying it into the sky, hundreds of feet in the air like a toy. Then his massive talons opened, releasing it earthward. It plummeted, picking up great speed as it fell, until it struck the earth, forming a giant crater before the company. They sought cover as rocks and debris flew around them with force.

Garold swung low for attack, releasing a blast of flame that melted much of the ground about the beast turning it to hot molten rock. An enormous yell came from deep within the hole. A giant limb appeared from the depression as the beast attempted to claw its way from the earthen pit. It was bleeding heavily and grew enraged as it crawled forward on all fours, attempting to rise.

Verion covered the distance in seconds, his sword and shield hoisted high. The beast began to rise, attempting to stand as Haldira swung a trail of fire toward a massive forearm. The ancient, magical blade hewed the creatures hand from its wrist, cutting through flesh and bone in one strike.

Torlen let loose a shout of pain and anger that filled the air and shook the ground itself so violently that several warriors and companions toppled to their knees and recoiled in horror.

Jinarl, Eldon and Murn arrived at that moment to begin their assault as archers sent shafts raining down through the air, most bounced away harmlessly. Some remained stuck in the beasts thick skin but did no damage.

Murn hacked freely with his axe at the creature's leg while Eldon echoed his movements on the other. The blades struck true time and again as deep wounds bled freely from the creatures legs.

The beast swung its clawless arm high above Verion, attempting to smash him into the earth. He could not escape. Quickly he raised the dragon shield overhead and braced himself for a death blow that would surely come. Thoughts of failure came to him as he watched the giant arm fall from above with speed. The blow struck with a dull, soft thud.

However, he had no time to marvel at the shields magic as he quickly rolled away while light blasts danced over his head. They struck Torlen's face once more as the creature readied for another assault.

Again, the sky darkened momentarily. Garold struck the giant from behind as he gave forth a massive roar that spilt the air with a deafening sound. Torlen was sent tumbling over and over again, arms and legs flinging erratically as he went. The dragon gained great speed before striking and no creature, regardless of size, could have withstood such impact without toppling.

The beast struck the ground with great force, its face pummeled into the earth as it came to rest, disoriented and bewildered momentarily.

Verion ran quickly forward, nimbly catching hold of the creatures horns and swinging himself unto its head, his feet firmly planted between the sizeable horns.

In that instant, the beasts forearm made a massive sweep of the ground. Spikes caught Murn and Eldon squarely. They flew through the air as lifeless dolls, striking a broken mountainside with hideous thuds.

"NO!" shouted Katima as the scene unfolded in mere seconds. Yet, it came to her in slow motion. She watched helplessly as the pair flew twisted and broken landing with dull, horrible thuds. She rushed to her fallen husbands side, as Nira went to Eldon. Aleeza quickly followed the pair with Qnara in tow.

Hexart's warriors rushed to the creature swarming like ants round his feet, body and head. Their pikes, axes and swords slashed and stabbed at the enraged beast as it tried yet again to reach its feet.

As it stood, the monster raised a foot from the earth and stomped quickly downward again and again. Many warriors perished with each blow. Yet, their attack continued with relentless fury. Their wrath built with each strike.

Then, at once, the beast went silent. It stood shuddering, teetering to and fro. Its arms twitched and the knees quivered wildly. It stood in utter noiselessness as all movement nearby stopped.

"RUN!" yelled Jinarl as the creature wobbled then fell slowly earthward.

An earth shaking thud resounded for a league as the beast slammed into the ground.

Verion, who was perched atop the beasts head, dove from the falling creature. He fell helplessly from high above, twisting and tumbling, gaining speed as he plummeted toward the twisted mountainside below.

The company watched in horror as the sight unfurled in the blink of an eye. Aleeza's scream piercing the stillness was all that was heard.

Then suddenly, his fall was stopped as giant talons closed around him, carrying him forth. Garold climbed into the sky, circled gently and glided to a smooth landing, setting Verion on firm ground once more.

Verion rushed passed the fairies to his wounded companion's side. His heart was filled with worry and anguish yet his face was stoic and devoid of expression as he approached. He stared into Murn's eye and grasp his arm waiting for a response of any kind. Immeasurable grief stole his breath away as he knelt beside the giant.

Murn smiled back weakly, his eye barely open, fluttering wildly as he focused on Verion's face.

"I see your ancient gifts have protected you," said Verion, tapping on the Cyclops's armor.

"He will live, though he has many broken bones" said Katima, her eyes still wet from her tears.

"And you, my lord," said Verion, turning to Eldon. "Your dragon scale saved you from death or serious harm."

"He, too, is broken badly. Rest must be taken, for they should recover their strength," said Nira, her voice softly entering Verion's ear. He simply nodded in response.

"What happened to the beast?" asked Eldon wheezing for breath that was painful in coming.

"It is dead. In large part due to your bravery," said Verion. "The tale can be told later, rest now my friend. Be silent and know the company is safe, but many have perished from the warriors."

Verion turned to the gigantic form of Garold who looked on with great interest. He bowed low to his savior then lowered to one knee before him.

"Mighty King of all dragons," said Verion aloud. "Unending gratitude will forever be yours, for my life has been spared by your graciousness. Long have I desired to lay eyes upon the father of all my beloved winged guardians. Our battle would have been in vain without your aid."

"King Verion, son of Parta, keeper of D'Enode's dragons, bearer of Dragon's Breath, you are held in high esteem for your care and love of my children's children. I shall always be at your beck and call. Simply send my name forth in your thoughts and I shall hear, no matter the distance. Fare thee well, my young lord. Until we meet again."

The gigantic form of Garold launched effortlessly into the air, winging its way northward. His great shadow covered all who stood before it. His massive wings made little sound as the dragon climbed steadily higher until disappearing into the clouds.

Verion rose and walked to the fallen form of Torlen, staring at the massive lifeless beast.

Once, you were a powerful being much like in our tales of legend. Yet you chose wicked ways and greed over pureness and love. If we would have but met ere evil took you, surely I would have bowed before your greatness and gave worship to you. Never would I have foreseen bringing about your downfall. Sorrow fills my heart for you, he thought sadly.

"Lord Jinarl, I require your aid," said Verion. "I cannot free my sword."

Jinarl came to his side. He gazed at the protruding hilt of Verion's sword. Silently, he summoned Dragons Might once more and grasped Haldira, pulling it free from the creature's skull with one tremendous heave.

During the attack, Verion pointed a flaming Haldira downward and drove it though the creature's head, bringing its quick death as it fought the ground forces.

"Your sword, my Captain," said Jinarl, presenting it with both hands, hilt first.

"Many thanks, my friend," said Verion as he retrieved his sacred blade. "I was unable to free it from the beast before I fell. My mind was filled with plunging to my death."

"The gods graced us this day and they surely bestowed blessings upon you," said Jinarl, resting his hand on Verion's shoulder.

Verion turned to Hexart who stood surveying the battle field near the crushed and broken warriors. Nearly four hundred had been slain under the crushing blows. Creatures and human alike lay dead.

"It is a small price to pay for freedom," said Hexart softly. "They fought with honor and died free. Nothing more could have been asked of them. We shall honor their memory forever."

Verion remained silent as he placed a hand on Hexart's shoulder and stared at the bodies before him. Great sadness came upon him. Remorse choked a lump in his throat, leaving a foul taste on his tongue.

"We shall lay them to rest in peace and glory," said Verion. "They shall not lie here forever in a forsaken place this way."

"Can we cover them, as we did with Baytor?" he asked, turning to Katima.

"Indeed," she replied. "They will be protected from any evil, as it was with Baytor. They will have magic upon them forever. It shall remain hallowed until the end of days" she said, waving her hands in the air.

Slowly, the earth rose up covering the mass of bodies that lay before the fairy. It glowed momentarily then faded. Green grass and purple flowers grew and bloomed instantly. Then, a tall lone tree sprang forth from the highest point of the rise, displaying leaves in full splendor.

"None shall disturb this site," said Verion to Hexart. "We will remember their sacrifice in tales and songs of my people. This, I promise to you. They shall be named the Fallen of Torlen."

Hexart knelt before Verion, taking him by surprise. His head tilted to the side as he stared openly at the warrior. He bade him rise and smiled widely.

"My people will journey to this site each year on this day to pay homage to the dead," said Hexart loudly for all to hear. "Long live the company for their gift. Long live our Captain."

"Should we desssstroy SSSelonoth next my lord?" said Turlk from the crowd.

Verion ran his fingers through his hair as he paced, his mind searching for an answer. *Why attack Selonoth now*, he thought. *After all, Holnok has already fled to Morog. It is him we seek, not the thralls at the battlement. We should press forward to finish our quest. Yes, that is what must be done. No good can come from attacking his minions, we can hunt them after both their masters are dead, which shall be sooner than they know.*

He turned to face the company. All stared openly at him as he sighed and began to pace once more. Verion's mind strayed to his previous quest. When, like now, he was looked to for answers. He never declared himself as leader, yet all turned to him for answers. It puzzled him for there were far more powerful races by his side, especially the fairies. How did he become sole counsel, he wondered. Leadership was thrust upon him and he had no intention to shun away from it. So he continued to pace and think.

Besides, as a future king he knew advice and counseling skills would be required to lead his own people. Though, secretly he fought with the part. Many lives depended on his choices, most of whom were his dearest friends. Already over six hundred lives were lost.

His head began to throb as his temples pulsed rhythmically. Turning his focus back to the situation at hand, he came to a conclusion. One he prayed would be the correct choice. Slowly he twisted and turned his head from side to side, then he sighed and prepared to speak.

"My companions, I believe a great errand is upon us. We must press onward to Morog," he said solemnly. "We shall find nothing at Selonoth but thralls and Holnok's minions, most of which have already fled. Let us finish this quest as planned. We must defeat the evil that is upon our lands and not falter. Though I believe our road shall be much worse from here. If Holnok desires the Six, then he shall have them. To Morog it shall be."

A sudden brilliant flash of light focused the company's attention to the rear. Delthas and Laveena stood before them, quiet and solemn.

"You have brought an end to our son," said Delthas softly, standing before the company expressionless.

Instantly, Verion felt fear grip him. What if Delthas and Laveena carried anger in their hearts for the slaying of Torlen. Were they here for revenge. They are peaceful people, yet Verion knew killing their flesh and blood must have created ire and pain in them toward the company, Verion in particular. He prayed he wouldn't be turned into anything unnatural or sent to some distant isle to live in exile for all his years to come. He felt powerless to control what was about to happen. Even with his mighty sword and friends about him he realized he was no match for the ancients if they decided to punish him.

He stepped forward hesitantly, then gulped and took a deep breath before he spoke.

"The beast that was once Torlen is no more," he said, summoning every ounce of his courage. "I will carry remorse for you in my heart until my end of days. The grief within you is unimaginable. But, I did what needed to be done. Do not hold any other responsible. For, it was my sword that slay him and I alone gave commands. If you hold ire against any, it is I that shall pay the price. Do as you will with me," he said, lowering to one knee and awaiting his fate.

Laveena stepped forward and stared at Verion for a silent moment. She extended her soft, white hand to him. He looked upon it with hesitation then accepted it gently as she helped him rise.

"Young lord," she said. "My race does not seek revenge. Torlen chose his own destiny when he strayed from our teachings and knowledge. He abused his power and magic to bring evil to your world. His death came from his own doings. You were simply the catalyst for his demise. No blame is placed upon you or the company. Though, it is indeed very brave of you to accept any wrath that would have come."

Verion stood speechless. He was unsure if happiness welled within him at being spared from becoming a ground crawling creature or if shock overtook his senses at the calmness of Laveena.

Either way, relief swept over him that he would not meet his end this day.

"We have come to take our son home," said Delthas. "Behold his true form."

Delthas waved his hand slightly. There, before the company stood a handsome man with smooth features and long brilliant white hair. His smile was mesmerizing to gaze upon, with eyes as brilliant as ever and the color of the sea.

"This . . . is our son," said Laveena softly. "He is our true son, not the beast lying before you. His soul is pure and untouched like snowflakes from the sky. His evil died upon your sword, yet he lives within our minds as the form you see now. Mourn not for him. Peace has taken him once again as it was during the innocence of his youth. Lust and greed have left him. He is free to walk in Valla with O'Tan and E'Lenoria.," she said as the vision quivered and faded slowly from view.

Eldon placed his arm around Nira as she wept. Aleeza took Verion's hand as she came to him. Renara and Setorin joined their parent's sides.

"We have done what we set out to do," said Renara. "My brother has been stopped from possessing or destroying your world. Now we shall leave you. You must face Holnok and his forces without our aid. Seek us on the return journey in the Forest of Dreams. There, we shall await you in Madaria."

Before Verion could speak, he covered his eyes at the flash of light that took the four Ancients from his sight. Again, he was momentarily speechless. He knew the Ancients promised aid to stop Torlen and they indeed did that, but still, Verion was despondent at seeing them depart.

Another brilliant flash came from behind the company. All turned in preparation of attack. They saw Torlen was gone. The bloodied beast had vanished, gone without a trace. The land showed no signs of death or battle, only the mound remained. Even the crater was gone.

The company gawked openly at one another. All heads swiveled to stare at Verion, who stood quiet and still.

"Let us rest here to pay final honor to the dead," he said. "At sunrise we move for Morog."

Camp was made quickly as the company and remaining warriors greatly desired food and rest. Now, food would now be a concern as Verion pressed onward. Marching to Morog was not part of the original plan and totally unprepared for. Though, he did have magic on his side. *The journey could never have gotten this far without the fairies and now I must rely on them yet again*, thought Verion. *Many days journey lies ahead and supplies run low. We now hold only simple breads and cakes. Not enough to feed us all. The fairies shall need to give us great aid along the way. Without them our journey will be impossible, for many leagues lay in both directions.*

"Indeed we shall, young lord," said Katima as she came to him. "Though we cannot summon food itself, we can make what we carry seem as a small meal. Silnoy is also carried with us."

"Your grace is accepted with open heart, my lady," said Verion. "Our road shall be long and slow, yet we must go forth. Hunger shall be a grief we must deal with."

"I shall do all I can. You speak the truth of a treacherous road and many nights before us. It shall be filled with despair and gloom. I have foreseen it."

"Can you see the outcome? Shall we prevail in our quest. Does Holnok fall."

"It cannot be seen. Clouds and haze keep the vision from me. Yet I sense death and horror await us all. Evil's fate is not within my sight."

Verion turned from her and stared eastward again as he fell silent. Then, he could bare it no longer and turned his gaze to the ground. Again, he held his Jewel to soothe his mind.

The moon was but a sliver in the sky. Though, it did not crest the mountains until well after midnight. Early night held absolute darkness, neither star nor moon shone above. Qnara's magic summoned fires that burnt bright and warm.

Verion felt alone and isolated. Involuntarily, his eyes were drawn to the east again. He saw no lights in the distant Selonoth. *Has evil fled the fortress? Should I be weary of forces issuing forth while we rest, coming upon us unseen?* he thought.

"There is no need for worry young king," said Qnara as she came to his side, sitting next to Katima and speaking softly. "No malice shall be upon us this night. We are free from harm. Rest well my friend. Strength of heart and mind shall return with the new day."

Verion could do nothing more than muster a smile and attempt to sleep. He rose and bade good night and found his bedroll.

Morog

The red stone glowed brightly, tracking the unknowing company as they moved forward through the barren, stony land. The High Lord had no knowledge his precious magical crystal had been betrayed many days prior. Yet he watched with great interest all the same.

Holnok gently lifted the Stone of Sight from its staff. Mixed emotions swept over him as he tucked it within the folds of his cloak. He was joyous Torlen fell to the outlanders. Hope rose quickly within him again. His intentions to dominate returned to him with force. Yet, now he stood in total fear of the Six and their power, an ancient power that would be seeking him even here in the deepest depths of Morog. Then confidence slowly crept back into his mind.

The outlanders will never penetrate this fortress, he thought. *This is not Mindaloth. They will not succeed here in the birthplace of wickedness. They will die before the fortress, overwhelmed by my forces. I will hold the Six shortly and my visions and dreams shall come to pass.*

Morog was raised ages ago using evil magic which still protected it. Holnok was certain fairy spells and magic would not work here, no matter how powerful. Perhaps even the Six will be rendered useless against him. Though, panic still gripped his heart. He pushed the overwhelming doubt from his mind. Though, after witnessing the battle with Torlen it struck dread within him. The outlanders were perhaps more dominant than he was lead to believe. It was no wonder Torlen held such desire for their trophies, he thought. Now,

Verion carried a magical shield as well. His best laid plans were in jeopardy once more.

How is it these vermin seem to defeat my every attempt to overcome them. I grow tired of the failure of my forces, he thought as he began to pace. *But, here I am at my strongest. Morog shall repel their futile attempts and I shall see their end once and for all. Then we shall see who reigns supreme over the lands.*

A low growl came from outside Holnok's door. He swung it open to face a Gorlan named Gundon pacing the stone hallway. The creature stood on its hind legs, instantly lowering to all fours as Holnok addressed him.

"They approach, my trusted ally" said Holnok quietly. "They bring the treasures to our very door. Prepare your forces to destroy them all, especially the fairies. Slay them first, then the Six shall be yours for the taking. Wait! Slay Fenorl first, then the fairies. Your master shall reward you well if this is done."

"We have seen the pointy-eared ones powers," replied Gundon. "They are daunting. The humans carry ancient weapons, while fire falls on us from the sky and warriors swarm us with biting axes, swords and spears."

"Then, you are unwilling to serve your lord," asked Holnok with sarcasm. "The great Gundon, leader of all the Gorlan, cowers before the man-things. Have you grown weak. Perhaps it is time for another leader of my trusted force."

"We live to serve our creator, my lord" replied the Gorlan. "I fear none of them. Yet, they are powerful, many of our kind will fall. Victory shall be ours in the end, I swear it."

Holnok cared little for the number that would be slain, he would simply create more when needed. His only concern was having the beasts return with the treasures and seeing the outlanders dead. His long held dreams would become reality.

"Then my friend, prepare for battle. They will draw close soon. We must be ready," said Holnok, staring westward. "Tell me Gundon, have any of our forces returned from the outlander villages yet? Do they carry treasures that I may decorate my hall with? Did your kind have their feast?"

"Nay, my lord," said Gundon with a growl. "As you have seen in the Stone, our forces met heavy resistance. Most will not return.

The outlanders are skilled in battle despite their puny size. Their strength and cunning were underestimated. We did not find the fairy city either. Our forces never reached Hatar, the outlanders seemingly rose from the ground to slay us. I am unsure what magic they possessed. Few ever reached the city before they were cut down. In Quantar, the humans slew us from tree tops. We never saw or smelled them. Eldarn was the worst. Many skilled swordsmen and archers awaited us. Even their women slew us. They saw us approach from the Watching Hill and took us unaware. The Ancients must have hid them from us or gave them strength and each had a dragon circling overhead, slaying all before we reached the enemy."

Holnok's face went red as his voice began to grow in volume. Frustration came swiftly.

"Then you failed me!" he said loudly. "We were to strike fear in their hearts forcing the Six to choose. But, why would they fear a force that cannot even reach the cities themselves."

"Ancients and dragons stood by their sides," said Gundon with a growl. "They turned us to ash, or made us disappear with but a wave of their hands. Tens of thousands or more went to each city, a mere nine hundred returned from each."

Holnok could no longer contain his frustration. He shouted at the top of his lungs. Anger rose within him as he paced furiously on the smooth black stone floor. His fists were clenched tightly as he mouthed silent words to himself.

"How is it so that six young outlanders cannot be captured and brought before me," asked Holnok aloud, speaking more to himself then to Gundon. "It should be a simple enough task."

"They have great powerful aid by their side, master," said Gundon. "Their dragons roast us alive, we are defenseless against their fire. We fear nothing, not even magic, yet they repel us even with great numbers against them."

"So they do, my Commander," said Holnok, regaining his composure. "I will have a great plan in place before the company arrives at Morog. Fear not, for their end will be here before these walls. Your forces shall be redeemed and none of the outlanders will leave alive. I hold great wrath for my former forces. Ensure they know the might of your horde. Leave none alive."

Gundon howled loudly as he stood on his rear legs.

"Stand ready for you orders," said Holnok with a wry smile. "They will come with the sunrise, after I have taken time to make the plan of their destruction."

"Our blades will be sharp, my lord," said Gundon. "We shall not fail you. All shall pay the price for entering your lands."

"See that you do not Gundon," said Holnok softly. "This world shall be ours, and you shall receive a just reward. Perhaps a land of your own that suits you, or gold and silver if that is your desire."

"Shiny metal does nothing for the Gorlan. We would relish hunting the outlanders at our whim, if it pleases our master," said Gundon with a low growl.

"So it shall be. Hold close to your heart that the vermin is here to serve me. Do not thin their ranks too greatly. I must have those strong of back to do my bidding. Kill the weak and old, I care not for them. This I grant to you."

Gundon seemed pleased as he licked his lips and growled a low rumbling sound as he made his way to the adjoining hallway. Undoubtedly, he reported the news to his awaiting clan, for many howls and baying echoed from the depths of the great fortress.

Meanwhile, anxiety grew in Holnok. He envisioned sitting upon his throne as Morog's minions spread his will throughout all the lands. All races would bow before him. Then, suddenly, Verion's words came into his thoughts. Could he regain his honor and live among the outlanders as a man with honor? Would they accept him after all the malevolence he brought to them? Secretly, he wished his father had never taken an evil path. What would his life had been like if wickedness hadn't taken his father's heart.

This is absurd, he thought. *Outlanders are good for only one thing, serving their High Lord.* Then, Fenorl entered his mind as jealousy filled his heart. He paced slowly in the grand hall, wringing his hands as he went.

That treacherous worm, he thought. *How dare he betray his master. He will regret his decision to abandon my side, fleeing to the doomed outlanders. He shall fall with them when all is done. I despise him even more so than Verion himself. I will decorate my chamber with both their heads. They can stare forever upon the Six that will hang opposite their lifeless eyes.*

He began to see the outlands beneath his rule with the Six finally under his control. Glorious thoughts came clearly now as he paced to and fro. Survivors of the raids served his wants and whims without question. His great black fortress stood amidst the barren broken ground and the fairies had been destroyed. Nothing more could he desire.

Holnok's shrill laughter echoed from the walls. His mind filled with domination and glory once more as he strode into the hallway. Striding from his room, he entered the hallway leading to Sartol's chamber, where he found the aged wizard pouring over old scrolls.

TOWARD THE ENEMY

The sun spread its golden glory over the land as the company shouldered their packs. The dragons circled above as Verion shielded his eyes staring overhead. Unspoken pride welled within him, bringing a smile to his lips. He felt confident with the guardians nearby. Their eyes could see movements from many leagues away. It was nearly impossible to have forces come unseen upon the company unless magically protected from sight.

Verion did not believe Holnok had magical powers on his side. He would have surely used it against them by now. He was grateful such forces were by his side in the form of the fairies and the Six. Yet, secretly he feared unseen power other than those that stood with him. The subtle displays of astonishing strength of the Ancients brought an understanding even the Six could be challenged by such potency.

He silently thanked the gods the immortal race held no desire for domination, except of course Torlen. But, he paid with his life for his corruption, a fact that would never leave Verion. Even in years to come Verion would see the slain beast lying before him along with a wavering image of the once glorious immortal man he once was.

Holnok was his only concern as he pressed forward to the crossing of the mighty Bilana River, which still lay four days march. His mind filled with visions of the ancient evil fortress of Morog. Could a mixed company of outlanders besiege the battlement? Humans rarely dared approach the evil place, at least none that lived to recite the tale. Uncertainty sprang into his thoughts as he trudged southerly across the wastelands of the Tortured Lands.

The fairies cast healing spells upon the land as they went. Telesta used the power of the Dragons Aura to send waves of sparkling translucent blue light forth in her effort to speed the earth's recovery.

Verion revisited the Bottomless Lands years after its upheaval and destruction by Holnok. The valley healed itself. Though, this came by the power of the united Six along with great magic from the fairies and the Aura. Once again green grass sprung from the ground, trees grew tall and strong, and clear water flowed freely. Its beauty had been restored and became a refuge for all types of birds and beasts. Foxes, squirrels and deer roamed freely throughout the land. Now, he wished the same for this land as well.

Again, as years before, the fairies cast magic here and there as they went, with Telesta close behind using the Aura for its purpose of good.

Verion smiled at their work. *The Six are a wonderful gift,* he thought as he strode onward. *They shall not fall into evil hands. It would spell the end of all we know if they were bent for fell purposes. They must remain unsoiled. This healing shall all be for naught if we fail in our quest. For evil will trample and destroy the land once more. Now though, they must face the company before doing their damage. Perhaps we should have delayed our healing until all is done. Though, I mean to see the end this time,* he thought.

Then, Katima came to his side as he was deep in thought, walking silently for awhile. Then she spoke after reading many of Verion's thoughts.

"Holnok does not simply wish to take control of the Six any longer. He wishes your death, as well as Fenorl's. Great hate burns within him for you both. I have sensed it," said Katima, as she drew close to Verion. "You are his bane. His attention has turned away from the fairies for now. As long as one of you lives, it will be so."

"Then I am pleased I could be of service to your race," he said with a half hearted smile. "At least Holnok shall turn his efforts on finding the company rather than seeking Avior. Even if it were discovered somehow, he could never break its magic. His forces would stand no hope of victory against your people. Your kind holds unseen powers I am sure. Ones which are stronger than any witnessed in ages, save for the Ancients themselves. It would be sheer folly to attempt to breech Avior."

"Indeed, his waning attention is one gain to my people. Yet, it will bring another attempt to take the Six from us before we reach Morog. Holnok does not wish for the company to ever lay eyes upon the wicked place. I believe he shall send forces to met us once more. Though since he resides in the wicked place, he has become harder to read. Evil spells must be with him."

"Long ago my father poured over old maps of the east. I remember them well. If the land has not changed I imagine Holnok will attempt to block our path near the river crossing. Perhaps just inside the outskirts of Morog, or near the ancient bridge if it still stands. That is where I would plan an attack. During the crossing, we are defenseless and forced to walk with only a few men abreast. Our cover is little if any indeed exists. We should make a plan before our arrival."

Verion's thoughts went to the dragons as he summoned Jenopta and Karnell.

"Go forth my trusted friends," he said. "Fly south to the great Bilana River. Evil forces may lie in wait for us there, I believe. Take no actions against them. Await our arrival and report what you see. Battle will be upon us soon. Go now and stay safe young ones."

Roars broke the morning silence as the two dragons winged southward with speed. Their shapes quickly passing from sight, rocking from side to side as they went.

"We shall not be taken unaware," said Verion. "I mean to end this when we reach Morog. Holnok will not escape this time, for he has no place to flee. Though, I carry an ill feeling since we ignored Selonoth. Yet, I did not wish for the trail of evil to grow cold. He could take up its ways again if he escapes once more. I pray the wise choice was made."

"Indeed," said Nira as she joined the duo. "You made the right decision, Brother. Though I have troubling thoughts of late. I sense Holnok possesses magic. Whether it is his own or aid stands by his side, I am unsure. Either way, we go forth to face it."

"Even after Torlen?" asked Verion. "All magical power should have died with him, except for small trinkets which could do us no harm I venture to guess. The only evil in Morog is the place itself."

"Brother, we speak of Morog. It was, and remains, the most wicked place on earth. Who knows what dark magic or horrible things Holnok found there. Perhaps even more powerful than the Six themselves," replied Nira.

"No power could rival the Sacred Six. Dragon Magic has blessed it and we have proven its power for destruction and healing as well. Now, with Torlen gone, I am sure there can be no rival. Good shall prevail. It must for the sake of D'Eonde itself. Holnok cannot be allowed to escape again."

"My young lord Verion, do not hold faith evil cannot be as powerful," came the fairy queen's voice into his mind. "Lest ye forget fairies fought in the Battle of Ages, seeing firsthand the power Welkar summoned from Morog. It is dreadful, malicious and stronger than you can imagine. Take great care in your journey."

Verion's sureness in himself and the quest quickly dissipated. Once again, dread of facing magic welled within his heart. Who could now stand by his side for aid? Torlen was gone. Was the evil magic from Morog indeed more powerful than the Six? Did Holnok find magic there that could be turned against the company. Could he counter it with the fairies or the Six, he wondered.

He halted the company for a brief rest, allowing him time to ponder what may lie ahead. The queen's warning repeated itself over and over in his mind, until he could bear it no longer. Calling to move after little rest was his only recourse, for now fear grew rapidly in him.

As they plodded forward once more, the fairies, Nira and Verion walked together and spoke of the road before them. Verion knew their guidance could be trusted. He would of course speak to the company and have their opinions as well. But, since he stood the chance of confronting potent magic from Morog, he desired those who knew the subject best.

After some time, Verion called the companions together and spoke openly.

"Trusted friends," he began. "We have endured much together, not only during the quest to Mindaloth, but this journey as well. I seek your counsel on the road and perils stretching before us. We," said Verion, sweeping his arm in the direction of the fairies and his sister, "have discussed several options. All of which I will share with you now and ask for your wisdom on these matters."

"We trust in you, my lord," said Eldon. "I thank thee for the chance to speak, but there is no need. I will follow whatever plan you put before us. I walk beside my Captain with a light heart. There is no fear within me."

"Here, here!" said Jinarl. "Many times I thought us doomed. Yet, here we stand side by side. I, too, will follow where you lead without question. Your keen wits have brought us this far. I say we should not stray from them now. I am with you as well."

"Though I am your betrothed, do not let that sway you in my words," said Aleeza. "I would follow you to the ends of the earth if you but asked. We all believe in you and the cause. Our life friends speak the truth. I am beside you no matter the danger or where it leads us."

Murn stepped forward with Zarah by his side.

"We have decided the same," he said with a smile that made his eye squint. "We go onward to complete our quest. Our only question is that of Selonoth. What shall become of it?"

Verion was stunned. He expected a barrage of questions and doubt from his friends. Yet, he had but one to answer. One which he had already given great thought to. Still, the answer eluded him. He thought the best course, as always, was to be open and speak truly.

"Honestly, I am unsure," he said truthfully. "First, I thought of destroying it, bringing it to the ground. Then I held the notion if the land was healed men could inhabit it for their own, stretching the safety of our borders even further to the East. Though I imagine few would dwell there after evil occupied it. It would remain forever tainted."

Then, a sudden thought came to Verion. He gave a quick start as if pricked by a dagger point, then turned to the warriors by his side.

"What say you to having Selonoth for you own?" he asked apprehensively to the warrior leaders. "One of your race could have the kingdom you deserve. Though granted, it may not seem a great prize to you."

"We thank thee for the offer," said Turlk. "But, we hold no desssire for a fortresss in rocksss. Our flatlandsss are held in our heartsss."

"We love hills and mountains," said Snarat. "Holes in ground suit us best. We no care for walls and towers. Yes, caves and tunnels are best for Orna. Give thing to Crutad."

Then Verion turned to Hexart and raised a quizzical looking eyebrow.

"If my fellow warriors hold no stock in the evil halls of Selonoth, the Crutad shall claim it for their own," said Hexart. "We accept your offer, Captain. My kind shall occupy its halls."

"Creatures could still dwell deep within the tunnels and halls, my lord," Verion reminded him. "Wickedness may not be wholly cleansed from within. Evil may reside there yet. Caution should be used."

"We will sweep through the fortress and eradicate any vermin that remains hidden from us," said Hexart grinning. "It shall be a pleasure," he said, smiling wider.

"Nira, speak to Ono if you can," said Verion quickly. "We shall have him carry word to the Crutad that Selonoth is theirs for the taking."

A cheer went up from the human warriors for the prize they had been gifted.

"Again you bestow great gifts upon us, my lord," said Hexart with a low bow. "Our reward shall become the eastern most kingdom of men, if you are willing to have us. Danger upon the lands to our west shall need to pass the Crutad first, and that shall be no easy task."

"Your people have fought and died by our side," said Verion solemnly. "How could I refute such bravery and sacrifice. It is the outlanders who will honor you and your men. They will speak of you and your kind in tales," said Verion with a sweep of his arms over the warrior clan. "Safety of our lands shall be in the valiant hands of Master Hexart and the Crutad."

"Now, let us press onward," he said, turning to all before him. "Urgency grows greater with each step. We must confront the malice that lay before us. Onward to Morog."

The sun gleamed brightly overhead as the company turned southerly, weaving through the broken, evil smelling lands that sweltered with heat. The host moved untiringly until shadows lengthened as night closed in with speed. Much needed food and rest were called for from the weary travelers.

Verion drove the company doggedly throughout the day and could go no further. Camp was made quickly with warm fires burning brightly. Thoughts of quelling the fires for fear of giving away his position came to his mind but he was comforted by the dragons overhead, No danger would come upon them unseen. He decided to enjoy the respite from evil no matter how short lived it may be.

Verion refused to let hunger nag at him as he nibbled on the last of his food. Now his pack lay empty except for the remaining cakes and bread. He pushed the thought of a warm meal from him and let his mind drift freely.

The creature warriors sat among themselves enjoying their human voices as they ate. Verion smiled as he listened to the various hissing from the Zarns and the broken speech of the Orna. Again, he remembered his first quest when he slaughtered thousands of their kind. Remorse swept over him as a wave splashing over rocks. *These feelings cannot be put into words,* he thought. *I destroyed so many of their kind, still, here they sit by my side ready to die in battle along with me. They follow my commands and trust my words to the end. I feel I owe them debt of some sort. What can I give them? A debt must be paid for my own hearts sake. But what? What could I give them.*

"They worship you as their savior," said Nira, her voice breaking his thoughts. "Regardless of the hurt we did to their kind, they were saved and set free. They performed their evil ways to please their master. Now they sit by our side as comrades in arms. Stay your despair, for it is not needed. They love their freedom as do the race of men and have you to thank for it. Tis already a noble gift bestowed upon them. They ask for nothing more."

Verion sat quietly as his sister spoke. He stared into her eyes that now glowed brightly in the dancing firelight.

"You are wise beyond your years, Sister," said Verion truthfully. "It is no wonder the people of Hatar love you. Though I have not openly confessed it in quite some time, I share their love as well. I could not have asked for a wiser, more beautiful sister than you."

Katima came by the duo's side as they spoke. She remained standing wearing a empty expression. After a long uncomfortable silence, she spoke.

"Aris has spoken to me," she said. "She commands me to say word has returned from the cities. Evil did not fare well. All races, guarded by dragons and with Ancient counsel, did great damage to the host before them. Most of your kind are safe, however some paid with their lives. Thus far it is unclear who lives or who perished."

Verion was torn. He rejoiced evil had been repelled, yet anxiety took him over his parents safety. Again thoughts of Cytan and Rolnor entered his mind. Do they still live? Did Raza and the many other friends he gained in each city during his visits fare well? Many were not warriors, simply peaceful folk living their lives the best way they could.

He stood suddenly and began to pace. Waves of throbbing pain slowly built in his head as he mumbled softly, turning this way and that as he went. A gripping desire to summon Trimlin and fly to Eldarn entered his mind but he quickly forced it from him knowing it was folly.

"I am weary. I take my leave now," he said abruptly as he strode from the fire to his bedroll. He curled next to Aleeza, but no sleep would find him this night. Anger kept him awake throughout his rest, anger toward Holnok and Torlen. Now, Torlen was no more, only Holnok remained. *Evil will end during this journey or I will perish trying to defeat it*, he thought. *Never again shall we live in fear or any of our people die in war.* Finally, sleep took him. Weariness washed over his mind and body regardless of his attempts to quell it. He fell fast asleep.

The morning dawned cool and crisp as pale light slunk from the eastern horizon. Slowly it made its way to the camp as it stretched across the broken landscape to touch upon them.

Verion's mood was foul this morning. Worry, hunger and dread slowly wore down his senses and stole his energy as he suppressed his feelings deep inside, keeping them from being read by the others. Though he realized, as usual, it was futile. For, Nira and the fairies were too strong as he was well aware of. He grew frustrated and angry at himself for allowing Holnok to escape during the siege at Mindaloth. The constant battle to hide his feelings slowly took its toll on his emotions. He grumbled to himself as he slipped on his boots.

He moved the company at speed through the lands, trying frantically to forget the news from Aris. He wished no word came at all, it would have been better, he thought.

My mind is laden with many burdens as it is. I pushed thoughts of my homeland from my mind to keep it clear for the evil before us. Now, it is at the forefront once again. It is agony, though I must not despair. Besides, the Ancients lent aid to us all. I am certain my family lives yet. I would know in my heart if they had fallen. Yes, I am sure I would know.

With that, he seemed satisfied. He strode forward, still struggling, yet confident in his thoughts of loved ones survival. He spoke to no one and desired no company as his stride lengthened as if trying to outrun his grief and gloom.

Before long, sounds of flowing water came to his ears. Instantly, panic beset him. This was the crossing he feared, for the river was wide and mighty. The company would be helpless if attacked here.

Karnell sat by the edge of the river awaiting Verion's arrival. The dragons thoughts entered his mind abruptly. The two young guardians had tirelessly patrolled the lands until the company's arrival.

"Rider, there is a stone bridge two leagues to the east," he said. "The evil ones must cross there, for the waters are deep and unforgiving here. There is no sign of any crossing place other than the bridge."

"Well done my trusted friend," said Verion. "We shall make for it with speed. Do you see any of the enemy?"

"Nay, rider" replied the dragon. "There is no movement about you." With that said, the dragon returned to the air.

Verion instantly turned to halt the company, passing the news to them all.

"We make for a bridge two leagues to the east," said Verion. "Karnell has found our way. There is no sign of the enemy as yet. Take food and drink as we move. We will not stop, for I will not be in the open longer than needed. It would be folly."

Turning quickly, he strode east, following the river which now stood before them. Verion crossed the Bilana River many times since his quest into the Bottomless Lands years ago. He came to love the blue, rapid waters. Here however, they seemed blackened, almost sentient with evil flowing within their depths. It lay darkened before him as he trod beside its banks.

Verion's face was anxious, then sadness swept over him. He wondered if the evil spread upstream to infest the waters near the Shimmering Lands. Anger slowly replaced sadness. He hated Holnok for causing such grief and destruction on a land that once lay beautiful and glorious in tales of long ago. Though, it had been ages since Welkar marred this place for the building of Morog, it remained disfigured since. Holnok simply came to restore it to its former malicious form.

Irritation drove him forward at a maddening pace. Unbeknownst to him, the others fell behind, except for Murn, whose giant strides kept him easily near. Seeing this, he halted, surveying the lands while waiting patiently, yet remaining silent. There before him, less than half a league away, the mighty river split. The Lonost came from the south, joining with the Bilana. Together they flowed easterly beyond sight. The stone bridge lay near their union, joining one evil land to the other.

Caution was used during Verion's approach, even though Karnell reported no sightings of Holnok's horde he was uneasy and did not trust the openness. Verion stared at the dark rock stretched before his feet. A vial feeling swept upon him, he stepped back in revulsion of setting foot on the terrible bridge. It seemed cursed and repulsive. He knew the minions of Morog used this bridge to bring their malevolence into the west. He yearned to destroy it as soon as the company passed. Though it had no life within it, he dreaded the black stone all the same.

With his courage gathered about him, he strode into the lands of Morog. Shortly after the last of the company passed, Verion readied himself to have Qnara to place her magic upon it to destroy the wicked thing. Even the sight of it caused despair and hatred.

"Though I share your feelings," said Qnara, "I believe it would be unwise to destroy our escape route. For, we are unsure if any other way leads us to our homes. This may well be our only way out. If it is gone, the connection shall be severed."

"Well met," said Verion. "Your wisdom and counsel is helpful, my lady. I was momentarily overwhelmed by my hate for these lands and its thralls. Though I am aware they could simply build yet another bridge, it would be more symbolic than not to fell it. It shall stand for now."

Qnara met his eyes and simply smiled, placing her hand gently on his shoulder.

Verion turned to gaze upon the company. They appeared weary and worn. He called for rest and a meal as the sun dropped below the horizon to his left. The lengthening shadows stretched their dark fingers toward the company as small fires sprung forth within the camp.

Total darkness encompassed the companions as they took their meal. Only firelight gave them comfort. No stars or moon shone in the sky above them, making Verion tense. It was disconcerting he could not lay eyes upon the guardians in the blackness. Light was totally obscured by a blanket of gloom that concealed all before it. Even the smalls fires seemed to fight for life while putting forth little glow.

Hunger played heavily on Verion's mind. The bread was gone, only the cakes remained. He named them Fairy Cakes, since not only was it simple but it was true, for the fairies held to their word and placed a spell upon their food stores. They tasted delicious and filled a grown mans belly with a few bites, however he secretly longed for a hot meal. Silnoy would be his last resort once the cakes were depleted. That time would come far sooner than he hoped.

The warriors did well on their own. They brought many simple foods which the fairies also gave grace too. The Orna and Zarns ate nearly anything they found for it was their way. Though at the start of the journey, they acquired a taste for man-food as they called it. Though now there was none to be had among them. Even Verion wished for some stew or meat that would satisfy him. Nonetheless, he held his grumbling stomach in check and never spoke a word of hunger.

"Trimlin," said Verion quickly as rising worry gripped him. "Are you above me, for this darkness takes my sight."

"Yes, rider," replied Trimlin. "Keltora and I circle above you. We see you plainly. The young ones are guarding you on the ground as they rest. They form a circle close by you in the night."

Verion breathed a sigh of relief. His confidence returned with the news from his guardian, though the murkiness dampened his spirits considerably.

EVIL MAGIC OF SARTOL

"I have found them!" exclaimed Sartol as Holnok entered his chamber. His face beamed with a mixture of pride and wonderment.

"Found what?" asked Holnok as his curiosity peaked. "You speak in riddles old man. Say what is on your mind."

"My lord, the great Welkar left many magical potions and spell books hidden within the fortress. I have discovered a great cache of them. See here," said Sartol with a sweep of his arm. "My powers may have been taken when I was outcast, but I hold hope it can be restored using ancient evil magic. I am sure the secret is held within our treasures."

"So, old man, you might be of some use to me after all," said Holnok with a slight smirk. "It would have been a tragedy to waste your life as sport for the Gorlans."

Holnok began to pace within the wizard's chamber as he mind filled with a plan for immediate use of the old man's restored talent. *Hidden magic and spells could be of great use*, he thought.

"The Stone of Sight has shown me the outlanders have reached my lands. They crossed the bridge and now head for my fortress. Little do they know what awaits them," said Holnok as hideous laughter came from his lips. "Make them regret their choice of coming against me.

Summon a storm that will assail them and turn them back from whence they came. You must separate them. The Six shall not unite again. Make them pay a penalty for daring to come hither. You are able to fulfill your master's wishes can you not?"

"Of course my liege," Sartol said. "As you command. It shall come forth with the dawn."

"See that it does Sartol," said Holnok. "The outlanders must come no further. Drown them, strike them down with lightning if you must, but do not let them pass any deeper into my lands."

"I will begin immediately, Sire," said Sartol. "You shall not be disappointed, my liege."

"Very well," said Holnok, eyeing the old wizard closely. "Do not forget the Gorlans are always hungry. Let that thought guide you during the endeavor."

Holnok spun and prepared to leave, then stopped in his tracks. He slowly turned to the wizard and looked him over one final time.

"You must protect the fortress," said Holnok coldly. "With all the newfound knowledge you acquired it should be a simple task. Also, make it so the fairies have no power here among my lands. Let them come against me as the rest of the pathetic outlanders, then we will indeed see if they are as powerful as they believe."

"But my lord, there are volumes upon volumes here," said the old man. "It would take many . . ."

"I care not for your reasoning," snapped Holnok. "Follow your masters wishes or perish after I hold the Six and have time to deal with you once more."

Holnok turned to the door and strode from the chamber, his boots clacking as they struck the stone hallway leading back to his main hall.

*　　*　　*

Sartol hid his hate well. Holnok never suspected the old man harbored secret disgust for him, much like Baytor did when he served as commander.

When the old man knew Mindaloth was going to fall, he escaped through the tunnels with many of Holnok's thralls. Yet, he returned to his master. For, he had no home to flee too. Now, in Morog, he felt powerful once more, ready to regain his self worth even if evil ways paved his path. He wished for greatness and would not let Holnok stand in his way.

The old wizard pulled an ancient leather bound book from a nearby shelf, set his spectacles firmly on the bridge of his nose and began to read. After Holnok's departure, Sartol sat smiling inwardly. He realized his master hadn't noticed that the old man seemed to be growing younger as the days went by. Many new spells and magic were now at his disposal and he ensured they were put to good use. Especially the few he kept secret to himself. For, the volumes were discovered many months ago and Sartol spent his days and nights pouring over them learning every secret and spell he was able. As he grew younger his mind became keen and the magic was far easier to store away in the recesses of his mind.

Though he held the books close to him and revered their knowledge, he retained and secretly practiced much of it unbeknownst to Holnok. If he was ever forced to flee Morog, he would ensure the Books went too. Great spells and power lay within them all and he had volumes yet to memorize. With that, he set to his master's wishes and would return to his precious Books as soon as able.

*   *   *

Meanwhile, Holnok stood staring to the west, knowing the company was now within his grasp. His desire became maddening as he began to pace frantically. Indecision gripped him tightly, for he was torn between allowing the company to draw closer, then encircling them in a ring of death or sending his minions to retrieve them at this very moment. But, his immediate plan to scatter them to the four winds so he could slay them one by one before they united against him suited him for now. Yet, worry gripped him, for he held no faith in the wizard.

Ancient magic or not, he was faithless the old man could stop the company. Again, he thought of his defeat at Mindaloth. Sartol was of little use to him there. In fact, he was all but forgotten. Since his return he could indeed be helpful if all he spoke was true. Could his decipher the ancient language of Welkar to aid in his cause. He greatly doubted it. We shall see, he thought. Then, he grew angry. He felt surrounded by incompetence.

"I will control my own destiny and bring glorious victory to Morog," said Holnok aloud as his ire rose quickly.

Then calmness took him. He gathered himself and clutched a thin golden chain and amulet that hung loosely round his neck. With his eyes closed he began to concentrate on Verion.

Hear me, Verion of Eldarn. I know you draw nearer even now. I see you. Abandon your folly and join me here in the fortress of Morog. None could stay us from our destiny. We would stand side by side as we sweep over the lands making them our own. Look at your companions about you. What do they offer you? Love and friendship you say. I say nay. They are murderers and villains. I would be your true ally, for I know your power. It lies not in your sword or shield, it is your mind. For, you are certainly wiser than I. Your counsel would be of great benefit to me. I call to you now. There is no need for us to fight as enemies. Join me. Come to me my lord.

Holnok released the amulet and sighed deeply, then opened his eyes. Again, his gaze went west. He wore a wry smile as he stood satisfied at his work.

"You will come to me, I feel it," said Holnok. "Your heart and mind shall be mine, just as your precious Fenorl served me, you shall too."

Hideous laughter echoed from the parapet, sweeping down across the darkened land beneath him.

Then, footfalls broke his joyous moment. He spun to see the wizard before him.

"I have done as you asked," said Sartol with a large grin. "The storm moves their way even now. Observe, my lord," he said, pointing a bony finer to the northwest.

The Battle for Morog

Verion attempted to rest, knowing the dragons protected the company from the ground and air gave him assurance he could rest peacefully. Then, suddenly, a voice came to him. It's harmonious sound rose in his ears, bringing its sweet melodic tone deep into his mind. He lay entranced as the charming words bound him.

He tried frantically to resist, but to no avail. The more he fought the sound the tighter it held him. Holnok's voice filled his mind involuntarily and his will to resist was gone. He sat stunned and dumbfounded, listening as the evil lord uttered a call to unite.

Unexpectedly, the voice was gone as quickly as it came. Zydor rushed to Verion's side as he shook his head, clearing the music from his mind. His eyes appeared glassy and distant as he slowly rubbed his forehead as the fairy knelt beside him.

"My lord, are you well," asked Zydor as he grasped Verion's shoulders. "I heard an fell voice on the wind, ringing with hatred and malice. I saw your distress. What did you hear?"

"It was Holnok," said Verion softly, still attempting to clear his head. "He spoke to me."

The companions gathered round Verion. Zydor brought attention to them both and summoned the friends, who were now filled with worry as they stood helpless over him.

"Of what did he speak?" asked Zarah. "How can you hear him, he holds no such power."

"He called to me, wishing me to abandon the company and stand by his side," said Verion softly. "I could not resist his voice, though struggling mightily, it held me. It was glorious to hear, much like that of the Ancients themselves. He beckoned me to join him."

"By his side!" shouted Murn. "Madness, I say! He knows his destruction is coming to him, only days away now. He cowers in his fortress and seeks to dissuade our mission."

"No," said Nira quickly. "He does not hide any longer. He is confident and remains proud even as we draw close. There is no fear in him any longer, for I believe he discovered many ancient evil things within the walls of Morog. His power has grown. This is but a small taste I am afraid to say. Now that Torlen has been slain, he feels he is master once more."

"Was there more, my lord," asked Milar. "Does he know we are in his lands now. Why does he reach out to you alone. Perhaps it was a dream."

"He believes my mind will aid him in some way, helping make plans to conquer D'Enode for his own. In his heart he must know it's folly, for never would I . . . ."

Verion was abruptly cut short by Telesta's voice rising in panic and terror.

"Look," she shouted. "A fell power comes for us. Take shelter!" she yelled, pointing to the southeast.

"That is no ordinary storm, seek haven. RUN NOW!" yelled Verion.

Dark clouds rolled through the sky with amazing speed, finding the company quickly.

Thunder reverberated above them as lightning lit the air with jagged, broken earthward strikes, sending dirt and rocks scattering though the night. In the thick gloom, some barely missing the companions heads. Pelting rain fell in droves, driven by incredible wind. Blackness overtook what little daylight remained.

He searched the ground before him. There was no escape of the terror that came against them. The only hope was the dragons. He rushed to their sides and commanded them to spread their wings. The warriors and company alike huddled beneath their shapes as best they could as they closed their wings about them. Even as Verion tried to speak, the wind forced his words into his throat. He made his way to the fairies side, pushing his thoughts into their minds.

"During our first quest you ended a storm, can you halt this insanity?" he yelled above the wind and thunder. "The mighty river rises quickly. It will sweep us away. We have no time to flee and there is no place to go if we could, there are too many of us."

The water began to rise in waves from the river banks as the ground quickly turned to mud, sliding and moving before Verion's eyes. He wondered if it would soon come to life and swallow the company like some ancient unforgotten evil beast of a distant age.

"We will try," came Katima's voice into his mind. "It comes upon us by unknown evil magic. I do not know if we can conquer it, though we will try."

The fairies held hands in a small circle and chanted silently as the wind howled against them. and the driven rain pelted them with a fury.

"It is no use," she yelled above the wind. "The spell is too powerful. It comes from Morog, I am sure. We cannot break the enchantment."

Hopelessness swept over Verion. He knew the dragons could not carry the entire company to safety and the lightning could be their death if they took to the air. He felt trapped and bewildered, his mind worked frenziedly trying to conceive a plan.

As he readied himself to give the command to flee a flash of light focused Verion's eyes to Renara. She stood mere feet away from him amidst the rain and howling wind, yet she was untouched by either. She remained beautiful and unsoiled as she stood smiling and raised her hands above her head. Instantly, the storm broke asunder. Sunlight came upon Verion's face as he gazed in wonder while sopping wet.

The waters receded instantly and the mud returned to hardened earth. The sky was cloudless and clear as the sun blazed overhead.

He strode forward and lowered to one knee.

"Many thanks, my lady," said Verion still kneeling with his head lowered, water dripping from his hair. "I held no hope of seeing you again until our return journey."

"My parents will not agree with my interference," said Renara. "I have grown fond of all of you and it was difficult to sit idly by while you were in peril with no hope of escape. My aid should not be spoken of if we meet again. Though, I imagine my actions are already known. Farewell for now, stay vigilant and safe."

Before another word was spoken, Verion raised his arm against the flash that took Renara from their sight.

"Let us move quickly," said Verion. "Our quest has taken a far more perilous turn if Nira's prediction is true. Now we face evil magic as well as the fortress itself. Do not despair, carry faith in your hearts. We will prevail, I have foreseen it. Move forward my friends."

Verion thanked the dragons for their protection as they launched into the air, then he shouldered his pack and strode to the south. He was sure Holnok would be furious his plan failed. Not only was the storm split apart but Verion's mind had not been swayed to leave the company. He smiled at Holnok's mounting failures, it gave him high hope. Then, he remembered advice given to him by Renara not to become overly confident for it could lead to the company's downfall. He suppressed his happiness, trying to focus on the land stretching bleak and empty before him.

The day passed quickly without further attack or magic coming against them. Even with the storm broken, the skies again grew dark and foreboding once more. Time was lost as he pressed forward. He was unsure if it was early afternoon or dusk. They traveled many leagues before calling a halt for a small meal and needed rest.

Sleep came in fractured pieces. Did he sleep past the sunrise or does darkness never leave these lands, he wondered. Either way, he desired to move forward. Urgency grew in him with each step. He fought to keep his emotions under control, for he was gripped by dread and hate.

Unseen malicious powers were now set against the company, he was sure of it. He despised attempting to combat an unseen foe. He felt tired and worn as the companions and warriors trudged forward. Weariness would not leave his body, though he was unclear if it came from magic or the journey itself. His legs moved relentlessly onward though his body desired rest.

The land became more broken as they moved eastward. The travelers were forced to climb treacherous dark hills that seemed to reach the sky itself. Thick black clouds lay high overhead, no sun would shine through or dare disturb their hold on dimness and gloom that surrounded the company.

Verion moved begrudgingly forward. Glancing back, he saw only the Orna could navigate this terrain without much effort. They loped along seizing hand and footholds where he saw none. His muscles burned and grew sore from the constant up and down of the treacherous slopes. He felt as if he was trapped in a living nightmare to which there would be no end.

"Nira," said Verion softly as she came to his side. "Do we have magic set against us? I must know" he said. "Never before have a felt so lifeless and drained of my will."

"I am unsure," replied Nira. "I feel the storm was work of fell magic, now however, I sense none. Holnok keeps unseen powers against us I believe, he must. Yet, I know not if he possesses it or he holds aid near his side. He has become unclear to me once more. I will seek counsel from the fairies."

Then the sweet voice of Aris entered Verion's mind. It rose sharply and became crystal clear, causing him to halt in his tracks.

"Young lord," she began. "Renara has visited me and we have spoken of all that has happened. Do not despair, for my daughter has grown even more powerful than Holnok could have foreseen. She will aid all you do, though it may be unseen. Renara has granted her new powers to advance the cause and your company. Press forward with hope."

Verion turned and smiled at Qnara as they marched forward. Faith in the quest soared once more. Steps seemed lighter and quicker now, though darkness was all around him. Time slipped away and he no longer knew how far the company traveled, or if day or night was yet upon them. This was the most disconcerting to him. It wore away at his mind and body. He rested when weary and traveled endlessly with the company following closely behind him.

He was not certain how many days passed or if it was yet the same day. Vaguely, he remembered calling for camp to be made several times. Yet, it mattered not, for time seemed to have stopped. He struggled mightily with it all as it slowly wore down his faith.

As they peaked yet another hillside, it came to him. Morog drew within sight. Any happiness or confidence he possessed fled. It was horrible to behold. Enormous black iron gates were closed tightly. Great towers rose high above the land, mocking his gaze upon them. Thunderous drums and noise rose from within the ramparts, shaking his will to go on. Two great walls stood before him, the first lower than the second with a vast moat of blackened water lying between them.

A dark, smooth bridge stretched the width of the water, joining the inner gates to the outer. Foul smells met his nose as he drew near, causing him to recoil. The smooth, polished black rock seemed alive. Even in the darkness the stone seemed to carry a dull shine, like hate itself was held in the rock.

Verion hid his shock and disbelief well. The fortress seemed impenetrable to him, even if the Sacred Six were turned against it. This was not Mindaloth, he thought. Pushing the rising panic deep within him, he turned to the company. Frustration mounted, gripping him tightly, for no plan was in place on how to gain entry. In Mindaloth, he obtained help from the enemy itself. Baytor, Hexart and Ono mainly. Now however, he held no such hope of luck being with him.

Verion could feel eyes upon him. Even with the battlement far from him, he felt their malice reach out to him, engulfing him as he stood motionless. The stares bore into him with a burning ferocity, making him draw back. Crushing disappointment rose up, clutching his heart with force. He felt defeated and alone. He wished to flee to the west, never to return.

"We have come this far only to be thwarted," said Verion. "I see no way to gain entry to this," he said, pointing to the malevolent fortress. "Hope is lost, despair has taken my heart."

"Hold tight to your faith, my lord. We shall not sit here and await our death from the masses within," said Murn. "There must be a way to secret ourselves into the keep."

"Magic will do us naught," said Qnara. "I have attempted it. There is an ancient evil power upon these walls. Even with Renara's grace upon me, I cannot break it."

"Failure shall not greet us if we draw near the walls," said Zarah. "We must go forth and bear the unhappiness rising from before the fortress. Mayhap we find a passage unlooked for."

"I know a path we may take," said Fenorl suddenly. "I shall lead the way if my lord commands me so. Yet, I dread the bowels of Morog once more."

All eyes focused on his expressionless face. Fenorl cast his eyes to the ground.

"How is that possible?" said Verion. "You memory of this place was taken from you."

"Indeed it was. Yet, unbeknownst to the company, before our parting, I begged Renara to use her powers to restore portions of my memory. Many horrible things came to me. I cringed and cowered before her, then hid my face and wept. Then, hate grew within me not only for my former self but for Holnok as well. I have seen the depths of Morog when I spirited him to safety after the downfall of Mindaloth. I hold a secret spell to unlock a door hidden on the easterly side of the battlement. Follow me if you will, for we shall steal ourselves into the fortress and finish this as it should be."

"Stay yourself," said Zydor. "I am not ready to put full faith in your secret entrance if you possess memories of your old life. How do we know you are still true to our cause. Why is this the first we have heard of your recollection."

Fenorl hung his head, shut his eyes and sighed heavily.

"In my heart, I knew it would come to this," said Fenorl. "Search my heart Zydor, probe my thoughts if you must. See I am true, unchanged. I belong to Eldarn and claim Verion as my king. No evil dwells within me any longer, or ever again. Though I knew some would doubt me."

"During our journey forth, Fenorl held many chances to betray us. Yet he held true to our cause and purpose never once deceiving us. Even fighting with valor by our side. I trust him and shall stand by his side," said Murn. "I do not doubt his word."

"I trust him with my life, I made a bond with him," said Verion, stepping forward. "I will follow Fenorl without fear and shall go by his side without any aid if I must. Choose now, time is quickly waning for our safety here before the gates of doom."

The company stood frozen momentarily. Nervous glances were exchanged between the companions, though none spoke openly. Then, Murn stepped forward.

"I am by your side as well, Fenorl," he said, placing his helm atop his head. "Come, let us be off."

"We shall all go," said Katima. "Aris spoke to us concerning Fenorl's courage. She foresaw his worth and valor in our quest. I do not doubt her words or visions, neither should any of you."

With that, all nodded their heads in approval. Slowly they began their descent to the land that lay mostly flat before them now. They set off for the rear of the fortress, turning eastward once more. They trod across the broken, hateful land as full darkness came upon them. No longer was it simply dim, it had grown to total blackness.

Verion knew the spell was still upon them for they remained unseen by Holnok. At least he prayed to O'Tan they were. Perhaps that is why no force came against them as they stood within sight of the fortress. He was unsure, but thankful nonetheless. Though, if Holnok gained evil powers why were they unhindered? Wouldn't the masses march against the Six, here before the walls of his fortress? Were they indeed seen but not considered a threat, or they were walking into a trap. Could it be one that Fenorl set?

It confused him, though he pondered it little. His mind was occupied with staying undetected and alive. He marched forward through the darkness and maddening sounds of the drums. The company trudged tirelessly through the blackness, drawing ever closer to the walls. Then, Fenorl halted.

"It is here," he said, running his hand over the smooth walls. "The entrance is before us."

Verion saw nothing but slick black stone. He gave a puzzled look to Fenorl, though it went unnoticed in the darkness. A desire to feel for a hidden door ran through his mind, yet he resisted, not wishing to touch the fortress itself. Turning quickly to the company, he spoke.

"Hexart," he said quietly. "There are too many to venture within the walls. Stay your warriors here. If we are trapped in the fortress flee to your lands, for you could do no more. Hold us a clear path of escape if you are set upon. You will have dragons overhead to aid you. Hold no doubt you are well protected."

"I will stay as well. Magic should be by their side." said, Zydor as he turned to kiss Qnara softly. "Return to me soon, my love. I shall give what protection I may to the outlanders and warriors."

"The Six to my side," said Verion. "I do not know what awaits us inside these black walls, but we must hold faith. Do not separate at any cost. We could remain trapped here forever if we lose one another."

He reached inside his tunic, pulling forth the Jewel of the Tareen. He concentrated momentarily as dim light sprang forth.

"Do what you will, Fenorl," he said with a smile. "Our lives are in your hands now."

Fenorl walked to the wall and placed his hands upon it and spoke softly, yet it seemed to echo and reverberate through the lands.

"Dauk Nah Ish Tol Crima Ol, Dauk Nah Rik Ta Crima Rek," he said thickly.

The words caused Verion to step rearward. The language seemed so evil to his ears he cringed. He knew it had not been heard in ages, if indeed ever, by any outlander. It burned into his mind as he listened helplessly. For the first time in his life he knew true fear from mere spoken words.

He gazed into Fenorl's eyes as he turned to stare at him. In the light of the Jewel, they seemed grey and distant. Like another held Fenorl's body and mind, though it quickly passed and they became clear and bright once more.

Suddenly, a large rectangular door took shape on the cold, lifeless wall. Fenorl reached out and pushed it open with ease. No sound issued forth as the door swung inward.

"I shall lead," he said commandingly. "For I believe the way is known to me. Verion speaks wisely, remain together, for there are many paths which lead to certain death for us all. They hold dark things yet unseen by the eyes of men, save Holnok himself. Come, we must not tarry."

Hesitation gripped Verion. Was this indeed a trap? Could he be leading the company to their capture or death? Did Fenorl revert to his evil ways now that his memory had been recalled?

"I will follow, my friend," he said, hiding his sudden misgivings. "Stay alert, all of you. We enter as one, we shall depart the same. Come, the gods are with us this day, I sense it."

The floor made no sound as they stepped upon it. It seemed alive and not willing to allow sound or light to disturb the malice seeping from it. Verion flinched at each step, feeling the fortress itself would give his position away if it could. How dare he, an outlander, enter this evil place. He held his Jewel before him as he went, lighting the way. The mighty wizards jewel faltered not, even in the depths of Morog.

As Verion gazed about his surroundings he saw many stairs leading from the hallway. Some climbed toward higher levels of the fortress and many turned downward into the bowels of nameless places that held things he did not care to imagine. Yet, Fenorl held steady to his path for a great distance. The walls remained smooth and cold as the company slunk forward. He tried desperately to avoid touching the stone. Irrational fear swept over him if he would brush the cold, black rock.

Then, many voices came toward them. Verion instantly dimmed his light and stood frozen.

Footfalls were heard plainly, pattering against the stone as they drew nearer quickly. Moments before, Verion spotted a stairway. Deciding it was his only choice, he grabbed Fenorl's shoulder, pulling him backward down the descending, winding stair.

Darkness lay thick about the company as they ran their hands over the walls to maintain balance. Verion grew forlorn. Much time passed before he relit his jewel out of hope to view some direction or tunnel to escape his rapid descent. He spiraled downward for a great distance, losing hope with each step.

Foul smells and fell sounds began to reach his ears as he slowly made his way downward. Traces of dim light began to grow near the tunnel's end, causing fear and panic within his mind. Instinctively, he gripped his sword, listening intently while moving forward to the light.

"Stop," he whispered. "We dare not go further. Nothing good can come from this. We need to climb upward toward Holnok, not downward where the darkness grows even thicker."

His words echoed from the walls as if he shouted them aloud. He shrunk at their very sound, then fell motionless for a long while, waiting to be discovered or pursued. Finally, he moved, turning quickly to began a journey upward. Sweat beaded his brow as he climbed tirelessly. Panic welled within him as his heart pounded within his chest. *Precious time has been wasted*, he thought. *Certainly the company will be discovered. Hope shall be lost in this maze.*

Eventually the stairs reached the hallway once more. He felt he had been climbing for hours. His legs burned and were weary, yet he could not stop to take rest. Thoughts of a brief respite disappeared quickly as he feared being taken unawares from behind, for he was unsure if the company was discovered and perhaps followed from below.

Once in the level hallway, Verion turned and spoke to Fenorl, who had fallen behind.

"Come, lead us," he said. "I can make no sense of this maze in the near dark. My jewel is of small aid in this labyrinth of stone and steps, though we would be blind without it."

Fenorl joined him and pressed forward once more. Then after many steps, he stopped abruptly before an ascending stairway.

"Here, we must climb here," he said, sounding nervous and worried. "This leads to the upper levels near Holnok's chamber. Come, quickly my friends."

Verion's head swiveled to gaze at his companions. Many eyes glared back at him through the light he carried in his hand. Again, he prayed to O'Tan he was not leading his trusted friends to their death. He turned quickly and followed Fenorl, pushing thoughts of hopelessness from him.

The company climbed at a slow, cautious pace. The drums grew louder now, reverberating from the walls, even shaking the floor beneath Verion's feet. Their slow, methodical rhythm pounded in his head, nearly driving him mad at times. His mind switched to the warriors outside. Were they engaged in battle? Had they been discovered yet? Will the quest prove fruitless?

What madness led me here? What did I hope to accomplish by entering Morog itself? I shall never find Holnok within these walls. I only lead my trusted companions to their doom. Fool! Thrice cursed fool. There must be another way! We should turn and flee while we still live. Perhaps we can draw Holnok out to do battle in the open. At least we would stand a chance of victory there, he thought wildly. His emotions tumbled out of control. Yet, he could not keep himself from thinking of despair and terror. He began to shake and tremble uncontrollably.

Then, he remained motionless as Qnara moved to his side. Her hand grew warm as she placed it softly on his shoulder. She drew near to his ear and whispered softly.

"I sensed a spell was put upon you. It has been broken and shall trouble you no more. My magic will protect us all the best it can. It was not Holnok himself. We have other powers at work against the company. Most of which are far above his ability," she said.

"Can you use your charm to tell us which direction to take?" he asked. "I feel time is against us. It is only by luck we have not been discovered yet, though I feel our blessings are stretching thin. In this blackness we could be pursued and not realize it until we were caught in a trap."

"I sense Holnok is still far above and unaware we are here. He stretches his power toward to all lands searching for us. We must go forward, my lord," said Qnara.

Verion rose up and began to climb the black passage once more. The company quietly fell in behind him as they pressed forward with new determination. Up many steps they went, seemingly ceaseless in their length. Still, they climbed on undeterred.

Again, his thoughts were his own. He knew powerful magic was on his side, including Renara's aid through Qnara. Fairies accompanied him, Murn was close, his wife and sister were within arm's reach. The magical dragon shield was on his arm and Haldira hung by his side. The power of the Six gave him hidden strength. He began to feel dominant, even here in the heart of malice.

His legs powered up the stairs, propelling him forward. He moved with purpose, though quite uncertain where it would take him. The company quickly reached another level, then another and yet another. *Holnok shall not be found here in the lower reaches of the fortress for he holds no love of his thralls and minions. They were nothing more than an end to his means*, he thought. So, he continued the ascent, traveling unhindered.

As he stepped onto the next landing, a wide open hall lay before him. Cold, stony darkness met him there, freezing him instantly. Quickly, he called Fenorl to his side. At that moment the drums stopped, giving an unnatural quiet to the chamber. Even the slightest whisper echoed from the black floor and walls within.

"Where are we?" asked Verion simply. "Can you tell? We must know."

"The Great Hall of Welkar," replied Fenorl. "Two other hallways lead away from here, both are level and unpatrolled. None dare enter here without permission. The one that lies left leads to the Seeing Room where Holnok spies on you with the Stone of Sight, further past that sits his bed chamber. The other leads to the fortress itself, to a maze of doorways. Some of which have not been explored yet."

"Does anyone sense Holnok, I must know his whereabouts," asked Verion.

"He sits in his chamber with the Stone," said Katima. "He may watch us even now, I am unsure if he can see us or we are hidden from him."

Making an instant decision, Verion pulled a cloak from his pack, a magical gift from Rolnor he received during his first quest. Slipping it on, he disappeared instantly.

"If I do not return, flee. Take the dragons and return home, scatter the warriors and await battle in your homelands, for it will surely follow my discovery."

Murn groped a large hand out in the darkness, trying desperately to find Verion. He caught his shoulder and gripped it.

"Have you taken leave of your senses," whispered Murn. "It is madness to approach him now. Simply wait for Holnok to show himself, then strike him down from afar, here in the blackness he loves. It would be an easy task for the fairies, or an unlooked for arrow. I shall do this thing."

"Tis true," replied Verion, "it would be best. Yet, I feel a need to look into his eyes. I need to stand before him, so he knows who it is that brings his downfall. Stand steady, I shall return."

With that, Verion slid from under Murn's hand and was gone. Murn cursed under his breath.

"We cannot sit here cowering in the dark," said the giant. "Follow him. We must guard the stairs and hallways. Move forward with your eyes open wide. Cry out if you see movement."

The company slowly emerged into the hall. Moonlight shone through a window to their right as it slipped from behind high evening clouds. It sent faint light skittering across the floor onto an ornately carved chair near the back of the chamber. Several banners hung silently on each side of the room. Great dark marble columns upheld the polished ceiling which seemed immeasurably high in the dim light. Beastly stone figures sat atop small pillars lining either side of the immense hall. No beauty was seen within. No wood, silver or gold shone within the bounds of the great room. Only malice and wickedness lived here, as it has been for hundreds of years.

The company broke into three groups, spreading out to cover all entrances. None could enter or depart unseen, though it was a certain trap if the ways were blocked.

Suddenly, the sound of a creaking door filled the empty chamber, echoing loudly from the walls. Qnara quickly waved her hand, ensuring each of the company remained undetected. She placed a more powerful spell over them, hiding them yet again, regardless of any magic Holnok possessed. Yet, all stood fast for fear of detection.

Then, a dark figure strode from the hallway, stopping instantly as he entered the chamber. He stood motionless as his eyes searched each inch of the hall. Advancing slowly, a smile came to his face as he strode to the throne chair, lowering himself gently into the seat. Again, his eyes methodically covered the hall, seemingly impervious to the near darkness. Then, he spoke softly as his hand gently touched upon his sword hilt.

"Let us face one another, young lord Verion," said Holnok calmly. "Do you wish to slay me unseen, hidden from my sight? Would you sneak upon me and drive a blade into my heart? Come, face me, for there is much to speak of."

Verion's eyes went wide under his cloak. *How was Qnara's spell broken? Perhaps Holnok is even more powerful than an Ancient.* Fear rose rapidly in his throat. *Holnok does hold magic,* he thought quickly. Indecision gripped him tightly as he struggled for a plan. Thoughts of dread and death filled him quickly. He stood frozen for what seemed like hours before Holnok's voice echoed within the hall once more.

"Come now Verion, you are not frightened of an old man are you," said Holnok, tauntingly.

Verion slid from his cloak and pack in a darkened corner, the sound instantly drew Holnok's attention. His eyes darted to the spot the young king stood still shadowed and hidden.

"So, you would murder me cloaked in magic I see," said Holnok, his grin growing wider. The feeling of invincibility grew within him. "You have done what I believed impossible by entering Morog itself. Though unsure how you accomplished it, nonetheless, here you stand before me with a drawn sword no less."

Struggling mightily with his thoughts, Verion pressed into a corner. The music numbed his mind, making it impossible to think clearly. He desperately tried to speak, yet, no words came from his lips. He shook his head trying to rid himself of the harp tune.

Then, another voice broke his trance. It came forth as a proud, regal sound here within the confines of malevolence. Verion couldn't help but hear its strength and pride.

"I, too, have entered Morog," said Fenorl. "You may entice Verion, but your words have no hold on me any longer, even with your new magic. We have come for you Holnok."

Holnok sprang to his feet, his eyes wide with fury. His hand grasped his sword. Then, calmness took him as he lowered himself into the seat once more. He thought better of facing two attackers alone, yet a plan was firmly planted within his mind.

So, the coward returns," said Holnok, wearing a thin, pale smile. "How many more lie hidden in the shadows like frightened beasts. Surely there are more of you. Will they not step forward to greet their lord. Appear before me and swear your allegiance."

Qnara lifted her spell as the company appeared before Holnok. His eyes went wide in disbelief, yet he remained motionless, sitting proudly on his throne chair. He mindlessly stroked his sword hilt as he spoke again.

"You are a crafty bunch for outlanders," he said sarcastically, hiding his astonishment well. "Long have I desired to have you stand before me. Now the Six is within my grasp and I shall have them at last. Rejoice! It is a glorious day. Though, first I should pay thanks for ridding me of Torlen. He was indeed bothersome to my plans."

"We will rid ourselves of you as well," said Murn. "Now, you cannot attack from the shadows. You stand before us for all to see. Your presence draws no fear from us and your thralls cannot save you now."

"Ah, the giant speaks for himself," said Holnok dryly. "I thought perhaps Verion would need give his permission before you were so bold. Does he not control you all? You mock my thralls for their servitude, yet, your company stands before me as mindless followers of a future king to a mere peasant village. What good can come of it. For, I see only death and misery if you refuse to stand by my side. Join me now and become kings and queens."

The harp music now began to grow within each of the company as Holnok pushed his unseen power outward. Some stood opened mouthed as others were expressionless with no desire but to hear Holnok speak. His plan was working perfectly. Once the company removed the spell they were powerless against his voice. A fact which he took full advantage of as he continued,

"Why would you grant this mere outlander power to govern a mighty Malmak? Your race is well known for being brave, fierce warriors. You, yourself, have slain many of my minions. An ancient race such as you should bow to no man. Then, there are the fairies. The beautiful, immortal race with powers well beyond that of a villager from the west. Your people could wipe these so called warriors from the earth. Yet, you protect him and keep him safe from harm, at his bidding no less. You hide his dragons from my sight and aid his cause without question. Why do you do these things?" asked Holnok, though it was a rhetorical question. "Long have I desired to know the secrets of your city and behold your magic. Come, join me and we shall share secrets."

"We do these things from friendship and life bonds, which of course, you could not understand. Your rule is through intimidation and fear. What know you of spoken oaths and camaraderie. You are faithless to all but yourself," said Telesta.

"You mark me as a villain then, one that holds no honor or courage. Nay, I say. For you are the cursed races. Yet, I extend an offer to join me here in Morog. Together we could possess this world. Your loved ones would be spared and we would own this earth. Imagine the glory of your own kingdoms and the power over life and death. You have but to lay down your trinkets and stand by my side and it shall be so."

Silence fell heavily upon the company. The walls seemed to close about them, squeezing away their breath as they stood motionless, while Holnok's voice echoed in their minds.

"Come now, are there none here who will step forth and receive a just reward from their High Lord," he said, before breaking into a low laughter which carried through the hall, filling every corner with its shrill sound.

Verion's head pounded as he put forth great effort to push the music away yet again. His eyes focused and refocused on Holnok sitting in his throne chair. He turned his concentration to the jewel that lay round his neck. It began to grow warm and brilliant under his tunic. Then, he pulled it forth and held it aloft as a great wave of light illuminated from it, sweeping across the floor, walls and ceiling in a radiant flash.

Verion thought he heard the room cry out in horror or pain and move under him as if it sought to escape the light. Never before had such pureness and power been loosed within Morog.

Holnok was taken aback, temporarily blinded by the light.

The company quickly regained their senses and drew swords as one.

"Your magical words shall not ensnare me," said Verion, breaking from his trance. "I have come but for one purpose, to serve justice upon you. Now, you shall answer for your crimes against all the free lands or perish here."

"Justice you say! And who here will judge me, great lord," asked Holnok. "You? Perhaps a fairy or a Malmak, even our visitors from the sea or plains. Will they hold my fate in their hands? I say nay again young foolish boy. You now trifle with things far beyond your pitiful powers."

Suddenly, Holnok's demeanor changed to threatening and malicious. His eyes flashed grey and cold as he locked unblinking stares with Verion.

"In this fortress you stand in the birthplace of evil and ancient power. Do not think you can simply slip from my grasp. I will have the Six now. Give them to me or I will summon forces to my side, ensuring your death. You are but a handful of young cretins and imps. Bandy not with my power, for it is greater than you imagine."

"As is mine Holnok," said Qnara. "I possess powers which even you have never thought possible. Summon your forces and you will die before they reach the doors to your hall. You have no magic that will protect you from *me*."

"Such a lovely race, the fairies are. How could one so glorious and beautiful threaten me with death," asked Holnok as he regained his composure.

"Enough talk!" said Murn, his eye wide with frustration. "Slay the worm where he sits."

Murn moved with remarkable speed, raising his axe and rushing forward to the throne chair.

Holnok raised his hand and thrust it forward. Murn's body was thrown rearward across the chamber like a discarded child's toy. He met the wall with a sickening thud, dropping to the floor motionless as his helm bounced across the floor.

Eldon shouted a war cry as he charged unseen from the darkness. Holnok had been so preoccupied with those before him, never did his head turn to see danger from the sides. He barely escaped, springing from his chair as Eldon's sword swung mightily. It neatly removed the top most portion of the chair back, level with the spot Holnok's head sat moments before.

The High Lord raised his hand once more, ready to thrust it forward. But this time, he was too late, his powers did not aid him before Verion's flaming sword met his right arm, hewing it neatly below the elbow.

Holnok's mouth fell agape, though no sound came from his lips. His face was twisted in pain and horror as he stared at his wound. He fell to the cold stone and writhed in agony. Disbelief flooded his mind as he staggered to his feet and ran wildly to and fro. Stumbling, he came before Verion and sank to his knees, staring blankly, sweat pouring from his face.

"Your evil ways shall end here this day," said Verion, pointing the flaming blade at Holnok's chest. "Morog has fallen. You are finished, now your crimes shall be answered for."

"Kill him, before he escapes or summons aid," yelled Jinarl excitedly.

"Lord Jinarl, you know I shall not slay a defenseless human being," said Verion.

"He is not human," cried Telesta. "He is a monster, a beast. Slay him. He would do no less to us."

"Hear me, all of you. None shall harm him. Though I greatly desire it myself, I shall not allow it. Look at him," said Verion, nodding to the moaning form behind him. "He is broken and pitiful." Old images of Fenorl after Keltora's rescue flooded his mind.

Then Holnok found his voice amidst the angry onslaught of voices.

"I shall hold no mercy for you," spat Holnok. "You will all die a horrible, painful death, a thousand times over." Then, he sprang to his feet and raised a hidden dagger overhead, dropping it quickly toward Verion's back.

His progress halted instantly. The dagger fell from his hand, clattering away on the stone floor. A horrible gurgling sound emanated from his throat as he clutched the protruding arrow now stuck there. His eyes scanned wildly about as blood ran over his cloak and tunic. Then, he saw Fenorl with a raised bow. He reached out helplessly with the stump of his arm and gurgled loudly, then crumpled to the floor, never to move again. As he fell, a red stone rolled from his cloak.

Verion gazed at it with much interest. Even in the dim light, it seemed to reflect the tiny bits of light it captured in the near darkness. Slowly his hand went toward it. When it lay nearly within his grasp, a voice rang in his ears.

"Leave it! You know not what evil is held within it," said Telesta. "Fell magic it is. One we could never contain."

"It is simply a crystal. Perhaps the Stone of Sight," said Verion. "Renara said it once saw the future. It could do so again. We should hold it for our own."

"She also said it was bent for evil by Welkar," quipped Nira. "Let it be, Brother. It is not for good, only evil."

Even as the High Lord lay still, his body was engulfed with light. Dim at first, then gradually growing in brilliance until it was unbearable to gaze upon. As the light faded his form had disappeared from before the company.

Qnara and Katima rushed to Murn's side as he lay still. His giant hand still held his axe tightly. His grey skin had gone white and pale.

While all rushed to Murn's side, Verion quickly tucked the crystal within his pack, then grabbed up the giant's helm and rushed to kneel beside his friend.

Nira quickly slipped her pack from her back, rustling with fury. She pulled forth a phial, a gift long ago from King Rolnor, her father-in-law.

"Upon receiving this gift, the king spoke that one drop could heal even when inches from death. I have never used it. It is called the Potion of Healing," said Nira as she gently lifted Murn's head. She unplugged the phial and gently eased two drops passed Murn's open lips as Qnara chanted an unknown spell.

Verion knelt by the giant's side and rested his hand on his armor, waiting for a sign of life. Never before had he experienced such grief and loss. Even during the death of Baytor his emotions had not been so overwhelming. His throat tightened furiously as he choked back a frustrated yell. His eyes blurred, yet he refused to let himself weep.

Silence gripped the company. Only soft sobs from Katima were heard.

Then, a deep moan came from the Cyclops as his eye opened and his arms moved slowly. His large body began to stir as he stared openly at Verion.

"What . . . what . . . happened," asked the groggy giant as his hands rubbed his face.

"Holnok is dead," said Verion simply. "The rest I will let your wife explain to you. In the future, let cooler heads prevail," said Verion with a large smile. "Twice during the same adventure you nearly left my side for Valla."

Murn shook his head vigorously as Verion laughed softly. Though thankfulness filled his heart. A great wave of relief swept over him as the Cyclops began to stir.

"Well done, Sister," said Verion, beaming with pride. "Your knowledge and quick actions were indeed useful once more."

"No, Brother," said Nira calmly. "We must thank the king for his gift, that is what saved our friend. That, and Qnara's added powers." Qnara simply bowed her head in response.

Then Verion turned to Fenorl, who knelt silently by Murn's side. His face was filled with amazement and awe as he rose to greet Verion, who now drew near.

"It was foretold your courage would show itself. I owe you my life, my friend," said Verion, as he placed his hands on Fenorl's shoulders. "We would have certainly met our death before the fortress, for none here could penetrate the walls without you."

"You owe me nothing, my lord," said Fenorl. "For you have already repaid any debt you believe exists. Many times over. A chance was given to me by a future king to prove myself and become a man of honor once more. Without his trust and faith in me, my life would have been for naught. Consider us even, my King. If anything, I am in your debt."

With that, Fenorl bent to one knee and lowered his head.

Verion gently helped him to his feet and stared thoughtfully into his eyes before speaking.

"None shall ever doubt you again," said Verion, smiling broadly. "Certainly not I. The prophecy of Aris has once more came to pass. The quest would have failed without you."

"We are not clear from danger yet," said Nira. "We are in the heart of Morog and though Holnok is dead, evil surrounds us. We must move, quickly."

Suddenly, the chamber door swung open. Sartol's babbling voice preceded him as he shuffled into the setting of death.

"My lord, I have found it, I have . . . ." he said, before stopping in his tracks and letting his sentence trail away.

His face twisted in a mixture of horror and confusion as his eyes scanned the scene before him. Then, panic gripped him as he began to shout.

"Intruders, Intrud . . . ." he yelled, before a sparkling ball of light came from Katima. It struck him squarely in the chest, slumping him to the ground instantly.

"Flee!" yelled Murn, who now stood at the rear of the company, fully awake.

The companions vaulted to the winding stairs, descending as rapidly as their feet allowed. Great drum beats now reverberated from all around them as a horn blast overpowered the rhythmic sound.

"We have been discovered," yelled Verion. "Fenorl, lead the way, quickly!"

"Fenorl pushed to the front of the company and ran headlong down the stairs. He traveled at a breakneck pace with Verion behind him, the lit jewel held high. Down and around they went, crossing halls and passing doorways. Again, time stood still as they ran. Every inch they traveled seemed to lead into darkness.

Verion thought they had overrun the entrance in the gloom. But, he trusted Fenorl implicitly. Nonetheless, he began to feel trapped. Each step looked the same as the last. Any second they would encounter the thralls of Holnok coming to the horn blast or call of the drums.

Then, Fenorl skidded to a stop. Abruptly he turned left and shouted over his shoulder.

"Here, it is here," hollered Fenorl. "Quickly, follow me."

Verion brightened the jewel as they ran recklessly to the end of the dark tunnel. Coming to a stop against the cold stone wall before them, Fenorl's voice echoed his chant.

"Dauk Nah Ish Tol Crima Ol, Dauk Nah Rik Ta Crima Rek," he muttered as the rectangular door took shape. Quickly, Fenorl pushed through it with the company close behind.

Horror met them as they emerged. The warriors were beset by thousands of Holnok's forces. The dragons blasted the earth, scorching the outer edges of the horde with fire. Ringing steel and shouts of battle filled the air. Agonizing screams came to Verion's ears.

He pulled Haldira free and gripped his shield tightly, then charged forward, summoning the sword's magic once more. Fenorl sprinted by his side, with the company close behind. A war cry came from the companions as they quickly advanced into the mass of flesh and steel.

Qnara remained still and cast a spell around the company. Many of the horde were trapped outside her shield, the remainder were ensnared by her magic that now surrounded the Six. Those blocked from the battle fled under the wrath of the dragons which circled furiously above cutting down all before them. Still, fierce fighting and great labor was needed to purge the enemy from within the protection.

The fairies banded together, side by side and began to aid the warriors that hacked and hewed at the ensnared forces, who now dwindled quickly. Bodies littered the ground, blood stained the earth beneath their feet. The battle was a melee as good and evil melted into one mass of flesh.

Finally, it was over. The last of the wicked forces had been cut down. The company was victorious. But at what price, Verion was unsure. He quickly surveyed the battle scene, searching for his companions and warriors alike. A bloodied Hexart knelt by several of his fallen warriors. Snarat helped his wounded counterparts to their feet. Turlk was nowhere to be seen. Verion searched frantically for the Zarn leader. Then, he found his broken body. He fell during the fray.

Verion knelt by his side, pulling his traveling cloak from his pack and covered his lifeless form. Then suddenly, a shriek broke the air. He sprang to his feet, sword in hand and rushed to the sound. The company gathered round as Verion arrived. Qnara wept openly over the still form of Zydor. Many arrows pierced him as he defended the warriors during the attack. He, too, fell in battle.

Only sounds of Qnara weeping broke the silence among them. Verion asked Zarah for her cloak and stepped forward to cover the fairy's body as well.

"I am uncertain what to say to ease your grief, my lady," said Verion sadly. "He fought bravely and with honor. Many here owe their life to his courage."

"Nethala anor tol etsa Valla mino falwen, vesto," said Verion softly, as he knelt by Zydor's body.

Qnara held her tears and stared openly at Verion. Her face was a mixture of sadness and awe.

"You have learned our speech well, my lord," she said. "Many years it has been since we have taught you our words, yet still it remains with you. Honor is carried in your heart. You pay tribute to a fallen fairy in his own tongue."

"I hold the highest regard for your race, my lady," said Verion. "I would bring Zydor back to you if I but possessed the power to grant it."

This, I know to be true," she said solemnly. "Even with Renara's grace in me, I, too, hold no such power. Let us gather the dead. Yet again, we must lay them beneath our protection forever."

The remaining warriors and the company carried the dead to a great mound before the evil walls of Morog. Many had fallen against the massive horde of the evil fortress.

Though the sun did not shine, Verion's brow beaded with sweat as the task was carried out. The company worked tirelessly throughout the remainder of the day. Then, a great spell was placed upon the mound which was forever known as the Despair of Morog. It became a sacred sight to many who stood before it that day and forever after.

Verion stood gazing upon the knoll with a saddened heart as the lone tree spread its branches.

"The dark day has ended. The enemy was slain or has fled before us. They now fly to parts unknown. Morog was their birthplace so none know to where they go. Perhaps we shall lay eyes upon them yet again. Though I hold great hope it is not so," said Verion.

He felt responsible for the death around him, especially Turlk and Zydor. Though the decision that left Zydor behind to protect the warriors was his own, Verion still grieved. Sadness welled within him as he stared at the great hill which had flowers in bloom. Then, Qnara and Katima joined his side.

"Do not allow such thoughts into your mind," said Qnara. "They each died valiantly and for a cause they believe in--freedom from evil."

She reached to Verion's head to remove his dark thoughts. He moved away and stared into her eyes.

"Allow my grief to disappear on its own doing" he said. "I am grateful for your attempt to aid me. Though, I must grieve in my own fashion. It is indeed strange to your kind to allow me such sorrow, yet it is part of my nature."

Darkness enveloped the company as Murn approached the trio. A chill wind came from the east as he rested a large hand on Verion's shoulder. The blackness shrouded their forms as they stood side by side, staring at the great mound in the faded light.

So my friend, tell me what words you spoke over Zydor," asked Murn quizzically.

"May your immortal soul rest in Valla forever more, friend," he recited for the Cyclops.

"I am joined with a fairy and I cannot speak the tongue as well as you," said Murn, attempting to lighten Verion's mind and heart. "Strange indeed, I know."

"Nay, my friend, it is not an oddity as you believe. I have always thirsted for all things new to me and relish holding the knowledge. I cannot say why though. Perhaps it is in my blood."

"I hold little of such deep matters. Though in fact I hold great respect due to your thirst for all things unknown to you. It is one of great honor and joy to each race. We bestow knowledge upon you and it is never forgotten," said Murn with a smile.

As they spoke, the company slowly gathered about them. Night now held the sky in its tight grip. Even the moon and stars hid their faces behind the thickening clouds.

"So, what of Morog, my lord," asked Milar. "Shall we bring about its end."

Verion turned to stare at the huge silhouette of the fortress behind him. Even in the darkness the battlement was visible to his eyes. He began to pace, alternating his gaze between the ground and Morog. The night crushed around him as he focused on a decision.

It is ancient evil that should be destroyed. Yet, it could serve as a monument to those that sacrificed themselves during the fight for freedom. None would dare enter here again. Holnok's minions have fled to lands unknown. It lies empty and bleak for all to see. Perhaps it could stand as a reminder to forego evil dreams of domination. If we could cast a spell upon it to keep the wicked ones from entering this place again, it would serve as a landmark.

Verion felt all eyes burning into his muscular frame. As he paced, he grew increasingly uncomfortable at being watched. He turned to his company with a small smile.

"We should all have a voice in what happens here," said Verion. "We choose its fate as one."

"It must be destroyed as with Mindaloth," said Murn. "The power of the Six must be brought to bear against this vile place. Not one stone or iron bar should remain."

"Morog cannot stand. Think of the horror and pain it has brought to not only us, but our ancestors as well," said Zarah. Eldon slowly nodded in agreement.

"Use the Six to make certain wickedness has no home any longer," said Jinarl. "We must bring it to the ground."

After much lengthy discussion, Verion decided its fate. He knew allowing Morog to stand would only invite future evil to take up its residence, spell or not. A fate he had no intention of allowing to pass.

"Gather around me, my friends," said Verion as he plunged his sword into the ground. "It is time to summon and join our powers."

Each of the bearers placed a hand on the sword hilt and extended their hands to each others shoulders, forming their human circle.

"Quelo fon pera thesa," they chanted in unison as an orb of light swirled and rotated violently in the center of the ring. Then came the whirlwind with its brilliant colors silently engulfing the sphere. Mixing together they became a beautiful collage of dancing light that gave forth no sound. It rocketed into the sky to fall and engulf the seemingly indestructible black fortress.

The tumultuous whirlwind dazzled and sparkled as it spun with ferocity. Its speed grew until the walls began to shake and crumble. Towers fell and walls slid, their pieces caught in the violently swirling winds as it tore the very foundation into mere bits of rock. The fortress slowly disappeared from view as it was overwhelmed by the magical winds. Then, it was gone. Nothing remained, not even a pebble of the once heinous place. The airstream twisted and turned, still dazzling and sparkling from within, before it launched skyward and disappeared from sight.

"It is done," said Verion as he pulled his blade free from the earth. "Morog shall only live in tales and memories now. Our races can live without the threat of evil from this ancient place."

"The dragon magic held within the Six is more powerful than the most potent evil ever known," said Qnara. "This is why both Torlen and Holnok forfeit their life in pursuit of the treasures they were not meant to hold. Lust for world ending power and domination held them."

Verion turned to Fenorl, who stood gazing and smiling at the vacant space before him.

"You saved my life this day. Now, I believe I am in your debt for a home in Eldarn. I gave my word to you, so shall it be," said Verion. "I am glad to be by your side for this moment. You above all others here should feel your burdens have lifted forevermore."

"I feel . . . free. At last my haunting visions can be gone. My nemesis is no more," said Fenorl, smiling broadly now. You were right, my lord, I held no magic or special power, yet all the same he is gone. It is over at last."

"We are all free once more," said Verion as he turned to the company. "Evil has been driven from this land as it was before. Now, none remain to carry on the dark ways. Let us return home and celebrate."

As in Mindaloth, the fairies, with Telesta by their side, cast healing spells upon the earth as Verion spoke. Grass and flowers began to sprout and grow before their eyes. Mountain settled and smoothed their sides, the jagged, sharp edges disappearing. Clouds broke asunder allowing the brilliant sunlight to warm the earth. Trees and shrubs flourished and bloomed. The once dark pools now held crystal clear blue water. Verion smiled and turned to the company once more.

Hexart, Snarat and the remaining warriors circled about the companions as Verion looked on confused. The two leaders approached the bearers and lowered to one knee with bowed heads.

"We swear allegiance to the Six. Your tales will be told in our clans until the end of time. We join the alliance of free men," said Hexart. "The work and misery here today shall never be forgotten, even by our children's children."

"Yes, we swear too," said Snarat. "The nasties are gone. We live in debt of men."

"You live in debt of no one, Snarat. Your warriors fought and died along side fairies and men alike," said Verion. "All of your races will be welcome in our lands from this day forward. Now, I believe we should journey to our own homes. We have been gone overly long. I yearn for the treed mountains of Eldarn."

So it was the company began the long trek to their lands.

"We are homebound once again, my friend. You have done well. We will ride again soon, I give my word," Verion thought as his mind reached out to his circling dragon.

A bellowing roar came from overhead as Trimlin responded to his rider's thoughts. All six dragons roared their approval simultaneously.

Verion strode forward of the company and warriors, beginning to move westward as the shout of Captain came from behind him. Inwardly he smiled at the day's work. Though, deep within him sorrow seized his heart from many losses of good men and creatures alike.

RETURN TO THE WEST

The company moved forward until daylight gave way to darkness. Camp was made as they lit small fires and ate what food they possessed, which by now was simply Fairy Cakes. Quiet voices filled the night. Grunts, cackles and broken human voices came from the Orna while low conversation rose from the Crutad. The Zarns hissed from afar.

Verion was filled with joy. Yet, his thoughts turned to Zydor. He was torn with guilt at the death of not only the fairy but Turlk as well. The scene of Zydor lying pierced with arrows and Turlk's broken body haunted him. His brow furrowed deeply as he sat alone with his misery and guilt. Closing his eyes and trying to drive their images from his mind worked to no avail.

Then, a gentle hand came to his shoulder. Nira's smiling face stared down at him. A half hearted smile broke on his lips, while inwardly he held great joy at her company.

"Speak your worries, Brother," said Nira softly. "I sense your thoughts. You blame yourself for the death of our friends. Yet, many died by their sides. We will never know their names, but all the same they are gone. Each fought with free will and the desire to stand by your side in combat. Mourn if you must, but it shall not alter the fact they will not return. Their races are unbound from the evil that spread from Morog. You could not have stayed the course of what came to pass. They rest now in Valla or wherever their race holds belief in."

"Your words are comforting and wise, Sister," said Verion. "Nonetheless, I feel sadness for Qnara. Her life partner was taken from her and it was partly my doing. How can I face her again, filled with shame and pity?"

"Yes, she laments her loss, but she does not place blame. Neither should you," said Nira, smiling once again. "You need not shun her. As companions we have shared much, including a journey to Mindaloth and now two other wicked places. Through it all, she has stood by our side, knowing full well the risks. Zydor knew also. He defended many lives before falling."

Verion sat in silent contemplation for some time. Finally, he rose. He placed a hand on Nira's shoulder and smiled, then walked to the fire to warm himself. Weariness from thought and despair took him. He found Aleeza and curled next to her sleeping form, no longer wishing for any thoughts to enter his mind this night.

Rising early, he strode atop a nearby rise to watch the young dragons chase one another in flight while Keltora and Trimlin circled slowly watching for remaining danger at ground level. Verion was sure the company would venture to their homelands free of distraction. Nonetheless, knowing the guardians filled the air put him at ease. He smiled as the youngsters blew small fireballs at each other, lighting up the pre dawn sky. An occasional roar came from their parents to correct them when needed. The scene lightened Verion's heart and brought joy as well.

Striding to the camp, he began to rummage in his pack for a cake. It was his final one, which he gave to Aleeza and settled for a sip of Silnoy for himself. Wafting aromas came from the Orna, Zarn and Crutad camp as well. Some of which he was perfectly content not partaking in, even if they offered. Nonetheless, he made a mental note to visit each campsite before they took to the trail again.

After his liquid meal he proceeded to each of the warrior sites as he intended, spending time at each. Speaking to all clans was a pleasant surprise, for on top of the gratitude they showed, he learned a great deal about the warriors. Then, sudden remorse gripped him as he listened, for only two of his friends had been lost, but together the clans lost great numbers of their strength. A selfish feeling swept over him as he thought of the reality of losing over fifteen hundred warriors. He grieved for all, but two in particular. How do Hexart, Snarat and the Zarns feel after losing over five hundred each? Now the Zarn's were leaderless as well. Shame filled his heart and mind as he sat and spoke and sat amongst them. It became known that Tordan would replace Turlk as leader of the Zarns.

Finally, he called to move. The sun showered its splendor upon the grass covered earth as the company stepped lightly away from camp. Trees cast shadows before them, which grew long and thin beneath the rising sun. Each step brought relief and lifted spirits, knowing they drew closer to their homelands with every footfall. Days passed quickly and uneventfully as they marched toward the bridge at the great river. The fairies and Telesta healed as they went. Finally, they crossed the mighty Bilana River and once more entered the land of Selenoth.

No sign of the twisted lands remained. Trees had sprouted and grown thick and tall, grass covered the earth as the sun smiled upon it. Gurgling brooks and streams brought joyful sounds to Verion's ears as he went. Wild shrubs and flowers dotted the landscape for as far as he could see. Knowing that Qnara had carried Renara's grace and power with her undoubtedly helped speed the healing. For it was a wondrous transformation. All signs of evil had been swept away. Only one exception remained.

He stared at the bridge one final time. It was his only reminder of the evil that once thrived here. Again, as he stepped from the wide connector that joined two previously evil lands, he paused. Thoughts of destruction entered his mind again, yet he stayed the thoughts. He turned to Katima and ask her to cleanse the bridge.

She beckoned Qnara to join her as they held hands and chanted softly. The stones blackness began to slowly, reluctantly fade giving way to grey, then a brilliant glistening white. It was wiped clean of all evil and filth that once occupied and possessed it. Verion smiled, turned westward and strode onward without looking back.

The night grew colder as the cloudless sky began to turn dim. Another camp was made as the weary travelers enjoyed respite from the day's journey. They covered many leagues that day before resting for the night amongst the tree laden slopes. Their bedrolls were spread on grass.

"We shall reach Selenoth soon," said Hexart as he approached Verion. "There, my warriors will take up home as promised. The western most outpost of men. Surely my people have swept clean the land and the fortress itself of any remaining evil. You must visit often my friend. Perhaps you could accompany us on our annual journey to pay homage to the great mounds of the dead that have been raised."

"I shall indeed," said Verion as he placed his hand on Hexart's shoulder. "Your people have fought valiantly and died with honor. I would be proud to pay tribute to their memory while by your side. I also carry a strange desire to lay eyes upon the innards of the fortress itself."

They stood silently gazing westward as the orange glow of the sun sank beneath the horizon, leaving them in utter darkness.

Suddenly, a flash of light broke the stillness. Swords were drawn and voices raised as the night was shattered by the blinding light. Renara stood before the dumbfounded group. Most instantly dropped to one knee and bowed their heads, except Verion. He drew close, then bowed low before the Ancient.

"Your destiny has been fulfilled young outlander king," she said softly to him. "You have defeated Holnok himself and laid Morog to ruin. Only the wizard Sartol escaped with the knowledge of the ancient evil place, and it shall serve him no use any longer. Your work is done. As before, my parents have no knowledge I stand before you, so my time is brief. Know that when you reach Madaria you will receive my parents warmest welcome. All of you will. You have done well, Lord Verion."

"I do not stand alone. My trusted companions kept me from harm. It is they who should be honored, not I. Our mission would have been for naught if not for each of them. I admit a longing to see Madaria and my home once more burns within me. The days will pass quickly now. We shall arrive in many days march. Perhaps we could receive a welcomed rest there if we are so allowed."

"So you shall," said Renara, still emanating a white light about her. "My parents draw near. I shall await your arrival. Farewell King Verion."

Another flash of light momentarily sundered the night and Renara was gone. Silence and the black night encompassed the camp once more. Verion stood a long while staring at the spot where she stood.

King Verion, he thought. *Though, someday I will rule Eldarn it seems odd to be called king by another. My father is the rightful king, I am only an heir. Yet, I am already treated as such by my companions. It makes me uncomfortable and feels out of place. Nonetheless, I shall not let it change me. Also, I pray to the gods Renara receives no retribution for aiding our cause. It would seem wrong somehow to punish her.*

Verion's thoughts were broken by the sound of shuffling behind him as the group rose from their knees.

"Let us take rest and move at first light," he said to the unblinking eyes before him. "We draw closer now and I, too, long for home. Good night to you all. I take my leave."

With that he turned away to find Aleeza and his companions. After a hearty meal, he rested once more. Though, he fell asleep with Renara in his thoughts.

Rising early, he pushed the group onward to the north as the sun began to climb steadily, so it went for many miles. The landscape bore no resemblance of the once horrific lands that the travelers had passed through previously. They traveled freely through glorious and beautiful lands that appeared shaped by the gods themselves as the sun shone brightly overhead.

Within several days march they drew within a league of Selenoth, for the company marched tirelessly forward until the battlement became visible. They stopped only for sleep and a few bites of Cakes or drink.

Now, the future king held mixed emotions. Anxiousness at seeing his home swelled within him, yet sadness took him at the first of several partings.

Hexart and his remaining Crutad warriors gathered round Verion to hear him speak. He stared forward searching the battle hardened faces of the fighters and smiled, then turned to face Hexart.

"May blessings from O'Tan and E'Lenoria be upon you and your people, Hexart," said Verion. "I will return to visit as often as I may. Eldarn is always open to you, my brother in arms. My people shall always welcome you."

"Blessings to you as well King Verion, my Captain," said Hexart with a bow. "You all shall live forever in our tales and songs as the warrior king, my friend."

"It is with sad heart I say farewell, for you will be missed. I take my leave, for many leagues travel still lie ahead on our path," said Verion as he grasp Hexart's thick forearm.

Verion turned westerly and began to march once more. Behind him many voices raised in cheers and shouts of farewell. Then, a Crutad war song came from the mass as pikes and spears beat the ground in steady rhythm. It reverberated through the hills as the company slowly faded over a small rise between distant peaks into the tree line.

The company moved for five more days in slow fashion until reaching the border of the Bottomless Lands. Again, there was no likeness to the lands Verion crossed on his first quest. The broken, horrid earth was gone. Green grass lay thick under his feet and tall trees surrounded him. Blue skies replaced the once darkened mass that hung above them with malice. Only beauty was his to behold now. They had become known as Quardoth, the Healed Lands.

Here, Tordan, Snarat and the remaining warriors would depart. Verion was given the way to find both the homes of the Zarn and Orna. He had never laid eyes on either of their lands to the south. He began to anticipate the journey to a new land. One that was unseen by any of his race.

"Go with speed and the luck of your gods to watch over and protect you both," said Verion. "You have fought with bravery and fearlessness. I am proud to call the Orna and Zarns my friends. I shall admit your losses grieve me greatly, my friends."

"We honor king always. Great warrior he is. Orna here if ever king need us," said Snarat is his broken way. "Our caves and holes not much to men, but you come visit Orna. Much good food for you." At that, Snarat broke out with a gurgling cackle and swayed from side to side with a large grin on his crooked face.

"We sssstand by your sssside too, lord Verion," hissed Torlan. "Turlk shall be misssed, but hisss memory will live forever among our people."

"As well it should, Torlan," said Verion. "All lands are open to you now. You know the way west to Eldarn. Honor and welcome await you there. We would celebrate your arrival. Fare thee well, friends."

Spears and shields clashed together as the company departed from the Bottomless Lands into the Forest of Dreams. They slowly disappeared into the thicker woods as the noise behind them gradually faded. The company moved forward at its original size, less one, Zydor.

Verion was pleased to have the thick forest about him again. He felt at home and peaceful now. The bliss felt upon entering the forest from the west returned to him. Creatures of all types still roamed freely about. Clear blue streams flowed here and there, gurgling peacefully as they flowed to their destination. Verion felt younger, as if much worry and weight had been lifted from his shoulders. His pack bore no weight on his back and his steps had spring in them. He smiled heartily for the first time in weeks.

Then Brandor entered his mind. His trusted mount waited for him in Madaria. This made his smile grow even more. His eyes instantly turned to the skies to catch sight of the dragons passing overhead. Joy now filled his heart.

He called for camp to be made as night approached rapidly. Much conversation was to be had between the friends as they sat and ate in the safety of the forest. Talk of evil was averted, only joyous memories and future hopes were spoke of. Sleep came easily to all this night. Verion was unsure if was aided by one in the company or perhaps an Ancient, yet, he didn't seem to care as he closed his eyes and slept soundly the entire night.

Warming rays of the sun were well into the sky before Verion stirred from his bedroll. He yawned and stretched as if he slept for days in end. He felt invigorated and hungry.

No sooner had he thought of food when Setorin and Renara appeared to him in a flash. There before their feet were large baskets of food. Meats, fruits, breads and many things Verion did not recognize sat before him.

"A gift to recover your strength," said Setorin. "Madaria is still many leagues away. This should aid your journey. For, it has been days since you ate a solid meal."

"Your aid is welcomed. It has been long indeed since I have tasted food. Only by the fairies aid and grace did we endure this long," said Verion. "We owe them a great deal."

"Pleasant journey, my friends," said Renara, then was gone in their usual flash.

Quickly the companions beset the baskets and began a fire for hot cooked food.

Aleeza brought her husband a heaping plate as he rose. Before allowing him to hold it she kissed him gently, then placed the overly laden meal in his hands.

"I imagine you are famished," she said with a smile and a wink.

"Indeed," said Verion simply as he kissed her softly. "I see some things have returned to as they were. I shall admit Silnoy will be hard pressed to pass my lips for some time to come."

He ate ravenously. Even the food tasted better here in the forest, he thought as he chewed.

Laughter was heard and many smiles graced the faces of the company as they pressed onward toward the home of the Ancients. Verion walked hand in hand with Aleeza as they marched in happiness.

The lands rolled gently up and down for many leagues. Grasslands with dense tree cover lay spread in all directions. Verion relished in the shade beneath the wide reaching branches of the hardwood trees. Leaves fluttered in the soft breeze as squirrels chattered noisily overhead, chastising those foolish enough to brave entering their territory.

Verion was blissful. The lands in every part of the world where evil had once lived had now been healed. Only burial mounds stood as solitary reminders of battle. Though, they too were grass and flower covered. One would be hard pressed to find them unless you knew where they stood. Katima once said purple wild flowers would bloom upon them. No other place in D'Enode would they be found. They signified fairy tears for the loss of the valiant.

Finally, after several days of similar travel, they reached the outskirts of the city. Madaria stood before them in all its glory and splendor. It was more beautiful and magnificent than Verion remembered. He stood admiring the view for some time before Nira's voice entered his mind.

"Come Brother, it is time for a needed rest," she said. "We have traveled many days since our quest. A bed and hot bath water will feel joyous indeed."

Verion stepped forward through the force field without hesitation. He instantly turned to the stables to find Brandor. A loud neigh met him as he entered. Again, after some time he was spurred to the city by Nira, for he was joyous at seeing Brandor once more.

As he exited the stables, four Ancients stood before him. He stopped and lowered to one knee and bowed his head.

"I come to you as your servant, if you will have me," said Verion. "I have caused the death of your son. I must pay that debt with my servitude if you so require it. Do with me as you will."

Movement and speech within the company stopped instantly. All eyes turned to him, then to the Ancients. None could believe their ears, they were taken off guard from his impromptu outburst. They began to fidget nervously as they awaited an answer.

Verion thought of this debt for many days, keeping his thoughts to himself, speaking to no one. He had hidden them well as the companions traveled. Now, he had determined that his service was the only small way he could be free of guilt. Even if it cost him dearly. He waited on bent knee for his fate.

"Rise future king of Eldarn," said Laveena softly. "I know this thought has troubled you for quite some time now. Yet, Torlen chose his own path. You played no part in his choice to turn to wicked ways. There is no debt between us. He would have slain you all if not for your actions. Fear not, for his true form which you have seen is at peace once again."

"Come, we shall feast and speak of the future," said Delthas.

The company gathered round the table that held their first counsel. Smells of blooming flowers and the forest itself wafted through the air, filling Verion's nostrils. He smiled outwardly as he sat listening to the sweet, musical voices of the Ancients.

"Will you stay among us now that peril has passed?" asked Verion abruptly. Instantly, he felt ashamed at his outburst. Even so, it was a question he greatly desired an answer to. "Knowing you have seen all that transpired will you return to the Mystic Isles since evil has been driven out."

"You have spoken to Murn of evil have you not?" asked Laveena. "Evil never truly dies, it simply fades for a time. Is that not true? We came before you to stop our son from destroying your world. That has been done. Now, we shall return to whence we came. Though, as you know, we see all from the Isles. Your races must shape and form this world and become stronger and more powerful together, without our help, young lord."

"I have already visited Selenoth and Morog. All the lands about them have been healed. The stain of malevolence has been washed away. Now stands green fields and meadows. Mountains are filled with birds and beasts alike. All that remains of your journeys are the mounds of the dead, which I have hallowed for eternity, even after the fairies blessings," said Delthas.

"Hear me outlanders," continued Delthas. "Evil will never leave this earth as long as men hold power and treasures dear to them. No magic known can end lust and greed from embracing those that will have it. Tis sorrowful indeed, yet it is the way of men. Jealousy, struggles for supremacy, and violence will plague your race forever. You have stayed the current threat against your people. Holnok and Torlen are dead, yet someday one will take their place. Perhaps the malicious monster that is named evil will not be seen again in your lifetime? Or it may rear its head and strike like a wild beast without warning. Though, grieve not young lord, for brave and true hearts shall not be denied their destinies."

"Then you will return to help us once again?" asked Murn quizzically.

"For thousands of years we have not meddled with your race, until Torlen forced our involvement. Once we return home we shall come hither only when your kind conquers hate and the killing of its own kind. For, our love of the children of O'Tan and E'Lenoria are great indeed. Yet, we will not stay you from the sins that grip all races," said Laveena with a gentle sadness in her voice.

The room fell quiet after she spoke. Verion's joy left him. He knew in his heart he would never lay eyes upon the Ancients again, yet he tried to keep hope alive within himself. He stared at the blank faces around him, sensing the emotions and thought of his companions were much akin to his own. This deepened his sadness even more.

"Do not despair Lord Verion," said Renara as she broke the silence. "After the quest from Mindaloth, your company united many races previously set asunder from one another. That was no insignificant task, young king. You have made great strides. Greater than anyone of this world has taken for hundreds of years. There is hope to be had with all that sit now at this table. Despair is for those that hold no hope. Each of you sitting before me keeps the dream alive. That is a wonderful and joyous thing. Many will follow your words, for they hold faith in you. Continue your quest for peace, it is never-ending."

Again, silence lay thickly over the company. Each turned to stare at the other. Smiles slowly replaced the frowns worn moments before. Verion's mind raced with thoughts of a united world at peace and harmony with one another. He smiled outwardly once more.

Conversation continued late into the night. The moon waxed full overhead as the travelers, weary from their journey, desired rest. Each was led to a comfortable room where they slept soundly and peacefully.

The company remained in Madaria for seven nights, learning much about the ways of the Ancients, their beliefs and philosophies on peace and life itself. When time to depart finally came, none did so with vigor in their strides. The moment was bittersweet for all, including the Ancients themselves, though they showed little outward sign of it.

Verion sat atop Brandor and smiled reluctantly. He waved to the foursome standing before him. Then, Laveena's voice entered his mind.

"We shall watch you and take great interest in your world's progress. You may use the crystal I sent with you to communicate with us if need be. It was given to you alone because you shall have the greatest role in the peace of the all lands. Guidance shall always be yours for the asking. Farewell for now young King Verion."

Verion turned his mount westward toward Avior and rode forward without looking back. Images of a united, peaceful world danced in his mind. Hope lessened the pain of parting. Yet, sadness played a cheerless song in his mind as he moved steadily west.

The company reached the E'Lenoria Mountains and began the steady winding ascent. Once over the peak they would be in the Shimmering Lands once more. Again, Verion's tracking skills proved invaluable as he retraced the same path used to reach the Forest of Dreams. This time however the pace was more relaxed and there was no weight upon his shoulders. He traveled carefree and at peace as Brandor moved gently under him.

Gynexa and Jarnea glided high above the mountains as he turned his gaze skyward. Eight other shapes sat perched atop the ridge of peaks. The lands were safe and the dragons had returned. He smiled as he rode onward. Then, he began to think of Aris, the Fairy Queen. His smile faded into a frown.

It is difficult enough to face her daughter Qnara each day with the guilt of Zydor's death on my mind. Now, I must stand before the queen herself. She is too powerful. I will not be able to hide my thoughts from her. She knows all that is in my mind. Though, I have nothing to keep from her except my guilt. I shall not look forward to our meeting. Though, I do admire and respect her race, I pray this alters nothing between us, thought Verion as he moved steadily with Brandor walked steadily onward.

The company made camp after many hours of riding over the summit. Finally, they reached the forest floor below as darkness shrouded the depths of the woods. Verion knew if he entered the forest the sparkling trees would give enough light to travel to the city. Yet, he was weary and sore. It had been many weeks since he sat in a saddle for an entire day. His legs were tight and he desired a warm meal and rest. Silnoy and Fairy Cakes had been forgotten after his stay in Madaria, now a hot meal would warm his belly.

After much food, he stretched out beside his wife. He lay on his back watching the moonlight dance from the dragons scales as two youngsters circled tirelessly above. Then, small sounds reached his ears. *Voices,* he thought. *We are waylaid!*

"Alarm! Foes are upon us!" he yelled, shattering the night. "Arise and draw swords."

Much shuffling and scurrying was heard. Shouts broke the stillness as ringing steel came from the camp. The company quickly gathered round Verion, prepared for battle.

"Eldon," whispered Verion. "Darkness does not affect your sight, what do you see, quickly."

The Willon began to slowly scan the forest. Abruptly, he stopped and pointed to a large cluster of thick, ancient trees.

"There are four figures, there," he said, still pointing. "Two stand upright, two are beasts. Though, I see no weapons and they remain motionless like statues. Perhaps my eyes play tricks on me. They could be Zenex and riders."

"No, Lord Eldon, your eyes are true to you," came a soft voice from the tree line in the common tongue. "We have no weapons, we come to you unarmed. No harm shall befall you, we simply wish to greet your Captain and his company, the slayers of Torlen and Holnok."

"Who are you, speak!" said Verion. "How do you come by news of our venture. Show yourself. Why lurk in the shadows and darkness, come forth so I may lay eyes upon you."

As the two figures approached, night gave way to a small light within the circle of the company. From the edge of the light came two shapes Verion recognized instantly as Tharnils. Raza had been carving wooden effigies of them when they first met years ago. Now, he lay eyes on the living animals themselves as they stood mere feet away. They were indeed as beautiful as the woodworker had portrayed them. Their thick fur rustled gently in the soft breeze. With long snouts, powerful legs and intelligent eyes they peered at the company. The top of their shoulder tood higher than Verion's head. It was an immense, beautiful animal, yet fierce looking as well.

The slender figure of a woman followed by a tall, thin man stepped forward. They dressed in flowing robes much like that of the Ancients. Only, their color was of the forest itself. Dark greens layered neatly with lighter greens and soft browns hung upon them. No bright colors were found. Gold, yellow, silver and white were not to be seen.

Again, Verion thought of the Ancients, for as the intruders came forward their skin was smooth and flawless, shining pale in the dim light. They, too, held a captivating beauty that one could not resist. He found himself staring openly, his sword point dropped to the ground as thoughts of battle or harm left him.

"I am Xana, this is Yanor, my beloved. We are of the Tareen. Long has it been since our race was seen. Our people have returned as promised now that Ancients, our creators, have graced D'Enode one again. In truth, we have just appeared before them making ourselves known. We have spent many days in Madaria after your departure. Then we chose to lay eyes upon you ourselves."

Verion and the company, though stunned, knelt before the two with bowed heads and lowered weapons.

"Rise, lords and ladies. We will answer your questions, for we know there are many within you. The Tareen have returned, rejoice," said Yanor. "Come, let us speak with nothing hidden from one another."

"Your race departed long ago, why? Now, you return. Will you stay among us once more," asked Verion as questions flooded his mind. "Where do you hail from, none have seen the Tareen. Only in legends did you exist. Yet, we still sing of your kind and tell tales of your power and magic."

Verion stopped suddenly, realizing all eyes were upon him. Embarrassment swept over him as his face grew flushed in the dim light.

"Delthas and Laveena commanded us to hide ourselves until the time of their return. Now we have come forth again to visit our descendents the fairies and all other races as well. We departed from you by command of our creators to allow your kind to grow and prosper without aid. You all have done very well indeed. Queen Aris and the fairies have grown well beyond expectations. All races have united and joined in friendship and evil has been driven out. Our home is in the Dark Forest, many leagues south of Eldarn. None dare venture there for it brings dread and fear to them, so we remained hidden and unseen for countless long years."

"Thousands of years have passed since the Fading Years," said Nira. "Long have races worshipped the Tareen. Though now, the fairies earn our respect and love in your stead. Your return will cause great joy and celebration throughout D'Enode. All will rejoice."

Verion subconsciously rubbed the jewel beneath his tunic as Xana spoke.

"Yes, my lord," said Yanor. "You hold the beloved jewel of our people. It is called Simil and shines with the power of goodness. Only those pure of heart my bear it hence. It beckoned to you, did it not? It chooses wisely."

Verion nodded awkwardly, but remained silent as he began to recall the first time he lay eyes on the jewel. Raza gifted it to him as it glowed brightly when it neared Verion's hand.

"Indeed," said Verion. "It lay warm and brilliant in my grasp. Never has it failed any want or desire I ask of it. I have learned much of it during this journey."

"Then, you have blood of the Tareen within your veins," said Xana. "Only those that bear our lines may command it so. It heeds no other."

Verion felt as if he was physically struck. *It cannot be,* he thought. *I am a simple warrior, not a descendent of a wizard or witch. Lo, is that why Nira and I were born with the power of seeing. Could it be? Do I hold magic within me. Why have my parents never spoke of it. Do they even know? I yearn to know more, every detail.*

"So you shall," said Yanor. "All will be explained in time. Though now, you should take rest.

If you will have us, we shall await your arrival in Eldarn. There we will speak yet again, at length."

"I shall hold great anticipation until our next meeting," said Verion. "There is much I would know. Eldarn will welcome you. Seek the king, my father. Parta will rejoice."

"Special love go to our children, Katima and Qnara. It has been overly long since we walked among the fairies. Though they believed we faded from the earth the time has come to greet them. However, now we must depart, for there is more that beckons our attention."

The company lowered to one knee once more, heads lowered.

"Rise, friends," said Xana. "Our grace shall be with you all. Long have we awaited our reunion with the races of D'Enode. Our love for you all is endless. Never doubt the joy we hold at our return. Farewell, for now we are off to visit our children in Avior."

A soft, warm light engulfed Xana and Yanor. It grew more brilliant with each passing moment, until the company shielded their eyes. Then, the Tareen were gone.

After much talk among the company, they chose to rest and move at first light. Anticipation now filled their hearts and minds. Verion tried to sleep, yet it eluded him.

It was then the voice of Aris came to him, the sweet music filling his mind.

"Welcome, Verion. I await your arrival with much anticipation. Know your family is safe in your homeland. They fought valiantly during the siege of Eldarn. Though Zydor rests with his ancestors now you must remove the chains of guilt you bear so heavily. They serve no purpose other than to burden your mind needlessly. He fell with honor. Come, Avior awaits you. The city is now visible once more. Seek and you shall find it with ease."

Verion drifted into a solid sleep after the fairy's voice faded. He woke refreshed and free of worry. After a hot breakfast he swung into his saddle with ease. The company journeyed for two more days until finally a clear path came before him. As the company rode westerly Verion suddenly recognized the spot he met Aris several times.

"My city lies this way," said Qnara as she took the lead, striking the plain path before her.

Swiftly, the company approached the secretive city of Aris and the fairies. Verion cherished Avior and the living forest which helped protect it. Amazement and admiration combined to form a deep love of the fairies home and its people.

Aris stood smiling near the cottage that the company was familiar with. Verion named it the 'Cottage of Want.' For it grew in size or provided restful sleep and food as need or want arose. He was fascinated by its magic and the astonishment never faded from him.

"Greetings my friends," said Aris with a soft smile. "Come, let us eat and speak of your journey. It is of great interest to me. Though I have seen much, there are some things even I could not see. We must also discuss the return of the Tareen as well. Our creators have returned to us after ages."

Food and drink were quickly brought before the travelers as they seated themselves, except for Qnara who stood in consult with her mother. As the company accepted an offer of another full plate and cup, Aris led Qnara down the passageway to the rear of the large room. Minutes later, as light conversation began from the friends, both fairies reappeared smiling.

Verion grew pleased at seeing Qnara wear a smile once more. It had been many days since her face glowed with happiness. He wondered if Aris put a spell on her own daughter to remove her pain and grief of Zydor's death. His guilt and worry flooded back to him in an instant.

"Once again we celebrate the destruction of the foul work of Holnok. Though, this time he shall not return. The world has been cleansed of his evil ways and lust for treasures he was not meant to possess. You all have fought with honor and strength. My people shall sing songs of your deeds for ages to come," said Aris. "Your names are now ones of legend."

"Yet, you know my heart is heavy with sadness for the fallen," began Verion. "I would . . ."

Aris raised her hand, causing Verion to stop mid sentence.

"Young lord," she said. "There is no need to dwell on death. You need not hold your burdens any longer. All here are saddened by the loss of those we held dear. A lament shall be sung in their honor. Yet, our remorse will not return them to us. Remember them in your heart where they shall live forever. Sadness cannot plague your mind. You have many things to occupy your thoughts and time will heal your grief. Go forth and further the unification of this world as you have dreamed of so often. There is much work to do."

"Agreed," smiled Murn, his eye growing wide. "People have grown closer then they have been in ages. Because of you my Captain our races are united as they were long ago. Still, there is much to do. We all stand by your side with aid to your dream. Or rightly, each of our dreams."

A chorus of shouts and cheers came from the company that remained silent until now. Each friend's thoughts rushed into Verion's mind. Hope grew in his heart, making him smile yet again as he had done often in the passing few weeks.

"My friends, it is indeed my dream to have D'Enode united forever, though it is not entirely my doing. It comes from the sacrifice of those we will see no more until we visit Valla itself. I have played a very small part in this undertaking. Yet, I humbly accept your praise and vow to work ever harder to realize peace among all races until my time fades from D'Enode," said Verion.

"That will be far longer than you have ever dreamed possible, young lord," said Aris, smiling.

Verion cocked his head slightly, unsure of Aris's meaning. *I am only a man. My life shall end as with any other of my race. My time on D'Enode is no greater than any other.* He poised himself to ask many questions, though he remained silent for the queen continued.

Then, Aris slowly turned to Fenorl, who shrank slightly under her gaze.

*   *   *

Fenorl knew the fairies, the queen in particular, had been aware of his evil deeds from the beginning. Katima and Qnara had told him as much during the journey after his cleansing. As Aris stared at him with her steady, penetrating gaze fear swelled within him. He believed his past might indeed come back to haunt him regardless of the outcome of the quest. That even with the killing of Holnok he had not been redeemed in her eyes. He sat silently awaiting his fate. His confidence and pride fled him as he became flushed and anxious. His dreams of a life with his Captain in Eldarn began to slowly fade before his eyes. Sweat beaded his forehead until he felt he could endure no more. He was mere seconds from rising and leaving the table when Aris's calm, gentle voice wafted on the air once more.

* * *

"A special place is now held among my people for you, Fenorl," she said, smiling. "You have proven your worth and courage to all here. None will ever distrust you again. Many doubted your value," she said, shooting a quick glance at Murn. "Yet you proved yourself many times during this journey. Fenorl you shall remain and now be known and sung about for ages."

"I deserve no such praise my lovely Lady," said Fenorl humbly, fidgeting slightly as he spoke. "I simply put an end to our tormentor. Which, if I may be so bold, would not have been possible without my companions beside me. They held faith in me even when I kept little within myself. The company has restored that which was lost."

The companions remained still and silent as Aris slowly turned and departed. Verion smiled at Fenorl, nodding his head in agreement. Happiness welled within him for his friend. Finally, he thought, he receives praise other than my own. Never again shall he be troubled with dishonor.

The evening drew on as the companions let worry and grief slip from their burdened shoulders and minds. Once more, time was lost. Verion no longer knew if day or night was outside of the cottage door. Yet, in Avior, the fairies could control the conditions if they desired, including whether it was light or dark.

Nonetheless, he grew weary and wished for rest and to have a clear mind once more. He bade the company sleep at their leisure and bid them return refreshed. Departing with Aleeza's hand in his own they slipped silently from view and soon after, all followed.

Upon rising from a deep sleep, Verion felt more refreshed than in a very long time, even after his rest in Madaria. A smile graced his face as he strode into the common room from the previous night. Most of the company was up and about. They greeted him jovially as he approached with wife by his side, both wearing happy grins.

Immediate discussion of the Tareen began. Their sudden appearance and return to D'Enode were the most talked about. As the conversation progressed, Aris and several fairies Verion had never seen before appeared and joined in as well. They were introduced as the High Council of Avior, the elders of the Protected Realm.

"Behold," she said. "Joy has returned to all, especially in Avior. Last night you were weary from travel so we held our talk. Now we shall openly speak of the Tareen. For we have been visited by Xana and Yanor. We bowed before them and gave great welcome. Many of our people wept upon hearing the news. Long have we thought their line faded from earth and memory. Now by the grace of the gods, they have returned to us."

These words shocked Verion. It seemed impossible a powerful being such as the queen of the fairies would bow before any race except perhaps the Ancients themselves. Yet the Tareen were not only forbearers, but held potent power as well, even more so than fairies.

That day a great celebration was held. Avior was alight with song and music, lasting well into the night. Verion and the companions delighted in the festivities and partook of much food, ale and song. He summoned forth the dragons as well, knowing their love of the fairies. They received great attention and gave many rides skyward. Finally though, the night drew to an end as the city fell quiet once more. The company found their rooms and slept well, but not before Aris put forth an invitation for all to remain in the Protected Realm until their hearts desired to take leave. The companions gratefully accepted her invitation, with Verion taking particular delight.

Before he discerned time, eleven days and nights disappeared. On the twelfth day his overwhelming desire to see his homeland and his parents spurred him to set foot on the path leading to Eldarn. He thought often of his family since the attack from Holnok's minions left him wondering if they had survived.

As he spoke of his desire to depart the company, none would part from him. So it was, the following morning would be their last in the exquisite, hidden city.

Verion felt joy at the thought of seeing his parents, yet sadness took him as always when departing this mystical place. Words could not express the reverence and love he held for the fairies. Though he tired many times, the words would not come.

Aris knew this and quietly came to him as he stood alone gazing into the high tree tops.

"Again we say farewell, young lord," she said. "I know your thoughts and I, too, hold no joy in your departure. For, you have brought my people much joy and happiness with your presence and thirst for our knowledge. They adore you and the dragons as well," she said with a thin smile. "You shall be missed by us all, especially Qnara for she holds you in high esteem."

"Tis true, I love your people next to none save my own," said Verion. "I shall return as often as allowed. Perhaps you may journey to Eldarn. You are forever welcome in my father's lands. We would rejoice at your coming. For now, all races are welcomed and shall be treated as honored guests, the fairies in particular. Without your powerful magic our quests would have resulted in failure. Qnara saved many lives as well, she is held in high favor."

The pair fell silent for a long while as Verion gazed at his surroundings with the queen by his side. Slowly, one by one, the company joined them. None spoke aloud, though Verion read sorrow in each of their thoughts. Leaving the Protected Realm tore at their hearts, though many desired their homelands, it did not ease the sorrow and despair of farewell.

The company rose early the following morning. Horses were laden with ample supplies from the fairies, though none were burdensome. The gifts bore no weight upon the mounts backs and were easily carried forth. Farewells were long and sorrow filled for all when time came.

"Until our paths cross again my friends, I bid thee farewell," said Qnara as she stood by Aris' side. "Each of you will be under our watchful eye. You simply need to close your eyes and utter my name and I shall answer."

"Most gracious and kind hosts," began Verion. "It is with heavy heart we leave your fair city and your kind. Though each of us longs for our own lands, leaving Avior behind is difficult indeed. You shall be in our hearts and thoughts each and every day. I bid thee farewell with a vow to return as quickly as I may."

Verion reined Brandor to the west and slowly steered him to the path appearing before him. He turned for one final glance over his shoulder at a smiling Aris and Qnara. Then, unexpectedly, his eyes went wide. There, next to Qnara, stood a glowing figure sheathed in white light. Zydor stood smiling at Verion, hand raised in a farewell wave.

Verion shook his head and refocused on the fairies and Zydor had vanished. No word was ever spoken to his companions of his vision. Though, he smiled and never looked back again.

Over the Mighty Helix

Within several days of carefree travel, the company reached the Helix River. The dragons soared overhead as the remaining companions steered the ferry to the eastern shore of the river. Here, four of the company prepared to depart for the sea port of Tarsis, the home of the Arton people.

"Once before on this very spot we bade farewell during our first quest. Yet again we stand together and prepare to go our separate ways with heavy hearts," said Telesta. "Though we greatly desire to feel water beneath us it shall be with sorrow we go forth."

"There is no need for mourning, my lady. Our parting is only for a short time. The dragons will ensure we are never long apart, no matter the distance. It is less than two day's ride between our lands," said Verion.

"True enough, my Captain," said Jinarl. "Nonetheless, you shall be missed. I believe the next visit belongs to us. We shall come to Eldarn after we have spent time with our own people. I long to feel the sea once more and grow happy."

"We shall look to the sky each day," said Verion smiling as he grasp Jinarl's forearm. "As always, you will be most welcome among the land dwellers and fellow warriors."

"Tell Father I miss and love him and we shall visit soon," said Zarah to Eldon. "Take good care of yourself, my Brother. Much longing fills my heart to see our city once more. Look for us before the fall season."

"Father will be pleased to see you both," said Eldon. "He speaks of you daily and I believe you are in his every thought. Your people miss you as well, they will rejoice at your return. There will be great celebration."

Brother and sister embraced as Luntar, Jinarl's dragon landed beside the group.

"Milar, my quiet friend," said Verion. "Though often you have remained silent your valor has shone through in many actions. Proudly I would stand by your side in any adventure. Visit us in Eldarn often, for I would enjoy your company."

"Before this journey, my friends had spoken highly of you," said Milar quietly as he swept an arm to his friends from Tarsis. "Often, I would silently believe no such man could exist, that they embellished their tales for my sake. Yet, since traveling with you for many weeks and standing by your side in battle, I believe their stories were incomplete. They should be even grander yet, my lord. Never have I met someone as worthy of the title of king. Your people shall be blessed."

Verion was amazed this quiet man before him spoke at length. Rarely had he voiced more than a few words during the trek unless directly addressed. Smiling, he placed his large hand on Milar's shoulder and bid him farewell.

"I shall send Eptus and Karnell with you for your journey home. They can return at their own speed when you have reached Tarsis. They are worthy dragons and will enjoy the exercise and they have never seen the sea that you so dearly love," said Verion, smiling.

His mind quickly reached out to the youngsters, giving them instructions for their travel. Within moments the two dragons landed next to Luntar. They purred while waiting patiently for their new riders to mount.

More farewells and oaths of friendship were spoken, until finally the dragons had riders upon their backs. They roared as they took flight northward, circling once above Verion, who spoke silently to them. He wished them well and a speedy return home.

The remaining companions, now numbering seven, mounted and rode westward for the Caves. Though, not before Verion paid respects to the spot where Murn's brother Bolo had fallen during their last quest.

Verion knew this moment was of particular discomfort to Fenorl since it was his treachery that led to the fray at this very spot, thereby causing Bolo's death. It took several long moments before Fenorl could even bear to face the site. Finally he came to Verion's side with Murn in tow.

"I hold no hate for you any longer, my friend," said Murn, resting a giant hand on Fenorl's back. "I dearly miss my brother and would enjoy his company yet again, but it is not to be. He died an honorable death in battle. That is a Malmak's dream. You were Natrae then, now you are Fenorl and you carry my friendship with you outlander."

"Long ago, when my heart was pure, never could I have done such a deed. Yet, evil took me and held tightly. Now, I have been released from my horrible dream and regained my honor and the scourge of Holnok is gone. Proudly do I stand beside you as a companion and life friend, Murn," said Fenorl softly.

"So be it. The name of Natrae shall never be spoken in the Caves again. Though Fenorl shall receive high praise indeed. Slayer of Holnok you shall be named and great welcome shall be yours when you grace our home."

Fenorl stood silent, gazing at the spot of Bolo's death, then he turned from it with his head hung low.

After several long moments, Verion called to mount and head west. Joy grew again as the thought of his friends opening their hearts to speak of the only remaining burden came to pass.

The path wound steadily upward for some distance turning ever more northerly. The trees stood tall as the forest grew close about them. Though unlike the forests of Eldarn, Verion still enjoyed this land. It felt much like home. The lands were not as mystical as Avior or Madaria, yet it was still wrought with beauty and wonder. Birds twittered to and fro, beasts moved at will as they rode forth.

Caves of Doom, he thought. *It would only be thought so if evil entered here, then they would certainly understand the name. It would then be fitting. But, there is no doom here. Only green trees, flowers, grass and wildlife. Each land holds its own mystique and charm and none are unwelcomed to me. Even as I ride, the eastern lands have been healed. Perhaps someday soon I shall revisit them to see their beauty in its full glory after the trees have grown even taller yet.*

Shadows began to lengthen as the travelers moved steadily forward. A chilled night breeze met them as camp was made, causing Verion to don his cloak. Katima magically lit the wood

Verion collected, for he was famished and greatly desired a meal. Nira retrieved pots and pans and began preparation of food and drink the fairies sent. Dim evening light gave way to darkness lying thick about them as the companions ate their fill. Talk went into late night. Many stars shone brightly overhead as the group prepared for their needed rest.

The morning dawned pale and warm. Verion stripped his blanket back and rolled over to rise silently. His gaze went westward where home, comfort and his parents lied in waiting.

Anxiousness swept through him, but he suppressed it well. To busy his mind, he began preparing breakfast for all.

Murn came silently to his side causing Verion to startle. Being deep in thought, he was taken unawares of his approach.

"Pardon, my lord," said Murn. "Forgive me for giving you a start."

"All is well, my large friend," replied Verion. "My thoughts were drifting. I saw images of . . ."

"Home, I would venture to say," said Murn, interrupting.

"Indeed. You know me well, giant. I long to see my parents and Eldarn. The road will seem lengthy, though I know each moment draws me closer," he said.

"I shall miss your company after your departure. Though, I know it shall not be overly long until I lay eyes upon you once more. After all, I have a dragon now," said Murn with a extremely large smile, making his eye squint.

Verion remained silent as he laid a hand on the Cyclops' shoulder. He, too, would miss Murn's company. Of all his companions, he held the giant the closest. His fierceness, wisdom and friendship were next to none. There was a certain unspoken bond the two shared that Verion had never known before.

When breakfast was over and supplies stowed, the sun had risen high. It was mid-morning before the travelers decided to move onward. Growing warmth greeted them as the sun burnt brightly in the cloudless morning sky.

Verion's cloak was gone and his sleeves were partially rolled upward. His heart was lifted as he drew ever to the west. Yearning to lay eyes upon the Dimlor Mountains arose in him. The simple act of seeing them would bring great peace, no matter how many leagues he needed to travel to arrive there. Each day he strived for a new goal. Today's goal was the Caves, then it would be the City of Life and so on until reaching the Dimlor's. He knew home would be a mere three days ride from the foothills near the Watching Hill. That of course, was his final goal.

The sun began to fade far sooner than Verion expected, yet they rode on until darkness was nearly upon them. In the fading light they went in single file along a worn trail leading northward. Finally the road ceased rolling up and down, climbing to a flat spot that made for a suitable camp.

Many thoughts occupied Verion's mind during the passing day, though they were mostly happy ones this time. Still, some sadness and sorrow found its way into his mind. However, they didn't last long for he refused them and forced them out.

Within days of pleasant journeying and conversation they came into sight of the caves that were Murn's home. Verion was relieved to be able to take rest in a soft bed again, yet he dreaded the upcoming departure. Nonetheless, he would relish the time he had with Murn, his clan and Katima as well.

One day blended into another. Verion learned more of rock carving, for it fascinated him to shape a piece of stone into a work of art, no matter how big or small. Karth, Murn's brother, spent much time with the new dragon and the company as well. Nira, grew even closer with Katima and Aleeza. Murn was thrilled to receive more dragon flying lessons as Verion and the Malmak clan looked on. However, Verion thought the Cyclops possessed an uncanny ability for balance and grace when riding, even more so than in combat. Nonetheless, he honored his friend's request for training.

Fourteen days passed until farewells were spoken. The dragons and horses were well rested and fed, growing anxious for another leg of the journey. Verion however, did not carry the same anticipation.

"Go westward with good hearts," said Murn. "Do not despair, for time shall pass with speed. Katima and I will visit soon, you have my oath." Murn wore a smile, but Verion read his true thoughts. He knew his large companion was filled with anguish, the same as his heart felt.

"May blessings be upon you," said Verion. "You have my sworn word we shall meet again soon. Take good care of your new dragon as well." He pointed to the purple shape floating above on the wind currents.

"Indeed I shall," answered Murn. "Now our visits shall be far easier and more frequent. Farewell."

Then, Murn walked to Fenorl, resting his large hand upon his shoulder. His eye roved over his onetime enemy, who now sat proud and straight.

"You will be welcome when you visit again," said the Cyclops. "I beg forgiveness for any hurt done to your honor by my words or actions, but I pray you shall understand why it came to pass that I held anger. I was mistaken."

"I understand now why my king thinks so highly and admirably of you, giant," said Fenorl, smiling broadly. "None could hope for a more trusting and worthy companion as you. I am proud to ride by your side . . . friend."

Verion was not surprised by the exchange, for he knew Murn genuinely meant every word as did Fenorl. The two had grown close during the quest and until their last days it was so.

As the travelers turned to depart Verion vaguely heard Murn shouting something about a surprise at the river. It made no sense to him at the time. He simply waved, shrugged and continued onward.

The five companions turned southerly toward the lower leg of the Helix River and none looked back. Verion hid his sadness well, even blocking his mind as best he could from his sister. Though, even without the amulet's power, he felt she knew his grief as they rode in utter silence.

At length, Fenorl began soft speech with Eldon and Nira. Gentle laughter was heard rising from behind Verion. Still, he carried dark thoughts while replaying many past events since his departure from Eldran. Disappointment and frustration filled his mind. He thought of Turlk and Zydor's death, departing Madaria and Avior and naturally of Murn. Holnok's death face appeared to him as well. Battle cries rang in his ears as his brow furrowed. He rode mindlessly until Aleeza joined him and begged for rest. The company covered many leagues that day as he sat deep in thought, riding forward giving no heed to the others around him. He smiled a false smile and called for a brief respite.

After a lengthy break where good food and drink was had, his mind cleared considerably. Vigor returned to his step once more. Once remounted and under way he felt relaxed and at peace for the remainder of the day. Dark thoughts had fled him, his spirits were high once more.

Soon, shadows grew long and thin as the sun hid itself before the travelers. The sky grew dim and cold as evening fell quickly while they trod southerly along a barely perceptible trail. Eldon's eyes saw it clearly as he rode in the lead, followed at lengthy intervals by his companions.

Verion held a burning desire to see home, which caused his relentless journey to the west. He rode until he could take no more. He was sore and weary of travel. He called for camp to be made as moving forward was now impossible, darkness finally engulfed them. The campfire sprang to life as he struck his flint and tinder. Much conversation poured forth once all pots and pans were emptied, cleaned and stowed.

It brought great joy to sit before an open fire with his life friends and discuss something other than evil. They spoke of carving stones and rocks, metallurgy, future plans and other things that sprung forth in their minds, regardless how trivial or large they seemed. Happiness was their only thought or desire.

The moon was bright and full before Verion realized he was mentally and physically exhausted. Rest came easily this night to the overly tired travelers, Verion in particular slept well, completely draining his mind's thoughts and letting go of sorrow for the time being.

The morning came too quickly for his taste, though he desired to move. Several days travel still lay ahead before reaching the City of Life. At least they would make the river crossing during this day, that alone would make him feel as if he gained ground toward seeing his home. That was his goal for the day, the River. Knowing he would spend several days at both Aleeza's home and Hatar did not lift his spirits, for it delayed his homeward journey even longer. Yet, he took great pleasure in visiting both cities and their people. He made a silent promise to himself to visit Raza this time. The kindly old wood worker was special to Verion, even before he gifted him the Jewel of the Tareen. He had taken an instant liking to the old man from the moment they met. His jovial ways and pleasant demeanor were quite refreshing.

Before long the company curved steadily southward, now turning their faces to the mountains. For most parts the path was straight and wide, horses could be ridden side by side for a great distance. It narrowed in spots, forcing the travelers to resort to single file. Nonetheless, conversation that began during breakfast continued the entire day. Verion was light hearted once more. Knowledge of Eldarn's safety set him at ease. Pushing any thoughts of home as deep as he could, he pressed forward with an outward smile.

In this fashion, the day passed quickly. Before long, sounds of swiftly running water reached his ears. *The dark waters of the mighty Helix are not far off now,* he thought. Then, as Murn had said, a great surprise came to him. As he reached the river a new sight filled his vision. Now he understood the giant's parting comment.

A massive stone bridge now spanned the waterway. It was heartily made of stone and rock, standing high, wide and strong. Its width was easily broad enough for four horses to ride abreast of one another.

Only the Malmak could build such a structure, he thought, marveling. *But when did they make time to complete this. Most of the clan must have started work shortly after our crossing to the east. It would have taken weeks to complete. It is beautiful to be sure. Only a Malmak could fashion stone with such precision and strength.*

It was then Verion realized how long he had been away from home. If Murn's clan had more than enough time to build this amazing thing during their absence he must have been gone longer then he realized. Sadness slowly returned to his mind again, though he gave a futile attempt to push it away.

As the companions mounts clopped happily across the bridge, Verion forced a smile. He began to think that not only was he enjoying a effortless journey but he saw flowing water beneath him again. The seafarers from Tarsis entered his mind as he slowly rode to the opposite shore.

That thought also turned his mind to the dragons. He reached out to Trimlin to check on the young one return from the north. Both arrived during the darkness of the previous night The dragons were once again at full strength and overhead.

Concealment was no longer on his mind. The remaining companions rode free of worry and unhurried toward their destination. Though many minions had escaped from Morog and perhaps Selonoth as well, Verion went onward without a care knowing his sister with her powerful sight was beside him. No danger would come to them unseen.

Two days passed, each much akin to the last, before their travel brought the company to the outskirts of the land of the Quantar. Immediately, even before greeting the king, Verion made good his promise by spending several hours with Raza in his tiny workshop. As always, his visit was highly enjoyable, for Raza's tales were not only entertaining but his mannerisms brought a large smile to Verion's face. The tale of the city's siege was recounted for Verion in detail.

The old man insisted on hearing the tale of the company's latest quest. This of course, took no small amount of time. During which, Verion found himself immersed in feelings and emotions he struggled so mightily to suppress during his trek. Now, he found a great solace in having them said aloud. It swept away great weight from his mind and shoulders as he spoke. New strength came forth in his voice as the tale was told, no longer did it bring dread and sorrow to him.

Finally, after an exceedingly lengthy farewell, the future king took his leave and proceeded to Cytan's home. The remaining travelers were seated in the familiar hall, placed on either side of the dining table.

"Many pardons, my King," said Verion with a low bow. "An overly long visit with Raza delayed my arrival, my liege. There was much to discuss since our last visit. Forgive me."

"Ah, Raza," said the king. "He is a delightful fellow. I visit him often for I cherish his work and the stories as well. Aleeza made mention of your visit, I held no hope of your return until the sunrise," said Cytan, smiling softly. "No pardon is needed my young lord, for I, too, have been lost in conversation with Raza on many occasion."

Verion chuckled softly as he placed himself in an empty seat next to the king. Food and drink were brought before him quickly. He felt famished, asking for another helping within minutes. Much talk was had that night of the journey and the defense of the city when evil forces came against it. To Verion's delight, Cytan bore a message from his parents that all was well, both were safe as he already knew and

Eldarn was never breached by the wicked forces unleashed against it.

"Again you have returned safely with my beloved daughter. If all the riches in my kingdom could be given freely to you, I would do so gladly for your gift," said the king.

"Sire," said Verion, standing to bow low. "You owe me nothing. For my vow was if I drew breath your daughter would return unharmed and so it is. Never would I ask for payment, for there is no debt in guarding the one I love so dearly. Though, without her, I would not be standing in your presence now."

Aleeza rose to gently kiss her husband, who felt growing embarrassment as his father in law looked on smiling. Then conversation returned as the king summoned more food and ale for the company.

"Not only have you brought home my daughter, but Fenorl as well," smiled the king. "Long has it been since we have laid eyes upon one another. In your absence the entire tale was told of not only the journey and the Tareen's return, but of Fenorl as well. My brother's son has returned to me whole and a new man. Perhaps, if I may say, even better than before."

Cytan then told the tale of battle for Quantar. Verion learned that Zot, Ono's mate, carried warning to the city before the attack, shortly before the Ancients appeared to give counsel. They prepared well for the evil onslaught, placing the most skilled archers atop the trees, hidden from sight in two separate locations. Dozens more stood fast at ground level with many skilled swordsman by their sides.

The wicked forces, after attempting several unsuccessful charges into the unseen force, broke asunder and fled, only to be cut down by the second force laying in wait. The hunters became the hunted. Cytan himself led the charge that raged at ground level. Dressed in his royal battle armor, the king bade his cavalry charge headlong into the fray before them. As the enemy fled, the dragon cut them down as they crossed the flowing river. Mere handfuls escaped to return to their master with ill news of utter defeat.

Verion's respect for the kindly king grew even more after the tale. From his first meeting with the king, he imagined Cytan held no love of battle, yet now his sword prowess was told by each member of the kingdom many times over. Speaking to several combatants who fought valiantly in the fray or witnessed the scene, Verion learned the king was fearless and skilled with not only horse but sword as well.

Minute after minute, hour after hour fell away until nine days passed in the blink of an eye. The travelers then decided to press westward once more. Lengthy farewells were spoken in the great hall and again sadness took Verion's heart, for Aleeza was Cytan's only child and she now lived in Eldarn, leaving the king alone. Though the stately man showed only happiness for his daughter, Verion knew loneliness held his heart on occasion.

Once outside, before descending the stairs which opened into the courtyard holding their mounts, Verion forced an outward smile, vowing to return as often as he could spare. After all, the dragons could bear the pair hence in less than a day's ride. Trimlin, reading his riders thoughts, roared overhead, making Verion smile genuinely. Gently turning Brandor's head to the west, he nudged him forward toward his next goal, Hatar.

The Bewildered Lands of the Quantar were forested with wide ancient trees that Verion adored. Their thickness and sheer size were impressive enough, but they also seemed sentient in many ways. Unlike the Protected Realm where the trees responded to your wants, these seemed to moan and sigh in a gentle breeze, almost as if they spoke as you drew near. He would make time to call for rest near one as often as possible, for he was fascinated by them and often caught himself speaking aloud to them as he rode.

Several times he thought, or imagined, they would sway or rock in response to his voice, even on a windless day. He was uncertain if it came from weariness or want for the behemoths to answer.

Eventually, the ancient trees gave way to younger, thinner, but no less impressive trees that filled the lands. He remembered these lands with reverence. Not only was it his wife's beloved homeland, but it was much akin to Eldarn as well. The sights, sounds and smells relaxed him as they pressed slowly onward. Knowing two days travel remained until reaching the ancient bridge spanning the lands between Hatar and Aleeza's home, he rode ever slowly to savior every moment.

The path wound steadily upward for a great distance before starting a gradual descent to the valley floor. There, Verion called for camp as night came quickly upon them. Shortly before he lay for his night's sleep he walked hand in hand with Aleeza through the tree line. It helped wash his anxiety from him before he attempted to close his eyes. It worked perfectly this night.

As morning broke upon the group, Verion had already risen and prepared breakfast for all. They swung into their saddles light hearted and full. The path took them over many gentle rises until it turned straight westerly for a way. They had left the trees behind and now rode in the flat lands that stretched before the crossing.

The bridge came into view far earlier than Verion wished. Mixed emotions swept through him, for he was leaving a land he loved, yet he drew closer to his parents with each step. Again, an outward smile appeared as the horses shod feet clopped noisily over the stone structure. Quickly the landscape changed to that of beautiful flatlands which held, at first appearance, nothing more than cactus and tumbleweeds. That was Verion's impression many years earlier when first setting eyes upon this land. Yet, he knew if one would simply open their eyes to see the crystal clear flowing streams, beautiful flora, and natural appeal, the land is incredibly satisfying and held much beauty of its own.

The site of the Battle of Ages would not be far away. Yet, they would likely bypass the battleground. Many years earlier, he stood by Nira's side as she used the Dragon's Eye to behold a ghostly vision of the battle. Though generally avoided, Verion did not fear the spot as many did. The others held no wish to visit here, so he was sure it would be bypassed on this trip as well. Perhaps he would return here on Trimlin when the time was right, for now he pushed it from his thoughts.

Sun's rays bore on them relentlessly as they traveled. With little cover to be had, the company grew warm and uncomfortable during the days and chilled at night, requiring fires to be lit and well stocked. Secretly his wished for a tree to shelter under, yet he held no qualms with sleeping on the hard ground beneath the stars themselves. However, an occasional cactus needle or thorn required one to place their bed roll with extreme vigilance. Within two days of relaxed but steady travel the walls of Hatar came into view.

King Rolnor stood before the travelers as they reached the stairs to the royal hall, making Verion smile. He was greeted by the kings usual crushing embrace. After a hearty meal and much casual conversation, all tales were repeated for the benefit and delight of the king, who sat enthralled as he listened intently, especially of the return of the Tareen. Then, the king began his tale of the attack of Hatar. He spoke of the news of his enemy coming forth to destroy the city. Verion learned Ono brought warning to Rolnor, who prepared quickly as well. As with the City of Life, an Ancient came forth with great counsel before the fray.

Holnok's forces knew little concerning the concealment skills of the flatlanders. Hundreds lay hidden in wait for the forces from the east, which were easily caught within Rolnor's net of death. There was no place to turn, they were surrounded by forces largely unseen. Arrows and spears slew them by the score within the circle, they fell one atop another during the carnage.

Then, a great wave of speeding horses bearing riders came forth to smash the assault, sending many fleeing, only to be cut down by the dragon as they took flight to the east. Very few escaped their fate, for the main force was easily trapped and given no quarter, rarely even seeing a glimpse of their attackers, save the horse charge. As with Cytan, Rolnor himself led the way, hacking and hewing all before him. He rode forth in kingly glory upon Enobella, his trusted mount. Most cowered before his wrath, those foolish enough to face him, perished. No spear, arrow or sword found either as they were blessed by Ancient magic before the battle began.

As with the Battle of Ages, a great burn pit was made. Weapons and bodies alike were piled deep into it and set ablaze. Verion's path to Hatar took him far above the pit, so he rode unaware of the mound that now stood as a reminder of the combat. It was simply called the Pit of Death.

Verion spent many days in Hatar, for he was unsure when he would lay eyes upon Nira, Eldon or the king again. He visited the smithy who had not forgotten him. There, he took great pleasure in the working of metal again. His mastery of metallurgy was well known and much revered in Hatar.

Again, time drew near for final farewells. Fourteen days passed since his arrival. Verion could contain his longing for home no more. It gripped him like a vice, never relinquishing its hold. He and Aleeza prepared to depart with heavy hearts. Now, Keltora would stay behind with some of the young dragons and Trimlin would journey with the remaining brood to Eldarn.

The three travelers, with dragons overhead, departed for Eldarn. They started on a straight northerly route thought that led to the pass through the Whispering Mountains. There the road would take a westerly turn to Eldarn. The four day journey would seem an eternity, yet it burned brightly in Verion's mind.

Danger was no longer upon them and Verion thought long about the dragons, deciding to send them onward to Eldarn. They earned the right to see their home and take a well deserved respite from battle and death, he thought. With a single thought he gave Trimlin the command to go forth and await their arrival. Bellowing roars reached his ears from the dragons as they spun and looped high above, then disappeared into the high riding clouds.

"Long have I waited to call one place home," said Fenorl suddenly as the dragons left his sight. "You have given me reason to live, my king. My debt to you will be everlasting, until I draw my dying breath. Allegiance to you and your queen will never fade."

"My friend, who has come through death and evil to become a respected man of honor, you owe me nothing. For it was you yourself who has proven worth and honesty beyond that of most men. We shall set to work on your home shortly after our arrival. Until then, you shall stay in our house as an honored guest," said Verion, staring squarely into Fenorl's eyes.

Fenorl's mouth fell agape as Verion smiled kindly at him. The future king took an immense liking to Fenorl since Ancient magic had been placed upon him. Even after he voluntarily recalled some of the past painful memories, his heart was true to good and pure ways now.

The path climbed slowly toward the pass. Trees began to close in on either side, growing thicker as the trio traversed the sloping trail. They rode until the yellowing sun sank behind the Dimlor Mountains. Verion dismounted and readied for camp thinking yet another goal had been reached. Only one remained now.

Then, through the silence of the night, flapping wings approached from the west. Verion sprang instantly to his feet and called for quiet. His eyebrows lifted slightly as a smile came to his face, for he knew the familiar sound of Ono's flapping wings.

Two bulging eyes shone through the blackness as Ono's winged form became clearer as he neared the firelight. He hovered before Verion, then landed and bowed awkwardly.

"It is good to set eyes upon you, my lord," said Ono in his high pitched, squeaky voice. "I bear news from Eldarn. Your parents send greetings and await your arrival with much anticipation."

Verion's heart leapt in his chest. Happiness overwhelmed him and he could no longer contain an overly large smile. Images of his homeland and parents flooded his thoughts, yet he composed himself to long enough to kneel and speak to Ono, gently patting his head as he did.

"Many thanks, my winged companion. Your news brings great joy and lightens my heart as well," said Verion. "We shall travel three more days until reaching Eldarn. Take word that we will travel with speed. Once again your aid is invaluable to me, little friend."

"I gladly serve in any way you require my aid," said Ono. "Your mother and father have shown me much kindness since my arrival in Eldarn several weeks ago. I will do this task in honor of your family, including the Lady Aleeza," Ono said, bowing toward Verion's life partner.

"Ono, I marvel at your ways," said Verion truthfully. A smile came to his face as he drew closer to the winged creature. "You do not serve me, it is I that bow to you. Never have you shown distrust in me, save but our first meeting. Your knowledge of Holnok and his ways saved the people of D'Enode from being overwhelmed by evil during our first quest. Even on this adventure you proved more worthy than any magical weapon held by any of us. The free peoples of this world owe their freedom to you as well as Zot. I learned you warned Hatar and Zot spread word as well. Yet more feats worthy of my praise to you and your kind."

The little creature stood unblinking for several moments before fluttering his wings with excitement.

"Again, you do me honor," said Ono. "I shall carry your words to Eldarn as you ask. There shall be a celebration upon your return. A festival to rejoice the downfall of Holnok. Until then, may your road be smooth."

"Farewell my small, honored companion. Look for our coming on the eve of the third day. The distance shall be bearable now due to your news. Travel well, noble one," said Verion as he rose to full height.

Ono bowed awkwardly once more, then rapidly flapped his wings and hovered before the trio. After one last look, he turned westward and disappeared into the night.

Verion felt the world was right. Only joy filled his senses. All dread and despair was forgotten. His pace would increase for the remainder of the trek, yet each step would be at peace. He kissed his wife's cheek, then turned to firmly grasp Fenorl's forearm wearing a large smile all the while.

"Come, let us rest, though honestly I doubt sleep shall find me this night. Soon we shall be home and celebrate our reunion. I imagine Fenorl, that you will be the guest of honor," said Verion, smiling broadly. "It was by your hand that evil was brought to its end. No doubt tribute and accolades shall be bestowed upon you. The hero of D'Enode, Slayer of Holnok."

Even by firelight Verion could see Fenorl's face grow flushed with embarrassment.

"My lord, I wish no such tribute. I simply wish to live among free, honorable people once more. Yet, I will accept it all the same if you wish it. Though many risk their lives by my side, it is not wholly my credit," retorted Fenorl, sheepishly, his eyes staring at his feet.

"Nonetheless, you shall be hailed a hero to be sure. Praise will be yours above that of the company, for you dealt the blow to end evil. Now let us attempt to rest, morning is not far off."

Verion fetched his bedroll and drew close to Aleeza, sleeping more soundly than he had since resting in Avior. The morning dawned warm as a slight breeze carried the sounds of the familiar forest to Verion's ears.

Smells of home are indeed wonderful, he thought. *I have the Dimlors beside me, the forest I have spent my youth in lies to the front and a clear path is before me. Only if I sat at home with the company around me could things be more joyous.*

After a hearty breakfast, of which Verion received two heaping helpings, they mounted and pressed forward. They traveled carefree with much conversation and laughter during the remaining three days until Eldarn came into sight. A sudden urge to burst into a gallop held Verion tightly, yet he held his emotions in check. The horses whinnied loudly, announcing their arrival, as many shapes stirred restlessly about in the streets. Cheers, shouts and many voices rose in the air. It seemed every breathing soul was out and about to welcome home their future king and queen and the stranger that rode beside them. Then, through the throng, Verion saw his father and mother moving to the forefront.

There had been no celebration during the previous quest. For the most part people were unaware evil was unfolding. The company had driven Holnok from Mindaloth with little knowledge to the western world of his expanding malice. However, once the tales were told and spread throughout the lands, Verion and his company became heroes. This time, with the unification of all races, news traveled quickly and was readily shared. The companions adventure had already become legend even before their arrival home. Undoubtedly, some tales were embellished to the point of extraordinary, thought Verion while frowning momentarily.

After greeting his parents, he was swarmed by well wishers. The words hero, champion, conqueror and many others were bandied about. He noticed Fenorl seemed overwhelmed by the attention, he felt a need to end the clamor as quickly as possible. Yet, he held no desire to end Eldarn's joy, so instead, he quietly snuck from sight with his wife and Fenorl in tow.

After several hours, with light now gone, the people found their homes once more. What with the festival planned for the following evening and the set up and preparation needing all day, they required their rest. Eldarn fell silent once more. Meanwhile, a light burnt brightly at the king's simple home as he entertained his son, daughter-in-law, and a newly acquired friend in Fenorl.

The future king listened intently as his parents retold their tale of the great battle of the Watching Hill. He was praised for his foresight of the need to rebuild the battlement. Many questions were asked by the trio and parents alike until the dawn was mere hours away.

Exhaustion came to Verion as he prepared to climb into bed in his own home. Aleeza was sleeping soundly as Verion led Fenorl to a small, comfortable room that lay at the end of a long hallway. No words were spoken between the two. Verion simply patted Fenorl on the back and departed.

Verion slept until early afternoon, quite late for him. He enjoyed rising early and working a full day, but there was no guilt in his heart for his late start this day. Before breakfast he visited Trimlin and the young dragons, thanking them once again for their efforts during the quest. He was overjoyed at seeing them once more, even though it had only been a short time since their departure while on the trail, he still hated being seperated from them.

All that day party preparations kept the town quite busy. Tents, games, and a great deal of food were brought in and readied for the festivities. An enormous cook pavilion was erected, filling the small valley with the most wonderful aromas that were smelled for a league in any direction. Of course the main attraction for some, besides welcoming home the guests, was undoubtedly the ale which flowed freely and in great quantity.

Later that evening the party began, it was one of particular splendor, being remembered for many a year to come in Eldarn. Even large banners were strung here and there throughout the town, which of course signified the importance of the event.

Between cheers and hollers of welcome the town folk called for a speech from their future king. Not being one for such things, he spoke briefly but found time to talk of a home building for his companion. Shouts of volunteers went up among men and women alike. This pleased Verion for the simple fact the voices rose heartily even before much ale was consumed. He knew all of Eldarn accepted Fenorl as one of their own. After all, they were warriors and Fenorl proved himself on several occasions. He, too, was worthy to be held in honor. Firing the arrow that slay Holnok carried much weight among the warrior folk.

In honor of the deed, Verion cast the finest sword and shield seen in many days gone by. Both were made from Costium, the hardest metal known. The blade was long and sharp, the shield broad and wide. This pleased Fenorl above all else, for his Captain forged them with his own hands. The sword he called Galmirest, Blade of the Sun for brightly indeed did it shine. The shield bore the name Vilnar, for in Eldarn tongue it meant Pure of Heart.

Fenorl was given the name of Sir True Shot. For even some of the most skilled archers in Eldarn would have been hard pressed to hit their target in those circumstances. After all, the company was in near darkness and fear would have taken much of their heart. Yet he felled the High Lord with one perfectly placed arrow. The name, though odd to some, was meant to give high honor, never a jest or disrespect. So, Fenorl wore it proudly.

UNEXPECTED NEWS

Five days after the celebration, an expanding glow appeared in Verion's home as he sat comfortably enjoying his morning meal. Xana and Yanor stood before him in his own living room.

"Forgive our sudden intrusion," said Xana. "We wish to speak privately. It is time to learn the truth of your powers and talents that lay still hidden within you. Nira is aware of her potential since we have visited. Great power is within her, magnified by the Dragons Eye. She could easily bear as much power as a Tareen, as do you. However young lord, you have not even begun to explore the magic within you.

"Magic, within *me*," he asked quizzically. "My only power is the Jewel and sword. Now I also bear the shield blessed by Delthas himself. I am simply a warrior, nothing more."

"You may indeed believe this is true, yet it is folly," said Yanor. "Please show me Simil, I very much wish to lay eyes upon it. It is very valuable and powerful to my people. It is a treasure that had been lost to time. Though now, it hangs round your neck. We are greatly pleased for its return."

Verion slowly slid the necklace from beneath his tunic, removed it and held it aloft. It swung dangling before the Tareen who smiled at one another and nodded in unison. It glowed brilliantly as Verion laid hands on the jewel itself.

"Place it on the table, my lord," said Xana. "Now, summon it to you. It will obey and go to its master."

"Master?" said Verion, surprised and unsure if he heard correctly. "I simply use it for light when needed and it allows me to speak to animals and the like. Though, I will admit, return from Morog without its aid would not have been likely."

"Try, Verion. You must. Unlock your inner strength and we shall teach you all the secrets within the Jewel," said Xana with a slight plead in her voice. "There is much you do not know yet. Our greatest and most powerful of the Tareen once carried it much like you do now, but that is another story."

Verion lay the jewel gently on the polished wooden table top and stepped several paces away. He opened his hand, closed his eyes and began to concentrate. Within seconds the necklace leapt from the table into his open palm. Slowly, he opened his eyes in disbelief. Turning to gaze at his visitors, they stood smiling with pride and joy.

"Well done!" said Yanor excitedly. "Mastering that feat could have taken many long months. Never would I have imagined such power on the first attempt. You may hold even more command than your sister. Your destiny is indeed to be superior to any other before you."

"I . . . I . . . never dreamed of such things," stammered Verion. "Is what you say true. Does your blood flow through my veins. Do I hold hidden powers?"

"Yes, young Master," smiled Xana. "The Gilarn are the oldest race of men. Long ago, when the world was still young, your race journeyed here from across the sea. You were one united race then. Once you touched upon the shores of the Sea of Songs you spilt asunder. The Arton, as they became known, held deep love of water and remained to build the great port of Tarsis. The others, traveled far to the south searching far and wide, finding deep love for the wood and mountain. Finally they set to building Eldarn and became known as the Elmar."

"But not before a small band traveled to the East, where they stumbled upon our sanctuary in the Forest of Dreams, for then it was unhidden. Then, a most wonderful thing happened. Gelmonor of the Elmar met and fell in love with Arnep of the Tareen," said Yanor with excitement in his voice.

"They were not meant for one another," continued Xana. "Yet, they fled our home and protection to live here. The council nearly stripped Arnep of her powers. But Laveena interceded and stayed their decision. Saying their love was meant to be. So it was, that Tareen blood entered the Elmar line. Together they made many sons and daughters. Gelmonor sat on the throne for countless years with Arnep by his side, her being immortal and using her powers to grant her beloved long life. Their children became the rulers of your kingdom for thousands of years. Your father is a direct descendent of Gelmonor himself, as are you. Arnep's blood flows through you as well, akin to your sister."

"Then, this is why I have the Seeing ability," said Verion, speaking aloud to himself. "Tareen blood flows within me. And the jewel . . . it is true, it calls to me and does my bidding."

"And much more as well," answered Xana. "You may hold more skills and power than you can imagine. All of which in time, we shall teach you to harness and control. Mighty magic is at your disposal, deep within you. Hence the reason the company looks to you for leadership, for your line is one of great kings, queens and just rulers. It is a given ability through your blood."

Verion sat speechless as the room fell silent for a long while. He rose, pacing slowly round the square floor, glancing at Xana and Yanor occasionally, mumbling to himself as he went. The Tareen sat patiently, reading Verion's every thought as he stared at the Jewel round his neck. At great length, he spoke.

"Teach me all you will, for my desire to do good is great indeed. Once king, I shall carry on the tradition of fairness and justice that has ruled my people for ages."

"Your reign will be long and prosperous Lord Verion," said Xana. "Arnep magically blessed your race with long life. Did it never occur to you why your father ages little. Or their parents. They are nearly four hundred years old, with your mother and father being nearly two hundred of your years."

Verion's knees went weak. He had never known this fact, it staggered him. Then, horror set into his mind and anxiety like he never knew took him, making his knees weak with anguish.

"Aleeza," he cried. "What of Aleeza, she is . . . is . . ."

"Human," replied Yanor softly. "Her life will end as any other woman of your kind. She shall die a humans death from her long years and age."

"No, it cannot be! You must help me. Save her, give her a gift to stay by my side. I beg you. You needn't make her immortal, simply let her live until I fade from D'Enode as well," pleaded Verion. "I must have her by my side, she is . . . . is . . . everything to me, my breath, heartbeat and life itself."

"We cannot," said Xana. "Though . . . there is a way, perhaps. Hand me your crystal from Laveena. I shall keep it safe and return as soon as I may."

Verion sprinted to his room, returning within seconds clutching a clear, small crystal in his hand. It was cut in the shape of an oval with many facets that held and twisted any light striking it, turning it more beautiful than Verion had ever seen. Yet it went unnoticed as he quickly slid into Xana's hand, who, within seconds, faded from sight.

It was nearly more than Verion could stand. He paced frantically, then tried sitting, which served no purpose at all. Quickly he paced once more, totally ignoring Yanor in the process.

The wizard was forgotten yet he looked on smiling all the while.

After what seemed like days to Verion, Xana's glowing form took shape quickly. Barely able to breathe, he stared openly at her, yet dared not speak for fear of the answer. Time hung motionless as his palms grew slick with sweat. He opened his mouth to speak, then froze as Xana spoke.

"I have spoken to Laveena," she said softly, handing the crystal to Verion. "She wishes to speak to you."

No sooner were the words out, than Laveena's flash of light took Verion's sight. After rubbing his eyes, the Ancient stood before him in all her splendor. He bowed instantly and dropped to one knee.

"I beg thee all powerful Laveena. Do not take my beloved from me long before my time comes as the years draw on. Let her sit by my side until my life is spent. Nothing more shall I ask of you. She is all I desire or need in this life. I had no knowledge of the length of my years, do not leave me empty and forsaken of love, of *her* love. My life shall be pointless and forsaken without the one I cherish."

"Rise, king of Eldarn. Long ago, when Gelmonor stole away with Arnep, I stayed the Tareen from taking her power, for I saw a love never to be repeated in time. It was my wish they be united together for many years. Only good would come from it. I swore never to give another such a gift," said Laveena as she gazed into Verion's eyes.

Horror registered on his face, realizing Aleeza could not stand by his side. His throat tightened as grief and panic took him, clutching his very heart and soul. It was impossible to stand for his knees went weak yet again, his body drained of all energy and will.

"Yet, before me is a future king on bended knee asking for the same offering," said Laveena, never taking her eyes from Verion's. "I grant you this gift from my heart. For I have watched you together for many years and your love is perhaps even deeper than that of your kin. Never have I seen such happiness and joy within this world. Your betrothed shall be blessed by my grace. It is already done," she said with a wave of her hand.

Verion wept openly as happiness, relief and love swept through him, mounting to a crescendo he could no longer bear. A great desire to embrace Laveena came to him, though reason held him back.

"Though I have nothing to gift to you in return, forever shall I be in your debt. You may ask anything of me and it shall be done," said Verion, regaining his composure.

"There is one thing," said Laveena. "The Stone of Sight. I wish to hold it."

Verion's eyes instantly went to the floor, like a child caught stealing or lying to his own parents. Slowly, he shuffled from the room, returning within moments with the crystal outstretched to Laveena.

As Verion released the crystal, it hung suspended, hovering before the Ancient's hand. A deafening, shrill scream filled the room as the stone turned round and round with incredible speed. A blackness was expelled from within as it twirled. Neither mist nor solid, it writhed and twisted before Laveena, struggling to escape or break free from her magical grasp that held it.

She slowly handed the Stone to Verion before turning her gaze to the soundless squirming mass. Standing silent for a long while, it seemed the two were communicating, for the black shape remained hanging yet undulating and calm now. Then, in a flash, it was gone.

"Wh . . . wh . . . what was that," he asked, still stunned. "Was it alive?

"That, was dark magic far beyond any you have ever faced. You were foolish for touching it, your sister gave wise counsel. Nonetheless, by bringing it to me it shall never be touched by evil hands again. I have restored the stone to its original purpose. One which Yanor and Xana will show you. Now young lord, the only gift I require is your fair and just rule when your time comes to bear the crown of your royal forefathers," she replied. "Fare thee well, young king. We shall meet again."

With that, a flash took Verion's sight yet again. As he refocused Xana and Yanor stood smiling before him.

"I am forever indebted to you as well. By your blessing and favor I have been granted all I desire on this earth," said Verion, bowing low.

"Nothing is owed to us, young lord," said Yanor. "We are your kin, it was meant to be. Now we must bid farewell. We shall return and begin your training ere too long."

Before Verion could speak, the duo faded from sight, leaving him alone in an empty room once more. Then, he wondered if the entire event was a dream. It felt surreal. Questions by the score arose in his mind. First and foremost was going to be a lengthy talk to his parents on why their lifespan was hidden from he and his sister. Then of course would be why the bloodlines from the great Gelmonor were being kept secret.

Aside from that, Verion was ecstatic. It seemed illusory to him Aleeza had been gifted with long life as well, they would be together for hundreds of years to come. He decided it was time to share the events, so he went forth and sought her out. First, he darted to his room and stowed the Stone and crystal in their hiding places he made, then scrambled for the front door.

He found her with Gynexa, they landed nearby and she strode to him smiling. Husband and wife kissed gently as he found her hand, leading her inside. There, they sat and talked for hours on all that the day's happenings brought forth.

Months later, Verion and Aleeza settled in to a routine of dragon training and normalcy once more. As promised, Fenorl received his home, one of the largest in town, even after his objections it is was too big for simply one man. Verion on the other hand took great pride in the dwelling since he designed and built a good portion of it himself. He even went as far to improve a local cave for Ono and Zot, who now also took up residence in Eldarn.

Regular visits to and from his companions were a common occurrence. Murn and Katima were seen frequently in Eldarn and became town favorites, for Murn became quite animated when he told a tale, which enthralled and often frightened some of the town folk. Eldon and Nira, along with the dragons, visited once or more a month, as did the sea farers of Tarsis.

Even Orna, Zarn and Crutad alike came to Verion's home, sending many murmurs through the townsfolk of Eldarn. The creatures and men were quite intimidating even for a warrior race such as the Elmar, not to mention they were considered oddities at first. Yet, after time, it became acceptable for folk to be seen trading, talking or even drinking with the newcomers, as they were often called.

During one of Nira's visits in particular Verion learned of the possibility of yet another hatching of dragons. Which of course thrilled him since part of his dream was to have dragons return to prominence on D'Enode once more. This more than anything brought great joy and cause for celebration.

An elaborate feast was thrown to rejoice the tidings. It is said this particular party was even larger than the welcome home feast Verion received. Of course, the debate went on for quite some time, never to be solved. Though it was always a topic of conversation among the townsfolk at the local inn.

The Tareen returned often to hone Verion's skills, most of which were unknown to him. He grew powerful and gained magical powers he kept hidden from all, except his closest friends and sister. During their visits the Tharnils came as well, freely roaming in and about town. It took many months before the townsfolk decided it was safe to venture outside when the creatures were out and about. Though none would dare ride them, the beasts managed to be fed quite well from the villagers.

VISIONS OF THE FUTURE

After learning much from the Tareen, Verion would sit alone after retrieving the Stone from its hiding spot and stare at it for a lengthy time. Trying to decipher the images that came before him turned into a form of relaxation.

A tall young handsome man that strode confidently about villages and towns would be seen. First he talked and laughed among the townsfolk then he became more withdrawn and sullen, his brow furrowed. Then, images of many dragons filling the sky were brought into focus. He gazed at beings never seen before, short and round they were. Yet sturdy and hearty looking. Some were smooth and others wore beards of some length, braided to lay upon their chests, even to the bellies.

A great castle with many ramparts and tiers was seen. It stood high above the ground and glistened with silver, gold and brilliant white. It was pleasing to look upon, for it seemed serene, lovely and peaceful. Flowers bloomed and trees grew tall and thick before it.

The castle faded to children playing with shouts of joy and loud voices rising in excitement as they chased one another about a perfectly manicured yard. One little boy and girl stood side by side petting a dragons neck before the vision changed to many of the companions faces. One in particular seemed distraught and worried, then expressionless and still. It became pale, cold and lifeless, then it was gone.

Verion sat and pondered all he saw, spending days in deep thought of the meanings of his visions. Often times his emotions were torn, for the laughing children brought him great joy along with images of many dragons. Still, impressions of a distraught companion left him worried and full of fear. Some, he did not understand at all. The castle and the short round men were a mystery, holding no special memory or any recognition.

Knowing the Stone merely foretold the future was of no help. Even Nira's Eye would show her images of things that could change or never come to pass at all. Were these visions of events that he would never see. Dreams perhaps. He was unclear and it tugged at his mind with a ceaseless nagging.

Raising his arm slightly, he summoned a drinking cup from a nearby table. It came into his outstretched hand and he drank deeply. He would not perform his newly found magic in front of his companions or visitors, in fact rarely letting his wife see his new powers. Yet, he had indeed been practicing his new art. Each time the Tareen would visit, he would take a newly learned skill and devote many long hours to it, attempting to master every aspect.

With or without his Jewel he could work wonders, though certainly he was much more powerful with it round his neck. He never parted from it, feeling empty and lost without it.

One of his largest joys and accomplishments was now he could speak to Nira with a simple thought no matter how great the distance. In fact, they spoke several days a week. Their bloodline bond had come full circle. Counsel was never more than a moment away for either of them. He found he could even speak to Aris at will, a fact he held great delight in.

The greatest surprise, and very enjoyable one at that, was Verion could now block his thoughts from all around him. With the exception of the Tareen or an Ancient, his mind was his own. No more would Nira, Jinarl, or any other ever sense his thoughts unless he desired it.

Overall, life was more pleasurable than Verion ever recalled it. It came to be he put Mindaloth, Selonoth and Morog out of his thoughts. Though, all had forgotten the old wizard Sartol.

SARTOL'S PLAN

The old wizard lay near death after the fairy's magical blast struck him, a blast that would have slain any other mortal man. Unbeknownst to the company, Sartol had evil enchantment upon him that spared his life. Though he barely escaped Morog before its destruction, he did indeed survive. Now, recovered from his injuries, he began to turn himself younger. Using the powerful dark magic he reversed his age nearly fifty years. Vitality coursed through his veins, strength filled every fiber of his being.

No longer could his aged eyes barely see a book page. His stride lengthened, his hair grew long and black and the once frail body became free of pain. Only in dreams would age ever touch him again. Great evil magic was now held within his mind. He also managed to save the entire volume of books he coveted.

Now, he wandered freely about the lands, for none knew him. He was simply another traveler for all intent and purpose. He chose the name Ormalt. For none alive remember the evil speech of Welkar, save the fairies and their kin. Little did the commoners know its true meaning, Death Comes Forth.

In this manner, hidden in a youthful body, great knowledge came to him. He learned of the different races and their ways and weaknesses, even becoming close with folk of high standing in many towns. All the while he plotted, ensuring his own plans would come to fruition when the time was right. He cast simple spells on the weak minded, making his words seemingly filled with truth and promise to grant their largest of dreams.

Word spread far and wide of this beloved traveler. People laid his wants and whims before him, never questioning his words of poison. Silently, secretly, he weaved a web of deceit and lies as he went. None ever doubted his intentions, which had turned dark indeed since he meddled with powers never meant to be discovered except by only the mightiest of wizards who could wield it or at least contain it.

Now, he thought, *I must simply bide my time until I can control them all. Holnok dared to take this world by force. I will simply take it for my own but for the asking. For, these fools are powerless against me.* Then, he laughed at all the work he had done.

If someone was foolish enough to cross Ormalt, they simply disappeared, never to be seen again. It didn't take long before hushed rumors began. At first, no one took much notice if one of the townsfolk would take an unexpected journey or vacation to visit relatives. But a few of the quicker witted ones started to wonder, and talk too. Simply because the travelers never returned from their extended stays, it brought much discussion and controversy.

"I believe they packed up and moved to Medson, the tiny town near Tarsis, up north," Ormalt would say. "Perhaps even East Kingsford out near the Old Lands." Every occurrence was neatly explained away, most of which sounded believable . . . to most.

Much debate went on for a long while over the issue. Of course, many folks enjoy wagging their tongues, so harsh words spread as fast as Ormalt's popularity did when he first arrived. Not all thought him the great Wish Granter, as some named him. In fact, no one ever recalls a single wish being gifted or given.

Somehow, that never stopped the believers. They loved the strapping, youthful man that came to visit as often as he could. However, very few ever considered how it was he could make a three day horse journey, overnight. In fact, he never came forth with a horse. When he appeared, he walked everywhere he went, they mumbled.

Often he strode forth within the towns, politely, casually greeting all he met. One rumor said he was in Barton one day and Nosk the next. The two lie more than ten leagues apart, some said. Others dismissed it as only talk and silly tales of gossip.

Thus it was Ormalt lived for a long while among those that grew distrusting for the most part.

Yet, none dared to confront him and most merely stayed away after they grew frightened. Words such as odd, queer, amiss, and more were used regularly when discussing his behavior.

Ormalt heard, but did not care about the rumors, for time was approaching to put all the long hours of planning into motion. He had grown powerful enough and learned more than his share of useful knowledge. He also held much of Morog's great dark magic on his side.

Author Biography

Being the second book in a trilogy, The Evil of Torlen, as with any series, shows character growth, not only emotionally but through their powers as well. The first book, entitled Dragon Code: The Fall of Mindaloth is available from Author House. My personal view of writing is much like life itself. You make mistakes and learn from them. So it is in the writing industry.

With each book I spend countless hours before the computer. Each writer pours out their heart to give you, the reader, a glimpse into our imaginations with each word or line written. Our sincere hope is to have an effect on you in some small, or large, way. We all have different tastes and styles we adhere to. With that said, I wish to gratefully acknowledge those who enjoy the Dragon Code works. Even as I write this a third book is in my computer files, along with another novel totally unrelated to the trilogy. From the bottom of my heart I thank those of you that support my love of writing and truly hope you enjoy the words within these pages.

As for myself, I retired from the United States Air Force in 2000. It was an experience I would not have traded for the world. It shaped me into who I am today. Giving more than twenty years of your life to one cause is a profound thing. Memories were formed that shall never fade from my mind. I respect all military services and my hat is off to all of you. You're all heroes.

I began writing by enrolling in two courses on 'how to' write children's books. The first was beginner level and the latter, advanced. From there it grew to freelance articles, some of which I still do for the local newspapers. Then, I realized I could do more. A long smoldering desire rekindled itself to actually write a fantasy novel, thereby creating my own world. Much like those I read about in my youth, hence, the second installment of Dragon Code.

As this book goes to print it will provide various methods to contact me. E-mail, web site, facebook, etc… are available if any of my readers choose to contact me. I read it all and will answer promptly. I am never far from a computer and shall see your messages daily and will respond quickly. Again, simply because I can't say it enough, thank you to each and every one of you who reads and enjoys this book. Please feel free to contact if you have the desire too. I will answer you as time allows.

With the deepest respect for any fans I pick up along the way, I want you to know that your support goes far beyond any words I could write here. Thank you all.

CPSIA information can be obtained at www.ICGtesting.com
Printed in the USA
267271BV00001B/3/P